Italian

A proposal of marriage…from a hot-blooded man, born under the Italian sun

Three passionate novels!

In February 2007 Mills & Boon bring
back two of their classic collections,
each featuring three favourite
romances by our bestselling authors...

ITALIAN PROPOSALS

The Venetian's Proposal
by Lee Wilkinson
The Italian Doctor's Wife
by Sarah Morgan
The Italian Doctor's Proposal
by Kate Hardy

SINFUL SECRETS

A Secret Vengeance by Miranda Lee
Sarah's Secret by Catherine George
Morgan's Secret Son by Sara Wood

Italian Proposals

THE VENETIAN'S
PROPOSAL
by
Lee Wilkinson

THE ITALIAN
DOCTOR'S WIFE
by
Sarah Morgan

THE ITALIAN
DOCTOR'S PROPOSAL
by
Kate Hardy

MILLS & BOON®

*MILLS & BOON and MILLS & BOON with the Rose Device
are registered trademarks of the publisher.
Harlequin Mills & Boon Limited,
Eton House, 18-24 Paradise Road, Richmond, Surrey, TW9 1SR*

ITALIAN PROPOSALS
© by Harlequin Enterprises II B.V. 2007

The Venetian's Proposal, The Italian Doctor's Wife and *The
Italian Doctor's Proposal* were first published in Great Britain by
Harlequin Mills & Boon Limited in separate, single volumes.

The Venetian's Proposal © Lee Wilkinson 2002
The Italian Doctor's Wife © Sarah Morgan 2003
The Italian Doctor's Proposal © Pamela Brooks 2003

*ISBN 10: 0 263 85144 3
ISBN 13: 978 0 263 85144 1*

05-0207

*Printed and bound in Spain
by Litografia Rosés S.A., Barcelona*

THE VENETIAN'S PROPOSAL

by

Lee Wilkinson

Lee Wilkinson lives with her husband in a three-hundred-year-old stone cottage in a Derbyshire village, which most winters gets cut off by snow. They both enjoy travelling and recently, joining forces with their daughter and son-in-law, spent a year going round the world 'on a shoestring' while their son looked after Kelly, their much loved German Shepherd dog. Her hobbies are reading and gardening and holding impromptu barbecues for her long-suffering family and friends.

Don't miss Lee Wilkinson's exciting new novel, *Wife by Approval,* out in April 2007 from Mills & Boon Modern Romance™

CHAPTER ONE

'PLEASE come in and take a seat, Mrs Whitney.'

Tall and slender in a navy suit, her corn-coloured hair taken up in a smooth knot, Nicola found herself ushered into a room that was solidly old-fashioned. Plum-coloured carpets, heavy velvet curtains, and above an empty fireplace a wooden mantel that held a ticking clock.

After coffee and condolences, Mr Harthill got down to business. 'The last time my client was in London he asked me to draw up a new will. In my capacity as executor, I can now tell you that you are the sole beneficiary of that will.'

Staring across a polished mahogany desk at the saggy-jowled solicitor sitting impassively in his brown leather chair, Nicola could only manage to stutter, 'I—I beg your pardon?'

'You are the sole beneficiary,' Mr Harthill Senior repeated patiently. 'When all the formalities have been observed, you will be a wealthy woman.'

A polite letter summoning Nicola to the West End offices of Harthill, Harthill and Berry had merely stated that Mr John Turner had passed away some three weeks earlier, and that if she would call she would learn 'something to her advantage'.

Shocked and saddened by the death of a man she had known for such a short time but liked immensely, she had kept the appointment.

The news that John Turner had made her the sole beneficiary to a fortune she hadn't been aware existed had come as a bombshell.

'But why me?' She spoke the thought aloud.

'I gather that Mr Turner didn't have any children of his own...'

No, John had never mentioned having a family.

'As well as his business interests,' Mr Harthill continued staidly, 'my client's estate includes the proceeds from the sale of his London home, and a small *palazzo* in Venice, known as Ca' Malvasia. He and his wife were very happy there, I understand.'

The London house Nicola had known about. John had mentioned his intention of putting it on the market, saying it was too big and too empty and he was hardly ever there. But his 'small *palazzo*' in Venice she hadn't. Though she was aware that John's deceased wife, Sophia, had been Italian.

'Is that where he died?' was all she could think of to ask.

Mr Harthill, used to euphemisms and looking a little distressed by her plain speaking, answered, 'No. Ca' Malvasia has been shut up since his wife passed away some four years ago. My client was in Rome on business when he suffered a fatal heart attack...'

She hoped someone had been with him. That he hadn't died alone.

'It wasn't totally unexpected,' the solicitor went on, 'and he had made provision. In the event of his death I was to give you this package, which I believe holds a set of keys to the *palazzo*.'

He handed her a small, thick envelope sealed with tape which bore her name and the address of the Bayswater flat she shared with her friend Sandy.

'If you wish to view the property I can put you in touch with my Venetian counterpart, Signor Mancini, who has been the family's solicitor for a number of years. He will be only too happy to help with your travel arrangements and show you the *palazzo*. Should you decide to sell, he can take the appropriate measures to have it put on the market.'

Sounding as dazed as she felt, Nicola said, 'I'll need to make some plans…take time off work.'

'Of course.' Mr Harthill rose to his feet to show her out. 'If I can be of any further service in the meantime, please let me know.'

'Thank you. You've been very kind.' She smiled at him. A smile that brought warmth to her heart-shaped face and lit up her green eyes.

A beautiful woman, he thought as they shook hands, and tragically young to be a widow. Even a rich one.

When Nicola let herself into the flat Sandy, a small vivacious redhead, was waiting, agog with excitement.

'I've made some tea. Come and tell all.'

Friends since their days at business college, and flatmates for the past three years, the pair were complete opposites. One an introvert. The other an extrovert.

Even before her young husband's fatal car crash Nicola had been quiet and self-contained, a woman who tended to stand alone in the wings and watch.

Whereas Sandy, outgoing and outspoken, was at her best bouncing off people.

In what seemed to be a case of role-reversal Sandy worked from home, as an information consultant, sitting in front of a computer screen in what she described as solitary confinement, while Nicola liaised with people, travelling almost non-stop as a conference organizer for Westlake Business Solutions.

Together they went through to the bright little kitchen and sat down at the pine table, where Sandy poured tea for them both.

Nicola accepted a mug and said simply, 'John made me his sole beneficiary. It seems I'm going to be a wealthy woman.'

Sandy gave a silent whistle.

'Apart from his business interests and the money from the sale of his London house, there's also a small *palazzo* in Venice.'

'You're joking!'

'No, I'm not.'

'Did you know he had a place in Venice?'

'No, he never mentioned it.'

'Sure you haven't got it wrong?'

'Certain. It's called Ca' Malvasia. I've even been given a set of keys to it.'

Taking the padded envelope from her bag, Nicola tore off the tape and tipped the contents on to the table.

As well as a bunch of ornate keys on an iron ring there was a small chamois pouch with a drawstring neck and a letter.

While Sandy examined the keys, Nicola unfolded the letter and read in John's small, neat writing:

Nicola, my dear, though we've known each other just a short time, you've been like the daughter I always wanted, and your warmth and kindness have meant a lot to me.

In the pouch you'll find Sophia's ring. Since she died I've been wearing it on a chain around my neck, but now I sense that I haven't got much longer I'm lodging it with Mr Harthill.

It's a singular ring. My darling always wore it. She was wearing it the day I met her. She once remarked that if any ring possessed the power to bring its wearer happiness, this one did. For that reason I would like you to have it, and I truly believe Sophia would approve.

Though we had both been married before, she was the love of my life as, I hope and believe, I was hers. We were very happy together for five wonderful years. Not long enough. But perhaps it never is.

In your case, I know your time with your husband was very brief. You're desperately young to have known so much grief and pain, and I'm only too aware that anyone who loses a loved one needs time to mourn. But remember, my dear, no one should mourn for ever. It's time you moved on. Be happy.

John

Blinking away her tears, Nicola passed the letter to Sandy, and, while the other girl read it quickly, picked up the chamois pouch and unfastened the drawstring. Tilting the pouch, she gave it a slight shake, and a ring slid into her palm.

Both women caught their breath.

It was exquisitely wrought, with twin ovals of glittering green stone sunk at an angle in the softly glowing gold setting.

'I've never seen anything like it.' Sandy's face held awe. 'What's it meant to be?'

Her voice unsteady, Nicola said, 'It looks like a gold mask, with emeralds for eyes.'

'Try it on,' Sandy urged.

With a strange feeling of doing something portentous, Nicola slid it on to her finger.

After Jeff's death she had lost weight to the point of becoming gaunt, and it was just a fraction too large.

'Even if it's only costume jewellery it looks fantastic!' Sandy enthused. 'Though it may be a little too spectacular to wear to the local supermarket.'

'You're right,' Nicola agreed. 'It would look more at home in Piazza San Marco.'

'Are you going to wear it?'

'At the moment I'd be scared of losing it. But I'll certainly keep it with me.'

'You speak Italian, don't you? Have you ever been to Venice?'

'No.'

'Wouldn't you like to go?'

'Yes, I would,' Nicola said slowly. 'I was thinking about it on the way home. I've time owing to me, so I might take a holiday. Stay there for a while.'

'Glory be!' Sandy exclaimed. 'A sign of life at last. I'd about given up hope. You haven't had a holiday since Jeff was killed.'

'There didn't seem much point. It's no fun staying in a hotel full of strangers. In any case, it's too much like work.'

'But you won't need to stay in a hotel when you have your very own *palazzo*.'

Nicola half shook her head. 'I can still hardly believe it.'

Her smooth forehead wrinkling into a frown, Sandy remarked curiously, 'I wonder why John Turner never mentioned having a house in Venice?'

'Talking about it might have conjured up too many ghosts. He absolutely adored his wife, and couldn't get over her death. It's one of the reasons he worked so hard and travelled so much…'

Nicola had done the same, only to find that pain and grief couldn't be left behind. They had travelled with her, constant companions she had been unable to outstrip.

Though she'd never found it particularly easy to make friends, she and John Turner had met and, drawn together by circumstances and their mutual loss, become firm friends—overnight, almost. The immediacy of their friendship had never been discussed or questioned, just accepted.

'Though there was an age difference of over thirty years, John and I had a lot in common. I was very fond of him.

I'll miss him.' With a lump in her throat, she added, 'I'd like to see the house where he and his wife were so happy.'

'Well, now's your chance.' Sandy's tone was practical. 'Why don't you come with me?'

'I can't say I'm not tempted, but I've too much work on. Besides, Brent would hate me to go to Venice without him. Apart from believing that English women find all Italian men fascinating, he thinks Italian men tend to stare at English women... And while he might not mind them *looking*, if it came to bottom-pinching...'

'I rather hope it won't.'

'You should be so lucky!' Sandy said with a grin. 'So how will you travel? Fly, as usual?'

'I'm tired of flying, seeing nothing but airports...' With a sudden determination to lay her own ghosts, Nicola decided, 'I think I'll drive down...'

Jeff, who had been the elder by six months or so, had passed his own driving test and taught her to drive in a small family saloon when she was just seventeen. But since his death she hadn't driven.

'In early June the weather should be good, so I think I'll plan a scenic route and take a leisurely trip, stopping three or four nights on the way. I'd love to see Innsbruck.'

Hiding her surprise, Sandy observed, 'While not wishing to spoil your fun, I must point out that you don't have a car.'

'I can always hire one.'

'And I've heard the price of parking in Venice is astronomical. But I don't suppose you need to worry about it now. By the way, now you've money to burn I expect you'll want to live somewhere a bit more up-market?'

Before Nicola could answer, she added, 'Don't think I'm trying to push you off, but Brent is itching to move in. I've kept the poor lamb waiting because I wasn't sure how you'd feel about having an extra flatmate, and a man to boot.'

'So you've decided to live together?'

'For a trial period. If it works out we may get married. Brent would like to.'

'Well, let me know if you want to spend your honeymoon in a *palazzo*...'

Without envy, Sandy said cheerfully, 'I do like having rich friends.'

Signor Mancini, when notified of Nicola's intentions, had proved almost embarrassingly eager to be of assistance. Though she had assured him that it wasn't necessary, he had advised her where to stay, and gallantly insisted on making all the hotel bookings.

For some reason, and without ever hearing his voice, Sandy had taken a dislike to the man. She now called him 'the slimy git'. But, unwilling to hurt his feelings, Nicola had thanked him and, abandoning her busman's holiday, accepted his well-meant help.

The only thing she had vetoed was that he should meet her on her arrival in Venice and personally conduct her to the hotel.

There was really no need to take up his valuable time, she had insisted politely, and it would tie her to being there at a certain hour.

Her last planned stop before Venice was Innsbruck, and she arrived in the picturesque Austrian city in the early afternoon.

Signor Mancini had arranged for her to stay at the Bregenzerwald, a nice-looking modern hotel just off the impressive Maria-Theresien-Strasse.

Nicola parked her hired car in the underground car park and, leaving her main suitcase in the boot, collected her small overnight bag and took the lift up to the elegant foyer.

It was deserted at that time of the day, except for the

desk-clerk and a thick-necked, bullet-headed man sitting by the window, who glanced up at her approach.

Having studied her for a moment, he retired once more behind his newspaper while she completed the formalities and was handed her room key.

It was her first visit to the capital of the Tyrol and, liking Innsbruck on sight, she decided to see as much as she possibly could in the relatively short time at her disposal.

As soon as she had showered and changed into a cream linen dress and jacket she made her way down to the foyer again, to find the same man was still sitting there, intent on his newspaper.

Having collected a street map from the desk, she turned to go.

The bullet-headed man had abandoned his paper and, his gaze fixed on her, was talking into a mobile phone. Their eyes met briefly, and perhaps embarrassed to be caught staring—even absently—he instantly looked away.

Map in hand, Nicola made her way into the sunny street, and after getting her bearings set off to explore.

There were plenty of horse-drawn carriages offering sightseeing tours, but, needing to stretch her legs following the day's drive, she decided to walk.

The sky was cloudless, the sun warm enough to make her push up the sleeves of her jacket, but traces of snow were still visible on the surrounding Alps.

After a look at the milky-green, fast-flowing Inn river, she made her way to the old part of town. The Altstadt, with its famous golden-roofed balcony and bulbous-domed Stadtturm tower, was colourful and bustling with tourists.

Strolling through the narrow, cobbled lanes, she was stepping back to admire one of the painted buildings when the thin heel of her court shoe slipped into a crack between the smooth stones and wedged tightly.

As she struggled to free it she heard the clatter of approaching hooves bearing down on her.

A second later she was swept up by a pair of strong arms and whisked to safety, while the horse-drawn carriage rattled harmlessly past.

For a moment or two, shaken, she lay with her head supported by a muscular shoulder, vaguely aware of the feel of silk beneath her cheek and the fresh masculine scent of cologne.

Then, pulling herself together, she raised her head and said a trifle unsteadily, 'Thank you. Believe me, I'm very grateful.'

'It was, perhaps, unnecessarily dramatic…' His voice was attractive, well-educated, his English perfect with only the faintest trace of an accent. 'But I'm glad I was on hand.'

Her rescuer was darkly handsome, without being swarthy, and just looking into his face took what was left of her breath away.

Apart from the colour of his eyes, he was a lot like her husband. Jeff's eyes had been a warm, cloudy blue, whereas this man's were a cool, clear grey. His hair was thick and raven-black—cut just short enough to restrain its desire to curl—his face lean and hard-boned, with a straight nose and a firm, chiselled mouth.

As she stared at him as though mesmerised, he said, 'Now I'd better retrieve your footwear.'

Setting her down carefully, so she could lean against the plastered wall of a building, he stepped out into the roadway.

He was tall and broad-shouldered and moved with an easy, masculine grace. Well, but casually dressed, in stone-coloured trousers and an open-necked shirt, he could have been simply a holidaymaker.

But there was something indefinable about him—a kind

of sureness? An air of authority?—that convinced her he wasn't.

Having eased the shoe free, he carried it back. 'The heel's a little scuffed, but apart from that it's undamaged.'

Settling on his haunches, he slipped the court shoe on to her slender foot, before straightening to his full height—some six feet plus.

Looking down at her heart-shaped face, with its pure bone structure and flawless skin, he commented, 'You still look shaken…'

She was. But not for the reason he imagined.

'What you need is that panacea for all ills, a nice cup of tea.'

His hand beneath her elbow, he led her round a corner to the Stadsbiesl, a tiny restaurant with overhanging eaves and white stucco walls. Its tiled roof sloping every which way, the old building leaned, supported like an amiable drunk between its neighbours.

A tunnelled archway gave access to a small sunny courtyard with three or four unoccupied tables covered with red-checked tablecloths.

'But perhaps, as you're fair-skinned, you'd prefer to be indoors?' he asked.

She shook her head. 'I love the sun and, so long as I don't do anything foolish, I tan quite easily.'

'Then al fresco it is.'

He helped her off with her linen jacket and hung it over the back of her chair.

The moment they were seated a white-coated waiter appeared with a pitcher of iced water and two glasses.

'Just tea?' Nicola's companion enquired. 'Or would you like to try a plate of the delectable cakes they serve here?'

'I had a late lunch, so just hot tea with lemon, thank you.'

He gave the order in fluent German, though she felt sure it wasn't his native tongue.

As the waiter moved away she remarked, 'You seem to know the Stadsbiesl well?'

'Yes. I eat here from time to time.' Studying her, he added, 'Your colour's coming back. Feeling better?'

'Much better.'

'On holiday?'

'Yes.'

'Is this your first time in Innsbruck?'

'Yes.' Reluctantly, she added, 'Though I'm only staying for one night. I'm on my way to Venice.'

'From England?'

'Yes. I'm driving down. Taking the scenic route.'

'It's a magnificent run over the Brenner Pass.'

'I'm sure it must be. I'm looking forward to it.'

But not so much as she had been.

Their pot of tea arrived, strings and tags dangling from beneath the lid. It was accompanied by a silver bowl of sugar cubes and another of thinly sliced lemon. On each bowl there was a pair of silver tongs shaped like twin dragons joined at the tail.

Indicating the pot, he suggested, 'Perhaps you'll pour?'

'Of course. Lemon and sugar?'

'Just lemon, please.'

She filled both cups, and passed him one. Then, made unusually clumsy by the knowledge that he was studying her, she dropped a piece of lemon into her own, so that it splashed tea down the bodice of her dress.

Getting to his feet, he felt in his pocket and produced an immaculate handkerchief. He dipped the corner into the pitcher of water and leaned over her to rub gently at the orange-brown stains.

Though his touch was light and impersonal, every nerve-ending in her body responded, and she felt her cheeks grow hot.

He moved back and, his head tipped a little to one side,

studied the results of his ministrations. 'There are still one or two faint marks but nothing too obvious.'

'Thank you,' she said in a strangled voice.

'It was my pleasure entirely,' he responded, straight-faced.

Uncertain whether or not he was laughing at her, she gathered herself, and, needing a topic of conversation, asked a shade breathlessly, 'Do you live in Innsbruck?'

'No, I'm here on business.' His eyes on her face, he went on, 'I live in Venice.'

'Oh…' For no reason at all, her heart lifted.

Still watching her, as though he was half expecting some reaction, he added deliberately, 'My name's Loredan… Dominic Irving Loredan.'

'Are you Italian?' was all she could think of to say.

'Half. My father was from the States, but my mother was Italian.'

So that accounted for the faint and fascinating accent she had noticed, and also for the eloquent way he used his long well-shaped hands when he was speaking.

'You're English, I take it?'

'Yes. I'm Nicola Whitney.'

He glanced at her wedding ring. '*Mrs* Whitney, I see.'

'Yes… No… Well, yes…'

Raising a dark winged brow, he commented, 'You seem a little uncertain.'

'I—I'm a widow,' she stammered.

Perhaps afraid of pitying exclamations, or maybe because to say it aloud made it all too real, this was only the second time she had voluntarily admitted her widowhood.

'You're very young to be a widow,' he remarked evenly.

'I'm twenty-five.'

'When did your husband die?'

'Three years ago.'

'And you're still wearing your ring?'

She still felt married.

When she said nothing, he pursued, 'Was his death some kind of accident?'

Because his question was matter-of-fact, unemotional, she was able to answer steadily, 'Yes. He was killed in a car crash.'

'So you're on your own?'

'I share a flat with a friend, Sandy.'

'He's not holidaying with you?'

'No, I'm alone… And Sandy's a *she*.'

Now why had she found it necessary to tell a complete stranger that? she wondered. Other people had made the same mistake and she hadn't bothered to correct them.

More than a little flustered, she hurried on, 'We met at college, and after Jeff, my husband, died she invited me to share her flat. I would have liked her to come with me, but she's a self-employed information consultant and she had too much work on.'

His manner casual, he queried, 'Are you in the same line of business?'

'No. I work for Westlake Business Solutions as a conference organiser.'

'Sounds very impressive. Are you good at your job?'

'Yes.'

The gleam in his grey eyes showed his appreciation of her answer before he asked, 'What qualifications are necessary for a job like that? Apart from looks?'

As he added the rider there seemed to be a slight edge to his voice. Or was she just imagining it?

She answered briefly, 'No qualifications as such.'

'Then what *do* you need?'

'A knowledge of how business works, a flair for judging what different clients want, and a certain originality. The ability to speak at least one extra language fluently is useful.'

'And do you? Speak another language, I mean?'

'Yes.'

'Do go on,' he said smoothly.

She shrugged slender shoulders. 'On the whole it's just hard work. Organising accommodation, conference facilities, a supply of suitable food and drink etcetera, and making sure everyone's happy.'

'Which I'm sure you do wonderfully well.'

This time there was no doubt about the edge, and, biting her lip, she remained silent.

'So where do you organise these conferences?'

'Worldwide…Tokyo, Sydney, Atlanta, Quebec, Paris, London.'

'That must involve a great deal of travelling.'

'Yes, it does.'

'And a good chance to meet people? The business delegates, for example?'

Disconcerted by his manner, and feeling a growing tension, she answered awkwardly, 'I usually only get to meet the people actually attending the conference, if things aren't going smoothly.'

'And of course you make sure they are?'

'As far as possible.'

Apparently sensing her discomfort, he sighed, and, leaning back in his chair, shook his head ruefully. 'Forgive me. I hope you'll accept my apologies?'

'For what?'

He gave a charming grimace. 'I shouldn't be grilling you about your life and work. You're on holiday and the sun's shining.'

The feeling of tension disappeared as though it had never existed.

And perhaps it hadn't. Maybe it had been all in her mind? Something to do with his resemblance to Jeff? Or the fact that for the past three years she had avoided socialising in this way, and so had lost her ability to mix and relax on a personal level?

'What do you have planned for the rest of your day in Innsbruck?' His low, clear voice broke into her thoughts.

'As much sightseeing as possible.'

'Alone?'

'Well, yes.'

'As my business is now successfully underway, and I'm alone too, perhaps you'll allow me to show you around?'

Her heart picked up speed and began to beat a tattoo against her ribcage while she decided what her answer should be.

She found him a fascinating and disturbing man. Disturbing not only because he reminded her of Jeff, but in a way she was unable to put her finger on.

Yet though her time spent in his company hadn't been altogether comfortable—and perhaps it was her own reaction to his explosive sex appeal that had caused her discomfort—she knew she didn't want it to end.

To hide the excitement that had suddenly made her feel like a girl again, she answered carefully, 'Thank you, that would be very nice.'

Whether he was amused by her primness, or pleased by her acceptance, she wasn't sure, but his white, even teeth flashed in a smile.

It was the first time she had seen him smile, and it added a thousandfold to his already considerable charm.

Dropping some *schillings* onto the table, he said, 'Then let's go.'

She gathered up her bag and jacket and they left the sunny courtyard, his hand at her waist.

Just that casual touch made her heart beat in a way that it had never done before. She had loved Jeff deeply, but they had been brought up together, he had been part of her life, so it had been a gentle, familiar caring. A feeling of warmth and safety rather than a mad excitement.

'Innsbruck is a compact city as far as sightseeing goes,' Dominic Loredan remarked as they emerged into the street. 'Almost everything of interest is here in the Altstadt—unless you'd like to see the Olympic ski jump, or the Europabrucke, Europe's highest bridge? Though tomorrow, if you head south on the motorway, you'll cross it.'

'I think, as time's limited, I'll stick with the historical part.'

'Then I suggest we start with the Hofburg Palace and the Hofkirche Chapel... That is, if you haven't already seen them...?'

'No, I haven't,' she said, no longer caring overmuch what she saw. Just being with this charismatic man was enough.

'They're just across the way from each other...'

His mouth was fascinating, she thought. It was a mouth that was at once coolly austere and warmly sensual. A clear-cut mouth that sent little shivers down her spine...

'Then later I'll take you up to Schloss Lienz for dinner.'

She dragged her gaze away from his mouth and, feeling her colour rise, echoed, 'Schloss Lienz?'

'The *schloss* dates from the sixteenth-century and has quite a turbulent history. To begin with it was a fortress, then it was used as a royal hunting lodge, now it's a first-class restaurant. From the terrace, which seems to hang in space, there's a superb view over the city.'

'It sounds wonderful.' Glancing down at the faint marks still visible on her dress, she added, 'Though I'll need to get changed first.'

'So will I. Where are you staying?'

'At the Bregenzerwald.'

'What a coincidence!'

'You mean you are?'

'Room 54.'

Hardly able to believe it, she marvelled, 'I'm in room 56.'

'Well, well… It seems coincidences are like swallows; they come in pairs…'

The rest of the afternoon passed in a haze of excitement. Nicola hadn't known this kind of happiness for over three years.

She found that Dominic Loredan was an easy and interesting companion, who proved to have an extensive knowledge of the city, an appreciation of beauty, and a dry sense of humour when pointing out the more droll aspects of the scenery.

When the pair had finally finished traipsing around the cobbled lanes of the old town, and seen most of what was to be seen, warm and a little dusty, they took a horse-drawn carriage back to their hotel.

Leaving her at her door, Dominic asked, 'How long will you need? An hour? Half an hour?'

Not having expected to dress up for dinner, she would have to go down to the car for her main suitcase. Even so…

'Just long enough to have a shower and get changed,' she answered quickly, begrudging even this amount of time spent away from him.

'Good.' Grey eyes smiled into green. 'I'll give you a knock in about half an hour.'

As she looked up at him he brushed her cheek with a single finger, and while she stood mesmerised, he bent his dark head and touched his lips to hers, a thistledown kiss that turned her knees to water and melted every last bone in her body.

Totally bemused, a hand to her lips, she watched him disappear into his own room. Then, like someone under a spell, she went into hers and gently closed the door.

CHAPTER TWO

FOR a little while she stood quite still, feeling again that most fleeting of caresses. Pulling herself together, she went to pick up her car keys.

Frowning, she stared at the empty space where she remembered them being before glancing around. Instead of lying on the chest of drawers, the keys, with their rental tag, were on the dressing table.

Perhaps she was mistaken? Maybe that was where she had left them? Or possibly one of the chambermaids had come in and moved them?

Whichever, the important thing was they were still there. So long as the car hadn't been stolen it wasn't a problem.

Stolen...

The implications of that thought made Nicola check her overnight case. A quick glance through the contents showed her passport and spare money were untouched, and so was her grandmother's jewellery box, which held most of the things she treasured.

Holding her breath, she released the catch and opened it. Everything seemed to be there. A small string of pearls Jeff had bought her for a wedding present, her grandmother's locket, the keys to John's house in Venice...

With a sigh of relief, she closed the lid and replaced the box.

Then, picking up the car keys, she took the lift down to the car park and hurried over to the blue saloon. Releasing the central locking, she moved to lift the lid of the boot.

It refused to budge.

Another press of the key released it. Which undoubtedly meant that it hadn't been locked in the first place.

Oh, but surely she'd locked it?

Or had she?

She lifted the boot lid, half expecting to see her case gone, but it was still there, exactly as she'd left it.

No, not *exactly*.

As if someone had closed it in a hurry, caught between the two zips where they met in the centre, was a small piece of material.

Opening the case, she looked inside. Once again nothing was missing. Everything seemed to be as it should be, apart from that tell-tale scrap of ivory satin that had been caught in the zip.

Eager to be off that morning, she had wasted no time in packing, so perhaps she had left that bit of nightdress hanging out?

But wouldn't she have noticed it?

Apparently not.

The only rational explanation had to be her own carelessness.

Yet the three things—the keys being moved, the car being unlocked, and the material caught between the zips—made a logical sequence that was very hard to dismiss.

Except that in the long run it made no sense.

If someone had got into her room and, finding the distinctive rental-tagged keys, gone to the trouble of locating the car and searching her case, wouldn't they have taken everything worth stealing? Including the car?

Instead there was nothing missing and the keys were still there. Which seemed to prove the whole thing was just a strange coincidence.

And coincidences did happen. Dominic Loredan being in the same hotel and having the room next to hers was proof of that.

Her thoughts having flown back to Dominic and the evening ahead, she lifted out the case, locked the car and hurried over to the lift.

Once in her room, having showered in record time, she donned fresh undies and a smoke-grey silk chiffon dress that Sandy had nagged her into buying, saying, 'You never know…'

It was a romantic dress, with a cross-over bodice, a long, swirling skirt and a matching stole. Shaking out the stole, which was lined with scarlet, Nicola hesitated, still unsure.

But recalling how, when she had hesitated at the colour, Sandy had exclaimed crossly, 'Oh, for heaven's sake! You can't go on wearing widow's weeds for ever', she made up her mind to take it.

Placing it on a chair with her small evening bag, she stood in front of the mirror to take up her thick, naturally blonde hair.

As she held the smooth coil in place on top of her head and began to push in the pins her eyes were drawn to her wedding ring.

Her task finished, she studied the thin gold band. Married for barely a year when Jeff was killed, she had now been a widow for considerably longer than she had been a wife.

As John had said, anyone who had lost a loved one needed to mourn, but no one should mourn for ever.

Maybe the time had come to let go of the past.

Slipping off the ring, she put it carefully with her other treasures.

Anxious to look her best—for the first time in more than three years—she picked up her cosmetic case and turned back to the mirror.

With somewhat darker brows and lashes, and a clear skin, she needed very little in the way of make-up. A dab of powder to stop her small straight nose from shining, a touch of green eyeshadow and a light coating of pale lipgloss and she was ready.

A knock made her snatch up her evening bag and stole and hurry to open the door.

Looking devastatingly handsome in a black tie and evening jacket, Dominic Loredan was waiting.

His gaze travelled over her from head to toe and back again, making her feel oddly shivery, before he remarked evenly, 'You really are the most beautiful thing I've ever seen.'

Just for an instant she had the odd impression that his words hadn't been intended as a compliment.

Perhaps he read the uncertainty in her face, because he took her hand and raised it to his lips.

The romantic little gesture and its accompanying smile smoothed away the impression, as the sea smoothed away footprints in the sand.

Her heart lifting, she returned his smile. 'I'm afraid I forgot to thank you for a lovely afternoon.'

Taking the stole from her, he put it around her shoulders and offered her his arm. 'The evening should prove to be even better.'

His sleek white sports car was waiting in the car park, its hood back, and in a matter of minutes they were making their way out of the city. Though the sun had gone, the air was still comfortably warm, and in the low-slung seats they were shielded from too much wind.

Soon they began to climb steadily, the view changing with every horseshoe bend. Stands of trees set in sloping green meadows... The flash of water and a roadside shrine bright with flowers... Wooden chalets, with a steepled church perched high on a bluff above them... Then, set against the magnificent backdrop of mountains, a turreted castle.

'The Schloss Lienz,' Dominic said.

'It's a real picture-book place,' she remarked delightedly.

'I'm pleased you like it,' he said gravely, as he took the winding road up to the *schloss*. When they reached it they drove through an archway into a vast cobbled courtyard. Set around it were metal sconces holding long torches that looked like enormous bulrushes.

Having helped Nicola out, he handed the car keys to a hovering attendant, and it was whisked through another archway, out of sight.

At this height the alpine air was appreciably cooler and fresher as she stood staring up at the grey stone walls towering above them. Seeing her slight shiver, Dominic thoughtfully adjusted her stole higher on her shoulders.

'Thank you.' She smiled at him, suddenly feeling cosseted and cared for, a feeling she hadn't experienced for a very long time.

At the entrance to the *schloss* they were greeted by a thick-set man with blond hair, who was, Nicola discovered later, the Baron Von Salzach.

In heavily accented English, he said, 'Good evening, Dominic. It is nice to see you again. Mrs Whitney, welcome to Schloss Lienz. If you will follow me, you have a table on the terrace, as requested.'

'Thank you, Franz.'

Their host led the way to the end of a large flagged hall and through a carpeted, chandelier-hung dining-room, where a quartet of musicians played Mozart and most of the well-dressed clientele seemed to be in decorous groups.

As they followed him Nicola noticed that several of the women with middle-aged escorts gave Dominic a second surreptitious glance, and her an envious one. As they reached a long, curving flight of stone stairs, Franz said, 'Please be careful. The steps are old and worn in places.'

The stairway led up to a flagged open-air terrace, which

held only a handful of widely spaced tables, four of which were already occupied.

'Out here it's somewhat less stuffy,' Dominic remarked *sotto voce*.

His sidelong smile convinced her he wasn't referring to the temperature.

When they were seated at a table set with gleaming crystal and a centrepiece of fresh flowers, the Baron said, 'I hope you will enjoy your meal,' clicked his heels, and departed.

Intrigued by the glowing charcoal braziers standing at intervals along the waist-high outer wall, Nicola remarked, 'They look so wonderfully appropriate.'

'As soon as the sun goes down they're necessary to keep the air comfortably warm,' Dominic explained. 'Though before they were installed, a couple of years ago, the hardy diner would risk pneumonia for the sake of the view.'

Gazing at the wonderful panorama of Innsbruck spread below them in the wide, flat valley of the Inn, she said, 'If you want my opinion, it was well worth the risk.'

'When all the city lights start to come on, you'll find it's even better.'

As they ordered and ate a superb dinner she found he was right. In the blue velvet dusk the glittering lights turned the twenty-first century into a fairy tale. While at the castle itself the lanterns on the terrace and the flaring torches in the courtyard below gave the scene a medieval feel.

Though he drank little himself, Dominic kept Nicola's glass topped up with an excellent Riesling that was light and subtle and easy to keep sipping.

Caught up in the magic of the moment, a magic that had a lot to do with the *schloss* but even more to do with her companion, she failed to notice just how much she was drinking.

During the meal he had steered clear of anything remotely personal, so it came as a complete surprise when, reaching across the table, he lifted her bare left hand and remarked, 'You've taken off your ring.'

'Yes.'

'Why?'

'I—I'm not sure,' she stammered, shaken both by his touch and his question. 'The time just seemed to be right.'

Something in his look made her go on to explain, 'I suddenly realised I'd been a widow for longer than I'd been a wife.'

Releasing her hand, he queried, 'How long were you married?'

'Not quite a year…'

Perhaps it was too much wine that loosened her tongue, or maybe, at long last, the time had come when she felt it a relief to be able to talk about the past.

Whichever, she found herself opening up to a perfect stranger in a way she hadn't been able to open up to anyone, except John.

'Jeff and I had a traditional white wedding on my twenty-first birthday.'

'But you'd lived together before that?'

'Virtually all our lives… Oh, I see what you mean. No, we hadn't lived together in that sense.'

Seeing his slight frown, she explained, 'Jeff's parents were my parents too. My *foster* parents. They had been my grandmother's friends for a number of years, and they took care of me while she was in hospital and after she died.'

'How old were you then?'

'Just turned five.'

'And your husband?'

'He was a few months older, and their only child.'

'They never tried to officially adopt you?'

'I think they would have liked to. They had hoped for more children, but they were well past middle-age when Jeff was born, so they would have been considered too old.'

'You had no grandfather?'

'He'd died the previous year.'

'What about your natural parents?'

'I'd never known them, and one day, having realised that most of my peers had a mummy and daddy, I asked my grandmother why *I* didn't. She sat me on her knee and gave me a cuddle while she explained that mine had gone away. Because of something one of my little friends had said, I translated ''gone away'' as ''gone to heaven'', and over the years my foster parents, no doubt thinking it was for the best, allowed me to go on believing they were dead.

'Then when I reached sixteen, perhaps as an awful warning, they decided I was old enough to know the truth. My natural mother, whose name was Helen, was my grandmother's only child. From the age of thirteen she'd been a bit wild, and she was barely sixteen when she discovered she was pregnant.

'It seems she wanted to have an abortion, but my grandmother was horrified and insisted on her going through with the pregnancy.

'She hated the whole idea of motherhood, and even before I was born blamed me for spoiling her life. When I was only a few weeks old she disappeared, leaving my grandmother to take care of me.'

'Your grandmother must have been quite young when she died?'

'She was in her middle fifties. She had some kind of minor operation that went tragically wrong.'

Running lean fingers over his smooth chin, Dominic remarked thoughtfully, 'So, with having the same parents, you and your husband must have been brought up like sister and brother?'

Made a little uncomfortable by the bluntness of the question, she answered, 'We were always very close. Though we spent most of our time together—we even went to the same school—we never argued or fell out... I can't ever remember not loving Jeff, and it was the same for him.' Smiling fondly, she added, 'He once told me he'd loved me since I was a scrawny five-year-old with big solemn eyes and a pigtail.'

'Didn't close friends think it strange that you never quarrelled like other siblings?'

She answered truthfully, 'I don't recall having a really close friend, apart from Jeff, until I got to college. As children, our parents didn't encourage us to mix much, and really we never seemed to need anyone else.'

'What about when you grew into adults?'

'You mean did we stay friends?'

'I mean when did you become lovers?'

'Jeff wanted us to sleep together as soon as I'd turned eighteen.'

'But you didn't?'

She shook her head. 'No... Though after he'd died I almost wished we had. It seemed such a waste of three years... But although our parents were kind, they were quite strict and God-fearing, and they seriously disapproved of anyone having sex outside marriage.'

'So what happened?'

'Jeff suggested we should get married, but we were due to start college and neither of us had any money. Eventually he decided to approach our parents and tell them we loved each other and wanted to be together.

'When he did, they said if we waited until we'd finished college—to be sure we weren't making a mistake—they would give us their blessing and pay for a white wedding and all the trimmings. That way they could be proud of us.'

Seeing Dominic's expression, she admitted, 'It must seem terribly old-fashioned, but we'd been brought up to respect their wishes, and living under their roof meant accepting their standards. Apart from anything else they'd been very good to me, and I didn't want to let them down, so finally we promised to wait.'

His grey eyes intent, Dominic asked, 'Surely a promise like that went by the board once you got into student accommodation?'

'The college was only just down the road, and in the circumstances it seemed sensible to keep on living at home.'

Dominic's flicker of a smile said it all.

Disturbed by that smile, she found herself defending the decision. 'It was what our parents wanted us to do. They said some of the students were a wild bunch and we'd be better off at home.'

'I would have bet on it.'

Before Nicola could make any comment, he pursued smoothly, 'So you finished college and had a white wedding... Then what?'

Unused to dissembling, she spoke the exact truth. 'I moved into Jeff's room.'

'Didn't you find being under your parents' roof somewhat...inhibiting?'

She had, more so than Jeff.

A little defensively, she explained, 'It wasn't how I would have chosen to do things. We'd both graduated with honours—Jeff in Design Engineering, me in Modern Languages and Business Studies—but neither of us had managed to get a job... In any case our parents, who had lived in rented accommodation all their lives, wanted us to stay with them until we could afford to start buying a place of our own, and Jeff was in agreement...

'I know that must sound a bit staid and unexciting...'

His voice almost angry, Dominic said, 'It sounds soul-destroying.'

Nicola flushed painfully.

Watching her colour rise, he apologised. 'I'm sorry, I shouldn't have made a remark like that.'

As lightly as possible, she said, 'That's all right. And it wasn't really so bad. At least Jeff and I were together…'

Then, wistfully, 'Though it would have been nice if we'd ever been able to move into a place of our own…'

'So you never succeeded in getting away?'

She shook her head. 'I'd managed to get an office job, but Jeff was unlucky. The company he'd joined made massive cutbacks, and he was one of the first to be made redundant, so we were still trying to save up when the accident happened.'

'Earlier you mentioned that after the accident you went to live with your friend Sandy?'

'Yes.'

'I'm surprised you didn't remain at home.'

'Our parents were killed in the same accident. The three of them were coming to pick me up from work when a lorry went out of control and hit them. We were all going on a family holiday.'

'So you were left with no one.'

'Sandy was very kind.'

'How did you cope with your freedom?'

She looked up startled. 'I suppose the answer's not too well. Though I never thought of it as *freedom*… It just seemed more like loneliness. I missed Jeff so much…'

'Having lived together for most of your lives, I suppose you were bound to. What was he like?'

'Very much like you.' She spoke without thinking.

The look in Dominic's eyes was swiftly veiled, yet she felt certain that he was far from pleased by the comparison.

Coolly, he said, 'Well, as you obviously loved him a great deal, I should feel flattered… Though I'm not convinced you know me well enough yet to compare us.'

'I—I meant in looks,' she stammered. 'Like you, he was tall, dark, and handsome…'

'A hackneyed phrase that can cover a multitude of sins,' Dominic observed mockingly. 'However, do go on.'

But as she described her late husband, visualising his face as she spoke and superimposing his features on the man sitting opposite, she knew her impression that they were alike was totally false.

The only similarity was the height and colouring.

Jeff had been over six foot, but compared to this man's broad chest and mature width of shoulder he had been... The thought that came to mind was *weedy*...

Feeling dreadfully disloyal, she pushed it away.

Both had hair that was a true black and wanted to curl, but while this man's was cut short and tamed Jeff's had been a boyish riot of tight ringlets.

He had still been boyish in many ways, his hands big-knuckled and bony, as though he hadn't yet grown into them, his face thin and sensitive-looking, with fine features and the air of a dreamer.

This man was anything but boyish. His hands were strong and well-shaped, with blunt fingers and neatly trimmed nails; his face was lean, with patrician features and an air of toughness and authority.

Jeff, by nature, had been kind and gentle and considerate.

Of Dominic's nature she knew nothing.

Yet looking at him now, and recalling the way he had adjusted her stole, she felt oddly certain that, like a lot of powerful men, he might well be tender and protective.

She missed that. The tenderness. The caring.

Watching her face, noting the wistful expression, and misinterpreting it, Dominic said, 'It's about time we changed the subject. You're starting to look sad, and talking about your husband can't be easy.'

'A short while ago, it wouldn't have been possible,' she admitted. 'But I think I'm finally coming to terms with his loss.'

That was the truth. Tonight, though there had been tricky bits, on the whole it had been relatively painless to talk about Jeff.

There were so many *happy* memories, and he would always have a very special place in her heart. But, as though a heavy load had been lifted, she no longer felt that crippling weight of grief she had carried for the past three years.

Watching her expression, Dominic said gravely, 'Welcome back to the world. What plans have you for the immediate future?'

'Short-term, I shall stay in Venice for a month or so. Make this holiday a new beginning. You see, I...'

His grey eyes were fixed on her face, intent, waiting.

On the point of telling him about John and her reason for travelling to Venice, she hesitated. Then, deciding she had done more than enough soul-baring for one night, changed her mind. 'I haven't taken a holiday since I joined Westlake, so I decided it was time I took a break.'

Their waiter appeared to ask if they wanted anything further and, after consulting Nicola, Dominic ordered coffee with cream for her, espresso for himself, and two brandies.

It arrived quite quickly, accompanied by a silver filigree plate of chocolates.

When the waiter had moved away on silent feet, Dominic asked, 'Have you ever been to Venice before?'

'No, though I've always wanted to. I've often visualised the warmth and colour, the wonderful old buildings, water everywhere, and crowds of people...'

'That about sums it up,' he said with a smile. 'Though the crowds are usually there only in the summer and at carnival time, and mostly in the touristy areas.'

'Then you don't find them a problem?'

'Not personally. There are many parts of Venice that hardly ever see a tourist—quiet backwaters, picturesque or decaying, depending on your point of view, where the ordinary Venetians live.'

'Have you lived there long?'

'All my life, apart from three years at Oxford and a year spent travelling. As I said, my father was from the States, but my mother's family have lived in Venice since the time of the Doges, when Italy was a great seafaring nation and one of the most prosperous settlements in Europe. Now, five hundred years past its heyday, Venice is still one of the most spectacular cities in the world.'

Noting that his voice held both enthusiasm and pride, she said, making it a statement rather than a question, 'And you like living there.'

'Yes, I do. For one thing it never becomes stale. There's always so much atmosphere, whether it's sunny, or rain-lashed, or there's a fog rolling in off the Adriatic. And in the evening Piazza San Marco is the perfect place for lovers. Something about the ambience makes couples of all ages sit and hold hands...'

The thought of sitting in Piazza San Marco holding hands with Dominic sent little shivers of excitement running through her.

Seeing that slight movement, he asked, 'Getting cold?' Before she could find her voice, he signalled the waiter, adding, 'I suppose it's time we were making a move. We've both got a fair drive tomorrow, and I could do with an early start.'

The bill paid, he rose to his feet and, with what she was beginning to recognise as his habitual courtesy, pulled out her chair.

Sorry that what had proved to be a magical evening was over, she allowed herself to be escorted back down the long, worn flight of steps, through the dining room and hall, and out into the flare-lit courtyard.

Dominic's car had been brought to the door, and, feeling

the chill of the night air, she was grateful that the hood was now up.

Cupping a hand beneath her bare elbow, making her pulses leap, Dominic settled her into her seat, then slid behind the wheel just as the Baron appeared and stood beneath the huge metal lantern to wave them off.

They both returned his wave, and a moment later they were through the archway and following the mountain road down to the valley.

Dominic drove with silent concentration as, their lights sweeping a path through the darkness, he negotiated the steep bends.

Nicola, very aware of his potent sex-appeal, thought only of him, and what tomorrow might hold when they reached Venice.

Feeling a thrill of expectation, she wondered whether he'd ask where she was staying, or suggest seeing her next morning before they each started their journey.

It would be lovely if he proposed having breakfast together...

She was still enjoying the glow of excitement and anticipation as they drew into the car park at the Bregenzerwald.

He helped her out and, a hand at her waist, accompanied her to the lift and pressed the button for the fifth floor.

When they reached her room she felt in her bag for the key and, having found it, fumbled to fit it into the lock.

She was starting to feel a little light-headed. Perhaps, as she wasn't used to drinking, she shouldn't have had a brandy with her coffee. But it was too late now.

'Allow me.' He took the key from her, and, having opened the door, handed it back with a smile.

'Thank you...'

She took a step into the room, and reached to put the key and her bag on the small table just inside the door. Then, with a sudden fear that he might just walk away, turned quickly to say, 'And thank you for a lovely evening. I've really enjoyed it.'

The sudden movement made her head spin, and, momentarily off balance, she swayed towards him and put her hands flat-palmed against his chest to steady herself. She could feel the warmth of his body through the fine lawn of his evening shirt.

Becoming aware that he had stiffened and was standing absolutely motionless, she backed away a step, saying huskily, 'I'm sorry.'

'There's really no need to be sorry... And I'm pleased you enjoyed the evening.'

Though the words were easy enough, there was a tautness about him, a look on his face that seemed to suggest a conflict of emotions, amongst them a touch of...censure?

It was gone in an instant, the smile back in place, convincing her that she must have imagined it.

A little awkwardly, she said, 'Well, goodnight.'

'Goodnight, Nicola.'

It was the first time he'd used her name.

Fascinated, she watched his mouth frame the syllables, and knew she wanted him to kiss her. *Needed* him to kiss her.

As though in answer to that unspoken need his hands closed around her upper arms and, drawing her towards him, he covered her mouth with his.

Though there was nothing diffident about it, his kiss was light, almost experimental, as though he was holding back to calculate her reaction before he decided exactly how to continue.

But once again her knees turned to water and her very bones seemed to melt, so that she was forced to lean against him for support.

His arms went around her, and as her lips parted helplessly beneath his he deepened the kiss.

It was like a brilliant flash of light, showing up both past and future, a revelation that was followed by a deep, black velvet darkness.

When he took her hand and led her into her room, closing the door behind them, she made not the slightest protest, conscious only of him and the need he had aroused.

Setting her back to the panels, one hand on the warmth of her nape, he bent to kiss her again while his free hand began to smooth over her slender figure: the small waist, the flare of her hip, the curve of her buttocks.

After a while the silk chiffon became an unwelcome barrier and, unzipping her dress, he eased it off her shoulders, allowing it to fall at her feet. Then his lips left hers to sensuously explore the line of her collarbone and the smooth skin of her shoulder.

When they reached the tender junction where neck and shoulder met, his kisses changed to little nibbling bites that made her stomach clench and her toes curl.

His mouth returning to hers, he unclipped her strapless bra and, cupping one of her small, firm breasts, brushed his thumb over the nipple.

While she was still struggling to cope with the sensations he was provoking, he bent his head and, having laved the other erect nipple, took it into his mouth and suckled sweetly.

She was suddenly into sensual overload, the pleasure so intense that she gave a little moan and, running her fingers into his dark hair, held his head away from her breast.

A moment later she was swept up in his arms and carried to the bed. The only light was from the street outside, but in the gloom she saw the gleam of his eyes as he laid her carefully on top of the covers and sat down beside her to take off what remained of her clothing.

CHAPTER THREE

IT WAS so long since she had been tenderly held and made love to, so long since she had felt the warmth of being needed, that far from objecting, half choked by eagerness, she would have helped him had it been necessary.

But his hands were both gentle and deft, and though he didn't linger, neither did he show the slightest sign of haste.

When she was totally naked, he said with a kind of urgency, 'Let your hair loose,' and, as she lifted her hands to obey, began to strip off his own clothes.

As her hair came tumbling around her shoulders, he sat on the edge of the bed and, running his fingers into the thick silky mass, began to kiss her again.

When he finally joined her on the bed, her arms were ready to welcome him, but stretching out beside her, he propped himself on one elbow, taking time to pleasure her, while he enjoyed a body that, he told her softly, was the loveliest he'd ever seen.

As he stroked and touched and tasted, she clenched and unclenched her hands, lost and mindless, caught up and engulfed by the kind of suffocating hunger and excitement she had never experienced in her life before.

Everything he was doing now only served to suck her deeper into a black and spinning whirlpool of desire, and by the time he made them one she was a quivering mass of sensations and desperate for the release that only he could provide.

Nicola floated to the surface to find it was broad daylight. The curtains hadn't been pulled to, and the early-morning sun was pouring in.

For a little while she lay half-asleep and half-awake, gazing up at the white ceiling, where a reflected sunbeam danced. She felt relaxed and contented in a way she hadn't felt for years.

She was trying lazily to brush aside the last clinging cobwebs of sleep to find the reason for her euphoria when, as though in answer, her mind was filled with thoughts of Dominic.

Memories of his dark, handsome face and the infinite rapture and delight he had given her came flooding back.

Her heart filled to overflowing, she turned her head.

She was alone in the bed, and his clothes had vanished. Presumably, for the look of the thing, he had gone back to his own room. But just the imprint of his head in the pillow beside her, and the recollection of his lovemaking, was as warming as the sun.

For so long the world had seemed a cold and lonely place. No love, no warmth, no joy. She had denied and suppressed all her natural needs, keeping her longings and emotions packed away in ice while life went on around her.

Now, as though to make up for the blows it had inflicted, fate had offered her a second chance of happiness.

A chance she had snatched at in a way that was not only completely unlike her but which, in her right mind, she would have regarded as wild and irresponsible.

In the normal course of events a new relationship would have moved forward at a steadier rate—getting to know one another, becoming friends, and then finally lovers.

But somehow they had skipped the first two stages. All she knew about Dominic was what she had discovered in a single afternoon and evening. That he was an excellent companion, intelligent and charming, with a dry humour and a curiously old-fashioned sense of chivalry.

She had no real idea what made him tick as a person.

After all her foster mother's dire warnings she had gone to bed with a man she had only just met; a man who was a virtual stranger. A departure from the norm that she was forced to admit was dangerous to the point of lunacy.

Though she couldn't regret a moment of it, she found herself wondering what on earth had made her behave so recklessly.

Too much alcohol had undoubtedly contributed, by putting her on a high and lulling her inhibitions. But if she was truthful, she knew the alcohol wasn't to blame.

She had found Dominic irresistibly attractive from the word go, and the whole magical evening—the drive, the *schloss*, the ambience, the good food and wonderful scenery—had all played a part.

A scene set for seduction.

Except that she couldn't blame him. She had *wanted* what happened. Probably more than he had, she admitted, recalling his first reaction to what she now realised uneasily must have appeared to be a come-on.

Perhaps if she explained to him that she wasn't used to drinking…? Or would it be better to say nothing? She didn't want him to feel guilty in any way, or think that she was trying to put the blame on him.

But why should there be any suggestion of guilt or blame? He certainly hadn't pressured her. She had been a willing partner…

And it had been *wonderful*. She sighed. As well as being a skilful lover, he had been generous and considerate and, remembering the controlled passion of his lovemaking, her heart began to beat faster.

Jeff's lovemaking had been kind and tender, warm and caring, but she hadn't realised until last night how much it had lacked passion. Or skill.

How much she had missed.

Her main pleasure, quite often her *only* pleasure, had been lying in his arms afterwards, happy that he was satisfied and contented.

Maybe it had been her own fault. Perhaps she had felt too inhibited to let go and enjoy the side of marriage that she was convinced her foster mother had secretly regarded as 'not quite nice'.

Things might have been different if she and Jeff had managed to get away—*get away*…she was using Dominic's words—but it was no use thinking about what might have been. That part of her life was over. Fate had written *finis* to it.

Now, at last, with John's encouragement, and having met Dominic, she was moving forward into a new, exciting, and hopefully much happier phase.

Thinking of Dominic, and recalling how he had mentioned getting an early start, she glanced at her watch. It was gone eight-thirty. He was probably waiting for her in the breakfast room, wondering where on earth she'd got to.

Pushing aside the light covers, she scrambled out of bed. Her discarded clothes, she noticed, had been picked up and placed neatly over a chair.

As soon as she had cleaned her teeth and showered she dressed in a light two-piece and flat shoes that she judged would be easy to drive in, and hastily repacked her cases.

Standing in front of the mirror, she saw a strange young woman with a smile hanging on her lips. A happy and excited woman, who had a glowing, heart-shaped face and sparkling green eyes.

With a feeling of *joie de vivre*, she smiled back.

She was halfway through taking her hair up into its usual neat coil when, recalling the way Dominic had run his fingers through it, her heart picked up speed and her hands started to tremble.

Telling herself not to be foolish, she finished pushing in

the pins and, leaving her luggage where it was, hurried to
the lift, eager as a young Juliet.

The breakfast room faced east and was light and airy,
with a crescent-shaped counter that held fruit and cereals,
rolls and croissants, ham, cheeses, and various preserves.

Three or four tables were occupied, and an elderly couple
were standing by the buffet debating in English whether to
have rolls or croissants. Dominic was nowhere to be seen.

So she was first down after all. Making up her mind to
tease him about it, Nicola helped herself to fruit juice and
a croissant, and sat down at a table for two. When a waiter
appeared, she asked for coffee.

By the time she had eaten her croissant and drunk two
cups of coffee, there was still no sign of him.

She went back upstairs and tapped at his door.

There was no answer.

Thinking he might possibly be in the shower, she knocked
harder.

Still no answer.

As she stood hesitating in the corridor, wondering what
to do for the best, a chambermaid appeared pushing a trolley
loaded with fresh bedlinen.

With a curious glance at Nicola, she opened the door of
number 54 with a master-key.

'The man who has this room…' Nicola said carefully, 'I
was hoping to speak to him.'

'He has gone, *fräulein*. The room is empty.'

'Oh.' Somehow they must have missed each other.
Possibly he was at the desk paying his bill.

Letting herself back into her own room, Nicola gathered
together her luggage and took the lift down to the foyer.

There were quite a few people there, including the bullet-
headed man she had seen the previous day, but no Dominic.

She paid her own bill and made her way down to the car
park. Having stowed everything in the boot, she locked the

car and crossed to the far bay where Dominic's white car
had been parked.

It was no longer there.

The realisation was like a blow in the solar plexus.

Surely he hadn't just gone without a word?

Hurrying back to the desk, she gave her name to the desk
clerk and asked, 'Did anyone leave a note for me?'

A white envelope with the hotel logo was produced. 'My
apologies, *fräulein*. It should have been given to you when
you checked out, but it was overlooked.'

Sinking into one of the maroon leather chairs, she tore it
open.

Written on a sheet of hotel notepaper, in a clear, positive
hand, it said simply:

A business commitment meant I had to make an early
start, and you were sleeping so peacefully when I left that
it seemed a shame to disturb you.

Have a good journey. I'm looking forward to seeing
you in Venice.

Dominic

I'm looking forward to seeing you in Venice...

But he'd never asked where she was staying, nor had he
told her where he lived.

In answer to his questions she had poured out her life
story, while he had told her virtually nothing about himself.
All she really knew was that he was a businessman who
lived in Venice.

Venice was a big city. A lot of people lived there.

As Nicola sat and stared blankly at the sheet of paper, it
was borne upon her that he had opted out. If he really *had*

wanted to see her in Venice he would have given her a phone number, told her where to contact him.

Her feeling of excitement vanished as if it had never been, and she bit her lip until she tasted the warm, sticky saltiness of blood.

After being cautious, inhibited even, all her life, she had thrown aside all restraints and behaved totally out of character.

Like the worst kind of fool, she had regarded their night together as *special*, the start of a wonderful relationship. But as far as he was concerned it had been just been a one-night stand.

If he had seemed caring and tender, it hadn't meant he *cared* in the slightest. Only that he was a good lover. To him she had merely been a woman who was willing, not to say eager, to go to bed with him.

He must be used to women throwing themselves at him. With his looks and charisma it probably happened a lot.

Recalling his momentary hesitation before he had kissed her, the look on his face that she was now convinced *had* been censure, she was filled with a sense of shame and humiliation. She had thrown herself at a man who must have felt little but contempt for her.

He might even be married.

She hadn't asked, and he hadn't mentioned it. But then, if he *was* cheating on his wife he wouldn't want to publicise the fact.

Thinking about it logically, as he was half Italian and living in Italy, he was almost certainly married, and probably had a family. Italian males tended to marry at a younger age than their English counterparts, and he must be somewhere in the region of thirty.

Feeling as if her heart had shrivelled inside her, she was about to drop the note into the nearest litter bin, when at the last instant she changed her mind and thrust it into her bag.

He had written it, it was the only tangible link, and somehow, although she knew she was acting like a weak fool, she couldn't bring herself to simply throw it away.

It was a beautiful day, with golden sunshine, a sky the colour of cornflowers, and a few white cotton wool clouds. But all the pleasant anticipation of the journey had gone as, heavy-hearted and bitterly ashamed of her actions, she drove out of Innsbruck and headed south for Italy.

Telling herself firmly that it was no use crying over what couldn't be altered, she tried hard to put Dominic Loredan and everything that had happened right out of her mind.

It was next door to impossible.

His strong, handsome face haunted her, and time after time she had to struggle to banish memories of his voice and his smile, his experienced hands and the touch of his mouth on hers.

However, by dint of concentrating on her driving and the magnificent mountain scenery, she managed to go for quite long periods without thinking of him, and she found the journey over the Brenner Pass both picturesque and interesting.

After a while she decided to have some music, and reaching for one of the tapes she had brought with her for the journey, slotted it in.

After a moment the first vibrant notes of a Rachmaninov piano concerto filled the car.

She hadn't been able to listen to that kind of music whilst living at home. Her foster parents had disapproved of Rachmaninov, thinking him too unrestrained.

Now, listening to the beautiful, passionate music, Nicola's thoughts turned once again to Dominic, and the night they had spent together.

She had awakened just as dawn was breaking to find herself held in the crook of his arm, her head on his shoulder, her body half supported by his.

He had been lying quietly on his back, his eyes open, his jaw covered in a dark stubble that made him look even more masculine and sexy.

Overjoyed that he was still with her, she had nestled against him.

His arm tightening in response, he had begun to fondle her breast, making her heart beat faster with pleasure and anticipation.

She had touched him then, tracing his ribcage, the muscles beneath the smooth, tanned skin, the line of his collarbone and his small, taut nipples.

Hearing his slight intake of breath, and wondering if her touch was giving him a fraction of the pleasure his was giving her, greatly daring, she had allowed her hand to wander downwards past the trim waist and over the flat stomach.

Turning his head so that his lips were brushing her hair, he had murmured, 'If you go on doing that you'll be in trouble.'

She, who had never in her life played this kind of lovers' game, had found herself asking provocatively, 'What kind of trouble?'

'Big trouble.'

'I think I can stand it.'

The words had ended in a gasp as he'd rolled her over, pinning her beneath him. 'Do you now?' he'd asked silkily.

Thinking of what had happened next, the pleasure they had shared before falling asleep again, made heat run through her. But rather than the heat of passion it was a burning humiliation.

Having stopped at a convenient roadside restaurant for lunch, it was late afternoon by the time she reached Venice and drove over the three-and-a-half kilometre Ponte della Liberta.

The built-up coastal strip had been flat and relatively un-interesting, and, apart from the bridge itself, this approach to the city seemed to be little better.

Then all at once its domes and spires began to appear, strangely beautiful and insubstantial as any mirage in the shimmering air.

Piazzale Roma, on the other hand, was as prosaic as any large square that was also a bus terminus. Edged by stalls selling cold drinks and hot dogs, chilled water melon and thin white slices of fresh coconut, it was hot and crowded and dusty, full of engine noise and diesel fumes, and the smell of fried onions.

No traffic went beyond the *piazzale*. All road vehicles were left either in the blocks of private garages or in the huge public car parks.

Unsure quite where to go, Nicola drew to a halt and hes-itated. A boy of perhaps eleven or twelve, wearing a torn T-shirt and sneakers, came up to the car and said through the open window. 'You English? On holiday?'

'Yes,' she answered a shade cautiously.

'I look after case while you park car. Then I show you where to get *vaporetto*.'

Dared she chance leaving her luggage with this brown-skinned urchin? Or would he disappear with it while her back was turned?

To give herself a moment to think, she remarked, 'You speak good English.'

'I learn from my cousin's wife. She 'as live in America long time. You put case here—' he indicated a flagged area by some stone steps '—I guard till you come back.'

Everything of real value was in her overnight case, and, used to travelling light, in this temperature it would be a boon if she *could* leave the big suitcase.

Seeing her waver, he urged, 'You OK… I no steal.'

'What's your name?'

'Carlo Foscari.'

He gave his name without hesitation. Making up her mind, Nicola opened the car door and started to get out. Her skirt rode up a little, and as she smoothed it over her knees she saw a short, thick-set man, with blue jowls and black hair, staring at her intently.

Recalling what Sandy had said about Italian males, she pretended not to notice.

Sun beat down from a cloudless sky and heat struck through the thin soles of her sandals as she lifted out her big suitcase and set it down in the gritty dust. When she looked up, the man who had been staring at her had vanished.

Opening her bag, she took out enough *lira* notes to hopefully make the ready cash more useful than a case full of clothing, and tore them in two. Giving one half to the boy, she put the other half back in her bag.

To her surprise, he grinned as he thrust them into the pocket of his frayed khaki shorts. 'I tell you no trust me.'

Grinning back, she asked in Italian, 'Would you, in my place?'

He gave her a look of respect. 'You speak Italian good, *signorina*…?'

'Whitney,' she supplied.

'Whitney…' He had a fair shot at it. 'But I practise my English…' Waving a grubby paw, he instructed, 'Go that way to long stay car park. I wait here.'

When she returned with a ticket and her overnight case, he gave her a cheeky grin. 'See! I no steal.'

'I should hope not,' she told him severely.

'This way,' he said importantly, and seized the big suitcase.

'You'd better let me have that,' she objected. 'It's too heavy for you.'

'Then I take small one.'

She shook her head.

'OK… I get help.' Putting two fingers to his lips, he gave a piercing whistle. 'Mario will come.'

Mario, a handsome young man with brown wavy hair and soulful dark eyes, appeared from nowhere.

'My brother,' Carlo explained briefly.

Nicola found herself escorted, one on either side, down the flight of stone steps to the Grand Canal and the landing-stage for the *vaporetti*.

Venice's main thoroughfare was wider than she had imagined, the sparkling water teeming with craft of all shapes and sizes, barges, motorboats, gondolas.

'See, it come.' Carlo sounded personally responsible for the arrival of the crowded water-bus which was approaching the landing stage.

Taking the torn *lira* notes from her bag, Nicola handed them to him. '*Grazie*, Carlo.'

Mario was appreciably older, eighteen or nineteen, she guessed, and a great deal better dressed. She was wondering whether to tip him when, as though reading her difficulty, he smiled at her, his teeth very white, and said, 'It was my pleasure, *signorina*.'

Glad that she hadn't hurt his feelings, she said, '*Grazie*, Mario,' and with a single smile made him forget the girl he'd been planning to take out that evening.

'Where you stay?' Carlo enquired.

'Hotel Lunga. Campo Dolini.'

'I know. You get *biglietto* to San Sebastian. Go down Calle Dolini.'

The *vaporetto* drew into the landing stage and bumped heavily a couple of times, before being moored. As they were practically swamped by the crowds streaming off it,

Carlo suggested hopefully, 'Tonight you wish for guide to see Venice?'

'*Non, grazie.*'

Looking disappointed, he persisted, 'Tomorrow morning, maybe?'

'No, thank you, Carlo.'

As she was carried forward by the surge of people waiting to get on the boat, he called, '*Ciao*, Signorina Whitney.'

By the time she had managed to struggle aboard and find a few feet of space to put her cases down, both Carlo and Mario had been swallowed up by the crowd.

As soon as the *vaporetto* began to move Nicola enjoyed the cooling breeze standing by the rail. Sun glinted on the pale blue-green water, and the light was so dazzling that she felt in her bag for her sunglasses.

The Grand Canal, picturesque and colourful in pastel hues, like a Canaletto painting come to life, was lined on either side with pale marble *palazzos*, baroque and rococo churches, and fine old buildings.

Some of them appeared to be sadly neglected, their crumbling steps and low-lying frontage blotched with patches of black, slimy seaweed. Yet, hauntingly beautiful even in their decay, they still held echoes of a former glory.

Though he hadn't been Italian by birth, this had been John's city.

It was also Dominic's…

The recollection brought a sudden lump to her throat, and she was still endeavouring to banish thoughts of Dominic from her mind when the boat reached San Sebastian.

Gathering up her luggage, she disembarked along with a small crowd of people, some locals, some obviously tourists.

Though the air seemed still and heavy, occasional little gusts of hot wind sprang up from nowhere, rattling the awnings of closed shops and swirling the dust.

Calle Dolini was a narrow street to the left, and she

walked along the shady side, putting the big case down briefly from time to time.

Away from the main *fondamenta*, and in the heat of the day, there was no one about apart from one man who was quite a distance behind her. Obviously in no hurry, he never caught her up, despite the stops.

When she finally emerged into Campo Dolini, she found that it was a quiet, dusty square surrounded by buildings with closed shutters.

What was obviously the rear entrance to Hotel Lunga looked distinctly unpromising, with crumbling stucco, narrow, shuttered windows and peeling doors.

Inside, however, it was positively luxurious, with polished marble floors and crystal chandeliers.

Standing by the desk in the foyer, she could see that the hotel's main entrance fronted on to a canal which ran parallel to the end of the *campo*. Steps led down to a private landing stage for the guests arriving by water-taxi.

Which of course, Nicola realised belatedly, *she* should have done. Though the *vaporetto* had been an experience she wouldn't have missed.

When she had checked in, she took the lift up to her third-floor room. It was cool and dim and spacious, with terrazzo flooring and the absolute minimum of light, modern furniture.

The windows were open wide, but the slatted shutters had been closed to keep out the sun. Opening them a few inches, she found herself looking over the *campo*, two-thirds of which lay in bright sunlight, the other third in shade.

As she stood by the window she noticed a man standing in the deep shadows at the far end of the square. He was of similar height and build to the man who had stared at her in the Piazzale Roma.

Her hand on the wooden shutter, she leaned forward to

try and get a better view. Squeaking a protest, it suddenly swung wide.

When she regained her balance and looked again, there wasn't a soul to be seen.

A glance in the *en suite* bathroom showed it was well-appointed, and, hot and sticky after her walk in the sun, she decided that her first priority was to shower and change.

As she stood beneath the warm water, smoothing shower-gel over her slick body, she remembered how Dominic's hand had explored her curves... How he had cupped her breast and rubbed his thumb lightly over the nipple, sending needle-sharp darts of pleasure through her... The way his tongue had laved the other nipple before his mouth had closed over it...

Shuddering, she tried to push the erotic imagery away, but already her whole body was growing alive and eager, every nerve-ending tightening in response...

With a sudden savage movement, she turned the water to cold, and gasped as the shock hit her.

Dried and duly sprayed with *Adventure*, the body mist Sandy had insisted on giving her as a 'seeing Venice present', she opened her case and found fresh undies and a silky sage-green dress with a loose matching jacket.

Deciding to abandon the rest of her unpacking until later, she slipped her slender feet into a comfortable pair of strappy sandals with a small heel, and smoothed on some sunscreen.

Then, having helped herself to a complimentary Pianta di Venezia, on an impulse she dropped the keys to Ca' Malvasia into her bag before setting off to explore.

Leaving the hotel by the main entrance, she paused on the sunlit pavement for a moment to study the map. Piazza San Marco, the hub of the city, was on the lagoon, and easy to find...

Abruptly, Dominic's tough, attractive face filled her mind, and the notion that he was almost certainly here, in Venice, maybe not too far away, was a bittersweet one.

Feeling as though her heart was being constricted by iron bands, she thought, If only things could have been different. He was the kind of man she would have been happy to spend the rest of her life with.

Oh, don't be such a fool! she berated herself crossly. How could she possibly think such a stupid thing? She didn't *know* him. And if she was right in her assumption that he was married, would she seriously want a man who could so casually cheat on his wife?

Pushing away memories of Dominic for perhaps the hundredth time that day, Nicola returned to the map to try and locate the house she could still hardly believe was hers.

Signor Mancini had told her that Ca' Malvasia was situated on Campo dei Cavalli, and quite close to the Grand Canal. He had added that the Rio dei Cavalli ran behind the property, so it was also accessible from the water.

Knowing that the Rio dei Cavalli should be easier to find than a square, she followed the curve of the Grand Canal scanning both banks… Yes, there it was—and, close by, the *campo*.

First thing in the morning she had an appointment with Signor Mancini, to be shown over Ca' Malvasia, but with a sudden surge of impatience, she decided that if she could find it now she would take a look at the outside at least.

She walked down the *fondamenta* and crossed a hump-backed bridge with ornate wrought-iron railings, and headed west.

The early-evening light was low and golden, scaling the crumbling stone and brickwork and slanting across water that, in the back canals, was the oily, opaque green of pea soup.

It didn't take her long to realise how easy it would be to

get lost in Venice. Away from the centre it was a labyrinth of narrow streets, the names of which were set high on the corners of buildings. Some were written in Venetian dialect, which made them more difficult to decipher.

It would no doubt have been a great deal simpler to have gone back to the Grand Canal and followed that, but she wanted to see the parts of Venice that tourists rarely, if ever, visited.

The everyday Venice that John had been familiar with. The Venice that Dominic knew and loved.

CHAPTER FOUR

MOST of the houses she passed en route had shuttered windows that gave them a blind, empty look. But the rattle of crockery and the sound of television suggested that many families were home and about to sit down to an early-evening meal.

Because of the network of waterways it was impossible to take a straight line so, zigzagging, crossing innumerable small bridges, she finally found an alleyway that led her to her goal.

At first glance, Campo dei Cavalli looked to be merely a quiet backwater with a few shady trees, but a handsome marble fountain in the centre, its four long-maned horses galloping through sea spray, spoke of more illustrious days.

Dominated on one side by a huge church, the *campo* appeared to be still and deserted, the only movement a swirling dust devil whipped up by a sudden gust of wind.

But as Nicola glanced around she saw a man with a mobile phone to his ear just disappearing into one of the alleyways that quartered the square. In such a setting it seemed incongruous.

Backing on to the Rio dei Cavalli were several old and handsome *palazzos*, whose intricate, lace-like façades and arched windows gave them a Gothic look.

Signor Mancini had mentioned that Ca' Malvasia backed on to the water, but surely none of those grand palaces could be the house she was looking for? Perhaps she had misunderstood, and it wasn't actually on the *campo*?

As she stood uncertainly, an old lady dressed all in black, her head covered by a lacy shawl, left the church by a small door set into the massive main doors and headed in her direction.

'*Scusi, signora,*' Nicola began politely, 'but can you help me? I'm looking for Ca' Malvasia.'

'It adjoins Palazzo dei Cavalli.'

Nicola could see no break in the façade of the palace the wizened hand was pointing at.

Seeing that blank look, the old lady, whose face was brown and wrinkled as a walnut, broke into a toothless grin. 'At one time Ca' Malvasia was part of the *palazzo*. There is the door.'

To the right of the *palazzo*'s imposing entrance, a flight of curved steps ran up to a black, studded door with a lantern hanging above it, and a series of long narrow windows on either side.

'*Grazie, signora. Buona sera.*'

'*Buona sera.*'

Nodding affably, the old lady went on her way, while Nicola tilted back her head and shaded her eyes to peer up at the house that was now hers.

Four storeys high, the top two storeys with balconies, Ca' Malvasia looked much bigger and far grander than she had ever imagined. There were no windows on the lowest floor, which suggested it was a boat-house, and all the upper windows appeared to be tightly shuttered.

She climbed the steps, and after feeling in her bag for the keys tried the largest in the lock. It moved quite easily.

Grasping the ornate iron ring, she pushed open the heavy door and took a few steps inside. After the heat and glare of the Campo dei Cavalli it was pleasantly cool and dark.

The air smelled slightly musty and vault-like, which wasn't surprising if the house had been closed up for years.

When her eyes had adjusted to the gloom, Nicola found she was standing in a marble-floored hall, with a beautiful central staircase.

The slatted shutters let in just enough light to enable her to make out several closed doors on either side.

Having got this far, it seemed a shame not to take a quick look at the rest of the house... Though the last thing she wanted to do was hurt Signor Mancini's feelings by preempting him...

But so long as she didn't open the shutters or disturb anything he need never know she'd already been here.

Her mind made up, she felt a little thrill of excitement.

There were electricity switches on the wall by the door, and without much hope she tried a couple.

Nothing happened.

Oh, well, she could at least get *some* idea of the layout.

Leaving the front door partly open, she crossed the hall and began to peer into the various rooms. Even in the shuttered dimness she could tell they were magnificent, with painted ceilings and antique furnishings.

At the far end, an arched door gave on to a wide stone corridor and what she guessed had once been kitchens and servants' quarters. She could just make out that a flight of worn stone steps disappeared upwards into blackness.

Returning to the hall, where a brilliant lozenge of light from the open door lay on the pale marble floor, she climbed the elegant staircase which led up to a gallery with four long, shuttered windows.

She had just reached the top step when a sudden loud thud made her jump. It was still echoing hollowly when she spun round to see that the slanting oblong of light had disappeared.

The front door was closed.

Perhaps one of those freak gusts of wind had swirled in? Or maybe the door's own weight had caused it to gradually swing shut?

Suddenly uneasy for no good reason, she hesitated, wondering whether to go down and open it again.

But that small amount of light would make no difference to the upper floor she was about to explore, and perhaps the door would be safer closed?

There must be a lot of valuable things in the house, and she had no idea of the opportunist crime rate in Venice.

The echoes had died away, and once more absolute silence reigned. For a few moments she stood, listening to that absence of sound until she fancied she could hear her own breathing and heartbeat.

Then, collecting herself, she moved to open the nearest door. The rooms on this floor, though large and grand by ordinary standards, were obviously the ones John and his wife had lived in.

Through the gloom she could make out that all the decors were light, and the furnishings relatively modern, though the doors, like the doors on the lower floor, had heavy metal handles and large iron locks, some with keys.

Everywhere had the dusty, deadened aspect that places seemed to acquire when they'd stood empty for a long time.

A stone archway beckoned and, wondering where the corridor led to, Nicola set off cautiously down it. Away from the faint light that filtered through the gallery's shuttered windows, it was even darker, and she moved with one hand on the nearest wall.

Above the faint rasping noise it made, she suddenly became aware of another stealthy sound.

A chill running through her, she stopped and turned, peering into the darkness, holding her breath while she listened.

There it was again, the merest brush of a footfall. The tiny hairs on the back of her neck rose.

Though in the close confines of the stone corridor the sound seemed to whisper around her, making it impossible to tell exactly where it was coming from, she knew someone must be following her.

Someone who was closing in on her.

Someone who was blocking her escape route.

Her breath caught in her throat, her heart pounding, she realised with sudden clarity that her only option was to go on. When she reached a door, it might be possible to lock it while she opened the window and called for help.

Feeling as though she was caught up in some awful nightmare, she turned and forced her shaking legs to carry her forward.

She had taken only a few hurried steps when a dark shape detached itself from the surrounding darkness and loomed up in front of her.

Far from following her, whoever it was had been lying in wait for her.

A strangled scream was torn from her throat, and, gripped by blind panic, she turned to flee back the way she had come.

'Nicola, stop!' a voice cried sharply. 'If you try to run in the dark you'll only hurt yourself.'

Before she could heed the warning her ankle turned under her, and she went sprawling, her head hitting the wall with a sharp crack.

When she regained consciousness she was lying full length on a couch, minus her jacket and shoes. A bearded, middle-aged man was bending over her, examining her left temple.

Straightening up, and addressing someone she couldn't see, he observed in Italian, 'Luckily it seems to have been just a glancing blow.'

Then, with the air of a conjuror producing a rabbit from a hat, he produced a pencil torch from a black briefcase and shone a fine beam into first one eye and then the other.

After due consideration he gave his verdict briskly. 'There is no evidence of any concussion, I'm pleased to say. Now, you mentioned the possibility of a sprained ankle...'

He bent to examine her left ankle, which was starting to swell.

She winced as his fingers pressed and prodded. 'Yes, a slight sprain. There may be a little pain and stiffness, some further swelling, perhaps, but again no long-lasting damage.'

Producing a small canister, he sprayed the affected area. It felt icy cold, and seemed to tighten around her ankle like an invisible tourniquet.

Replacing the torch and the canister, he said, 'I'll leave some painkillers. The patient should take two immediately, and then as necessary. If there should be any signs of nausea or blurred vision, perhaps you'll let me know as soon as possible?'

'Of course. Many thanks for coming so quickly, Doctor. Stefano will show you out.'

Though she couldn't see the second man, and had never heard him speak in Italian before, she would have recognised that voice anywhere.

Had recognised it, when it was too late and she was already embarked on her headlong flight.

'How are you feeling?' Casually dressed in light trousers and a sports shirt, his dark, attractive face serious, Dominic came to stand by her side.

'I'm fine,' she answered, trying to struggle into a sitting position.

The sudden movement sent her head spinning and she closed her eyes. No, she thought dazedly, the whole thing had to be just a vivid dream. It couldn't possibly be Dominic.

Opening them again, she saw that it was.

'I don't understand,' she said weakly, as he carefully helped her up and put a cushion behind her back.

'What don't you understand?'

'Anything... Where I am. What I'm doing here. Why *you're* here...'

'You're at the Palazzo dei Cavalli, and I'm here because this is where I live.'

Ironically, he added, 'In case you haven't realised yet, we're neighbours. I brought you back here after you passed out.'

She put a hand to her throbbing temple. 'But what were you doing in Ca' Malvasia?'

When he didn't immediately answer, she added, 'And how do you know we're neighbours?'

Coolly, he said, 'It would make sense to leave the rest of the questions until later. You've had quite a nasty shock, as well as a bump on the head. I'll get my housekeeper to bring you a cup of tea and a couple of the painkillers Dr Castello left. When you've had those, I suggest that you keep your feet up until I've finished my business. Then if you feel well enough we'll do some serious talking.'

Before she could make any attempt to argue he turned away, and a moment later the carved oak door closed quietly behind him.

Feeling as if she needed to pinch herself, Nicola looked around her for the first time. She was in a handsome, well-proportioned room which, in spite of the half-closed shutters, gave the impression of being light and airy.

It was furnished as a living room-cum-study, with an eclectic mix of old and new, and, despite its palatial grandeur, looked comfortable and lived-in.

But what was Dominic Loredan doing living here?

Well, why not? She made an attempt to rationalise things. He had said he lived in Venice. The fact that he lived in a *palazzo* wasn't too strange. Because of its former wealth and historical grandeur, a lot of people in Venice must live in a *palazzo*.

What was strange was that out of the whole sprawling

city he should live next door to the house that had been John's and was now hers.

Coincidences did happen, and truth, it had often been said, was stranger than fiction. But surely this was too fantastic for words? An unbelievable coincidence...?

Another thought struck her. Though it had been dark in the passage at Ca' Malvasia, and Dominic couldn't possibly have seen her face, he had known who she was. He had called, 'Nicola, stop!'...

Her musings were interrupted by an elderly woman dressed all in black, carrying a tray of tea.

Setting it down on a low table near the couch, she indicated two white tablets on a small saucer, and said in halting English, 'Signor Dominic say to take.'

'Thank you...?'

'Maria,' she supplied.

'*Grazie*, Maria.'

'You speak Italian?'

'*Si*.'

A look of relief spreading over her broad face, the housekeeper said in her own language, 'Dominic asked me to tell you that he will be with you in about an hour...' Picking up the silver teapot, she filled a porcelain cup, before going on, 'He said to remind you that when you have drunk your tea, he would like you to lie down and rest quietly.'

Though politely phrased, Maria obviously regarded her master's request as an order.

'*Grazie,*' Nicola said.

'Is there anything further you need, *signorina*?'

'*Non, grazie*, Maria.'

When the housekeeper had gone, Nicola sipped her tea and swallowed the tablets. Young and resilient, she was already starting to feel much better but, unwilling to rock the boat, she decided to rest as Dominic had asked.

Trying to ignore the questions that buzzed in her head

like a swarm of bees, she stretched out full length once more and closed her eyes…

With so much on her mind she hadn't expected to sleep, but when she opened them again Dominic was sitting on the edge of the couch, one arm resting against the back, looking down at her.

Though she was unable to decipher the expression on his face, something about his posture convinced her he had been there for a little while, watching her.

The idea was an oddly disturbing one. It made her feel vulnerable, at a disadvantage.

He had changed into a white shirt and a well-cut evening jacket, and, freshly shaved, his black hair still damp from the shower, he looked fit and vital and devastatingly handsome.

His grey eyes studying her face, he asked, 'How are you feeling now?'

'Fine.'

'If I remember, you told me that earlier, when it was patently a lie.'

'Well, now it's the truth.'

'Hungry?'

'Starving.'

'I find that reassuring. Are you happy to eat here…?'

She hesitated. The last thing she wanted to do was find herself eating with his wife…

'Or would you prefer to go out, if the ankle will allow it?'

'Are you married?' The words were spoken before she could prevent them and, horrified by the bluntness of the question, she stammered, 'I—I mean if you have a wife and family to consider…'

His smile faintly mocking, he said flatly, 'I'm not married. The only family I have is a younger brother, David, who is away on business until tomorrow.'

She felt almost faint with relief.

'So which is it to be?'

'Out, please,' she said breathlessly.

No matter what, it would be wonderful to get her first sight of Venice by night with Dominic at her side.

'Are you sure that both your head and ankle will stand it?'

'Quite sure.'

All at once she was filled with hope and vitality. Though there were a lot of questions still to be answered, none of them really mattered.

Dominic was not only unmarried, but somehow he had contrived to find her again, and the bitter disappointment of the morning had vanished as if it had never been.

'Let me see how steady on your feet you are.'

Holding out a hand, he helped her up, and waited with his palm cupped lightly beneath her bare elbow. Something like an electric current sensitised her skin, and she felt a shiver run through her.

Head bent, so he wouldn't see how much his touch affected her, she stood as instructed, ignoring the slight twinge of pain that shot through her injured ankle.

'No discomfort?'

'None,' she lied.

'Then I think you'll do. There's a bathroom through here if you'd like to freshen up before we start?'

'Oh, yes, please,' she said gratefully.

Her jacket, sandals and handbag had been placed on a chair and, gathering them up, she followed him.

He opened a door to the left and showed her into a room that Sandy would have unhesitatingly described as 'big enough to hold a ball in'.

It was luxuriously equipped and, suddenly feeling dusty and dishevelled, she asked, 'Do you think I could have a quick shower?'

'Of course.' Straight-faced, he added, 'If you need any help just give me a shout.'

When he had gone, closing the door behind him, she turned on the water and, after stripping off, stepped into the shower stall.

Careful not to get her hair wet, she showered as swiftly as possible, dried herself on a fluffy towel and, feeling greatly refreshed, pulled on her clothes, pleased to see that her fall hadn't marked them.

It took less than a minute to comb out her thick blonde hair and recoil it, and she was ready.

At her entrance, Dominic tossed aside the paper he'd been reading and rose to his feet. 'A woman of her word, I see,' he congratulated her. 'Feeling better?'

'Much better.'

'Then let's go. But to be on the safe side I'd like you to stay off your feet as much as possible.'

Nicola had presumed they would walk, but, a hand at her waist, he escorted her across a magnificent hall, through a door, and down a flight of marble steps.

Favouring her sprained ankle, she descended with care into what was obviously the main boat-house. There were several craft moored there, amongst them two sleek motorboats.

From the landing stage another few steps led down to where the nearest motorboat, which was tied to an iron ring set in the stonework, was bobbing about on the blue-green water.

He helped her in, and when she was settled, took the controls and headed up the Rio dei Cavalli to the Grand Canal.

Feeling as though she was in a dream, she studied his strong profile, the way the breeze of their passing ruffled his black hair, his long-fingered hands on the wheel.

She didn't care where they were going—she was with

Dominic, and that was enough— She asked, 'Where are we going?'

'There are many excellent restaurants in Venice, but as it's a nice evening I thought you might like to eat al fresco in Piazza San Marco.'

Remembering what he had said about that famous square, she said huskily, her cup running over, 'I'd love to.'

They disembarked at San Marco, but instead of holding her hand Dominic tucked it under his arm as they walked through the winding lanes.

'Palazzo Ducale, you'll certainly recognise,' he said as they passed the wonderfully ornate façade of the Doge's Palace. 'And the Basilica di San Marco and the Campanile you can't miss, but if you're not planning to leave Venice in a month the sightseeing can wait until another time.'

His words, and the casual way they were spoken, made a little chill feather across her skin. But at this early stage in their relationship she could hardly expect him to declare that he would never let her leave. Just the fact that they were together again should be enough.

Together again... But how had he known where to find her? What had he been doing in the Ca' Malvasia? Unless he'd seen her going in and followed her?

Though if he had why hadn't he said so at once? And why had he assumed that they were neighbours without her telling him anything about John or inheriting the house...?

All at once the questions were back, thick as wasps around a jam pot. 'Dominic...' she began.

Reading her mind with frightening accuracy, he stopped and put a finger to her lips. 'Explanations can come later, after we've eaten.'

Her heart racing, and made breathless by that lightest of touches, she resolutely turned her back on the questions.

Why spoil the evening by worrying? She would put the whole thing out of her mind until he was ready to tell her.

Simply enjoy being here with him, in this wonderfully romantic setting. Enjoy the happiness that Sophia's ring seemed to be bringing.

Though the sun no longer beat down, the sky, laced with ribbons of gold diaphanous cloud, still held a shimmering heat which hung like an inverted copper bowl over the square.

The café Dominic had chosen seemed fairly crowded, but in a trice a table was found for them and set up.

As they took their seats and ordered a flock of pigeons rose with a whirring of wings and wheeled, dark silhouettes against the brightness.

Sitting sipping a martini, looking at the wonderful façade of St Mark's and listening to the orchestra playing Neapolitan love songs, she burst out impulsively, 'I've never been so happy.'

For an instant he looked startled, almost disconcerted. Then a shutter came down and, his face wiped clear of all expression, he said lightly, 'Just wait until you taste the *soglione alla Veneziana*.'

When the waiter had cleared away the aperitif glasses and brought a carafe of chilled white wine, Dominic asked politely, 'Will you excuse me for a couple of minutes? I need to make a phone call, and I've forgotten to bring my mobile.'

'Of course.'

She watched as, tall and broad-shouldered, he threaded his way lithely between the tables and disappeared inside.

Day was dying now, swathed in the first blue-purple veils of approaching dusk, and the lights were coming on in the square. Music, talk and laughter swirled and eddied, while perfume and the aroma of roasting coffee mingled with a warm salt breeze from the Lagoon.

'*Buona sera, signorina.*' A strange young man was standing smiling down at her. 'Remember me?'

Belatedly, she recognised the white teeth and soulful brown eyes. *Mario*.

'Of course I remember you.' She returned his smile.

'You permit?'

Before she could point out that she was with someone, he had dropped into the chair opposite, his melting gaze never leaving her face.

'Did you find your hotel without difficulty?'

'Yes, *grazie*.'

'I should have come with you and carried your case. It was shameful of me to leave so beautiful a girl to make her own way.'

Made uncomfortable by his attitude, she said briskly, 'It really wasn't a problem.'

'And now you are here all on your own, on your very first evening—'

'But I'm not—'

In full flow, he carried on as though she hadn't spoken, 'I called at the hotel to find you, but they said you were not there. Then, as though it was meant to be, I find you sitting alone in Piazza San Marco.'

Seizing her hand, he added, 'It will be dark in a little while. You must allow me to take you on a gondola, show you what a very romantic place Venezia can be—'

Trying, without success, to free her hand, she interrupted, 'Mario, please listen to me…' Her words tailed off as she saw Dominic standing a few feet away watching silently.

The look of cold fury on his face made her flinch.

Seeing the movement, and following her gaze, Mario rose hastily to his feet, his eyes reproaching her.

'I'm sorry,' she said. 'I tried to tell you I wasn't alone.'

Dominic took a step forward and, with a muttered, *'Scusi,'* Mario lost no time in escaping.

'Dear me,' Dominic said, resuming his seat, 'I seem to have frightened your latest conquest away.'

Though he spoke lightly, and his face was now inscrutable, she could tell that he was still furiously angry. But surely there was no need for such an extreme reaction?

Wishing the little incident had never taken place, she said carefully, 'There's really no need to talk about conquests. He's just a young man who carried my case to the *vaporetto* earlier today.'

'He seemed to...shall we say...fancy his chances.'

'Well, I did nothing to encourage him, if that's what you're suggesting. He's a mere boy,' she added.

'Don't tell me you think age matters?' Dominic's voice had an edge to it. Before she could answer, he went on, 'And if all this young man did was carry your case to the landing stage, how did he know where you were staying?'

Aware of a little thrill of excitement, because he was acting like a jealous boyfriend, she told him, 'Carlo asked, so he could give me directions...'

Dominic raised a dark brow. 'Another one?'

'Carlo, who is Mario's brother, must be all of eleven or twelve. When I stopped in Piazzale Roma he offered to guard my case while I parked the car...'

By the time she finished describing the incident, Dominic had relaxed and was looking amused.

A few seconds later their food arrived and, back on an even keel, Nicola was able to enjoyed the meal, the wine and the sheer delight of being with him.

By the time they reached the coffee stage, the evening had turned oppressively hot and sultry.

Glancing up at the sky, which had darkened and grown heavy with massing columns of indigo cloud, Dominic remarked evenly, 'There's going to be a storm before too long, so I think it's time for a few questions and answers... If you'd like to begin?'

She started with the most puzzling. 'I don't understand how you found me... I can only presume you must have

seen me in Campo dei Cavalli and followed me into the Ca'
Malvasia?'

'Wrong on both counts.'

'You *didn't* follow me?'

'No.'

'Then you must have noticed that the door had been left
open and, knowing the house was empty, decided to come
in and investigate?'

Already he was shaking his head, his white smile making
it into some kind of game.

'But I heard it slam as I reached the top of the stairs.'

'I didn't come that way.'

'So how *did* you get in?'

'At one time Ca' Malvasia used to be part of the Palazzo
dei Cavalli...'

Of course. The old lady she had spoken to in the *campo*
had said as much.

'When they were divided, a communicating door was left.
I came through that way.'

Unable to credit it, she protested, 'You're not trying to
tell me that our meeting like that was a coincidence? You
must have known I was there—'

His eyes gleamed. 'Yes, I did. Or at least I knew you
were going to be.'

Aware that he was playing with her, she said shortly, 'So
it was your intention to lie in wait for me and scare me half
to death?'

'No, that wasn't my intention. I would have come downstairs to meet you, but I was held up. As it was, I'd just
come through the door at the end of the corridor, and when
I realised you were so close I was almost as surprised as
you were. Not *that* many women would have gone exploring
a strange house in the dark.'

'How did you know I was coming to Ca' Malvasia? I

hadn't mentioned it.' Another thought struck her. 'And how did you know exactly *when* I'd be there?'

'I've been having you kept under surveillance.'

'What?' she said stupidly.

Calmly he repeated the statement.

'You've been having me watched…?' Choking with indignation, she demanded, 'Since when?'

'For the last couple of weeks,' he admitted with no sign of remorse.

'But we've only known each other two days,' she said blankly.

'We only *met* yesterday, but I've known about you for some time.'

'What do you mean, *known about me*? And *why* have you been having me watched?'

'As we're going to be neighbours—that is, unless you decide to sell—I wanted to know exactly what you were up to, what kind of person you were.'

'How did you know we were going to be neighbours? I've never mentioned having a house in Venice.'

'I thought you were about to… The evening we were at the Schloss Lienz.'

Recalling Innsbruck, and all that had happened there, she said with difficulty, 'So it wasn't just by chance that you were staying at the Bregenzerwald and in the next room?'

'No, it was all pre-planned.'

Feeling her blood turn to ice in her veins, she asked, 'How did you manage it?'

'Signor Mancini arranged everything…'

Just the fact that Signor Mancini was involved explained how Dominic had known she was going to be his neighbour… And remembering how politely insistent the solicitor had been about selecting her hotels and making all her reservations, Nicola bit her lip. Sandy hadn't been far wrong when she'd referred to the man as a slimy git.

With a slight smile, Dominic added, 'Apart from our actual introduction, that is.'

'What if I hadn't caught my heel and fallen on you?'

'I would have found some other way to get to know you. But as fate took a hand…'

CHAPTER FIVE

COLD through and through, despite the heat, she said, 'As you were on the spot so opportunely, you must have been following me.'

'I was,' he admitted coolly. 'At that point, wanting to make personal contact, I gave Muller another job to do.'

Muller... As he spoke the name, in her mind's eye she saw the bullet-headed man who had been sitting in the foyer at the Bregenzerwald.

Then a different man, short and blue-jowled, who had stared at her in the Piazzale Roma, and who, she was now sure, had been watching the hotel and had followed her to Ca' Malvasia. A man who had carried a mobile phone—that was how Dominic had known what time she would be there—and in all probability had been responsible for the door slamming.

She shivered. The fact that Dominic had had someone watching her every move, and reporting back, was becoming frighteningly clear.

What wasn't at all clear was *why*...

Keeping her voice as steady as possible, she said, 'You seem to have gone to a great deal of trouble and expense to have me checked out...'

'And you'd like to know why?'

'Yes.'

'I thought you might have guessed.'

'It's obviously something to do with the house. Though I don't see why my possibly becoming your neighbour should count as—'

'There's a little more to it than that.' His chiselled mouth twisted in a mirthless smile. 'The thing that does count is the fact that you might possibly have become, in a round-about way, my stepmother.'

'Your stepmother?'

'I presume you would have married John, had he lived?'

'Married John…? No, certainly not. The idea is quite absurd!'

Her reaction was so instinctive that just for an instant Dominic looked jolted.

'So you had no intention of actually marrying him?'

'Of course I hadn't… But just supposing I had, how could that possibly have made me your—?' She stopped speaking abruptly.

He waited, his grey eyes on her face.

'Sophia was your mother.'

'That's right.'

'But John wasn't your father.'

'Right again. My mother was married twice.'

'Yes, I know, John said so. But he'd never once mentioned having any stepchildren.'

'I rather thought not. You didn't even blink when I told you my name. And of course *children* is hardly the word. David was thirteen and I was twenty-one when they met and married. I'd just returned from college, and it was rather sprung on me…'

She got the distinct impression that had he been at home at the time he would have done his best to prevent it.

'I was aware that my mother had met someone, but they hadn't known each other for more than a few weeks, and I'd failed to realise it was serious.'

Something about the set of his mouth made her hazard, 'You didn't like John very much?'

He avoided the question, answering obliquely, 'It didn't much matter whether I liked him or not. My mother didn't ask for my approval.'

Greatly daring, Nicola queried, 'If she had, would you have given it?'

'No.' Dominic's answer was uncompromising. 'It had all happened too quickly. I thought he was probably marrying her for her money... You see, all the money was hers. As an only child she had inherited the Loredan fortune. My father, Richard Irving, had worked hard and added to it, and when he died, my mother was one of the richest women in Venice.'

Troubled, Nicola said with certainty, 'John absolutely adored her. I don't believe for a minute that he married her for her money.'

'It's possible I was wrong... But for a while things were awkward, and when I returned from my travels there was some friction. That's why the *palazzo* was divided and Ca' Malvasia came into existence.'

'I'm sure they were very happy there.'

As though striving to be fair, Dominic admitted, 'They appeared to be, and he seemed devastated when she died.' Cynically, he added, 'Though that might have been because, instead of being able to control the whole of her fortune, he was only left a third of it. The other two thirds stayed in the family. The palazzo and one third came to me, the rest was put in trust for David for when he reaches the age of thirty.'

'But you couldn't have been thirty when your mother died,' she objected.

Flatly, he said, 'I was twenty-six, and wealthy in my own right. David was eighteen, and still a bit wild. Mother's intention was to preserve the family fortune...'

Suddenly realising exactly where this was leading, Nicola sat quite still.

'Which was why John Turner's estate was supposed to come *back* to the family when he died.'

'I see,' Nicola said slowly, while her heart seemed to shrivel inside her.

With just those few words Dominic had made his interests clear, and crushed any hopes she might have cherished for the future.

She wanted to put her head down on her arms and cry her heart out.

It seemed that even the house and the money John had willed to her weren't rightfully hers...

But in that case why had both the solicitors, even Signor Mancini, who was obviously working for Dominic, let it go through?

But perhaps Dominic's claim was on moral rather than legal grounds? If it *was*, that put things in a somewhat different perspective.

While she wouldn't like to be morally responsible for leaving someone poor who ought to have been rich, as it stood she wasn't seriously depriving either Dominic or his brother.

Both already had a third their mother had willed to them and, in addition to that, Dominic had admitted to being a wealthy man in his own right. If he simply wanted John's share to increase what was already a substantial fortune...

Though Nicola was quiet and vulnerable in a lot of ways, she was far from weak. From her grandmother she had inherited an inner strength, a fine core of steel that, when the chips were down, made her a fighter.

She sat up straighter, unconsciously squaring her shoulders. 'You say John's estate was supposed to come back to the family?'

'Yes.'

'And you blame *me* because it didn't?'

'Not altogether.' Sardonically, he added, 'A young widow has to think about her future.'

It wasn't the answer she was hoping for, and, disliking

the connotations, she harked back to ask, 'What exactly do you mean by supposed?'

'It was understood that it should.'

'All of it? But surely John must have had money in his own right? He once told me that the London house, which he'd recently sold, was the family home and had belonged to his parents.'

Looking less than pleased, Dominic said, 'Well, if not all of it, certainly the money Mother left him, plus Ca' Malvasia. That was the understanding.'

'Whose understanding? Yours? Or everyone else involved?'

'Everyone else involved, as far as I know.'

'As far as you know? Didn't you talk to John about it?'

'No, I didn't,' Dominic replied a shade curtly.

'Or your mother?'

'My mother was a woman who liked to run her own affairs.'

'And she would have considered it interfering?'

Watching his jaw tighten, Nicola knew she'd struck a nerve.

Ignoring the question, he said repressively, 'It was her wish that the Loredan estate should remain intact. Which meant that John's share, and particularly Ca' Malvasia, should be returned to the family.'

'Was that stipulated in her will?'

'It should have been.'

Those four words answered Nicola's question.

On firmer ground now, she fought back, 'If your mother had seriously intended her husband's share to be returned to the family, surely it would have been?'

His grey eyes cold as ice, Dominic said, 'I can only presume that she relied upon him to respect her wishes. And at that time it probably didn't seem necessary. He had no other family. No children of his own. No one to leave it to.

Who could have guessed that he would lose his head over a girl young enough to be his daughter?'

'You've got it all wrong,' Nicola informed him coldly. 'John didn't *lose his head* over me. There was absolutely nothing of that kind about our relationship.'

'You didn't love him?'

'John was special, and I cared about him. But I didn't *love* him, at least not in the way you mean. We were just good friends.'

Seeing a sardonic half smile twist Dominic's firm lips, she assured him, 'And that's the truth, believe me…' Then was angry with herself for sounding defensive.

'How long had you known each other?'

Convinced that he already knew the answer, she admitted, 'About six months.'

'Did you live together?' The sudden question was like a whiplash.

Green eyes flashed. 'No, we didn't! The whole idea is absurd! John was more than twice my age.'

'What does age have to do with it? Some women are able to attract men of any age from sixteen to sixty… As you've already amply demonstrated.'

The rider made her flinch. So that was the kind of woman he believed her to be, she thought despairingly. And the unfortunate episode with Mario had only served to strengthen that belief.

Dominic's reaction, rather than being the jealous anger she had read it as, had simply been a wholesome disgust.

Biting her lip, she said with difficulty, 'I can understand in a way why you think that. But you're quite wrong. I'm not like that at all. And as far as John goes, as I've just said, it wasn't that kind of relationship. We were each of us travelling, and during the months we knew each other we only met up three or four times. Occasionally he'd phone or write, and once we had dinner together when we both happened to be in London at the same time…'

'Do you honestly expect me to believe that's all there was to it? That it was quite innocent?'

'Whether you believe it or not, it happens to be the truth.'

'Why should a man who was far from being a fool leave everything he possessed to a girl he'd only met half a dozen times at the most? Of course, if he was besotted, and the girl had…shall we say *encouraged* him by promising to marry him…'

It was oppressively hot and sticky. Pushing back a wisp of hair that had escaped and clung damply to her cheek, Nicola denied firmly, 'He wasn't besotted, and I've already told you there was never any question of marriage.'

'So what did you promise?'

Almost wearily, she said, 'I didn't promise anything. John loved his wife very dearly and—'

'That might well be true. But she'd been dead for almost four years—'

'She might have been dead for four years, but he still hadn't got over her death.'

'He wasn't an old man. Only in his late fifties. He might well have considered taking a lover. Felt he needed a woman in his life—'

Nicola shook her head. 'You must know that John was already suffering from a bad heart.' Though aware that Dominic looked surprised, as if he *hadn't* known, she pressed on, 'The only thing he needed at that point was a friend. Someone in the same boat who could appreciate his loss and understand what he was going through…'

There was a far-off growl of thunder and sheet lightning flickered in the distance. The very air seemed to be holding its breath, waiting for the coming storm.

Her head had begun to ache savagely, and, feeling unable to cope any longer, she pushed back her chair and gathered up her bag. 'If you'll excuse me... I'm getting rather tired and I'd like to go.'

He rose immediately, once more the polished host. 'Then of course I'll take you home.'

'Thank you,' she said with stilted politeness. 'But there's really no need. I can get a water-taxi.'

'Not at all.' He was equally polite. 'I won't hear of it.'

Signalling a waiter, he paid the bill before offering her his arm.

Her ankle had stiffened up and was hurting, but, pretending not to notice the proffered arm, she set off towards the *piazzetta*, hurrying in her need to get away, disregarding the pain.

With Dominic keeping pace effortlessly, they walked a foot apart, like strangers, to where the boat was moored.

He jumped in first and turned. His whole attitude was challenging, and she was tempted to ignore the hand he held out to her.

But the amount of traffic on the lagoon was making the dark water choppy, and the small craft was bobbing about like a cork on a rough sea.

A flash of lightning silhouetted Dominic, standing with his legs a little apart, balancing with the grace of familiarity. Making it look easy.

Still she doubted her ability to step in unaided. It wasn't something she was *used* to doing, and if her ankle let her down and she had to be ignominiously fished out of the lagoon, he would certainly have the last laugh...

Admitting defeat, she took his hand.

As she stepped in, either the boat lurched or he gave a little pull, and, completely off balance, she fell against him.

He took her weight easily, and for a moment or two held her pressed against the length of his muscular body.

Finding her footing, she pulled herself free and, glad that

it was dark enough to hide her flaming face, sat down with a bump.

His soft laugh convincing her it had been no accident, but his way of paying her back, she sat in stony silence as they began their journey.

She hadn't mentioned where she was staying, but obviously he knew. Either Signor Mancini or the man who had been following her would no doubt have told him, she thought bitterly.

The low rumbles of thunder and the distant flashes of lightning indicated that the storm was still some way away; Dominic was taking the quieter canals and driving without haste.

Where two waterways intersected, they were held up by a red traffic light. As they waited for it to change to green, some warning sixth sense made Nicola query, 'We are going the right way?'

She saw his white teeth gleam in a mocking smile. 'I was taking the quieter route, on the grounds that at night it's more romantic.'

Wishing she hadn't asked, she relapsed into silence.

The back canals, with only a few lamps gleaming on the dark water, tended to look very much alike, and she soon lost all track of where they were.

Watching for the distinctive humpbacked bridge she had crossed earlier that evening, and the main entrance to the Hotel Lunga, she was taken by surprise when Dominic suddenly cut the engine and turned into a well-lit boat-house.

As he drew into the landing stage and reached to moor the craft, she cried, 'What are you doing? This isn't the hotel.'

'I never thought it was,' he assured her gravely.

Making an effort to keep the panic from her voice, she protested, 'But you were supposed to be taking me home.'

'This *is* home,' he said, as he handed her out and helped her onto the landing stage.

Jerking her hand free, she said bitterly, 'It might be *your* home, but it's not mine. I didn't want to come back here.'

Ignoring her protest, he turned and led the way up the steps and into the *palazzo*, leaving her little choice but to follow him.

When they reached the hall, he asked politely, 'Would you like to come through to my study for a nightcap of some kind?'

'No, I wouldn't,' she answered raggedly. 'I want to go back to the hotel. If you won't take me I'll get a water-taxi.'

'Well, you could—'

'I certainly will.'

'But I wouldn't advise it,' he carried on smoothly. 'As it's the height of the tourist season, you're hardly likely to get a room.'

'I've *got* a room.'

'Not any more. I told them they could let someone else have it.'

'You *what*?'

'I explained that as you'd had a slight accident while visiting Ca' Malvasia, I'd invited you to stay at Palazzo dei Cavalli.'

'I don't *want* to stay here!' she cried, overcome with agitation at the thought. 'Besides, all my belongings are still at the hotel.'

He shook his head. 'I asked for them to be brought over. You'll find that everything is in your room, waiting for you.'

'No, I refuse to stay! I'm going to get my things and leave.'

'It's almost twelve o'clock,' he pointed out levelly. 'You can't go walking around Venice alone at this time of night with a sprained ankle. And don't pretend there's nothing wrong with it, because I know quite well there is.'

'*Please*, Dominic…'

Quizzically, he asked, 'Is the prospect of being my guest distressing enough to make you beg?'

'I don't care to be the guest of a man who's convinced I'm nothing but a heartless, scheming gold-digger.' Her voice broke. 'I don't even know why you *want* me here.'

But even as she spoke she knew only too well why. It would enable him to keep her under surveillance more easily…

'Let's just say you fascinate me.'

He sounded sincere and, thrown, she momentarily dropped her defences.

Taking immediate advantage, he cupped her elbow and, urging her into his study, helped her off with her loose jacket before pushing her gently onto the couch.

Lit only by several standard lamps, the large, well-furnished room had an air of cosy intimacy that had been lacking earlier.

Crouching at her feet, Dominic slipped off her sandals. 'Now, let me take a look at that ankle.'

It had puffed up considerably, and become so stiff and painful that she was forced to bite her lip as his long fingers began to gently probe and press.

Clicking his tongue in annoyance, he said, 'I should have had the sense to make you stay indoors and rest it…'

In spite of everything it gave her the strangest feeling— a combination of excitement, desire and tenderness—to look down at his bent head. The thick black hair that gleamed with health and wanted to curl, the tiny ends that feathered into his tanned nape… Even the back of his neck was sexy…

Glancing up, he added, 'I think a cold compress is called for.'

His eyes lingered on her face, and as though what she had been thinking was written there for him to read she felt herself start to blush.

Finding it an unexpectedly sweet amusement to tease her, Dominic watched with interest while she turned red as a poppy.

Then, rising to his feet with effortless grace, he said, 'I'll only be a minute,' and disappeared through the door, leaving it open behind him.

Disturbed and angry with herself, she wished fervently that she could just get up and walk out.

But even if Dominic would allow her to, she couldn't go wandering round a strange city with nowhere to go and a storm brewing.

Though she hated the feeling of being a prisoner, she would be much safer here.

Or would she? It would all depend on what kind of safety she was thinking of…

He was back quite quickly, with a cold pad and a crêpe bandage which he applied with deft efficiency. Nicola was surprised by his competence. In her admittedly small experience of men, most of them could hardly cope with a sticking plaster.

Watching his lean, well-shaped hands tuck in the end of the bandage and fasten it neatly with a safety pin, she went hot, her skin burning as she recalled what pleasure those skilful hands could bring…

'There, that should improve matters.'

His voice made her jump.

'Thank you.' Aware that in her agitation she had sounded ungracious, she added jerkily, 'I'm sure it will.'

'Now, what about that nightcap?'

Eager to escape, she shook her head. 'I don't think so. Really… I'm ready for bed.'

'There's not much point in going to bed wound tight as

a spring. You're much more likely to sleep if you put your feet up and relax for half an hour while you have a drink.'

Though phrased as a suggestion, she felt sure it was an order and, convinced that if she didn't put her feet up he would have no qualms about doing it for her, she reluctantly obeyed.

'So what's it to be? A brandy?'

She shook her head. 'Something long, cold and non-alcoholic, please.'

He went to a sideboard that contained a small fridge, and after a moment returned with a glass of iced fruit juice.

'How's that?'

She took a sip and said, 'Lovely.' Then, on edge because he was watching her, sat rolling the beaded coldness of the glass between her hot palms.

Frowning a little, he remarked, 'You look as if your headache's come back?'

'Yes, it has,' she admitted.

He took a small bottle from his pocket, and after unscrewing the cap shook a couple of tablets into her palm. 'You'd better have another couple of these.'

'Thank you.' Obediently she put them in her mouth and, taking another sip of her drink, swallowed. They failed to go down and she shuddered as they dissolved bitterly on her tongue.

Well aware that he was still standing studying her intently, and needing something to say, she asked, 'Your housekeeper doesn't object to having an unexpected *guest* thrust on her?'

'Not at all,' Dominic answered evenly. 'For some reason she approves of you.'

'How do you know?'

'Because she chose to get your room ready herself. By the time I rang to make sure your belongings had arrived, she assured me that everything was in order.'

Discarding his jacket, he undid his black tie, leaving the ends dangling, and unfastened the top two buttons of his white silk evening shirt, exposing the tanned column of his throat.

Nicola shivered, recalling all too clearly how she had buried her mouth against it while his hands had roamed at will over her eager body...

Catching sight of her rapt face, and intrigued by it, Dominic watched as her pupils grew large and unfocused, her soft lips parted and a slight flush stained her high cheekbones.

Innocently erotic, she looked like a woman being made love to.

It had a powerful effect on him and, forced to leash his own sexuality, he wondered who the man was who had engendered that look. Possibly her husband. Though he doubted it.

Suddenly she blinked, and, coming back to the present to find his eyes were fixed on her face, hastily looked down.

Her small, straight nose was shiny and there was a faint dew of perspiration on her forehead and upper lip, while the lamp she was sitting under shone on her corn-coloured hair and cast shadows of her long lashes onto her cheeks.

She really was quite enchanting, he thought. No wonder John had been captivated by her. If only she was half as innocent as she looked...

But everything seemed to suggest that, far from being innocent, she was a clever manipulator who used her beauty to further her own ends.

Unconsciously, he sighed.

There was a gleaming coffee-making machine on the sideboard, and reaching for a small cup he made himself some espresso before taking a seat opposite his unwilling guest.

For a while they sipped in silence, then, picking up the

threads of their earlier conversation, he said, 'So John had developed a bad heart? Could nothing be done about it?'

'No, it was just a matter of time. You didn't know?'

He shook his head. 'But I find it interesting that *you* did...'

So he thought she had battened on to a middle-aged man whom she had *expected* to die.

After a moment, Dominic went on flatly, 'As soon as Mother's funeral was over he closed up the house and left. Apart from one brief exchange, we hadn't been in touch since.'

No wonder John had never mentioned having a family. Clearly there had been no love lost on either side, and after his wife's death there would have been nothing to keep him in Venice...

'Where and when did you two meet?'

Dominic's question broke into her thoughts, and, collecting herself, she answered, 'In Paris, at the end of last November.'

'Tell me about it.' Whimsically, he added, 'And I'm a glutton for detail.'

Well, if it was detail he wanted, he should have it.

'Linda Atkin, one of my fellow workers at Westlake, who was organising a heads of business conference in Paris, had been taken seriously ill with pneumonia... I forget which hospital the ambulance took her to. Possibly it was Saint Antoine's...'

Dominic's small twisted smile acknowledged her mockery.

'Anyway, at very short notice I was asked to fly to Paris and take over her duties. The conference was being held at the Hotel Honfleur, which is one of the older-type, greystone hotels in the Rue Rosslare, not far from the Champs Elysées...'

Holding up both hands in a gesture of surrender, he said, 'Okay, I'm sorry. I should have said *relevant* detail.'

Unwilling to let him have it all his own way, she asked, 'Suppose we have different ideas on what we regard as relevant?'

'I'll go along with what *you* consider is.'

With saccharine sweetness, she said, 'You're too kind.'

Judging by the gleam in his eye, he would have liked to take her over his knee, but he only said politely, 'Do go on.'

'There were some fifty delegates at the conference, which was due to start the following morning, and most of them had already arrived and been settled in. But as far as I was concerned, with not coming on the scene until quite late that evening, there was still a lot to check over. On the ground floor, next door to the conference facilities, there was a small office to work in, which was a great help. Unfortunately, some last-minute problems meant it was very late by the time I'd got everything sorted out.

'Tired, and none too warm, I was about to go up to my room, which was on the fourth floor, when I discovered there had been some kind of power failure and the lifts weren't working. Which meant I had no choice but to walk up...'

The whole place was silent and deserted at that time in the morning, and Nicola had almost reached the fourth floor landing when the sight of a man slumped on the stairs made her jump.

A middle-aged man, dressed conventionally in a grey business suit and tie, was sitting on the third step from the top, leaning against the wall, head bent.

Her first thought was that if he had had too much to drink she would need to call someone. But there had been no sign of any night staff.

As she hesitated, he muttered, 'Sophia,' and lifted his head.

He was a nice-looking man, somewhere in his late fifties, she guessed, with a lean, ascetic face, thick grizzled hair and hazel eyes.

It was immediately clear that he was ill rather than drunk. His face was ashen, the skin stretched tightly over the bones, and his lips were blue.

'How can I help?' she asked in English.

She was about to repeat the question in French when he answered, 'Tablets.'

'Which pocket?'

He made a fumbling gesture. 'Top, inside…' His face was contorted with pain and the breath rasped in his throat.

Sitting on the cold marble step beside him, she felt in his top right-hand jacket pocket and gave a sigh of relief when her fingers closed around a small plastic container.

'Two?'

'Yes.'

She shook two of the tiny white tablets into her palm and watched him clumsily pick them up and put them under his tongue.

Wishing she was carrying her mobile phone, she said quickly, 'I'll go and call an ambulance.'

As she half rose he grasped her hand with a kind of desperate strength, pulling her down again. 'Stay with me, please.'

The fingers gripping hers were like ice.

Wondering how long he'd been there, she said, 'You really ought to have some help.'

'N-nothing they can do,' he mumbled.

Afraid that if she left him he might somehow tumble down the stairs, she stayed where she was.

Holding his hand between both of hers, she tried to warm

it, while she went over in her mind how to do heart massage should it become necessary.

But the tablets appeared to be working, and after a little while that dreadful ashen look began to disappear and his colour gradually seeped back.

Despite the returning colour, she saw that his face looked pinched and cold.

It was freezing in the stairwell, which suggested that the central heating had stopped working at the same time as the lifts.

She herself was starting to feel chilled to the bone and, concerned for him, knowing it would be better if they could move, she asked, 'How are you feeling?'

'Better now. Just need to lie down.'

'Which floor are you on?'

'The seventh.'

Only too aware that there was no way he could climb three flights of stairs in that condition, she said, 'You'd better lie down in my room for a while…'

Once he was safely lying down, she could go in search of some assistance.

'It's quite close,' she added reassuringly. 'Just through this door and we're practically there.'

A quick look in her shoulder bag located her room key and she slipped it into the pocket of her suit before offering him her arm.

With her help he got unsteadily to his feet.

'You can lean on me,' she said. 'I'm much stronger than I look.'

Though he was quite tall, he was spare, and, his arm around her shoulders, they somehow made it through the door and the few steps down the carpeted corridor to her room.

Once inside, she steered him to the bed and drew back the duvet. He sank down on the side, and she slipped off his shoes and socks before helping him remove his jacket and tie and undoing the top two buttons of his shirt.

'Do you need anything else?'

'Nothing else.'

When he was lying down, she made him as comfortable as possible and pulled the duvet over him, before switching off the main light and adjusting the bedside lamp so that it didn't shine in his face.

'There, now you can get some rest.'

His eyes closed, he said huskily, 'Thank you, my dear. You've been very kind.'

She was about to move away when he reached blindly for her hand. Suddenly, urgently, he said, 'Stay with me. I don't want to be alone.'

'I should get some help… A doctor…'

'No use…' His fingers tightened painfully. 'Promise you won't leave me.'

Touched by his need, she said, 'I promise.'

Still holding his hand, she sank down in the small arm-chair by the bed and, leaning back against the cushion, waited for him to sleep…

CHAPTER SIX

WHEN Nicola opened her eyes and peered blearily at her watch, she found it was a quarter past six.

The man in her bed was still asleep. His breathing was easy, and she was relieved to see that his colour was good.

She felt stiff and cramped through sleeping in an awkward position. There was a crick in her neck, and her right arm had pins and needles.

One good thing was that some time during the night the heating had come back on and the room was comfortably warm.

Moving carefully, she collected a change of clothing and went into the bathroom, quietly closing the door behind her.

When she was showered and dressed, her hair taken up in its usual smooth coil, she returned to the bedroom to find her unexpected guest had awakened and was sitting on the edge of the bed putting on his shoes.

He looked up to smile at her. 'Good morning.'

'Good morning.' She returned his smile. 'How are you feeling this morning?'

'Right as rain, thank you.'

'I'm so pleased,' she told him, and meant it.

'I must apologise for all the trouble I've caused you.'

She shook her head. 'It was no trouble.'

'You gave me your bed... Where did you sleep?'

'In the chair.'

Seeing he looked worried, she reassured him, 'And quite soundly, I might add. I've only just showered and dressed.'

'Something I'm about to do.'

94

Recalling that he was on the seventh floor, she said, 'I'd better just check to see if the lifts are working again.'

To her relief they were, and she returned to report, 'Whatever the problem was, they seem to have fixed it.'

'Good. I'm afraid I'm not really up to stairs.'

Taking his jacket from the back of the chair, he shrugged it on, then coiled his tie and slipped it into his pocket.

Holding out his hand, he said, 'You've been very good to me, and I don't even know your name.'

'Nicola Whitney.'

'I'm John Turner.'

They shook hands gravely.

'Are you here for the conference?' she asked.

'Yes. Are you?'

'I'm organising it. A last-minute replacement for Miss Atkin, who was taken ill yesterday afternoon.'

'I suppose that means you have to start work very early?'

'Not too early. I got most of the details sorted out last night.'

'In that case, will you have breakfast with me?' A shade gruffly, he added, 'There still seems to be a lot to say.'

Since Jeff's death she had assiduously avoided social contacts, so she was surprised to hear herself agreeing, 'Thank you, I'd like to.'

'Then shall we say the breakfast room in fifteen minutes' time?'

After checking through the day's agenda, Nicola went down to the breakfast room, which was at the rear and looked over an enclosed garden.

It was still quite early, and the only other occupant was a man dunking a roll into a cup of hot chocolate while he read the morning paper.

The glass roof and the amount of windows suggested that the room had originally been built as a conservatory. This notion was reinforced by a pale tiled floor and a profusion of tall green plants and potted palms.

Skirting round a particularly luxuriant fern, Nicola chose a table for two over by the windows.

When, a moment or two later, John Turner walked in, freshly shaved and wearing a well-cut suit, it was like seeing an old friend.

He sat down opposite and smiled at her. His mouth and teeth were good, and she thought afresh what a nice-looking man he was.

A waiter appeared to take their order of orange juice, coffee and croissants, and returned almost immediately with a loaded tray.

While they spread *confiture* on the fresh, flaky croissants, they talked easily about the conference and the day ahead.

Nicola had poured their second cup of coffee before John introduced a personal note, by saying abruptly, 'With regard to last night… I must apologise.'

'Apologise? For what?'

'I have the distinct impression that I clung to you like a child.'

'There's absolutely nothing to apologise for,' she assured him.

'Thank you. You're very kind.'

'Isn't there anything…?' she paused uncertainly.

Reading her mind, he shook his head. 'Because of several different factors my condition is terminal, and every attack takes me a step closer. I know and accept that. But, while I was prepared to die, I suddenly found I didn't want to die alone. Perhaps it was the thought of going into the unknown…

'I've never been a religious man, and I can only hope that my wife was right when, on her deathbed, she promised she would be waiting for me.'

'Sophia?' Nicola said.

Looking startled, John asked, 'How did you know?'

'Last night when you were sitting on the stairs, you spoke her name.'

'I wanted her there with me… But instead you came, and I can never thank you enough.'

Then, with a determined change of subject, 'You must travel a lot in your job?'

'Yes, almost non-stop.'

'Don't you ever get tired of it?'

'Sometimes,' she admitted.

'I see you're married. Doesn't your husband mind you being away from home so much?'

Quietly, she said, 'My husband's dead. He was killed in a car crash.'

'How long ago?'

'Two and a half years.'

Reaching across the table, John took her hand. 'It doesn't get any easier, does it? It's three and a half years since my wife died, and I still miss her every hour of every day, as you must miss your husband…'

'So you and John forged an instant bond of sympathy?'

Dominic's quiet voice brought Nicola back to the present, and she blinked a little as the Honfleur's breakfast room, with its pale tiled floor and walls of glass, was replaced by the lamplit study.

'I'm sorry?'

He repeated the question.

'Yes, you could say that.'

'And I presume you went on to find out a great deal about each other?'

'Not exactly. John told me comparatively little about his private life. As I said earlier, he never once mentioned having a stepfamily. Or living in Venice, for that matter.'

'I wonder why not?'

'I think he still found it too painful to talk about Sophia and the past. We were in the same boat, so I could understand how he felt…'

'Then you really *had* lost your husband?'

As Nicola stared at him blankly, thinking that she must have misheard the question, he added, 'Or was that just a clever trick to gain sympathy and form a fast and easy rapport?'

Even then she wasn't sure she'd understood.

'I don't know what you mean,' she said.

'I mean, are you *really* a widow? Or is it just part of the act, so to speak?'

Every vestige of colour left her face, and, white to the lips, she said, 'I wish I could say it *was* just part of an act, but unfortunately I am a widow.' Her voice hoarse and impeded, she added, 'I told you all about my husband…'

'But how much of what you told me was actually true?'

Lifting her chin, she looked him in the eye. 'All of it. Every single word.'

Then, bitterly, 'Though knowing in what light you must have regarded me, I suppose I couldn't expect you to believe anything I told you.'

'I have to admit that by the time we left the Schloss Lienz I'd started to wonder if I could be wrong about you. Everything you'd said *sounded* convincing.'

Ironically, he added, 'In spite of all I knew to the contrary, I was almost on the point of believing in that innocent young girl—'

Suddenly furious, she choked, 'What do you mean, "in spite of all I knew to the contrary"? You didn't *know* anything. Because John left me his money, you *presumed* I must be a gold-digger who'd got her hooks into him. You jumped to conclusions that were completely false.'

A flash of lightning through the shutters and a louder

rumble of thunder brought their own touch of drama to the scene. The distant storm was circling round, getting closer.

'I'm sure you'd like me to think that you're as innocent as you look, but I'm afraid I can't.'

Stung, she said with blistering scorn, 'You've let the desire to hang on to your mother's fortune warp your judgement. You wouldn't recognise innocence if you fell over it.'

'But I can recognise *lack* of it,' he said evenly.

'What?'

'I can recognise *lack* of it,' he repeated.

His voice caustic, he went on, 'Surely you don't expect me to believe that someone as naive and innocent as you had painted yourself to be could later on that same evening throw herself at me quite so blatantly?'

Recalling all too clearly how she had swayed towards him and put her hands flat-palmed against his chest, Nicola felt her face flame.

'Or do you want to deny that too?'

'I know it must have *looked* as if I was throwing myself at you, but it was quite accidental. I just lost my balance.'

'Really?' he drawled.

'Yes, really.' Stammering a little, she tried to explain. 'I—I'm not used to drinking and I'd had too much wine, and then a cognac. It made me unsteady on my feet...'

His cynical expression told her clearly that he didn't believe a word of it.

'So you're saying it wasn't a come-on?'

'That's exactly what I'm saying.'

He smiled grimly. 'I suppose next you'll be swearing you didn't want to go to bed with me, and trying to blame me for seducing you?'

Looking down, she said in a small voice, 'No.'

Watching the fan of long, gold-tipped lashes flicker against the pure curve of her cheek, he echoed, 'No?'

'I've no intention of trying to blame you for seducing me.'

'I'm pleased to hear it.'

Gathering her courage, and knowing that her only option was to speak the truth, she went on, 'And though I didn't intend to invite it, I did want to go to bed with you.'

He raised a dark, mocking brow. 'Tell me, Nicola, do you feel the urge to sleep with every new man you meet?'

Her face burning afresh, she said, 'No, I don't. The only man I've ever slept with is my husband.'

'You mean apart from me?' he asked, a gleam in his grey eyes.

Lifting her chin, she agreed, 'Apart from you.'

Then, needing to convince him that she wasn't the kind of woman he thought her, she insisted quietly, 'Since Jeff died I've never so much as *looked* at another man.'

'Do you know, I could almost believe that?' he said with more than a touch of sarcasm.

'You *can* believe it.'

'Didn't you tell me that your husband had been dead for several years?'

'Three.'

'And you've been celibate all that time?'

'Yes.'

'A young and beautiful widow in need of consolation... Surely there must have been plenty of men who were interested?'

'Except for John, I avoided telling anyone I *was* a widow.'

Dominic's smile was twisted.

Recalling their first meeting, she added hastily, 'I mean until I met you.'

Desperate to make him understand, she went on, 'Apart from doing my job, I shut myself away from all contact with people. Men simply didn't interest me. I just wanted to be left alone to pick up the pieces.'

'Are you telling me that, as a young and healthy woman with natural needs, you didn't *miss* human contact?'

'If you mean sex—when you're grieving for someone sex becomes unimportant. It was the *warmth* of human contact, the *caring* that I missed.'

Her words held an unmistakable ring of truth, and for a heartbeat he looked distinctly shaken.

Then, his face expressionless, he asked, 'So if you had gone for three years without taking a lover, why indulge in just a casual romp with a perfect stranger?'

Feeling as if a giant hand was squeezing her heart, she stayed silent.

But, apparently intent on having an answer, he persisted, 'Or perhaps you're going to tell me that you felt I was *special*, like John Turner?'

'No, I'm not.' How could she tell him that? After he'd called it 'just a casual romp'.

'So why?'

'Too much to drink, perhaps. A sudden impulse. Or maybe a feeling that my time of mourning was finally over and I could start to live again.'

'Then almost any man would have done?'

'No!' Then, regretting her vehemence, 'It would have had to be someone I was really attracted to.'

'Ah! But then didn't you say your husband and I were alike?'

'I thought so at first, but I was wrong,' she stated flatly. 'You're not like Jeff at all. Not even in looks.'

He thought that over, before asking, 'All the same you were attracted to me?'

'Yes.'

When she failed to elaborate, he remarked silkily, 'I

thought you might have regarded me as another possible meal-ticket?'

'I don't need a meal-ticket.'

'Perhaps not, now your future's taken care of.'

'I never did need a meal-ticket,' she told him spiritedly. 'I'm quite capable of earning a living and taking care of the future myself.'

'Some women might consider that finding a rich and lonely man in failing health is an easy way to do it.'

'Some women might, but I don't happen to be one of them.'

As if she hadn't spoken, he went on, 'It's surprising how even an apparently level-headed man can be taken in by a beautiful face. Though isn't there a saying, there's no fool like an old fool?'

'John was far from being a fool. He *was* lonely, but even so, if I *had* been hoping to "take him in" I'm sure he would have known.'

'When did he actually tell you he was going to leave you his money?'

'He didn't. We never discussed money. I had no idea he was a rich man. The first I knew about it was when the solicitors wrote to tell me of his death and asked me to call in to see them.'

Then, knowing she would never convince him, and sick of trying, she swung her feet to the floor. 'Now, if you'll excuse me, it's been a long day and I really would like to go to bed.'

Dominic gave her a glinting, sidelong smile. 'But not alone, I hope?'

Wondering why a man like him wanted to take a woman he so obviously despised to bed, she said curtly, 'Definitely alone.'

'Oh, well…' With a shrug he rose to his feet, observing

casually, 'To avoid straining that ankle any further, I'd better carry you.'

'No!' Suddenly panic-stricken, she insisted, 'I can walk up. I don't need to be carried.'

Being carried up, held against his muscular body, would only weaken her resolve not to indulge in the kind of casual sex he had in mind.

And she mustn't *allow* herself to weaken.

To sleep with him again would destroy her pride and her self-respect. It would make her into the kind of woman he imagined her to be.

Despite the cold compress her ankle was still swollen and, realising it would be difficult to walk in heels, she decided to go barefooted. Picking up her sandals, she struggled to her feet.

She had taken just a couple of steps when her ankle let her down, and with a gasp of pain she dropped the sandals and grabbed the back of the nearest chair.

Dominic gave an exclamation of annoyance. 'Now perhaps you'll stop acting like a stubborn little fool!'

Before she could argue any further he had stooped and lifted her high in his arms.

In response, her stomach folded in on itself, every nerve-ending in her body sang into life, and her heartbeat and breathing both quickened drastically.

She was trying hard to appear unmoved when he gave her a sardonic glance and suggested, 'It would be a big help if you were to put your arms around my neck.'

Biting her lip, she reluctantly did as he'd asked, clasping her hands together behind his dark head. He had lifted her so effortlessly that, unable to believe he *needed* any help, she felt sure he was merely baiting her.

As he carried her across the hall and up a beautiful marble staircase that contrived to make the one in Ca' Malvasia seem relatively ordinary, her certainty that he was superbly fit was upheld.

His breathing had quickened only slightly, and she was oddly convinced that it was due to the feel of her body against his, rather than her weight. It verified the fact that, no matter how badly he thought of her, he still wanted her.

Why?

Or was it simply a case of any woman would do? But instinctively she felt that *wasn't* so.

When they reached the top of the grand staircase he turned left and followed a wide corridor hung with chandeliers. It was crossed by several smaller corridors and lined on either side with magnificent mirrors and paintings, and dark, elaborately carved doors.

He stopped in front of a door part-way along and, still holding her, said evenly, 'This is your room.'

There seemed to be no way of differentiating between them, and she wondered how on earth he knew which was which.

As though reading her mind, he asked, 'Is there something wrong?'

'Not really...' Determinedly looking away from the face so close to hers, she explained, 'Only it struck me that if I have to leave it I might have a problem finding it again...'

'It shouldn't be necessary to leave it, at least until morning. The old place has had a certain amount of modernisation, and all the rooms in this wing have an *en suite* bathroom.'

'Oh.' Feeling a bit foolish, she added, 'It's just that all the doors look alike.'

'At first glance they may *look* alike, but when you have time to study the carved panels you'll see that they're all different. Most of them represent Roman gods or deities, of which there were a vast number...'

With no change of tone, he queried, 'Perhaps you'd like to turn the doorknob?'

Unclasping her hands, she reached to do his bidding. While she turned the heavy metal knob, the fingers of the other hand brushed the short hair curling into his nape. Though thick and springy, it had the texture of silk. She wanted to keep on touching it.

Shouldering open the door, he carried her into a large, well-furnished room, where the hanging lamps had been left burning, and set her carefully on her feet. As he removed his hand it brushed against the side of her breast.

Though it seemed to have been accidental, just that casual touch made her nipples grow firm, and she found herself praying that he wouldn't notice the evidence of her arousal.

Luckily, his mind seemed to be on other things. 'All you need to do to know which is your room,' he continued, 'is look out for Janus.' He pointed to the central door panel, where a strong, mask-like carving showed two identical faces looking in opposite directions. 'As you can see he has two faces...'

With a strange inflection in his voice, he went on, 'I chose this room especially for you.'

As her colour rose, he added smoothly, 'But not for the reason you imagine...'

Smiling a little, he touched her warm cheek with cool fingers, destroying what remained of her composure.

'Janus is usually depicted with two faces as he is the guardian of doors, and every door looks two ways. January was named after him because he's also the god of new beginnings...'

New beginnings...

As she gazed at him, wondering if his words held some deeper meaning, he said lightly, 'When I asked what your plans were, didn't you answer that this holiday was to be a new beginning?'

'Yes, I did.'

And it had been. Though what had promised to be the start of a wonderful voyage of discovery had foundered on the rocks of Dominic's prejudice before it had even begun.

Then, because the need to know had been gnawing at her, 'I'd like *you* to answer a question now.'

'Very well. What do you want to know?'

The words practically tumbling over each other, yet instinctively careful how she phrased it, she asked, 'As you think so badly of me, why did you take me to bed last night?'

For an instant he looked disconcerted, then he admitted ruefully, 'I couldn't help myself. I wanted you so much that it was impossible to simply walk away.'

'I should have thought it would have been quite easy to walk away from a woman you had nothing but contempt for.'

'Oh, I wouldn't say *nothing* but contempt... I found you both disturbing and bewitching, and I was jealous of John... But, while I despised myself for feeling that way, I found I wanted you more than I'd ever wanted any other woman...'

She felt an almost fierce satisfaction. At least the *desire* had been mutual.

'I still do.' Standing quite still, he looked intensely into her lovely face. 'What do you want?'

She knew only too well what she wanted, and the recognition made her go hot all over.

His smile knowing, confident, he put his hands on her shoulders and drew her against him, eliciting by that simple act a more immediate and urgent desire than Jeff had ever evoked in all the months they had been married.

Reading her reaction, he bent his dark head to kiss her, but even as her lips parted and she felt her body grow limp and pliant her mind was suddenly clear, icy cool.

Jerking herself free, she said, 'What *I* want is for you to believe that I'm not the kind of woman you think I am.'

Though obviously startled, he made a swift recovery. 'I'd *like* to believe you're as innocent as the day is long, but in the circumstances that seems highly improbable... However, I'm willing to give you the benefit of the doubt while we get to know each other better.'

Stung, she said quietly, 'You really are an arrogant swine.'

He laughed, and with his index finger lightly traced her cheek and jawline. 'But you still want to sleep with me?'

Tempted almost beyond endurance, she clenched her teeth. But knowing that if she appeared to be easy it would only serve to confirm his bad opinion of her, she denied firmly, 'No, I don't.'

'Sure? It's one of the quickest and most enjoyable ways of getting to know one another.'

'Quite sure.'

'Pity.'

'Now, if you'd please go.'

'If that's what you really want... Goodnight, Nicola. Sweet dreams.'

'Goodnight,' she replied stiffly.

In the doorway he turned to say, 'Oh, by the way, I'm in the next room along. If you should happen to change your mind, there's a communicating door.'

As every nerve in her body tightened in response to that mocking invitation, the heavy door closed behind him with a slight thud.

Feeling oddly shaky, she wondered, Had Dominic been planning this? Was that the real reason he had given her this particular room? To make it easy?

Trying not to think of him, how close he was, how much she wanted to be with him in spite of everything, she looked around her.

Though it had a wonderfully ornate ceiling, the room was decorated and furnished with relative simplicity. Apart from several comfortable-looking chairs, there was a chest of drawers, a wardrobe, a dressing table, and a carved four-poster bed with a blue brocade canopy.

A quick glance showed that all her clothes had been unpacked and put away, and a short ivory satin nightdress and gown folded tidily and left on the counterpane ready for use.

Beside the four-poster was a bedside table with a state-of-the-art telephone on it. Thoughtfully, her small travel-clock had been placed there, alongside the book she had been reading and her grandmother's jewellery box.

On the far wall there was a pair of long, narrow arched windows, and with a little shock of surprise she heard the sudden vicious squall of rain that beat against them.

Hobbling a little, to protect her bad ankle, she crossed the room to the nearest one and folded back the shutters. The lamps shone on the window glass and made broken reflections of the room behind her in the wash of rain.

As, shielding her eyes, she looked over the dark canal there was a vivid flash of lightning. Its split-second eerie brilliance lit up the black water and the wrought-iron balconies and crumbling stucco of the *palazzo* opposite. It was followed almost immediately by a loud clap of thunder which echoed and re-echoed.

The storm had finally arrived.

While she wasn't afraid of it, the electricity in the air made her feel restless and edgy... As did the frustration caused by refusing to satisfy her newly awakened sexual needs.

There was a door on either side of the room, and she hesitated, wondering which led to the bathroom and which through to Dominic's room.

She felt a bittersweet longing to be in his arms, and if

she opened the wrong one and he was waiting for her she might not have the strength to tear herself away a second time.

And that would only compound the unfortunate picture he had formed of her.

A moment's thought reassured her, however. He had said the next bedroom *along*, so the right-hand door must be the one that led into his room.

There was a big old-fashioned lock on it, but there seemed to be no key, nor was there a bolt.

Still, she knew she had only her own longing to fight. Though Dominic was a red-blooded man, she was convinced that he would make no further move. Having issued the invitation, he would now stand back and leave it to her to decide whether or not to accept.

If only he hadn't got totally the wrong impression of her... But, realising only too well how things must *appear*, she couldn't altogether blame him.

Sighing, she wondered if she would ever be able to convince him that she was totally innocent. Or had fate brought them together only to stand on either side of an abyss that could neither be jumped nor bridged?

It was an unbearable thought.

Turning away from it, she opened the other door and found a large and luxurious bathroom, where her modest towelling robe and toilet bag were waiting.

Doing her utmost to push all her worries aside, at least for the moment, she cleaned her teeth and having removed the bandage from her ankle, showered with care.

Then, after brushing out her long hair, so that it tumbled in a pale silken mass around her shoulders, she donned her nightdress, turned off the main lights and climbed wearily into bed.

Its comfort welcomed her.

Switching off the bedside lamp, she closed her eyes, tired

to the point of exhaustion. It had been a long and wearing day, not only physically but mentally.

There had been the car journey, her first sight of Venice, the visit to Ca' Malvasia... And on top of all that she had run the entire gamut of emotions, going from happiness to despair not once, but twice. So much had happened that there had been no chance to think ahead, but tomorrow she would have to make some crucial decisions.

First and foremost, should she return home or carry on with her holiday?

But even as she asked it that question answered itself. There *might* be something she could do to make Dominic see her in a different light, and while there was still the faintest chance of changing his mind she couldn't bring herself to walk away.

And, recalling what Sandy had said about Brent moving in, she realised that returning to the London flat was no longer an option.

Which meant that when she did go back she would have to find herself some new accommodation, or else stay in a hotel...

The second most important thing was what to do about the Ca' Malvasia... Which reminded her that she had a morning appointment with Signor Mancini to be shown over it. An appointment that she would now have no compunction in cancelling...

Her thoughts growing fuzzy, she yawned...

Almost as soon as sleep claimed her, she began to dream...

She was in Ca' Malvasia, climbing the stairs. Everywhere was dark and silent and somehow menacing. She wanted to turn back but, as was the way of dreams, knew that she had no choice but to go on.

Moving like some wraith, she went through a stone archway and down a bare corridor. Away from the faint light that filtered through the gallery's shuttered windows it was even darker, and she felt her way with one hand on the nearest wall.

Above the faint rasping noise it made she became aware of another stealthy sound.

A chill running through her, she stopped and turned, peering into the gloom, holding her breath while she listened.

There it was again, the merest brush of a footfall. The tiny hairs on the back of her neck rose.

Someone was close at hand, creeping up on her, about to reach out of the darkness and touch her.

Suddenly drenched in icy perspiration, she gave a strangled scream and tried to run.

She had only taken a few stumbling steps when she came up against a solid wall. Heart pounding, sobbing for breath, she scrabbled at it blindly, frantically, feeling for a door. There *had* to be a way through to safety…

CHAPTER SEVEN

ALL at once a door opened, letting light stream in from the room beyond, and a moment later, finding her out of bed, Dominic had gathered her into his arms.

At first, still trapped in the web of panic, she struggled wildly.

Holding her with infinite care, he murmured, 'Gently, gently... It's all right... Everything's all right. It's just a nightmare.'

When she stopped struggling and slumped against him, trembling in every limb, he held her close. He could feel her ribcage heaving and her heart pounding.

Her head cradled against his chest, his mouth buried in her fragrant hair, he continued to murmur soothingly until the harsh sobbing breaths eased and her heartbeat returned to something like normal.

'All right now?' he asked, after a while.

'Yes, I'm all right.' But her voice was muffled and husky, and she continued to tremble.

He stooped and lifted her. 'Then let's get you back to bed.'

As he laid her on the bed and pulled the light covers over her the darkness and terror came crowding back. Cold, despite the heat, and still not fully awake, she clutched at his hand. 'Please don't leave me,' she begged.

'I won't leave you,' he promised.

Having closed the communicating door, he discarded the short silk robe he was wearing and slid in beside her. Then, gathering her to him, he settled her head on his shoulder.

*　　*　　*

When Nicola stirred and drifted to the surface there was an absence of sound, a quality of stillness, that suggested it was very early morning.

Still more than half-asleep, she was aware of a feeling of warmth and security, a sense of happiness that was all-embracing.

As she lay, little facts began to filter into her consciousness. One of her legs was resting against another hair-roughened leg, there was the weight of an arm across her ribcage, and her cheek was pillowed comfortably on a smoothly muscled chest.

After being alone for so long it was wonderful and, sighing, she nestled closer.

'Good morning.'

She opened heavy lids to find Dominic staring down at her. He was studying her intently, unsmilingly, his grey eyes fixed on her with a look that might have been mistaken for tenderness.

His handsome face was very close and she could see the absurd length of his lashes, the little creases beside his chiselled mouth and the dark stubble adorning his jaw.

As she gazed up at him he met her eyes and smiled into them. Then, putting a finger beneath her chin, he tilted her face so he could more easily kiss her lips.

Helplessly moved by a stirring that was part physical, part emotional, she responded to that kiss, felt not only on her mouth but in every fibre of her being, sweet and disturbing.

He made a little sound in his throat, a mingling of desire and satisfaction, and deepened the kiss.

Instantly she was caught up and carried away by a wave of *need* so powerful that it washed away any hope of resistance.

But it was need on more than one level.

From their very first meeting her feelings for Dominic hadn't been only sexual. He might be proud and arrogant and prejudiced, but she knew deep within her soul that intellectually and emotionally, as well as physically, he was everything she needed and wanted.

And more.

As he kissed her, his demanding, skilful hand moved down to cup and caress her breast through the thin satin of her nightdress.

After a moment he raised his head to say thickly, 'Satin's all well and good, but it's the silk of your skin that I want to touch.'

He began to strip off the unwanted nightdress.

Eager for his touch, she helped him pull the garment over her head and discard it.

Her creamy breasts were small and high and beautifully shaped, with erect dusky-pink nipples that invited his attention.

As soon as he had looked his fill, they got it.

He was a generous lover, and with only his fingers and his mouth he took her to the heights.

Obviously enjoying what was happening as much as she was, he continued to stroke and touch and taste until she thought there could be no further pleasure he could give her.

But then, surprisingly and sweetly inventive, he led her into new discoveries of herself that made her whole being throb and sing with delight.

By the time he lowered himself into the waiting cradle of her hips, sure she was sated, she thought only of him. But at his first strong thrust a spiral of bliss began to build deep inside: a spiral that grew and intensified until it exploded into dazzling fragments of ecstasy.

Though he had given her more pleasure than she had ever thought possible, when it was finally over she found her greatest joy was to cradle his dark head against her breast.

*   *   *

When Nicola awoke for the second time it was to instant and complete remembrance, and a jumble of warring emotions.

She had meant to sleep alone, and had almost managed it—until circumstances had conspired against her by bringing Dominic to her side.

Feeling her heart pick up speed, she turned her head, only to find that she was alone in the big bed.

Sharp disappointment and cowardly relief mingled. One half of her badly wanted Dominic to be still lying beside her, while the other cringed at the thought of having to face him.

Still recalling all the pleasure that had been lavished on it, her body felt sleek and well satisfied. Utterly content.

Her mind wasn't so happy.

As she lay staring up at the richly embroidered canopy, a sense of failure, of self-condemnation, gnawed at her.

How could she expect Dominic to believe that her actions since they had met had been wholly foreign to her? How could she expect him to believe that her relationship with John had been completely innocent when everything she had done pointed to the contrary?

She sighed deeply. If she told him the simple truth, that she loved him, he would never believe her.

She loved him... Her subconscious had put her feelings for Dominic into words.

She had loved her husband. But with hindsight she could see that her love for Jeff had been a gentle, familiar, one-dimensional emotion that had grown with propinquity and been nurtured by the need to love *someone*.

Whereas the love she felt for Dominic had been practically instantaneous. A strange and powerful three-dimensional emotion that had sprung to life fully grown and taken her over heart and soul before she had been aware of its existence.

Her quiet love for Jeff had been returned in full. But this passionate love she felt for Dominic seemed fated to be unrequited.

Pierced by the painful thought, she sat up.

The room, which overnight had changed from strange to familiar in the way that rooms did after a short acquaintance, was cool and dim. In the air was the scent of lavender, and sunlight slanting obliquely through the shutters made tiger-stripes across the counterpane.

Though it felt early, a glance at the watch she wore on her left wrist showed that it was almost a quarter to twelve, and she had already missed her appointment with Signor Mancini.

At that instant there was a tap at the door.

A shade uncertainly, she called, 'Come in.'

She was taken completely by surprise when Dominic walked in. He was wearing casual trousers and an open-necked shirt, and carrying a silver oblong tray.

'I hope I didn't wake you. I got up to make your break-fast.'

'No,' she said in some confusion. 'I really should have been up long ago. I had an early-morning appointment with Signor Mancini.'

'When I realised you weren't going to make it, I rang him.'

'Thank you.'

'I have Maria's permission to bring you a cup of coffee and a croissant, so long as I do it circumspectly,' he informed her gravely.

With a grin, he added, 'I imagine she thinks you'll be up and fully dressed by now. If she knew you were still in bed and stark naked, she'd have a fit...'

The reminder of her nakedness made Nicola blush and hurriedly pull up the counterpane to cover her breasts.

Dominic sighed. 'While modesty in a woman is seen to be a virtue, it can spoil a man's enjoyment.'

As she blushed to the roots of her hair, he went on, 'Though I must say Maria would approve. She's very proper. She's run the old place with a rod of iron since before I was born.' Ruefully, he added, 'We're all still scared stiff of her.'

The thought of Dominic being scared stiff of any woman, let alone his own housekeeper, made Nicola smile.

Her smile was enchanting. It lit her green eyes, added a breathtaking warmth and charm, transformed her face from merely beautiful to incandescent.

Standing quite still, he feasted his eyes on her. The mass of silky corn-coloured hair that tumbled around her shoulders; the long, slender neck; the smooth creamy line of her collar-bone; the way she had tucked the counterpane beneath her arms to prevent it slipping down...

Flustered by his steady regard, she jerked the counterpane even higher.

Seeing her discomfort, he put the tray supports down and settled it across her knees before coming to sit on the edge of the bed, warning quizzically, 'Don't tell Maria.'

On the tray was a small silver coffee pot, a jug of cream, a bowl of brown sugar, a cup and saucer and, lying on a white damask napkin, a single, perfect red rose.

She stared at it as though spellbound until her gaze was drawn upwards to meet Dominic's.

Grey eyes looked deep into green, conveying a silent message that made her heart swell with happiness. But all he said was, 'The rose is from me.'

'Thank you.' Her voice was husky. 'It's beautiful.'

And it was. Just past the bud stage, the velvety petals were a deep crimson shading to almost black, and the leaves a dark and glossy green.

As she lifted it up to smell its fragrance a sharp thorn pricked her finger.

She gave an involuntary exclamation.

He saw the drop of bright blood welling, and, taking the rose from her hand, tossed it carelessly onto the bedside table. Then, putting her finger in his mouth, he sucked.

Desire kicked low in her stomach and began to form a pool of liquid heat as she remembered the urgent and piercing pleasure of making love with him.

Round a mouthful of finger, he mumbled, 'Can't be too careful with roses.'

'It's quite all right, really,' she told him in a strangled voice.

Letting go of her hand, he said thoughtfully, 'Perhaps I should have made it a hothouse bloom after all...'

She shook her head. 'There's something so sterile, so artificial, about hothouse blooms. I much prefer a garden rose, thorns and all.'

He gave her a strange, almost enquiring look. 'Or maybe a gold brooch in the shape of a rose?'

All her new-found happiness shrivelled and died. 'You mean for services rendered?'

'I wouldn't have put it quite so bluntly. But you're such an absolute joy to make love to that if you *were* looking for a meal-ticket it would be well worth it.'

Feeling as if a cold weight had settled in her stomach, she said, 'As I told you last night, I'm not. Now if you'd please go.'

'Ordering me out is getting to be a habit,' he pointed out mildly.

Flushing, she said, 'I'm sorry. I won't be doing it again. As soon as I'm dressed, I'm leaving.'

He shook his head. 'I'm afraid I can't allow you to leave.'

'You can't make me stay here against my will,' she protested. But, remembering how easily he had dealt with her opposition the previous night, she suddenly wasn't so sure.

'It won't be against your will. If you consider the matter logically, I'm sure you'll come round to my way of thinking. You see, it makes sense from a purely practical point of view. This is the height of the tourist season and every hotel will be booked solid. You'll find it impossible to get any accommodation…'

Nicola was about to tell him she'd chance it, when he carried on evenly, 'But more important is the need to prevent any possible gossip.'

'Gossip?' she echoed blankly.

'News travels fast in such a self-contained community. Venetian society, and especially all my friends, would think it distinctly odd if the person who inherited the *palazzo* wasn't staying there.

'Call it family pride, whatever you like, but the Loredan name is an old and aristocratic one and still highly respected.

'Over the centuries several of the Loredan men became doges and wielded real power. The merest whisper that Sophia Loredan's husband had been foolish enough to leave such a bequest to a young woman the family refused to accept would soon cause a scandal, and that I will not allow.'

'Then I'll move into Ca' Malvasia,' she retorted. 'No one can object to me living there.'

'I can,' he disagreed quietly. 'You see the building was never legally divided. To all intents and purposes Ca' Malvasia is still part of the *palazzo*.'

'What do you mean, "to all intents and purposes"?'

'I mean I could claim it is. If the matter went to court it might take some time to resolve.' With a slight smile, he added, 'It's touch and go who would win in the end, but in the meantime I could certainly prevent you living there.'

He gave her a moment or two to think it over, before going on, 'Now, rather than putting us both to so much trouble, wouldn't it be a great deal easier to simply stay here until you make up your mind what to do with it?'

Already knowing the answer, she asked, 'What do you *want* me to do with it?'

'Sell it back to me.'

'For a song?'

'For the market price.'

'What if I don't want to sell?'

'Then I'll have a very beautiful neighbour.'

'Don't you mean a thorn in your side?'

He gave her a glinting look. 'There's little doubt you *could* be, if you so wished. But I'm rather hoping you won't go down that particular path. It's a great deal more pleasant to be friends…'

With just the slightest touch of menace in his voice, he added, 'And for your own sake, Nicola, I must warn you that I make a very unpleasant enemy to have.'

Yes, she had little doubt that he could be quite ruthless if he felt the need.

A shiver ran down her spine.

He saw that betraying movement, and smiled grimly. 'Now we understand each other, perhaps we can forget any slight unpleasantness and get back on an amicable footing?'

When she failed to answer, he smoothly laid it on the line, 'And while you enjoy your holiday and decide on your future plans you will be a welcome guest at my home.'

'Don't you mean a prisoner?' she asked bitterly.

'How melodramatic,' he mocked. 'Just try to think of the *palazzo* as a hotel.'

'I'm afraid I can't think of it as anything but a prison.'

'Well, at least it's a luxurious prison. Well suited to your preferred lifestyle… And of course it's an "open" one. There used to be dungeons in the old days. Still are, as a matter of fact, but now they're used for storing wine rather than locking up prisoners, so you'll be free to come and go as you wish.'

'But no doubt kept under surveillance?'

'I never do anything that I don't consider is necessary.'

He headed for the door, leaving her to interpret that as she wished.

In the doorway, he turned to say, 'Having dealt with any urgent business, I've decided to take the afternoon off, so I hope you'll join me for lunch on the terrace, at one...'

Though carefully phrased, she recognised it for what it was—a gauntlet thrown down to tempt her.

But before she picked it up she needed time to think...

'That is if your ankle is better...?' he added.

If she said it wasn't, he would no doubt come up and fetch her.

Deciding to play safe, at least for the moment, she assured him coolly, 'I'm sure it will be.'

'Good.' He went out, closing the door quietly behind him.

Feeling as though she'd been put through a wringer, Nicola lifted the silver pot with a shaking hand and poured herself a cup of coffee. She added a little cream and drank it abstractedly while she considered her options, of which there were few. Three at the most.

She could throw in the towel and go home at once.

But that option she immediately ruled out. Though she no longer had any hope of changing Dominic's mind about her, she wasn't going to let him just drive her away.

Her second option was to pick up the gauntlet and try to find somewhere else to stay—she didn't for a moment doubt that if he took the appropriate steps he could prevent her staying at Ca' Malvasia, though surely such a move would risk starting the gossip he was so keen to avoid?—but defying him would mean serious confrontation.

She would be taking a big chance if she called his bluff,

either over the possibility of gossip or him trying to take Ca' Malvasia away from her.

And of course there was always the danger that he wasn't bluffing and that she would end up in the middle of a scandal with nothing. With Dominic as her enemy.

Though, whether he was or not, what was the point of engaging in a long drawn out war of attrition? A war that, with the power Dominic wielded, would almost certainly end in her defeat.

Which left only the third and final option. She would have to bow to the inevitable and stay at the *palazzo*.

It would at least keep open hostility at bay and give her the time she needed to decide what to do.

Already she knew that she didn't want to part with Ca' Malvasia, and if it hadn't been for Dominic she wouldn't even have considered it.

But he wanted it back, intended to have it back, and looking at the matter from his point of view she could understand why...

Somewhere in the distance, a dog barked.

Roused from her thoughts, she glanced at her watch. Halfpast twelve. She didn't want to be late for lunch.

If she was to be his 'guest', at least for the next day or so, it would make life a lot easier if she tried to ensure that everything went as smoothly as possible.

Putting aside the tray, she got out of bed, and was pleased to find that her ankle felt almost normal. She was about to head for the bathroom when she noticed the rose lying on the bedside table.

It was still beautiful, but now she looked at it with vastly altered feelings, undecided whether to throw it away or simply leave it there to wilt.

But in spite of the fact that its gift had been just an empty mockery, she couldn't bring herself to do either. Picking it up, she carried it into the bathroom and put it in a glass of water.

When she had showered and cleaned her teeth she brushed out her hair, wincing a little as she touched the bruised area high on her temple. But she had been extremely lucky. It could have been so much worse.

Though it was pleasantly cool inside the shuttered rooms of the *palazzo*, she knew that outside the sun would be baking, so instead of make-up she applied some sunscreen and a touch of pale apricot lipgloss.

Then, after taking her hair up into its usual smooth, gleaming coil, she dressed in a simple sheath and flat-heeled sandals, and at five minutes to one, her defences firmly in place, sallied forth.

Having descended the grand staircase, she was hesitating at the bottom, wondering which of the many doors led outside, when a stocky, silver-haired manservant appeared.

With a stately bow, he said in excellent English, 'The master asked me to be on hand to show you to the terrace… So if you will follow me…?'

'Thank you.'

As she walked in the wake of the black-clad figure she discovered that the *palazzo* was even larger and more imposing than she had first thought. Altered over the centuries, and modernised in parts, it was built in a rectangle around a central courtyard and garden.

Outside there appeared to be no trace of the previous night's storm. The ground was dry, and the air was warm and still and scented with roses. On the steps that led down from the terrace to the garden, several small green lizards were sunning themselves.

In the centre of the paved court was a marble fountain, with water pouring from a tumble of rocks and a trio of long-maned white horses galloping through the spray.

This fountain and the one in the *campo* appeared to have

been designed by the same sculptor, Nicola thought, finding the sound of running water, with its musical splash and gurgle, oddly cooling and refreshing.

Wearing dark glasses, the sun beating down on his head, Dominic was sitting in a lounger glancing through what appeared to be a sheaf of business papers.

Nicola felt the urge to turn and run, but, endeavouring to look calm and collected—which she most definitely was not—she made herself walk towards him.

At her approach he put both the papers and the glasses aside and, every inch the polished host, rose to his feet with a smile.

When she failed to return his smile, he made a point of taking her hand.

Moved as always by his touch, but intent on staying behind her defences and treating him with distant civility, she let her hand stay in his for just a moment before withdrawing it.

His head tilted a little to one side, he studied her silky dress, patterned in subtle shades of green and grey, before remarking, 'You look delightfully cool and fresh... Which in this heat is no mean feat.'

Not knowing how to respond to his unexpected compliment, she found herself saying stiltedly, 'Somehow the fountain makes things seem cooler.'

'When I was quite small, though I knew it was strictly forbidden, I used to climb into it fully clothed and ride on the horses. Much to Maria's horror, I might add. One day when I refused to come out she was forced to wade in after me...'

Amused and intrigued by this glimpse of Dominic as a small and naughty child, Nicola found herself smiling, before it occurred to her that that was precisely why he'd told her the little anecdote.

Part-way along the terrace, where shrubs and vines provided welcome shade from the sun, a buffet table had been set up. It had a centrepiece of fresh flowers and was laid with starched napkins, monogrammed silver and crystal glasses.

Having settled her into a chair, he took a seat opposite and, watching her expressive face, grinned. 'I did tell Maria a *simple* meal, but this is the nearest she can get to a picnic. I think she seriously disapproves of eating in the open air. Now, may I pour you some wine?'

'No, thank you. In this heat I'd prefer water.'

'How sensible of you.' He picked up a tall jug and poured iced water into two lovely glass goblets.

'You must be hungry, as you've had no breakfast, so what will you start with? Something not too heavy? Seafood, perhaps...?'

Throughout lunch, as though his strategy was to disarm her and lure her from behind her defences, he talked lightly, easily, about a variety of subjects.

Determined to follow his lead, she answered in the same vein, and gradually found herself relaxing into the role of welcome guest that he had forced upon her.

By the coffee stage, after a remark Nicola had made about the beauty of the goblets, they had got on to glass-making.

'Glass has been made in Venice for over a thousand years,' Dominic told her. 'The furnaces were originally in the historic centre, but because of the risk of fire they were moved to the island of Murano late in the thirteenth century. There are still quite a few glass factories there, if you would like to see the glass-blowers at work?'

'Oh, yes, I would,' she said eagerly.

'Then, if your ankle isn't paining you at all, we could perhaps go over to Murano this afternoon. Of course these days quite a few of the factories are engaged in making cheap showy stuff for the tourists. However, there are still some real craftsmen about, able to produce the finest work... Things like this, for instance.'

He pointed to the clear, colourless *cristallo* container that held the centrepiece of flowers.

Shaped like a conch shell, and so fine as to be almost invisible, it was an exquisite piece of craftsmanship.

'It's absolutely wonderful,' Nicola said sincerely. 'Is it modern?'

'Yes. I bought it as a wedding gift for my mother and John. I don't think *he* cared for it much, but my mother loved it, and after she died he asked if I'd like to have it back.'

'I can't understand John not liking it. He had an eye for beauty.'

'Obviously.'

Angry with herself for making that incautious remark and providing him with an opening, Nicola bit her lip.

After a moment, he pursued evenly. 'There's something I've been meaning to ask you. As you and John were such close *friends*, why didn't you come to his funeral?'

'He'd been dead for three weeks before I was told about it. I'd been working away.'

Hearing the unmistakable ring of regret and sadness in her voice, Dominic suggested, 'Well, while you're in Venice, if you'd like to see where his remains are buried...?'

Frowning, she said, 'I understand he died in Rome?'

'Yes, he did. But as my mother had expressed a wish that they should lie side by side he was brought back to the family mausoleum on San Michele.'

'I'm so *glad*,' Nicola exclaimed fervently. 'It would have been what *he* wanted too...' Her voice faltered and her almond eyes filled with tears.

Frowning, Dominic queried, 'His death really upset you?'

Blinking away the tears, she took a deep, calming breath. 'Yes. As I've already told you, I was very fond of him.'

'Still, leaving you everything he owned must have made up for a great deal?'

'It didn't make up for losing one of the few people I could call a friend.'

As though trying to make a point, Dominic persevered. 'But surely being named his beneficiary must have been more…shall we say…*rewarding* than merely accepting gifts.'

'I don't know what you mean,' she informed him coldly. 'John never gave me any gifts.'

'None at all?'

'None at all.'

His grey eyes hard as granite, he asked, 'Are you sure about that?'

'Quite sure.' Desperately, she added, 'I would never have taken gifts from him.'

'That's strange, because I have every reason to believe that he gave you a gold ring. A Maschera ring.'

Nicola's face flamed. 'Oh, but he didn't give—'

'Don't bother to deny it. Though Muller was unable to find any trace of it when he searched your cases, I'm quite certain—'

'How dare you have someone search through my things?' she cried furiously. 'You had absolutely no right—'

'I have every right when I'm convinced you have something that doesn't belong to you.'

'So, not satisfied with labelling me a gold-digger, now you're calling me a thief!'

His lips tightened. 'That ring is very precious. I should have kept it safe—'

'So why didn't you?'

'At Mother's funeral I noticed that John was wearing it on a chain around his neck. I should have demanded its return there and then, but he seemed genuinely distraught and I couldn't bring myself to.

'He left Venice the next morning, and when I managed to locate him and ask for it back he refused to part with it. He swore Mother had given it to him on her deathbed—'

'Well, if that's what he says, then surely—'

Disregarding the interruption, Dominic went on with quiet certainty, 'But he was either lying or mistaken. I know for a fact that she would never have done any such thing.'

'What makes you so certain?'

'Because that ring is irreplaceable. It's a family heirloom. After John died it was the first thing we looked for, but there was no trace of it amongst his personal possessions.'

'So you immediately jumped to the conclusion that I must have it?'

'And I was right, wasn't I? Even though you're still trying to deny it.'

'I'm not trying to deny I have it. What I am denying is that John gave it to me—'

'So you're admitting you stole it?'

'I'm admitting nothing of the kind. If you'd only *listen* to me. Let me explain. He didn't *give* me the ring in the way you mean. It was in the packet that Mr Harthill, the solicitor, was keeping for me, along with the keys to Ca' Malvasia.'

'Did you know it belonged to my mother?'

'I knew it had belonged to John's wife.'

With quiet fury, Dominic said, 'He had no right to give it away. Apart from anything else, it's one of the few original Maschera rings still in existence, and that makes it practically priceless.'

CHAPTER EIGHT

'I SHOULD have realised it all came down to money,' Nicola remarked bitterly.

'Are you trying to tell me you didn't know it was worth a fortune?'

'I'm not *trying* to tell you. I *am* telling you. As far as I was concerned, it might well have been simply good costume jewellery. Until now I had no idea of how much it was worth.'

'It isn't just what it's worth in money. That ring has been in the Loredan family since the early seventeen hundreds. For generations it's been passed on to the wife of the eldest son. Or, if there are no sons, to the oldest daughter.'

'I see,' she said slowly.

'But you didn't feel guilty?'

Agitation brought Nicola to her feet, a bright flag of colour flying in each cheek. 'Why should I have felt guilty? I didn't know any of this.'

'Please sit down,' Dominic ordered quietly.

Sinking back into her chair, and only too aware that she sounded both resentful and defensive, she told him, 'All I knew was that the ring had belonged to John's wife and he wanted me to have it—'

She stopped speaking abruptly. Standing a few yards away, in the shadow cast by a thick vine, apparently eavesdropping, was a tall, good-looking young man with black curly hair.

She had thought at first that Dominic was like Jeff, but this man was even more so, and she was unable to take her eyes off him.

Seeing she was looking fixedly over his shoulder, Dominic turned his head. 'What the devil are you doing here?' he demanded curtly.

Unabashed, the younger man gave him a mocking glance and moved out into the sunshine. 'In case you've forgotten, I live here.'

'In case *you've* forgotten, you're supposed to be at an important meeting in Mestre at two o'clock.'

'I didn't forget. I didn't feel like going.'

Watching Dominic's jaw tighten ominously, he added hastily, 'Stomach pains. Been having them for a couple of days. Ever since I ate that lobster…'

'Save the excuses.'

'Look, I've asked one of the secretaries to attend the meeting and take notes…'

Dominic pushed back his chair and rose to his feet, anger in every line of his lean body. 'This meeting was set up to discuss Zitelle's new project. Sending one of the secretaries to take notes just isn't good enough!'

'Oh, Rosa's quick and accurate. She'll include all the salient points and give me a printout.'

'As Rosa happens to be Pietro's secretary she'll no doubt have her own job to do.'

'I'm sure she won't let me down. She's got the hots for me.'

A look of disgust on his face, Dominic said coldly, 'When I entrusted this to you I thought I'd made it clear that we need a personal presence there.'

'But I know next to nothing about Zitelle's new project—'

'You'd know a great deal more if you bothered to attend the meeting.'

'It's a damn sight too hot to be sitting in a boring meeting, especially as I don't feel well.' With a kind of sly defiance, he added, 'And I don't see *you* working.'

'I've been working from home.'

His eyes travelling appreciatively over Nicola, the new-comer remarked, 'Nice work if you can get it.'

'You'll keep a civil tongue in your head,' Dominic ordered sharply.

Then turning to Nicola, he said formally, 'I hope you'll accept my apologies. It's the height of bad manners to quarrel in front of a guest.'

'Oh, I'd hardly call it quarrelling,' the younger man disagreed lightly, 'just a demonstration of brotherly disharmony...'

So this was David. She had already guessed as much by the resemblance, but his remark confirmed it.

Like a small boy showing off, he added, 'And a spot of disharmony isn't to be wondered at when you come to consider how much the head of the house enjoys laying down the law...'

It was plain that David was hell-bent on annoying his brother, and Nicola got the distinct impression that her presence was making him a great deal bolder than he might otherwise have been.

But, his temper leashed, Dominic was once more calmly in control. 'Nicola, may I introduce my brother David? David, this is Mrs Whitney.'

Gazing into her eyes, David took her hand. 'It's a pleasure to meet you, Mrs Whitney...'

He really was a charmer, she thought—and didn't he know it?

'...or may I call you Nicola?'

'Please do,' she said carefully.

'I understand your husband's dead?'

'That's right.' Her voice was steady.

'You're much too young to be a widow. And far too beautiful...'

Still holding her hand, he added deliberately, 'I can quite

see why Dom invited you to stay. Though I must say that in the circumstances I'm surprised you agreed—'

'Are you intending to have lunch?' Dominic broke in abruptly.

'No. I ate at Leonardo's before I came home.'

Only too aware that Dominic was watching, Nicola made a determined effort to withdraw her hand.

Releasing it reluctantly, David smiled at her and carried on speaking as though there'd been no interruption. 'However, I'm glad you did. You'll certainly help to brighten up the old place.'

'I don't expect to be here for long,' she said a shade awkwardly.

'How long is *long*?'

She answered truthfully, 'Just until I have time to decide what to do about…things.'

'You mean selling Ca' Malvasia? Oh, but you mustn't do that. Why not move into the place? Become our neighbour? You've no idea how boring it can be living in—'

Dominic gave him a look that effectively stopped the flow of words; then, speaking into the sudden silence, addressing Nicola, he said formally, 'If you'll excuse me? I must give Bruno Zitelle my apologies and arrange to have someone else attend the meeting.'

Turning to David, he added grimly, 'But first I'd like a word with you.'

Drawing his brother to one side, he began to reprimand him. Though he spoke in an undertone, never once raising his voice, it was obvious that whatever he was saying was more than enough to seriously deflate the younger man.

In no doubt whatsoever which was the stronger of the two, Nicola watched the pair of them, noting the similarities and the differences between them.

They were each over six feet tall, but Dominic was more

strongly built and had a mature width of shoulder the younger man lacked.

Both men were raven-haired, but while Dominic's hair was cut short and tamed David's was an unruly riot of curls.

With less angular features, and blue eyes instead of grey, at first glance David appeared to be much the better-looking of the two.

But a second glance showed that his handsome face was spoilt by a self-indulgent mouth and a weak chin, and he had none of his brother's powerful attraction.

The conversation over, and after a brief glance in Nicola's direction, Dominic went back into the *palazzo*, while, a slight flush lying along his cheekbones, David returned to her side.

Removing his jacket, he tossed it carelessly onto the nearest lounger, and, dropping into a chair, said, 'Phew!'

'Laying down the law?' she asked sympathetically.

'Big time. As far as you're concerned, he's just warned me off so emphatically that, reading between the lines, I'd say he's fallen for you himself… No, on second thoughts, I'd *swear* to it.'

Feeling her face grow hot, she shook her head. 'I'm sure you're wrong. He doesn't even like me. In fact quite the opposite.'

'Then why did he invite you to stay at the *palazzo*?' David asked shrewdly.

Unwilling to go into details, she said, 'I think he wanted me here so he could…keep an eye on me.'

'And no doubt bring pressure to bear to get you to sell Ca' Malvasia?'

'Yes.'

'He does want it back very badly.'

'As he regards it as part of the *palazzo*, that's understandable,' she admitted.

'Will you part with it?' David asked curiously.

'I don't want to, but—'

'Then don't. He can't force you to sell.'

'Probably not. But as things are…'

'Don't let him bulldoze you into doing something you don't want to do. If necessary you should fight him all the way.'

If she hadn't felt the way she did about him, she might well have done. But, as it was, she didn't have the heart to fight.

What was the point? If she won, Dominic would almost certainly hate her… And she couldn't bear to live next door to him knowing he didn't want her there.

Watching the despairing look on her face, David hazarded, 'Afraid you wouldn't win?'

'I'm afraid it might be a hollow victory.'

'Big brother certainly knows how to intimidate people.' He grinned suddenly and admitted, 'When Dom gets really angry he frightens the hell out of me… And today he was livid. After he'd told me to leave you alone, he gave me a tongue-lashing for not being at that meeting, and for what he called "impertinence".'

Dryly, she asked, 'And you don't feel it was deserved?'

He groaned. 'I didn't think *you'd* be on his side.'

'I'm not on anyone's side. But you did go out of your way to aggravate him.'

'I can't seem to help it,' David admitted, with disarming honesty. 'He's so bossy, so arrogant, so damn critical of everything I do. He makes me feel humiliated, puts my back up…'

Nicola felt a quick rush of sympathy. She too had been forced to cope with the bossiness, the arrogance, the feeling of being humiliated…

With a spurt of impatience, he added, 'I wish I didn't have to work for him.'

It was such a relief to forget her own troubles for a bit,

and talk about his, that she found herself asking, 'Are you forced to work for him?'

He said ruefully, reaching to pour himself a glass of wine, 'If I don't work he won't give me an allowance. You see, he holds the purse strings. Though I ought by rights to have money, I can't get my hands on it until I'm thirty. Which is a blasted nuisance. I hate living in a mausoleum like Venice. As soon as I get the chance, I'm off to the States—'

Sounding bitter, he went on, 'But for the moment I'm stuck here without a cent, all because big brother persuaded Mamma that if I got my inheritance too soon I'd fritter it away.'

'*Did* he persuade her? I got the impression that your mother was a lady who made up her own mind about things.'

'Well, whether he persuaded her or she decided for herself, the result's the same. I'll be living like a pauper until I'm thirty…'

Hardly a *pauper*, she thought with a touch of wry amusement. Neither his well-cut suit and silk shirt, nor his hand-made shoes, had come cheap.

'You mentioned an allowance…'

'A mere pittance. And when I took a holiday Dom hadn't sanctioned he threatened to stop it.'

'Couldn't you work for someone else?'

'I tried it once, but the wages were laughable and they expected me to be there five days out of seven.'

'Tough!'

He grinned briefly at the sarcasm, before going on, 'At least while I'm working for DIL Holdings as the boss's brother I get quite a few perks, and when Dom isn't around I can do pretty much as I please.'

Nicola, who was no longer so sure where her sympathies lay, was about to suggest that he really wasn't so hard done by, when he asked, 'What are you doing for the rest of the afternoon?'

'Well, I don't really know...'

'Have you seen much of Venice?'

'No, I only arrived yesterday. Your brother did suggest a visit to Murano, but...'

'You won't see Dom again this side of dinnertime,' David assured her with certainty. 'Work's his god. He'll probably go over to Mestre himself rather than lose Zitelle's good will...'

Seeing Nicola's expression, he added quickly, 'It was the truth, you know. I have been having stomach cramps... Though Dom, who's a hard-hearted devil, obviously didn't believe me.'

Nicola, who hadn't believed him either, said, 'I'm not altogether sure I blame him.'

'I really don't know how someone so beautiful can be so unkind,' David complained sweetly. 'You ought to be all womanly sympathy.'

'I might be if I seriously thought my sympathy was justified.' Then, at his hurt expression, 'Well, it did sound a bit thin.'

'Tell you what,' he said magnanimously, 'I'll forgive the fact that you doubted me if you come out with me this afternoon.'

Reminding herself of her decision to make sure things went smoothly, she shook her head. 'No, I'd better not.'

'Because you don't think Dom would approve?'

'I'm sure he wouldn't.'

'So what if he doesn't? Are you seriously scared of him?'

'Of course I'm not scared of him,' she denied, just a shade too hastily, and seeing David's derisory grin gave way to the temptation to add, 'But I thought *you* were.'

'Only when he's around.'

Feeling a sense of camaraderie, and disarmed by the self-mockery, she said seriously, 'But you must know as well as I do that it would be asking for trouble…'

'We're free agents. To hell with him. In any case, how would he know?'

'If he came back and found both of us gone…'

'He won't be back. Once he's working, everything else gets pushed on one side… Surely you don't want to just sit here for the rest of the afternoon?'

With all of Venice on the doorstep, she didn't. Suddenly impatient, tired of inactivity, she wanted to get out and about.

If Dominic had said anything about returning, had asked her to wait for him… But he hadn't.

Seeing her waver, David urged, 'Oh, come on… You're not a prisoner, and we'll be back before he's even missed us.'

'Well perhaps for just an hour or so.'

'That's my girl!' he cried triumphantly.

Suddenly remembering, she said, 'But didn't you have stomach pains?'

'They're much better…'

'How convenient.'

'It's quite true that I *did* have them, so don't look so stern and accusing… Now, do you need to do anything before we start?'

'Just slip upstairs for my bag. I may need some more sunscreen.'

'You're in the east wing, presumably?'

'Yes.'

'Which room?'

As she hesitated, he hazarded with a sly grin, 'I bet Dom gave you the room next to his.'

Noting the confusion she was unable to hide, he added with a slight touch of malice, 'I must say I don't blame him. A communicating door comes in very handy.'

Then, hastily, 'There's no need to be cross. I'm only joking... Now, if you go up by the back stairs it'll save time, and you'll be less likely to meet anyone.'

'I don't know where the back stairs are.'

'Come on, I'll show you.' Picking up his jacket, he seized her hand and hurried her down the steps and across the courtyard to a small door at the rear of the house.

It opened into what were clearly servants' quarters, with kitchens and storerooms and a veritable maze of stone passages. Through another door was a flagged area with a flight of stone steps leading up to an archway.

Pointing upwards, David said, 'If you go through the archway and turn left, there's a corridor that leads straight to the east wing. It should only take you a minute or so. I'll wait for you here...'

Just in case we're seen together, hung on the air unspoken.

Feeling distinctly nervous, almost guilty, Nicola followed his instructions and came out practically opposite the door she now recognised as her own.

Once inside her room she breathed a sigh of relief. But it was absurd to feel guilty, she told herself firmly. It wasn't as if she was doing anything wrong.

Dominic might have warned his brother to stay away from her, but she and David were grown adults—and if, tired of being dictated to, he *wanted* to risk taking her out for an hour or two...

Ignoring the voice of common sense that warned her she shouldn't be a party to it, Nicola opened her shoulder bag and dropped a tube of sunscreen and some tissues into it.

She was just closing it again when, with a sudden shock, she recalled what Dominic had told her about Sophia's ring being priceless.

Unzipping the small compartment at the back, she took

out the soft leather pouch and put it into her grandmother's jewellery box.

It should be safe enough there for the time being.

Shutting the door quietly behind her, she hurried back the way she had come, her heart beating ridiculously fast.

David was waiting where she had left him. 'See anyone?' he asked.

She shook her head. 'Not a soul.'

'Good. I've got a boat waiting for us. This way.' He crossed to a stout oak door with an iron grille. Even before he drew back the bolts she could hear the surge and slap of water against stone.

The door gave access to a short flight of worn steps and a landing stage.

'This isn't the way Dominic took me last night.' She spoke the thought aloud.

'No, that would have been the main entrance. This is the tradesmen's,' he added with a grin.

Both the huge wooden boat-house doors were closed, but a narrow side door led to an outside landing stage where, to her surprise, a black steel-prowed gondola was waiting.

The gondolier, dressed in a red-striped T-shirt and a straw hat with a red ribbon, helped Nicola in while David followed on her heels.

As soon as they were settled side by side on the cushioned seat the gondola drew away.

Watching the boatman ply the long oar with marvellous dexterity, she remarked, 'How exciting. I must admit I hadn't expected a gondola.'

'I daren't take one of the motorboats in case Dominic misses it,' David explained. 'And Giorgio can come and go much more quietly than a water-taxi. With a bit of luck no one will realise we've gone.'

'I take it you often use this method of escape?' she asked lightly.

'Yes, I do,' he admitted with cheerful unconcern. 'It saves an awful lot of trouble and tiresome explanations. Being the younger son is a terrible trial... But we're out to enjoy ourselves, so I vote we forget our problems for a while...'

Only too happy to follow his lead, she relaxed and began to enjoy the strange movement of the gondola, which dipped and curtsied in response to the gondolier's single oar.

It was mid-afternoon and the sun was riding high in the sky. Apart from some red-faced, perspiring tourists there were few people about. Most Venetians, it seemed, had retired indoors to escape the sweltering heat.

Leaving Rio Cavalli, and moving from sunlight to shade, they threaded their way through a network of waterways, passing under bridges where the water was dark green and the shadows quiet and deep.

After a while Nicola became aware of the varied smells of the city: fruit, flowers, ground coffee, bread being baked, the sweet, heady scent of wine and spices... And all the time the splash and ripple of water...

She felt a sudden poignant sadness. If only she had been discovering this most picturesque and romantic of cities with Dominic beside her...

'This will do fine, Giorgio. We'll walk from here.' David's voice broke into her thoughts.

A moment later they drew into a gondola park where several of the gondoliers, their straw hats tipped over their faces, were taking a siesta.

When Nicola had been helped out a roll of lira changed hands, and after a low-toned conversation with their boatman David joined her on the *fondamenta*.

As the sun beat down mercilessly the stones they were standing on threw back an oven heat.

His jacket over his arm, perspiration shining on his forehead, he said, 'It's a damn sight too hot for walking about

sightseeing… Tell you what, why don't we take a dip instead?'

'A dip?' she echoed.

'If we go over to the Lido we can relax under a beach
umbrella and go for a swim.'

'That sounds wonderful… But we haven't got swimwear
or towels or changing facilities—'

'That's just where you're wrong. For convenience, I use
part of my allowance to keep a permanent room at the Trans
Luxor. An arrangement that big brother knows nothing
about. Come on.'

Taking her hand, he led her along the *fondamenta* to what
she presumed was the Venetian equivalent of a taxi rank,
and in a moment they were speeding towards the long, narrow strip of land that formed the Lido.

Once on the island, Nicola was surprised to find that,
unlike Venice, there were busy roads with cars and buses
and taxis.

David hailed a taxi for the short drive to the hotel, which
was a dazzling white building shaded by trees. Inside it was
cool and dim and absolutely deserted, except for a pretty
young blonde behind the reception desk.

As they crossed the marble-floored lobby David remarked
casually, 'Last time one of my girlfriends was here she left
her swimsuit in my room…'

Suddenly realising exactly what he'd meant by *convenience*, Nicola wondered whether she'd been wise to come.
But it was too late now. Having got this far, she could
hardly walk out.

'Gina's just about your size, if you'd like to borrow it?'

Far from enamoured with the idea, Nicola was about to
politely refuse when, indicating a small boutique just off the
main lobby, he added, 'Or if you'd prefer to have your own
you could choose one while I pick up the key.'

By the time he had picked up the key, which involved a

lengthy flirtation and a great deal of giggling on the part of the blonde receptionist, Nicola had selected and paid for a modest black swimsuit.

His ground-floor room was large and well-furnished, with French doors that opened on to the cool greenery of the gardens. Beyond was a private beach bright with umbrella-shaded loungers.

A room like this must cost a great deal to rent on a permanent basis, Nicola thought, deciding that his allowance couldn't be the mere pittance he'd described it as being.

As soon as the door had closed behind them he hung his jacket over the back of a chair and, having drawn the many-layered muslin curtains, began to unbutton his shirt.

'Perhaps I could change in the bathroom?' she suggested evenly.

Indicating a door to the right, he agreed with a mocking grin, 'By all means, if you're feeling particularly modest.'

Refusing to rise to the bait, she went, bolting the door after her just to be on the safe side.

The swimsuit, which fitted her to perfection, was nowhere near as decorous as it had seemed, the legs being cut high and the bust low. She stood for a few seconds trying to adjust it, before giving up the struggle.

As well as the white bath towels there was a pile of coloured beach towels, and after selecting a couple she ventured out, to be greeted by a low, appreciative whistle.

Dressed in red swimming trunks, and sporting what seemed to be an all-over tan, David looked both macho and sexy, and she could quite understand what women saw in him.

But as far as *she* was concerned, measured against Dominic's powerful physique and virile attraction, his brother couldn't compete. The sight of him failed to raise her pulse-rate one iota.

With a suggestive glance at the bed, he said, 'I thought you might fancy a little siesta first?'

'No, thanks.'

'Why not?' he sounded genuinely surprised. Then, as though just stating a fact, he added, 'A lot of women find me irresistible.'

'I believe you. I just don't happen to be one of them.'

'Go on, don't fight it,' he urged.

'I don't need to. To put it bluntly, I find you eminently resistible.'

'You certainly know how to hurt a man's feelings,' he complained with mock indignation.

Liking him for the way he'd taken her rejection in such good part, she said, 'But I do think you're nice.'

Perking up, he suggested, 'If you'd like me to show you just how nice I can be—'

'I wouldn't.'

'We don't have to go for a swim just yet,' he persisted. 'It'll be cooler in an hour or so's time, and there'll be less people.'

'I expect to be back at the *palazzo* in an hour or so's time,' she informed him crisply.

He sighed. 'Then I suppose we'd better get moving.'

The Adriatic was a pale, clear green and refreshingly cool, while the fine sandy beach was clean and golden and shelved gently.

Though most of the loungers were occupied they managed to find two free ones side by side. Enjoying the holiday atmosphere, the pleasure that sun, sea, and sand could bring, they alternately swam and stretched out in the shade, sometimes in companionable silence, sometimes talking idly.

Waking from a doze, and glancing around, Nicola realised that quite a lot of the loungers were empty.

'What time is it?'

'No idea,' David said idly, his eyes still closed.

'I'm sure it must be getting on. We ought to be starting back.' Jumping to her feet, she gathered up her towel and sunscreen.

Reluctantly he followed suit, and led the way through the tree-shaded gardens back to his room. As he unlocked the French doors he offered, 'You can have the bathroom first. Unless you'd like to share a shower?'

'This is no time for joking,' she said severely.

'What makes you think I'm joking?'

She sighed. 'You're incorrigible.'

With a grin he assured her, 'It's part of my charm.'

Going through to the bathroom, she stripped off her swimsuit. Her hair felt sticky with the salt water, and, taking out the pins, she reached for the shampoo.

As soon as she had showered and blowdried her hair, she pulled on her clothes and went back to the bedroom, her hair still loose around her shoulders.

'It's all yours.' Then catching sight of the expression on David's face, she asked sharply, 'What's wrong?'

'Have you seen the time?'

'No, I left my watch in my bag.'

'Take a look.'

With a sudden sense of doom she reached for her bag, which she'd left on a low chest, and felt for her watch.

Staring at the gold hands on the black face, she protested stupidly, 'No, it can't be six-thirty!'

'I'm afraid it is. We've blown it. There's no way we can get home before Dom. In fact, unless we're lucky, we won't be back in time for dinner.'

'Oh, Lord,' she exclaimed in dismay.

Gathering up his clothes, he said, 'Look, while I shower, I'll try to decide what to do.'

'What *can* we do?'

'I'll let you know when I've had a minute to think.' He disappeared into the bathroom, closing the door behind him.

Finding her small brush, Nicola was about to put up her hair when she realised she'd left her pins in the bathroom.

David returned quite quickly, fully dressed, his blue eyes bright, his damp hair clinging to his skull in tight black curls.

'Well?' she asked, without much hope.

'As far as I can see we've only two options. We either go straight back and brazen it out—but I tell you now I'm not much for that course of action; it'll mean being in the doghouse for weeks—or we play it cool.'

'What do you mean by play it cool?'

'Presumably by now Dom will know we're both missing. But he can't be sure we're together. We could have gone out quite independently... Now, my suggestion is this. We don't rush back. In fact we wait until everyone's in bed...'

'Oh, but—'

'We can have a meal out, see a little of Venice by night, then get a gondola back and slip in separately. If we go straight up to our rooms no one need ever know we've been together. Then, if we meet in the morning we greet each other like virtual strangers...'

'But won't it mean telling an awful lot of lies?' she asked unhappily.

'Why should it? If Dom asks me I'll tell him I've been over to the Lido... If he questions you, don't mention the Lido, simply say you've been sightseeing.'

'What if it doesn't work?'

He shrugged. '*If* it doesn't, though there's a good chance that it will, we might as well be hung for sheep as lambs... What do you say?'

She hesitated, disliking the idea of having to lie, even by omission. But she was at least partly to blame. If she hadn't been stupid enough to agree to go out with David none of this would have happened.

And if Dominic *did* discover they'd been together, after he'd warned his brother off, David was going to be the one to suffer the consequences. So if there was a sporting chance of saving the day…

'All right,' she agreed.

'That's my girl!'

CHAPTER NINE

DESPITE her unease, the return journey to Venice by water-taxi was an experience Nicola wouldn't have missed for worlds.

The air was golden and pellucid, and sun sparkled and danced on the lagoon. At David's urging she had left her hair down, and a warm breeze played with the heavy silken mass, blowing curly tendrils across her cheeks.

In the distance the historic centre, with its bridges and bell towers, its temples and palaces, lay like some magnificent backdrop, serene and enchanted against a deep blue sky.

'Isn't it *wonderful*?' she said over the noise of the engine.

'Most people think so.' David sounded indifferent.

Glancing at him, she saw he was completely unmoved by the beauty of the city.

'I suppose, having lived here all my life, I'm used to it,' he added.

Dominic was used to it, but as far as *he* was concerned Venice still hadn't lost either its loveliness or its fascination…

'One thing it does have,' David pursued after a moment, 'are some first-class restaurants. I thought we'd eat at Il Faraone, which is one of the best. They know me there, so we'll have no difficulty getting a table, and if we disembark at Accademia, it's quite close.'

Nicola's ankle had started to swell and stiffen up again, and putting her weight on it had become painful, so she was pleased not to have too far to go.

After disembarking near the Accademia Bridge and walking a little way, they turned into a narrow *calle* that lay in deep shadow.

They were part-way down it when some distance ahead a man coming towards them paused in the shadows to light a cigarette. The flare of the match briefly illuminated a thin, swarthy face with a hooked nose.

Seizing her arm in a vice-like grip, David swung on his heel and headed back the way they'd come.

Nicola felt a tingle of apprehension, sensing something sinister in the little incident. But perhaps she was just being over-imaginative? It could be simply that he had taken a wrong turning.

Though as he appeared to frequent Il Faraone that seemed somewhat unlikely.

A swift glance at his face only served to confirm her suspicion that something was wrong. 'David…' she began.

'It's all right,' he assured her. 'There's no problem. It was just someone I didn't want to run into. This way is just as quick.'

In spite of his attempt to shrug it off she could tell he was rattled. But, reminding herself that it was no business of hers, she said nothing further.

As she might have expected, Il Faraone was elite and stylish, with a well-dressed clientele and a striking Egyptian decor. When David had been greeted by name and made welcome they were shown to one of the best tables.

His smile slightly reckless, he ordered champagne, and when it arrived drank the first glass as though it were lemonade.

The menu was so large and varied that, after glancing through it twice, Nicola sought his advice on what Italian dish to try.

He answered abstractedly, as though his mind was on other things, and they were halfway through the meal before he seemed able to shrug off whatever was bugging him and give her his full attention.

Then, studying her face, he said thoughtfully, 'Apart from the fact that you're beautiful, I know hardly anything about you. Tell me about yourself.'

A little uncomfortably, she asked, 'What would you like to know?'

'What do you do? Or rather what *did* you do before you became a rich woman?'

Ignoring the rather snide way the question was phrased, she told him levelly, 'I'm a conference organiser for Westlake Business Solutions.'

'Was that how you met John?'

'Yes.'

'Did you live with him?'

'No. Nor did I persuade him to leave me his money.'

'I rather thought not. You don't seem to be the gold-digger type.'

He sounded sincere, and, her green eyes suddenly misty, she said, 'Thank you for that.'

'Did he love you?'

'No. He still loved your mother. We were just friends. We hadn't really known each other very long.'

'So why did he leave you everything he had?'

'I'm still not sure. Possibly because he didn't get on with—' She stopped speaking abruptly.

'The rest of the family?' David supplied. Then judiciously, 'Can't say I blame him, personally. Apart from Mamma, nobody else really accepted him, and he must have known it. Though leaving you the Maschera ring was really getting his own back with a vengeance...'

So David *had* been eavesdropping.

'Just for curiosity, have you decided whether or not to let Dom have it back?'

'There's been no time to think about it... I just wish it wasn't *worth* so much,' she burst out raggedly

Curiously, he asked, 'Then you really didn't know how valuable it was?'

'Of course I didn't. I'd hardly have been carrying it around with me if I had.'

'If you were carrying it with you, why didn't Dom's detective find it? I gather he searched your cases.'

'It was in my handbag,' she admitted.

David gave a long, low whistle. 'So you were *literally* carrying it around with you. It's just as well big brother doesn't know that. He'd have a heart attack... Though of course Mamma always wore it,' he continued thoughtfully, 'and no one queried how safe that was.'

Eyeing Nicola's bag, he raised an eyebrow. 'I suppose you're not still...?'

'No,' she said hastily. 'I left it in my room.'

'Safely hidden?'

'I put it in my grandmother's jewellery box.'

He nodded, before commenting with a certain degree of satisfaction, 'I must say Dom hasn't had it all his own way lately. What with being deprived of the ring, and Ca' Malvasia...'

'Not to mention the money.' She failed to hide her bitterness.

'I think the money's the least of his concerns. The lucky devil already has enough. But he does badly want the other two. The woman he's going to marry—'

'He's going to be married?' Even to herself, her voice sounded shocked, impeded.

'Ah!' David exclaimed. 'You're surprised because of what I said earlier, about him having fallen for you?'

Nicola took a deep, steadying breath, and remarked as lightly as possible, 'Well, it just goes to prove you're wrong.'

'Not at all. Until he and Carla are married he'll be allowed his little indulgences, so long as he's discreet and the Ferrinis don't get to hear of it.'

'When…?' She faltered, then went on, 'When are they going to be married?'

'So far as I'm aware they haven't yet set a date.'

Knowing she was just torturing herself, but unable to stop, she asked, 'How long have they known each other?'

'Practically all their lives. Though Carla's quite a bit younger than Dom—more my age. They've been unofficially engaged for over a year. But for some reason, though he admits it's high time he settled down and produced an heir, Dom has been dragging his feet.'

'I can't understand why. I wouldn't have done. Carla's a beautiful girl, and the Ferrinis, who were close friends of Mamma's, must be amongst the wealthiest families in Venice. There's also a branch of the family in New York, and they're not short of a dollar or two…'

He sighed. 'If you do decide to let Dom have the ring back I expect it will help to spur him on…'

Her heart like lead, Nicola said, 'I don't see what else I can do. I'd feel bad knowing not only how much it's worth but about the tradition.'

'I must admit I don't see the point of keeping up all these old traditions.' David sounded bored. 'Though Dom is pretty keen on it. He's always seemed to be in tune with the past…

'Whereas Carla's a thoroughly modern girl and probably doesn't care two hoots about the ring. But having Ca' Malvasia back would almost certainly make a difference.'

'You don't mean they'd live there?'

'No, but Carla's mother would. It's already been discussed. Signora Ferrini, who has been recently widowed, would like to sell the Ferrini family home, a huge crumbling place on the Giudecca, and be close to her only daughter.

Dom has already agreed that she could live with them in the *palazzo*, but she wants to keep her independence. If she was able to have Ca' Malvasia it would be ideal.'

Her despair complete, Nicola said, 'No wonder he wants it back so badly.'

'Well, in my opinion you'd be a fool to let him have it.' Then, as though sensing how low she felt, 'But let's forget about Dom and go and paint the town... What about a spot of dancing?'

'That would be lovely,' she said as brightly as possible, 'but I don't think I can. You see I sprained my ankle yesterday, and it's starting to play up again.'

'Which means no walking either?'

'Well, not too much,' she admitted.

'In that case I know the ideal way to spend the rest of the evening. We'll go to the Club Nove. We can sit and have a bottle of champagne while we enjoy the floor show... Oh, just a word of warning. Don't ever mention this to Dom.'

After taking them through a network of back canals, the water-taxi dropped them by a short flight of water-lapped steps which led into a narrow alleyway between high brick walls.

The alley gave on to Campo Mandolo, a rather grand square which, with several bars and open-air restaurants, appeared to be a venue for Venetian night-life.

On the right of the *campo* was a restaurant with a large group of people eating outside at tables set beneath a green and gold awning. Judging by the cake it was a birthday celebration, and there was much talk and laughter and clinking of wine bottles.

By the side of the restaurant was a black studded door with a metal grille. There was no name on it, and nothing to indicate it was a club.

Reaching up, David tugged at the old-fashioned bell-pull.

A face appeared at the grille, and after a moment's silent scrutiny the door was opened by a burly man in evening dress.

Leaning towards him, David said something Nicola didn't catch.

'What about her?' the man asked.

'This is Signora Whitney. She's all right. I'll vouch for her.'

The man nodded, and they were ushered inside and the door closed behind them.

Nicola found herself standing in a bare foyer, with a marble staircase leading upwards. As the man disappeared into a small cubicle David said, 'This way,' and led her up the stairs.

At the top of the stairs was another door with a grille. He rapped briefly with his knuckles, and once more they were silently inspected.

Nothing was said, but the door opened and they were ushered into a large room with luxurious ivory and gold decor and crystal chandeliers. At the far end was a dais with a black baby grand piano.

In front of the dais was a highly polished dance floor the size of a postage stamp, around which were scattered a dozen or so tables.

An elegantly dressed hostess appeared at David's elbow, and with a smile showed them to one of the few unoccupied tables.

She was followed almost immediately by a wine waiter with a bottle of champagne in an ice-bucket and two long-stemmed glasses. Easing out the cork with a nicely controlled pop, the waiter poured the smoking wine before moving away on silent feet.

Nicola got the impression that champagne was part of the usual routine.

Glancing around her curiously, she saw that some of the clientele wore evening clothes, while others were more casually dressed, but they all seemed to have one thing in common—money.

Leaning towards her, David said in her ear, 'Good timing. The floor show's just about to start.'

Sipping champagne, they sat and watched an extremely good show which included a brilliant illusionist and a Frank Sinatra look-alike.

After perhaps an hour, when the pianist was accompanying a husky-voiced blues singer wearing a gold-lamé dress, David began to get restive.

'Let's go through and get a bit of the action.'

'A bit of the action?' Nicola echoed uncertainly, as he pulled back her chair.

He grinned. 'There's no need to look so wary. I only meant a few rolls of the dice.'

So this was a *gambling* club. That explained the rather strange mode of entry.

Recalling his injunction not to tell Dominic, and feeling distinctly uneasy, she said, 'I'm sure this isn't wise. I really think we should go.'

'Don't be such a spoilsport,' he chided her. 'It's only a bit of fun, for goodness' sake. Look, I promise we won't stay long…'

Seeing she was unconvinced, he pulled a mobile phone from his pocket, 'If it makes you any happier I'll call Giorgio and ask him to pick us up in half an hour or so.'

He was clearly determined, and, unwilling to make a fuss, she waited while he had a brief word with the boatman, then reluctantly allowed herself to be shepherded into a side room.

Windowless, and brightly lit by harsh neon lighting, it was as large as the other room, but stark and businesslike, with nothing to distract the gamblers from their game.

There were quite a lot of tables—some set up for baccarat, some for dice games, others for roulette. Most of them were busy.

As they approached one of the tables a seat became vacant. Pushing her into it, David had a quiet word with the banker and was given a pile of pink plastic chips in exchange for what appeared to be an IOU.

On edge and anxious, she watched as he picked up and rattled the dice. 'I really need to win, so keep your fingers crossed.'

'Oh, I *will*,' she said fervently.

Fascinated in spite of herself, she watched as he began to roll the dice with a devil-may-care air quite at odds with the seriousness displayed by most of the gamblers.

Almost immediately he hit a winning streak. From then on it seemed he could do no wrong. 'You've brought me luck,' he said jubilantly, as he threw a double six.

'I'm glad,' she said. Then, urgently, 'Can we go now?'

'While I'm winning?' he sounded amazed.

'Surely that's the time to stop? Please, David. It's getting very late.'

Seeing she was really anxious, he said, 'Just another few rolls, then I'll pack it in.'

But, as though Lady Luck had suddenly withdrawn her favours, he lost on the next roll, and after one more win began to lose steadily.

No longer able to look, Nicola sat with her hands clenched until the banker finally called a halt.

Taking out a pen, David began to plead for a further chance to win back what he'd lost, but to Nicola's great relief the banker was adamant. There was to be no further credit.

His face set, David turned away, and they left the club in a brooding silence.

Everywhere was in darkness now, the bars and restaurant closed, tables and chairs piled together beneath the awnings.

They had crossed the deserted *campo* and were about to turn down the alley, which was unlit, when two men stepped out, barring their way. Both appeared to be brawny, but one was appreciably taller than the other.

'Before you go, we'd like a word with you.'

In the gloom Nicola could see neither of their faces clearly, but their menacing attitude brought a distinct chill of fear.

'Can't you make it some other time?' David asked with a bravado that almost came off. 'As you can see, I have a lady with me.'

The spokesman, who was the taller of the two, said, 'I'm sure she won't mind waiting just a couple of minutes.'

Closing in on David, they hustled him down the alleyway.

If they showed any sign of harming him she'd have to scream, Nicola thought desperately. But all she could hear was the low murmur of voices. A few snatches of conversation in disjointed sentences.

'Why not talk to me at the club...?'

'...disturb the other clientele. So what about it?'

'As soon as I can...'

'You shouldn't have been allowed to get in any deeper. Angelo's not pleased...'

'...pay, I promise...'

'How soon?'

'Another few days...worth his while...'

'He said tomorrow. No later than three o'clock.'

'I'll try, but I—'

'You'll have to do better than try. Angelo's getting impatient.'

They seemed to be returning, and Nicola heard the last few sentences more plainly.

'Remember what happened to the last man Angelo got impatient with.'

'What good would that do?' David sounded scared.

'It might serve as a lesson to others who run up debts when they haven't got the money.'

'But I *have* got the money,' he said desperately. 'Angelo knows that. I just can't get my hands on it at the moment.'

'Then you'd better find some other way to pay…and before three o'clock tomorrow.'

Emerging from the alley, the two men melted into the darkness, leaving David standing alone.

Mingled with her relief that they hadn't harmed him was a very real anxiety. There seemed little doubt that he was up to his neck in trouble.

As she rejoined him, he said with a jauntiness she was forced to admire, 'Sorry about that. Just two rather impetuous friends of mine.'

'Friends' was the last word she would have used, Nicola thought, but he seemed less alarmed by them than by the man he'd avoided earlier.

When they reached the end of the alleyway David gave a sigh of relief to find Giorgio's gondola was drawn up by the steps.

Without a word being spoken Nicola was handed in, and in a moment or two they were threading their way through the dark canals.

They approached the *palazzo* as silently as they'd left it, only the faint creak of the oar and the splash of water to give away their presence.

At the landing-stage David had a whispered conversation with the boatman before a roll of notes changed hands.

Then, putting his lips to Nicola's ear, he said softly, 'I'll go in first, to make sure the coast's clear. Just in case there's a problem give me ten minutes before you follow. Giorgio will tell you when the time's up. Be sure to bolt the door behind you, and use the back stairs like you did before. Once we're both safely in our own rooms no one can swear we've been out together.'

He gave her hand a quick squeeze. 'With a bit of luck we're home and dry.'

To Nicola, sitting waiting in the darkness as the seconds crept by and a balmy night breeze lifted her hair, ten minutes seemed an age. She could see the faint greenish glow of Giorgio's luminous wristwatch without being able to tell the time.

Silent and aloof, the boatman stood like a statue, plying his long oar to keep the gondola steady while the water slopped a little, like a cup of black coffee in an unsteady hand.

When he finally turned his head and gave her a brief nod, she whispered, *'Grazie,'* and allowed herself to be helped onto the landing-stage.

He was drawing away before she had let herself in.

Closing the door quietly behind her, she struggled to push home the stout bolts. Despite her care, both of them grated. In the silence the noise seemed terribly loud, and she stood for a moment, her heart in her mouth.

Then, plucking up courage, she climbed the dimly lit stairs and tiptoed along the corridor. The whole place appeared to be fast asleep, but she held her breath until she had reached her room and slipped inside.

She was endeavouring to close the heavy door quietly when, in the darkness, she misjudged the distance and it shut with a distinct thud.

As she stood there, frozen, the communicating door was thrown open, letting in a flood of light.

Dominic stood in the doorway wearing a dark silk dressing gown. Though his black hair was ruffled, she got the distinct impression that he hadn't yet been to bed.

'Where have you been?' he demanded.

His back was to the light and she couldn't see his face clearly, but there wasn't the slightest doubt that he was *furious*.

'Out.' In spite of all her efforts her voice shook a little.

Taking in the dress and sandals, the shoulder bag and the silken wind-blown hair, he said, 'That's obvious. And it's equally obvious that you've only just returned.'

'Yes,' she admitted.

'Come in here,' he ordered curtly. 'I want to talk to you.'

'Please, Dominic, can't it wait until morning?'

'No, it can't.'

Desperate to postpone the confrontation, she pleaded, 'But I'm tired and my ankle hurts.'

'That I can well believe,' he announced grimly. 'But you have some explaining to do, and I've no intention of letting you stand on the opposite side of the room while you do it, so come along.'

Knowing full well Dominic was capable of sweeping her up and carrying her across the room, Nicola dropped her bag on a chair and reluctantly moved towards him.

He stepped aside to allow her to pass.

Seeing his set face, and suddenly scared stiff of his anger, she hung back.

Seizing her wrist, he drew her inside and closed the door behind her.

She had somehow expected his room to be grand and imposing, but, agitated as she was, she was struck by the simplicity of the off-white walls, the plainness of the furniture. The only thing to echo his wealth and power as the head of the house was a magnificent four-poster with a scarlet and gold canopy.

'Sit down.'

'I'd rather stand.'

'Will you stop behaving like a stubborn little fool and do

as I say?' Though he still hadn't raised his voice, it cracked like a whip.

She sank down in the nearest chair.

Remaining standing, he told her, 'As soon as I'd arranged for someone else to take David's place at the meeting, and made my apologies to Bruno Zitelle, I came back, expecting to take you over to Murano, only to find you'd disappeared.'

'I—I'm sorry,' she stammered. 'But you didn't say you'd be coming back, and David thought—' Realising it was unwise to involve David, she broke off abruptly.

'What *did* David think?'

Carefully, she answered, 'Only that if you once got involved with work it was unlikely you'd be back. He said you might even go over to Mestre yourself, so I decided that rather than just sit there I'd go out for a little while—'

'But it wasn't "a little while". You've been out for hours. When dinnertime came and there was still no sign of you I began to think you'd...'

Though he failed to complete the sentence, she knew exactly what he'd been about to say. 'Gone? Left Venice for good?'

'It did cross my mind,' he admitted.

Though his words were almost casual, she was suddenly quite certain that he'd been *afraid* that she'd gone, that it had *mattered* to him.

For a moment her heart lifted.

Then with a pang she realised that it hadn't been *her* that had mattered, but the fact that she had the Maschera ring.

Sighing, she asked, 'So how did you know I hadn't gone for good?'

'I went up to your room and discovered your belongings were all still there. That reassured me for a while, but when you still failed to return I began to get seriously concerned about you.'

'Well, I'm sorry if you were concerned.' Deciding to fight

back, she added, 'But as you yourself said it was an ''open'' prison I could see no harm in going out to do some sight-seeing.'

'*Sightseeing*? Have you any idea what time it is?'

'Well, I know it's late but—'

'It's nearly half-past two.'

'Oh...'

'Anything might have happened to you!' With a kind of raging calm, he demanded, 'How could you be so foolish as to go roaming around Venice alone until the early hours of the morning?'

'But I wasn't...' Naturally honest, she made a very poor liar, and, realising she'd almost given David away, she broke off in confusion.

Dominic's eyes narrowed. 'Alone?'

'Roaming around. Quite a lot of the time I was sitting down because of my ankle.'

'Where were you ''sitting down'' until two o'clock in the morning?'

'I can't remember the name of the place...' Hoping she wasn't giving away too much, she added, 'I had a drink there, then stayed to watch the floor show.'

Her inquisitor changed ground with an abruptness that threw her. 'How did you get in and out of the *palazzo*?'

'I—I don't know what you mean.'

'It's a perfectly simple question.'

When, unsure what to say, she stayed silent, he asked, 'Did you leave and return by the main entrance?'

Guessing that the main entrance would have been locked and bolted before the servants went to bed, she stammered, 'W-well no.'

'So which entrance *did* you use?'

'I went and returned by boat.'

'I see... But not the way I took you last night.'

It was a statement, not a question, and, afraid of putting her foot in it, she once again remained silent.

'So who told you about the tradesmen's entrance?'

Trapped, she cried, 'I refuse to answer any more questions. As a guest here I've every right to come and go as I please, without being interrogated.'

He raised a black winged brow. 'Interrogated?'

'What else would you call it?'

'Perhaps if you'd told me the truth to start with…'

'I haven't told you any lies.'

'I'm satisfied that you've told me the truth *as far as it goes*. But I'm not a complete fool. I know you've been out with David.'

Then, surprising her, 'From the description you gave me of your husband, I imagine my brother is a lot like him?'

'Yes,' she admitted.

'Well, just bear in mind that, unlike your husband, David's a philanderer, a heartbreaker.'

'How kind of you to warn me.'

'So where did he take you?' The question came with the suddenness of an ambush.

'I've already said I won't answer any more questions.'

'As a matter of fact you don't need to; I can guess. You see, I'm well aware that David keeps a room at the Trans Luxor, over on the Lido… And the fact that your hair is loose suggests that you've either been swimming or indulging in some…shall we say…*indoor* exercise…'

Watching her eyes drop in confusion, and her cheeks grow hot, he remarked trenchantly, 'I can see I've guessed right. So which form did the exercise take?'

'As it's nothing to do with you, I've no intention of telling you.'

'I suppose I don't need to ask. David is no slouch when it comes to getting women into bed.'

'Neither is his brother,' she retorted. 'And at least David isn't engaged...'

As soon as the remark was out she wished it unsaid.

His grey eyes narrowing, Dominic queried, 'So what exactly did he tell you?'

Trying to sound as though she didn't care, she said, 'Only that you were going to be married.'

Then suddenly the pain and bitterness overflowed. 'I can quite understand why you want both the ring and Ca' Malvasia back.' Blinded by tears, she jumped to her feet and headed for the door.

He got there ahead of her and, his back to the panels, stood blocking the way.

'Don't rush off.'

Head bent, struggling to hold back the tears, she said thickly, 'Please let me leave.'

'Not until you tell me whether or not you went to bed with David.'

Lifting her head, the tears pouring down her cheeks, she cried fiercely, 'Why bother asking? If I denied it, you wouldn't believe me.'

'Try me.'

'Of course I went to bed with him! Knowing the sort of woman I am, what else would you expect?'

'But I *don't* know. I'm still trying to find out.'

'What does it matter? So long as you get everything back you regard as yours!' Sobbing now, she tried to open the door.

When he moved, she thought he was going to let her go, but instead he pulled her into his arms.

For a few seconds she attempted futilely to free herself then, giving up the struggle, she buried her face against his chest and proceeded to cry her heart out while he held her close and stroked her hair.

'Don't upset yourself,' he said softly. 'Everything will be all right, I promise…'

But he was going to marry a woman named Carla and nothing would ever be right again.

'Now, don't cry any more.'

Struggling for control, she drew back a little, and said with pathetic dignity, 'I'm sorry.'

'There's nothing to be sorry for.' Lifting her face, he wiped away the tears with his thumb.

That tender little gesture was her undoing. Fresh tears overflowed and ran down her cheeks.

Whispering, *'Cara mia,'* he pulled her close again, and began to kiss them away.

The yearning for him, the need she felt deep inside, began to grow, and with no reserves of strength left to fight it she was lost long before his kisses changed from being merely comforting to passionate and demanding.

When Nicola opened her eyes, the room, with its white-walled simplicity, looked totally strange—until she remembered that this was Dominic's room, and, though she was alone, this was Dominic's bed she was lying in.

He had called her *cara mia*…

But he shouldn't have done. He was engaged to be married.

She gave a little moan of anguish and despair. In spite of knowing that, she had allowed herself to go to bed with him yet again.

Would she never learn?

While she was deeply and passionately in love with him, Dominic cared nothing for her. He was simply assuaging his sexual needs while he waited to marry another woman.

No, that was hardly fair. She was making it sound as if he had simply *used* her. But, a lover of great tenderness and passion, he had given her a lot more than he had asked in return.

Remembering how he had spent half the night making sweetly inventive love to her, she shivered with pleasure.

Yet while she found their physical relationship infinitely and endlessly enjoyable, it was *loving* him that lit up her whole being, *loving* him that *mattered*.

But there was no hope of Dominic loving her. Though he'd been willing to take her to bed, his main interest was getting back the ring and Ca' Malvasia to facilitate his marriage.

Knowing and accepting that, to stay here would only be torturing herself. The sooner she left for England, the better. But first she would go to see Signor Mancini and take steps to formally hand back what she now realised John should never have left her in the first place. Then she would be able to leave Venice with a clear conscience.

CHAPTER TEN

HAVING reached a decision, though her heart bled at the prospect of never seeing Dominic again, she felt a little easier in her mind.

A glance at her watch showed it was almost eleven-thirty. If she was able to make an appointment to see the solicitor this morning, she could be heading out of Venice by early afternoon.

Getting out of bed and discovering the rest had improved her ankle enormously, she gathered up her clothes, which had been placed on a carved wooden chest, and hurried into her own room.

The solicitor's phone number was in her handbag, and Nicola forced herself to pick up the phone and ring his office.

When Nicola had given her name and mentioned that the matter was urgent, his secretary informed her that, though he was going out shortly, he would make time to see her if she could come over immediately.

While she showered and dressed as quickly as possible, her mind went back over the events of the previous night.

With a feeling of shame she recalled how, when Dominic had asked her if she had slept with his brother, beside herself, she'd lied and said she had.

Now, bitterly regretting her stupidity, she wished for David's sake that she had simply denied ever being with him. If he had got into serious trouble she would be to blame.

As soon as she was ready Nicola made her way down the grand staircase in fear and trembling. The last thing she wanted to do was run into Dominic. Though hopefully, at this time of day, he would be working.

To her great relief she reached the handsome front door and closed it behind her without having encountered a soul.

Outside the sun was shining from a blue, blue sky, and the air was filled with a golden warmth that lay on her bare arms like a caress.

When she had walked the comparatively short distance to the Grand Canal, she took a water-taxi to Calle Pino, where Signor Mancini had his offices.

The middle-aged driver was cheerful and garrulous and, saying she would only be a few minutes, she asked him to wait.

A board on the door of number *sette* informed any interested persons that the offices of Mancini and Coducci were on the second floor.

Nicola rang the appropriate bell and spoke her name into a small oblong grille. In response there was a slight crackle, and a tinny voice asked her to come straight up.

A second later, with a metallic click, the bolt was released and the door swung open a few inches.

The entrance hall was dark, and she reached to press the glowing light switch before closing the door behind her and climbing the marble stairs.

Signor Mancini, a short, silver-haired, dapper man, was waiting at the door to greet her with an outstretched hand and a great many cordial remarks, and lead her into his office.

Ignoring both the hand and the pleasantries, she gave him a cool, *'Buon giorno.'*

As soon as she was seated, he queried, 'How may I help you?'

Without hesitation, she told him exactly what she had decided.

'Everything?' He sounded startled.

'Everything,' she said firmly.

'Well, of course, if that's what you wish…?'

'It is.'

'Then I'll take the necessary steps to make it legal. Will you be remaining in Venice?'

'No, I'm leaving this afternoon.'

'Where can I contact you?'

'I'm not sure. I'll have to let you know.'

Wasting no more time, she rose to her feet, and headed for the door.

When they got back to the *palazzo* she directed the taxi-driver to the tradesmen's entrance, and again asked him to wait.

Once more her luck was in and she saw no one as she hastened up the back stairs. Her cases had been stowed at the bottom of the cavernous wardrobe and, having unearthed them, she placed them on the bed and started to pack her belongings.

Nicola was about to put her grandmother's jewellery box into the smaller case when she remembered the Maschera ring. She would leave that with a note for Dominic, she decided, telling him what she had done and wishing him every happiness.

Lifting the lid, she found the chamois pouch, but it only took a second to confirm that it was empty. A quick search amongst the other items failed to locate the ring.

Bitterness rising in her throat like gall, she realised that Dominic must have taken it. Either yesterday evening, when he had come to her room to check that her belongings were still there, or this morning while she lay asleep in his bed.

But, knowing how much the ring meant to him, perhaps she couldn't blame him? In his place she might well have been tempted to do the same.

Yet she knew she *wouldn't*, and she felt an acute sense of dismay and disappointment. To simply take it while her back was turned lowered him in her estimation. It wasn't the action of a man of honour.

Her hands not quite steady, she was packing the rest of her things when a knock at the door made her jump out of her skin.

Standing motionless, she held her breath, hoping against hope that it wasn't Dominic, and that whoever had knocked would presume she wasn't there and go away.

'Nicola…' It was David's voice. 'Are you there? If you are, for God's sake open the door!'

Hurrying across the room, she opened the door to find David, grey-faced and sweating, slumped against the jamb.

Shocked, she began, 'What on earth…?'

'Listen,' he said urgently, 'I want you to do something for me…'

'Hadn't you better come in and sit down?'

'No time. I must get back before they miss me. The doctor has just diagnosed acute appendicitis…'

So he hadn't been lying about the stomach pains.

'An ambulance is coming any minute to take me into hospital, and I badly need your help.'

'What do you want me to do?'

Biting back a groan, he said, 'I want you to go to Club Nove *straight away*. Ring the bell until someone comes. Tell them your name, and insist on speaking to Angelo in person…'

Thrusting a small, brown padded envelope into her hand, he went on, 'Give him this message and tell him I've sent it.'

'Oh, but I'm just—'

'Believe me, I wouldn't ask you to do it if I wasn't desperate. But Angelo won't waste any time. If he doesn't hear from me before three o'clock he'll send his thugs after me and I'll end up in the hospital's mortuary rather than the recovery room. Please, Nicola… You're my only hope.'

Reacting to the desperation in his voice, she agreed, 'All right, I'll do it.'

He nodded and, bent over in agony, his lip caught between his teeth, began to make his slow, shuffling way down the corridor.

Afraid he would collapse, she watched him until he reached the end. Then, thankful she had a taxi waiting, she thrust the package into her bag and hurried down the back stairs. On the way she passed a maid, who gave her a curious glance but said nothing. When the driver had helped her into the boat, she told him where she wanted to go, the engine roared into life, and a moment later they were heading up the Rio dei Cavalli. As they reached the Grand Canal a water-ambulance passed them, speeding towards the *palazzo*.

As soon as she was safely away from Venice, Nicola promised herself, she would ring the hospital and make sure David was all right.

When they reached the bottom of the alleyway that led to Campo Mandolo, she gave the driver a substantial tip and said, 'If you wouldn't mind waiting again, I'll only be a few minutes. Then, when I've picked up my luggage from the *palazzo*, I'd like you to take me to Piazzale Roma.'

'Certainly, *signorina*. You're leaving Venice?'

'*Si.*'

'You don't like our beautiful city?'

'Yes, I love it. I'll be very sad to leave.'

'Then you must come back soon.'

She managed a smile, and accepted his steadying hand as she disembarked.

The nearby restaurant was still busy with lunchtime customers as she approached the club's black studded door and rang the bell.

Inside, apart from the noise of the bell, which echoed hollowly, everything seemed quiet and deserted.

After perhaps half a minute she tried again, without success.

What was she to do if nobody came? If she failed to deliver the package before three o'clock would David's life really be at risk? Or had he been exaggerating?

Recalling the two men who had bundled him down the alleyway the previous night, she knew she couldn't afford to take any chances.

With renewed determination, she rang the bell a third time. Somewhere inside a door banged, and a few seconds later a tough-looking face appeared at the grille. It was the same man who had admitted them the previous night.

'I'd like to speak to Angelo,' she said steadily.

Sounding none too pleased, the man informed her, 'He always has a sleep after lunch.'

'I must speak to him,' she insisted. 'My name is Nicola Whitney. I have an important message for him.'

Dark, close-set eyes studied her distrustfully, and she thought he was going to refuse.

'*Molto importante,*' she stressed.

'Very well,' he growled. 'But he won't like being disturbed.'

Opening the door, he led the way across the bare foyer and up the stairs.

'Wait in here.' He unlocked a door to the left and, switching on the light, showed her into a small windowless office.

A moment later he had closed and locked the door behind her.

Resolved to stay calm, she took the envelope from her bag and looked around her while she waited. There were several grey metal filing cabinets, a cluttered desk with a sagging leather chair, an overflowing wastepaper basket, and a large, heavy-looking safe. The air was stale and smelled of cigarette smoke.

The lack of windows made her feel claustrophobic, and

as the seconds ticked past she found herself gripping the padded envelope tightly, feeling a growing nervousness.

It seemed too bulky to contain just a message…

Nicola was never sure when the suspicion entered her head, but suddenly it was there.

She recalled the little scene in the alleyway—David saying, 'But I *have* got money… I just can't get my hands on it at the moment.'

And the spokesman insisting, 'Then you'd better find some other way to pay…'

What if it was David who had taken the ring?

No, no, she couldn't believe he would take the priceless Maschera ring to pay his gambling debts…

Or would he? He was almost certainly desperate enough. And after their conversation in Il Faraone he had known exactly where to find it.

Could she bring herself to look inside the package and make sure?

If she didn't, Dominic might lose one of the things he treasured most, and it would be her fault.

With sudden determination she tore open the envelope. Inside was a message scrawled on a sheet of thick white paper, and a gleaming gold ring.

As she stared at it in horror she became aware of approaching footsteps, and an instant later she heard the key turn in the lock.

If Angelo didn't know what David was sending him, she might be able to brazen it out.

Her mind working like lightning, she thrust the package down the side of the wastepaper basket to hide it, and straightened up just as the door opened.

The man who came in was of medium height, with a thin, swarthy face and a hooked nose. It was undoubtedly the same man that David had taken such care to avoid.

And all at once Nicola understood why.

Though Angelo's appearance was almost weedy, there was something repellent about him, an air of cold ruthlessness that sent a shiver down her spine.

Fixing her with glittering black eyes, he said politely, *'Buona sera.'*

'Buona sera, signor.'

'You're Signorina Whitney, I understand?'

'Signora,' she said firmly.

'You have a message for me?'

'Si Signor, from David Loredan. He was unable to come himself. Unfortunately he has just been taken into hospital with acute appendicitis.'

'I would have thought David had too much respect for me to offer weak excuses.'

'It's no excuse, *signor.*'

The deep-set eyes narrowed. 'Why did he send you just to tell me that?' With a kind of grim humour, he added, 'Surely he doesn't expect me to send him a bunch of grapes?'

She smiled slightly. 'He was afraid that if you didn't know the true situation you might be tempted to act…shall we say…hastily… All he needs is a little more time.'

'He's been saying that for weeks.'

'Though David is a wealthy man, because of a proviso in his mother's will he's having a problem actually getting hold of his money.'

His voice almost a purr, Angelo said, 'I understood he was finding some other way to pay.'

Nicola's blood ran cold.

When she said nothing, Angelo demanded, 'So what is this "other way"?'

Drawing a deep breath, she said evenly, 'I'm afraid I don't know. With David being taken ill so suddenly we had little time to talk. He might have been planning to ask his brother for help.'

'From what I've heard Dominic Loredan is seriously displeased with David's profligate ways, and this time might well refuse.'

This time... So Dominic had bailed David out in the past.

Striving to sound confident, she said, 'Blood is thicker than water, *signor*, and I'm sure Dominic wouldn't want to see any harm come to his brother.'

His black eyes pinning her, Angelo remarked silkily, 'Though you speak our language with charm and fluency, you are not Italian, I fancy?'

'No, I'm English.'

'How do you fit into this? Which of the two men is your lover?'

'Neither,' she denied crisply. 'I'm simply a guest at the *palazzo*.'

'For a guest, you seem to know a great deal.'

'What I *do* know is there's no lack of money there, and it would be well worth your while to give David some leeway. Once he's out of hospital I'm sure he will find a way to pay what he owes.'

Then, with a confidence she was far from feeling, 'Now, if you'll excuse me, I must be getting back. *Buona sera, signor.*'

Shaking his head, Angelo smiled mirthlessly. 'I should like you to stay. In fact I insist on it. I'm convinced the thought of you being here will speed David's...*recovery*.'

So he hadn't believed her.

Raising his voice, he called, 'Enrico.'

The door opened at once, making it quite clear that the burly man who had admitted her earlier had been waiting just outside.

'Signora Whitney will be staying for a while. Make her comfortable in the back room. But first...'

Holding out his hand and addressing Nicola, he asked politely, 'If I may?'

It took her a second or two to realise he wanted her shoulder bag.

She passed it to him without a word.

Putting the bag down on the desk, he searched through it swiftly and efficiently, obviously expecting to find the ring. He paused to check her passport and driving licence before nodding to the burly man, who seized her arm and began to propel her towards the door.

'There's no need to use force, Enrico,' Angelo observed mildly. 'I'm sure Signora Whitney won't give us any trouble.'

Wanting to beg him to let her leave, but knowing it was useless, Nicola followed Enrico back down the stairs, across the foyer, and along a short passage.

At the end of the passage a couple of steps led down to a metal door that opened into what appeared to be a storeroom.

Thrusting her inside, Enrico closed the door with a clang, and a second later a key grated in the lock.

She felt a sudden surge of panic, a desire to scream and pound on the door.

But, having got this far, she must keep her head.

Standing quite still, her hands clenched into fists, she fought off the panic, telling herself firmly that no one would do her any harm. She was merely here as a hostage, and it would only be a matter of time before she was released.

When she felt calmer, she looked around her. Her prison was small and gloomy and filled with such a variety of junk that there was hardly any floor space left.

It had no windows; the only source of light was an ornate grille set high in a brick wall that, judging by the dank smell, backed on to a canal.

Wondering if there was any chance of escape, she looked around her for something to stand on. There were several packing cases, but they all appeared too heavy to move.

A long-legged rickety stool seemed to be the answer to her prayers and, setting it down as close to the wall as the surrounding clutter allowed, she climbed on it to examine the grille.

It didn't take her long to discover that though the metal was flaky with rust it was strong and set firmly into the surrounding mortar.

No chance of escape that way.

It seemed she was fated to stay here until David had recovered enough to miss her.

Unless she could attract someone's attention.

She had been right about the canal, but the waterway appeared to be stagnant and little used, and the backs of the buildings opposite looked for all the world like semi-derelict warehouses.

As she leaned forward to try and see down the length of the canal one of the legs of the stool suddenly snapped, and she fell, scraping her face against the rough bricks of the wall and landing on a pile of junk that was anything but soft.

It took her a minute or more to collect herself and find her feet. Then, making her way rather shakily across the only litter-free bit of floor, she sat down on one of the packing cases.

There was a burning pain down one cheek. Touching it gingerly, she felt the wet stickiness of blood.

Well, it was her own fault; she should have taken more care. And, like her previous accident, it could have been a great deal worse...

As the time crawled past on leaden feet her thoughts turned to Dominic and she found herself wondering what he was doing.

Had he missed her by now?

Yesterday he had been concerned about her. But today he was probably too worried about his brother to have given her a thought. She felt sure that, no matter how much trouble David had caused him, he *would* be worried…

A sudden movement outside the door and the sound of a key being turned in the lock made her look up.

Enrico was standing there. With a jerk of his head he motioned her to follow him.

Feeling bruised and stiff, she obeyed.

As they approached the office she heard Angelo saying, '…owes me a great deal of money.'

Then a low, attractive voice answering, 'When I'm satisfied that Signora Whitney is here and unharmed, I'll be prepared to discuss the matter with you.'

Enrico opened the door and propelled her forward. She stumbled into the room to find Angelo by the desk, facing a grim-looking Dominic.

She was wondering how he'd managed to find her so quickly when, taking in her battered appearance, he exclaimed, 'Dear God!'

'It's all right,' Nicola assured him hurriedly, as a white line appeared round his mouth. 'It was an accident.'

Seeing he wasn't convinced, she explained, 'I climbed on a stool to try and see through the grille. One of the legs broke, and I scraped my face on the wall…'

'They haven't hurt you in any way? Because if they have—'

'No… No, they haven't,' she assured him. 'I'm fine.' But her relief was so great at having Dominic there that though she tried very hard to appear totally composed she began to tremble.

Putting an arm around her, he announced with quiet authority, 'I'm taking Signora Whitney straight home. I'll see you tomorrow morning at ten o'clock.'

Angelo looked at him, weighing him up, then warned, 'It wouldn't pay to change your mind.'

'I'm not in the habit of changing my mind,' Dominic told him curtly.

'I'd like my bag, please.' Nicola was surprised by how normal her voice sounded.

'Of course,' Angelo said smoothly, and passed it to her.

Without another word Dominic escorted her out of the building and down the alleyway to where his motorboat was waiting by the water-lapped steps, moored to an iron ring.

Only then did she remember how she'd got there. 'I came by water-taxi and I asked the driver to wait...'

'Yes. When you didn't reappear, he had the good sense to come back to the *palazzo*. Thank the Lord I'd just returned from the hospital, and when he mentioned Campo Mandolo I realised where you must have gone, and at whose instigation.'

He looked so cold and angry that, biting her lip, Nicola relapsed into silence, and the rest of the journey back was made without a word being spoken.

When they reached Palazzo dei Cavalli he led her straight to his study and settled her on the couch. 'How long is it since you had anything to eat? Did you have any lunch?'

She shook her head.

'I'll get Maria to bring you something. A bowl of soup, perhaps?'

Her stomach churning, she said, 'I don't think I can eat anything just yet.'

'Very well.'

He disappeared into the bathroom to return after a moment or two with a small bowl and a first-aid box. Bending over her, he began to bathe her cheek.

Though his face was hard and set, his hands were as gentle and tender as a caress.

Tending to her injuries was getting to be a habit, she thought with wry humour, then winced as the antiseptic stung her raw cheek.

Pausing, he asked, 'Is it very painful?'

'No, not at all,' she mumbled, and saw a muscle in his jaw jerk.

He finished his ministrations by spreading on a fine layer of soothing ointment.

'Thank you,' she said. 'That feels a lot better.'

By the time he'd cleared away the things he'd been using, and dropped into a seat opposite, it was hardly hurting at all.

She had expected him to start questioning her, and had psyched herself up to answer, but, tight-lipped and oddly pale beneath his tan, he sat in brooding silence staring blindly at the floor.

Dismayed by his attitude, and with the strain of the day beginning to tell, she was finding it difficult to control her emotions.

Needing to be alone, she rose a shade unsteadily and said, 'If you don't mind I'd like to lie down for a while...'

He looked up, and she was shocked by the bleakness of his expression.

'I—I'm sorry you're so angry with me,' she stammered.

'It's not you I'm angry with. It's that idiot brother of mine for putting you at risk.'

He jumped to his feet, and a moment later she was in his arms, being held close.

She was amazed to find that Dominic—strong, imperturbable Dominic—was trembling.

His cheek pressed against her hair, he whispered, 'Dear God, if anything had happened to you... I don't know what I would have done.'

As his arms tightened convulsively, she gave a little gasp.

'I'm sorry, did I hurt you?'

'No... No, you didn't...'

But already he was drawing back.

'Dominic, I...' Only too happy to be in his arms, but

suddenly remembering Carla and unable to tell him so, she broke off in some confusion.

Once more in command of himself, he said evenly, 'Before you go, I want to ask you something. Why did you decide to leave without even telling me? Was it because of what happened last night?'

'Partly,' she admitted.

'What made you go to see your solicitor?'

'How did you—?'

'He phoned just as I was leaving to find you, and told me what you were proposing to do. I want to know why.'

As levelly as possible, she said, 'Because I've come to realise I have no right to things that morally belong to the Loredan family.'

'I must admit that was how I first thought of it. But now *I've* come to realise I was wrong. Therefore I've asked Signor Mancini to ignore your instructions.'

Sinking back onto the couch, she protested, 'But surely you want Ca' Malvasia back?'

'If you're willing to sell, I'll be happy to buy it back at the market price.'

'And the ring?'

His smile wry and self-mocking, he said, 'Though it may sound foolish, I'd always visualised giving the Maschera ring to the woman I loved and intended to marry...' After a moment, he went on, 'David was rambling just before they sedated him. He kept saying I should stop you taking it...'

She caught her breath. It sounded as if he had had second thoughts...

'So presumably you told him you were leaving?'

When, uncertain how to answer, she hesitated, Dominic said, 'Look, I know he came up to your room...' Then, urgently, 'It crossed my mind that you might have fallen in love with him?'

'No, I haven't fallen in love with him.'

She heard Dominic's sigh of relief.

'But you said he was like Jeff. You admitted you'd slept with him…'

'He *is* like Jeff, at least in looks. But I didn't sleep with him.'

'Thank heaven for that!'

'I only said I did because I was so upset.'

'Why were you so upset?'

'I didn't like the idea that for the past two nights I'd made love to someone else's fiancé.'

'But you did it again,' he pointed out quietly.

Flushing, she said, 'That's why I'm leaving.'

'I see. Would it make any difference to your decision if I told you that I had no intention of marrying Carla?'

When, hardly daring to hope, she waited, her eyes fixed on his face, he went on, 'I wanted to settle down, to have a wife and a family, but I seemed unable to find the woman of my dreams. Carla's a beautiful girl, and I'm fond of her, so eventually we drifted into an engagement. I might even have married her if I hadn't discovered, quite by chance, that she was in love with David.

'She has her pride, and she begged me to keep it a secret and just let things drift for a while… I agreed, though from odd things David has let drop I rather suspect that the interest might be mutual…'

Remembering their conversation in the restaurant, Nicola said, 'I'm sure you're right.'

'And of course they're more of an age,' Dominic pursued. 'Though if Carla does decide to take on that graceless young scamp she'll need to keep him firmly in order…'

'Won't her mother object?'

A shade cynically, he told her, 'I imagine that Signora Ferrini, who has a soft spot for David, would happily swap one Loredan for another. He may even be able to persuade her to move to the States. Which wouldn't be a bad thing.

It might keep him out of the clutches of men like Angelo Gallo…

'And, speaking of Gallo, would you like to tell me exactly what happened today? Why David sent you?'

'He wanted me to take…a message.'

'A message? Why couldn't he have phoned?'

Her mind going a total blank, she said nothing.

'So the message wasn't a verbal one?'

'No. An envelope.'

Sounding as if he was thinking aloud, Dominic said, 'Why go to the trouble of sending a note? Why not an e-mail or a text message? Unless there was something else in the envelope…'

He was too clever by half, she thought, trying to look calm and failing dismally.

His sharp eyes noting her confusion, he said, 'And presumably you know what that something was?'

'Yes,' she said reluctantly.

'Well?'

'Oh, can't you ask David?'

'I'm asking you. And I want an answer.'

Hating herself, she admitted, 'It was the Maschera ring.'

'You *gave* it to him?' Dominic demanded incredulously.

'No. He knew where it was and he must have taken it. I discovered it was missing as I was packing. I'd intended to leave it for you.'

Dominic groaned. 'No wonder Gallo let us go so easily. I'd willingly have paid him, but now he has the ring—'

Nicola shook her head. 'He hasn't.'

'What do you mean, he hasn't?'

'The envelope David gave me was quite thickly padded, which seemed unnecessary for just a message, and while I was waiting in Angelo's office I began to get suspicious…'

As steadily as possible she explained how she had opened

the package and disposed of it when she heard someone
coming, and what she had told Angelo.

'So that's why he kept you, to put pressure on David…
And unless he's come across it the ring's still stuffed behind
his wastepaper basket…'

'No. When I got rid of the note and the envelope I kept
the ring.'

'You kept the ring?' Dominic echoed incredulously.
'How did you manage to hide it?'

'I wore it,' she said simply, and held out her left hand.
The mask was turned into her palm, the back of her hand
showing only an innocent gold band on her wedding finger.

Lifting her hand to his lips, he kissed it. 'You're not only
beautiful and courageous, you're very clever.'

Warmed by his praise, she slipped off the ring and gave
it to him.

His eyes on her face, he asked, 'Don't you like it?
Wouldn't you prefer to keep it?'

She shook her head. 'I can't. It's a beautiful ring and I
love it, but it isn't really mine to keep. John should never
have given it to me.'

'What if *I* gave it to you?'

'But you should give it to the woman you marry.'

'So you want me to propose first?'

Feeling as though her throat was full of shards of hot
glass, she begged, 'Please don't joke about it.'

'I've never felt less like joking. Will you marry me,
Nicola?'

Unable to believe what she was hearing, she simply gaped
at him.

'I know it's sudden, but I also know that you're the
woman I've been waiting for. In spite of believing the worst,
I fell in love with you the minute I saw you…'

When, choked by happiness, she continued to stare silently at him, he said slowly, 'I had hoped you might be

able to forgive the way I've treated you... I'd even dared to hope that you might feel something more than mere attraction for me... But it seems I was wrong.'

She found her voice. 'No, you weren't wrong. I knew from the start that I loved you, that you were special.'

'*Cara mia,*' he whispered, and, sitting beside her, slipped the ring back on her finger.

Then, gathering her into his arms, he began to kiss her with a tender passion that melted her heart and more than made up for the times she'd been miserable.

After a while he raised his head to complain, 'When I asked why you'd slept with me, you didn't say anything about my being special.'

'I couldn't.'

'Because of what I'd said about John?'

'Yes. You see John *was* special, but in a totally different way. He was a friend, never a lover.'

'Why do you think he bequeathed everything, including the ring, to you? Was it to spite the Loredans?'

'I'm still not sure,' she admitted honestly. 'I hope it was just because he liked me. All he said in the letter he left was that he wanted me to have it.'

'Did you keep the letter?'

'Yes.' She reached for her bag and, after feeling in the zipped compartment, passed the letter to him.

While she watched him, he read what his stepfather had written.

Nicola, my dear, though we've known each other just a short time, you've been like the daughter I always wanted, and your warmth and kindness have meant a lot to me.

In the pouch you'll find Sophia's ring. Since she died I've been wearing it on a chain around my neck, but now I sense that I haven't got much longer, so I'm lodging it with Mr Harthill.

It's a singular ring. My darling always wore it. She was wearing it the day I met her. She once remarked that if any ring possessed the power to bring its wearer happiness, this one does. For that reason I would like you to have it, and I truly believe Sophia would approve.

Though we had both been married before, she was the love of my life as, I hope and believe, I was hers. We were very happy together for five wonderful years. Not long enough. But perhaps it never is.

In your case, I know your time with your husband was very brief. You're desperately young to have known so much grief and pain, and I'm only too aware that anyone who loses a loved one needs time to mourn. But remember, my dear, no one should mourn for ever. It's time you moved on. Be happy.

John

When he had finished reading it, Dominic passed it back and said slowly, 'I owe you an abject apology. As soon as I began to get to know you I felt I'd been wrong about you. But I had to keep pushing to be certain...' He sighed. 'I've given you a hard time. I just wish there was something I could do to make up for it.'

Greatly daring, she said, 'Well, there is one thing...'

'What's that, *cara mia*?'

'Tomorrow morning it would be nice to wake up with you in bed beside me.'

His white teeth gleamed in a smile. 'Consider it done. Though it might mean putting Gallo off until the afternoon... On the other hand, if I go and see him as arranged you could always stay in bed and wait for me.'

'What a wonderful idea.'

He kissed her, and asked, 'How do you feel?'

'Fine. Why?'

'I thought if you still want to lie down I might come with you.'

She pretended to consider the matter. 'Well, because of my bruises I'm sure I'll be more comfortable lying down than sitting.'

'Then what are we waiting for?'

'Suppose Maria catches us?'

'If she does, I'll leave it to you to smooth her ruffled feathers.'

'And how would you suggest I do that?'

Straightfaced, he suggested, 'You could always ask her to be bridesmaid.'

THE ITALIAN DOCTOR'S WIFE

by

Sarah Morgan

Sarah Morgan trained as a nurse and has since worked in a variety of health-related jobs. Married to a gorgeous businessman, who still makes her knees knock, she spends most of her time trying to keep up with their two little boys, but manages to sneak off occasionally to indulge her passion for writing romance. Sarah loves outdoor life and is an enthusiastic skier and walker. Whatever she is doing, her head is always full of new characters and she is addicted to happy endings.

Don't miss Sarah Morgan's exciting new novel, *The Sicilian's Virgin Bride,* out in April 2007 from Mills & Boon Modern Romance™

PROLOGUE

DOMENICO SANTINI slammed open the door of the exclusive clinic, his sensual mouth set in a grim line. Every muscle in his body was tense, every nerve ending responding to the anger that simmered inside his powerful frame.

He strode across the elegant reception area towards his brother's consulting room, totally oblivious to the rapt female attention which followed his progress.

Under strict instructions to allow no one to see the boss without an appointment, the receptionist half rose to her feet and then sat down again, her knees weak as she recognised the visitor. Even the threat of losing her job wouldn't have given her the courage to try and stop Domenico Santini.

And he knew it.

The self-assured stride, the arrogant tilt of that dark head and the bored, slightly disdainful look on his sinfully handsome face were the mark of a man who knew that his authority wouldn't be challenged.

He moved through the foyer with the lethal grace of a jungle cat, and the receptionist stared, feasting her eyes on the luxuriant black hair, the smouldering dark eyes and the muscular, athletic body.

The newspapers and gossip magazines didn't do the man justice.

He was staggeringly good-looking.

Ferociously intelligent, monumentally rich and wickedly handsome, Domenico Santini was every woman's fantasy.

'Don't even think about it,' her fellow receptionist drawled softly, following the direction of her gaze. 'He's way out of your league.'

'He's stunning.'

'He's also dangerous,' her friend muttered. 'He's a very famous heart surgeon, did you know that? Children's heart surgeon. What a joke! The man must have broken as many hearts as he's mended in his time. He only has to snap those clever fingers and women leap into his bed. Lucky them.'

It was a woman who was on Nico's mind as he opened the door of his brother's consulting room, pausing only long enough to check that he wasn't with a patient.

'I need to talk to you—' His tone was curt and he spoke in Italian as the brothers always did when they were alone together.

Carlo Santini leaned back in his chair, his dark eyes watchful. 'So—talk.'

Two years younger than Nico and generally considered to be the more approachable of the two brothers, he waved a hand towards a chair, but Nico ignored the gesture and instead opened his briefcase and retrieved a slim file which he tossed onto his brother's desk.

'Read that.'

Carlo stared at him for a long moment and then lowered his eyes to the file, opening it slowly and perusing the contents.

While he read, Nico paced across the room, his broad shoulders tense as he stared out of the window across the expensively manicured grounds of his brother's clinic. Occasionally he glanced over his shoulder, his expression impatient as he waited for his brother to finish digesting the contents of the file.

'So?' Finally Carlo lowered the file. 'This girl had donor insemination in my clinic.' His tone was noticeably cool. 'I don't know why you have a file on her, but if you've come to me for more information then you're going to be disappointed. You're my brother and I love you, but I won't discuss my patients with you.'

'This isn't a clinic matter, it's a family matter.' Nico's black brows met in a frown. He'd expected Carlo to react to the name in the file but he'd forgotten just how many women trooped through his brother's world-famous infertility clinic every year. 'And I'm not asking you to break patient confidentiality. Look at the name again.'

'Harrington. Abby Harrington—it doesn't ring any bells.' Carlo peered more closely at the photo. 'I've definitely never seen her before. She's gorgeous. There's no way I would have forgotten a face and a body like that.'

'Then let me jog your memory,' Nico's expression darkened. 'She was Lucia's friend at school. Remember the shy little mouse who we thought might have a stabilising influence on our dizzy sister?'

Carlo's eyes narrowed. 'Vaguely. What about her?'

'And do you remember what happened two years ago?' Nico's tone was lethally soft. 'Lucia came to me with a sob story about a friend who couldn't have children.'

Carlo frowned. 'Yes, I remember that. The woman was in her late thirties and her husband was infertile and—' He broke off and his eyes travelled from his brother's icy expression to the photo in the file. 'Are you suggesting what I think you're suggesting? This is *never* the same girl.'

'It's the same girl,' Nico growled softly. 'As you can see, Lucia's *friend* wasn't in her late thirties or happily married.'

Carlo winced. 'I'm beginning to understand your interest. If my memory serves me correctly, that was the one and only occasion that we've managed to persuade you to be a donor for my clinic.'

Nico's jaw tightened. 'Fathering children indiscriminately with no say in their upbringing has never appealed to me, as you well know.'

Carlo held his gaze. 'But you agreed to do it for Lucia's friend.'

Nico dragged long fingers through his luxuriant black

hair and gave a growl of anger and frustration. '*Dio*, I was totally taken in by her sob story—how her friend's husband couldn't father children and how devastated they were....'

Carlo stared at the file. 'And you really think that this is the same woman?'

Nico's mouth tightened. 'I know it is.'

Carlo let out a long breath. 'Well, if you're right, it certainly seems as though our little sister might have been economical with the truth,' he observed, his eyes fixed on the photograph in the file. 'She looks nearer twenty than forty.'

'She's twenty-four,' Nico ground out, 'but she was twenty-two when she came to your clinic—*twenty-two*.' His voice was raw as he emphasised the words. 'And she has never been married.'

'I didn't see her, Nico.' Carlo put the file down, his expression serious. 'Come to think of it, I think I *was* due to see her but then there was a family crisis and she had to see one of my colleagues instead.'

'That was cleverly arranged,' Nico said bitterly. 'Who do you think engineered the family crisis that kept you away from the clinic that day?'

Carlo pulled a face. 'Lucia?'

'If Abby Harrington had seen you personally, you might have refused to go ahead—at least with me as the donor.'

Carlo nodded. 'Because I would have known that you wouldn't agree to be a donor for a single girl.'

'But the doctor who eventually saw her didn't know that,' Nico concluded, his mouth set in a grim line. 'I suspect that Lucia had him wound round her little finger as she did the rest of us.'

Carlo shook his head in disbelief. 'She certainly thought it through.'

'If our little sister applied the same degree of thought and deviousness to a useful career then she might stop wasting her life,' Nico observed acidly. 'We all know what

Lucia is like when she wants something. She is manipulative and persuasive and she can be very, very difficult to resist. *Dio*, even knowing her as I do, I agreed to be the donor in her little scheme.'

Carlo fingered the file, his handsome face troubled. 'So how did you get this information? You know we have strict rules about confidentiality at the clinic. How can you be sure that this is your baby?'

Nico tensed and a hint of colour touched his incredible cheekbones. 'You know how strongly I feel about family. I wanted to check on the baby I fathered.' A muscle moved in his jaw. 'I knew you wouldn't give me the information I needed so I hired a private detective.'

Carlo frowned. 'But you didn't even have the girl's name. He wouldn't have been able to—'

'He's the best,' Nico interrupted smoothly. 'He found her. That's all you need to know.'

'And have you spoken to Lucia?'

'Not yet.' Nico's expression was grim. 'I'm going to see Abby Harrington first. Then I'll deal with Lucia.'

Carlo let out a long breath. 'Well, don't be *too* hard on our little sister. You're pretty strict with her, Nico.'

'If I detected the slightest evidence of common sense, I'd cease to be strict,' Nico said wearily, and Carlo nodded.

'I know—she's a total airhead and if it weren't for you she'd have come off the rails years ago because our father's too busy to notice her.' He closed the file and handed it back to his brother. 'I can't imagine how she thought she'd get away with it but I suppose there was a chance that you wouldn't find out the truth about Abby Harrington.'

'Evidently.' Nico's voice was clipped. 'Both of them must have assumed that I'd never follow it up.'

Carlo sat back in his chair, his dark eyes reflecting his concern. 'So now what?'

There was a tense silence and when Nico finally spoke his voice was hoarse. 'I want that baby.'

There was a deathly silence and for endless seconds Carlo didn't move.

Finally he spoke, his voice urgent. 'You can't do that, Nico.'

'It's my child.'

'I know that.' Carlo's eyes were fixed on his brother's face. 'And I also know what that knowledge must be doing to you in the light of what's happened to you since that baby was conceived. Nico, you've never really talked about it, but you know that if you want to—'

'I don't.' Nico's tone held a cold finality. 'I just want to talk about this girl.'

'We both know that it is one and the same subject.' Carlo said carefully. 'I know how strongly you feel about family but we both know that there's more to this than—'

'That's enough!' Nico's eyes were hard as he stared at his brother. 'This isn't about me. It's about *her*. And the child. *My* child. I feel a responsibility towards that baby, which is why I decided to check on how the family was getting on.'

'I can imagine how you must be feeling, but you agreed to be the father,' Carlo reminded him, and Nico lifted a hand to cut him off, his expression menacing.

'For a happily married couple. Not for a young, single girl with no financial or emotional support. I never would have agreed to father a child for a penniless schoolgirl!'

'She was twenty-two.'

Nico let out his breath in an impatient hiss. 'As far as her suitability for motherhood goes, she is a baby!'

Carlo looked at him through narrowed eyes. 'You've never met her. She might be a great mother.'

'I know everything I need to know about her,' Nico said flatly, 'and the more I know, the more determined I am to take the child away from her. She isn't a fit mother.'

'Calm down.' Carlo leaned back in his chair. 'That's a pretty serious accusation. What's the woman done?'

Nico gritted his teeth. 'Apart from conspiring with Lucia to lie to me so that I'd agree to father the baby? Well, for a start she puts the child in a crèche while she works as a nurse. If she wanted a child so badly, why is she working?'

'Nico, this is the twenty-first century,' Carlo pointed out quietly, his tone reasonable. 'Women work. Even women with children. And working mothers need child care.'

'She shouldn't have chosen to become a single mother if she didn't have the means to support the child,' Nico growled, and Carlo's eyes narrowed.

'Well, not everybody has unlimited funds. Maybe she had good reasons for wanting a child—'

Nico made an impatient sound. 'Why are you defending her? What possible reasons could justify a twenty-two-year-old wanting a baby? She has plenty of reproductive years ahead of her in which to marry a man and produce babies naturally.'

Carlo looked him straight in the eye. 'I'm defending her because I know that this isn't about her and the baby. Not really. It's about you,' he said softly. 'You are making this personal.'

'*Dio*, of course I'm making it personal!' Nico flashed him an impatient look. 'How do you think I feel, knowing—?'

He broke off and Carlo rose to his feet, watching his brother closely.

'You can't take her child, Nico.'

'Watch me.' Nico's expression was grim. 'And you're forgetting that it isn't just her child, it's *my* child. And according to my sources, the girl is in big trouble. She earns next to nothing as a nurse and she obviously doesn't manage her money well. At the moment she has been given two weeks' notice to find somewhere else to live because she can't keep up the rental payments. My sources tell me that she doesn't have enough money for anywhere else.

Soon my child will be homeless. Do you expect me to sit and watch while that happens?'

Carlo let out a long breath. 'I can see that the situation is less than ideal, but—'

'My child does not deserve a nomadic existence with a mother who clearly can't manage her finances well enough to keep a roof over her head,' Nico growled, and Carlo watched him thoughtfully.

'She might not be willing to give the baby up,' he pointed out, and Nico frowned dismissively.

'The girl is clearly struggling to bring the baby up alone. I suspect that she will be only too pleased to take a financial incentive in exchange for the baby. Clearly having a baby was a whim and the reality of life as a single parent has proved less romantic than she expected.'

'I think you underestimate the attachment between a mother and her child,' Carlo said quietly. 'Especially a mother who went to the trouble of having artificial insemination in order to conceive. She would have had a counselling session at the clinic and her reasons for wanting a child must have been good. I doubt that she will give the baby up lightly.'

'You're wrong.'

'Maybe.' Carlo gave a brief smile. 'But my advice is stick to mending hearts, and leave the serious business of baby-making to those of us with some understanding of the emotions involved.'

'I understand the emotions better than most.' Nico's teeth were gritted and Carlo gave a sigh.

'*Sì*, I know you do.'

Nico shrugged, his black eyes hard and cold. 'Then you'll understand why I am right to go after the baby.'

'I understand, but I don't condone it.' Carlo picked up the file again. 'Answer me one question. If Abby Harrington had turned out to be in her late thirties and happily married, would you be threatening to take the baby?'

Nico frowned as if the question was completely super-fluous. 'Of course not. I would have checked that they had everything they needed and walked away.'

But it would have been the hardest thing he'd ever had to do in his life.

'Then do the same thing now,' Carlo said quietly. 'You cannot take a child from its mother. Let it go, Nico. If you want family life, find a nice girl and marry her.'

Nico's eyes were hooded. 'Like you have, you mean?'

'I'm still auditioning for the role.' Carlo's dark eyes flashed wickedly and Nico raised an eyebrow in mockery.

'You feel the need to audition the whole female population?'

Carlo gave a rueful smile. 'All right, I'm the first to admit that, like you, I've never found a woman who can see further than my wallet.' His smile faded. 'But that fact doesn't make this right, Nico, and you know it.'

'I'm not seeking your approval.' Nico's tone was harsh. 'I came here because I wanted the answer to a question.'

'Which was?'

'I wanted to know if you were aware of her deception.'

Carlo shook his head. 'No. I didn't deal with her case and you should know me well enough to know that I wouldn't do that to you.'

Nico's expression darkened. 'Lucia did.'

Carlo shrugged. 'As we both know, Lucia is young and impulsive. And very spoilt by our parents. This was prob-ably another one of her whims.' He walked towards his brother and laid a hand on his shoulder. 'I know you don't take advice from anyone, but I'm going to give it anyway. Whatever reasons this girl had for deceiving us, she clearly wanted that child. Don't jump to conclusions. Are you ab-solutely sure she knows you're the father?'

'Of course she knows.' Nico was back in control, his

emotions buried under the icy exterior for which he was renowned. 'Lucia told me at the time that her friend drew up a list of qualities that she wanted in a father and I was the perfect match.'

His tone was bitter and Carlo sighed.

'Lucia adores you, Nico. She probably genuinely did think you'd be the best father in the world and you know that all her school friends worshipped you. She just didn't think it through.'

Nico's mouth tightened. 'She never thinks things through.'

'And as for the friend—if she does know, she clearly didn't want you to find out.' Carlo rubbed a hand across the back of his neck, clearly concerned. 'This is going to come as a shock to her, Nico.'

Nico's mouth tightened. 'Good.'

Abigail Harrington had deceived him. She was clearly a calculating, manipulative woman who was totally unsuited to motherhood. As far as he was concerned, the bigger the shock, the better.

CHAPTER ONE

'I HATE leaving her—she was a bit fretful in the night. I'm afraid she might be coming down with something.' Abby reluctantly handed her daughter over to Karen, the nursery nurse who ran the hospital crèche. 'Maybe I should have kept her at home, but they're so short-staffed on the ward that I just couldn't do it to them, and—'

'Abby, stop worrying!' Karen interrupted her gently and settled Rosa on her hip, her expression sympathetic and mildly amused. 'She looks perfectly healthy to me. I know you feel guilty about working but you don't need to. There are plenty of single mothers in the world and plenty of them have to work. She has a really great time here and you're a brilliant mother. The best I know.'

Was she?

Abby bit her lip, painfully aware that Karen didn't know the whole truth of Rosa's conception.

It was a part of her life that she never discussed with anyone.

And although it was true that there were plenty of single mothers in the world, there were surely very few in her situation. And because she never forgot that she'd chosen this life for Rosa, she was doubly determined to be the very best mother that she could be.

'It's so hard for you, being on you own. You must feel so lonely sometimes,' Karen said gently. 'I know you don't like talking about it, but do you ever think of contacting her father?'

'No.' Abby shook her head.

How could she? Because she'd been so desperate to have a baby, she'd chosen to do so without the traditional sup-

15

port of a man. Rosa's conception had been arranged with clinical efficiency and total secrecy, and she had absolutely no idea who the father was.

And that knowledge nagged at her constantly despite the fact that the pain of her own childhood had left deep scars and she was only too aware that having two parents was no guarantee of childhood bliss. She'd been sent to boarding school at the age of seven by workaholic parents keen to relieve themselves of a child they'd never wanted, so she knew better than anyone that two parents didn't necessarily make a happy family.

But that didn't stop her feeling guilty that she'd deprived Rosa of a father.

'You never talk about it and you're always so self-contained and independent.' Karen sighed. 'He must have hurt you so much.'

Abby bit her lip, unable to correct the misconception without giving away her secret. The truth was that Rosa's father hadn't hurt her at all. *She didn't even know him.* All she knew was what her friend Lucia had told her. That the donor was Italian and very clever. And as for being independent, well, she'd had to be. Unlike most of her peers, her parents had never been there for her so she'd learned to take care of herself.

'How's little Thomas Wood?' Karen settled Rosa more comfortably on her hip and changed the subject neatly. 'When's he going for his op?'

'Tomorrow.' Abby pulled a face and handed over a bag containing all Rosa's things for the day. 'That's the other reason I felt I had to work today. I need to give his parents some support. They're terrified.'

'I'm not surprised.' Karen shook her head, her expression sombre. 'I can't begin to imagine how it must feel to see your five-month-old baby going for open-heart surgery.'

'Yes.' Abby leaned forward to kiss her daughter one more time. 'Still, Thomas is luckier than some. We've got an Italian surgeon arriving today to spend a few months on the unit until they appoint someone permanently. He's supposed to be one of the best there is and he's going to be teaching and working on the wards for a while. He's doing Thomas's operation. With an audience of thousands, from what I can gather. I hope he's got steady hands.'

She stroked a hand over Rosa's head, marvelling at how silky her dark hair was. 'You promise to call me if you're worried about her? Even if she's just a bit off colour—'

'For crying out loud, Abby!' Karen gave her an exasperated look and waved a hand towards the door. 'Just go, will you? She'll be fine!'

Abby gave a faltering smile, cast a last longing look at her daughter and then forced herself to leave the brightly decorated crèche and make her way up to the paediatric surgical ward where she worked. As usual she had a dull ache in the pit of her stomach.

She hated leaving Rosa so much.

It was like a physical wrench that didn't seem to get any easier with time. Given the chance, she would have spent every moment of every day just playing with her daughter and cuddling her but circumstances made that impossible. She *had* to work. Fortunately she loved her job and knew how lucky she was to work on such a respected unit. She found the field of paediatric cardiac surgery stimulating and absorbing and she knew that once she arrived on the ward she'd put thoughts of Rosa to one side and concentrate instead on the sick children and worried parents who needed her care.

And in a way Karen was right, she reassured herself firmly as she pressed the button for the lift. Plenty of parents worked and their children didn't suffer for it.

She took comfort from the fact that Rosa was a happy, sociable child and being with the other children in the crèche provided her with an important source of stimulation.

As the lift doors opened she straightened her uniform and checked that her long blonde hair was securely fastened.

'Hi, Abby.' Heather, the ward sister, greeted her with a warm smile and gestured towards the side room. 'The Woods are biting their nails to the quick in there. Fortunately we're well staffed today so you should be able to concentrate on them and give them all the support they need.' She glanced around furtively and lowered her voice. 'And maybe you'd better check they understand everything that's happening. Mr Forster had a brief chat with them before he left but you know what he was like, poor thing. He never had any time for the parents and he was hopeless at explaining anything. They looked more confused when he came out than they did when he went in.'

Abby gave a wry smile. One of their consultants, Mr Forster, had just taken early retirement on the grounds of ill health, but it was widely rumoured that he had just been finding the job too stressful. It was certainly true that he'd always been hopeless at explaining. He used the same terminology that he used with his medical team so his patients never understood him. 'Perhaps the new surgeon will set an example.'

'Let's hope so. Thomas should be first on the list tomorrow and our Italian whiz-kid should be up later to talk to them.'

Abby's blue eyes gleamed with amusement. 'Whiz-kid' seemed a strange description for someone with such an awesome reputation who was doubtless crusty and grey-haired. She'd never met the man in question but she was sure that he'd long ago outgrown the 'whiz-kid' title.

Making her way to the side room, she tapped on the door and walked in.

Lorna Wood had Thomas on her lap and he was dozing quietly.

'Hi, there.' Abby's voice was hushed so that she didn't disturb the baby and Lorna looked up, her face pale.

'Oh, Abby, I'm so pleased to see you.'

'How are you doing?'

Not very well, by the look of her, but, then, that was hardly surprising in the circumstances. Abby couldn't begin to imagine how she'd feel if it was Rosa who was about to have major heart surgery.

Lorna pulled a face. 'I feel awful. Worried, panicky…' She spoke in an undertone, careful not to wake the sleeping baby. 'But mostly I feel guilty.'

'Guilty?' Abby's eyebrows rose in surprise and she closed the door behind her. 'Why guilty?'

The young mother shrugged helplessly. 'Because Thomas seems fine most of the time and I'm asking myself if all this is necessary. Am I doing the right thing by letting him have the op?' Lorna glanced at her, her eyes filling as she begged for answers. 'I know they keep telling me that he'll get worse, but why not wait until it happens? Why do the operation now?'

More evidence that Mr Forster's explanations had been less than perfect, Abby thought, hoping that the new consultant would have a better way with words. With Mr Forster they'd virtually had to provide a translation.

'I know that Thomas seems well, but waiting might damage the heart further,' she said quietly, and Lorna bit her lip.

'But how do we know that for sure?'

Abby took her hand and gave it a squeeze. 'I think you need to talk it through with the surgeon who is going to do the operation,' she suggested. 'He's coming to see Thomas later. I'll make sure that he knows that you're worried so that he finds time to answer your questions.'

Clearly, concisely and in language that could be understood by normal mortals!

Lorna shrank slightly in her seat. 'I don't want to bother

him,' she said quickly. 'He's an important man and I'm the least of his worries.'

'You won't be bothering him,' Abby said firmly, used to dealing with that type of attitude. She'd lost count of the times patients had told her they refrained from asking questions because they didn't want to bother the doctor. 'If there are things you don't understand then you must ask!'

Lorna pulled a face. 'I find doctors really intimidating. Especially surgeons who can operate on a child's heart.' Her eyes were round with admiration. 'I mean, can you imagine being clever enough to do something like that? I always feel as though my questions are stupid and I'm wasting their time. Mr Forster has explained everything to me once. It isn't his fault if I'm too stupid to understand.'

'You're not stupid, Lorna,' Abby said firmly, making a mental note to brief the new consultant fully. He needed to spend time with the Woods. And he needed to use simple language. 'If it would make you feel better, I'll make sure I'm there, too. And I'll make sure that he doesn't leave the room until you've asked him every question you have and fully understand what's happening.'

'This whole thing feels like a nightmare. I just wish this was all a dream and I could wake up,' Lorna muttered, and Abby leaned forward and gave her a quick hug.

'The worst part is the waiting.' She looked at the sleeping child and smiled. 'I need to do his obs—you know, temperature, pulse that sort of thing—but I'll wait for him to wake up. Later on I want to take you to the cardiac intensive care unit—we call it CICU—so that you know what to expect when Thomas comes back from Theatre.'

Lorna bit her lip. 'Is it very scary?'

'It can seem scary,' Abby said, her tone gentle. She knew how important it was to be honest with parents and to prepare them for what lay ahead. 'You know that when he first comes back from Theatre he'll have a tube down his throat to help him breathe and a drain in his chest, as well as a drip. The monitors can seem very high-tech and daunting but the staff on CICU are wonderful and I know they'll take good care of you and Thomas. We've a baby who has just had a similar operation to Thomas on the unit at the moment so I can show you what to expect and you can chat to the parents.'

'And after CICU he'll come back here to the ward?'

'Once the doctors feel he's well enough, they'll transfer him back here.'

Lorna cuddled the sleeping child closer. 'And will you still be the nurse looking after us? You're always so calm. Nothing seems to make you flap—the minute you walk into the room I feel less panicky. I don't think I could bear having anyone else.'

'When I'm on duty I'll be your nurse,' Abby assured her. 'We try and maintain continuity whenever we can.'

Lorna gave a weak smile. 'Our nurse. You're supposed to be Thomas's nurse but you end up looking after the whole family.'

'That's because the whole family is part of Thomas's recovery,' Abby pointed out gently.

The whole ethos of the ward was to give care to the whole family, in recognition of the stress on the parents when a child was undergoing major surgery.

'Give me a call when Thomas wakes up and I'll check his obs,' she said, picking up his chart and checking what had happened in the night. 'In the meantime, I'll track down this new consultant and make sure he makes time to see you.'

'I hear that he's Italian.' Lorna looked at her anxiously. 'Is he good, Abby?'

Abby thought of the eulogies that had been heaped on the man's head in the past few weeks and smiled.

'He's better than good, Lorna. The doctors here say that he's a legend in paediatric cardiac surgery. He's pioneered several different techniques and his results are astonishing.

That's why he's going to spend some time over here with us. Sharing his experience as well as filling in for Mr Forster until they make a permanent appointment. It happens quite often, believe me. In a way Thomas is lucky that he's taken his case.'

Lorna nodded and gave a wan smile. 'I just hope he's as good as you say.'

They shared a look of understanding, each knowing that, even in the most capable hands, operating on a child's heart always carried a risk. The challenge was balancing the risk of the operation with the risk of not correcting the defect in the heart.

It was midmorning when there was a sudden bustle on the ward and a group of doctors arrived, looking round expectantly.

'Is Mr Santini here yet?' Greg Wallis, the surgical registrar, glanced into the office and Abby shook her head.

'If you mean the new consultant, no, not yet—he's been meeting the team on CICU and he's due here any minute.' She frowned slightly and looked at Greg. Had she heard correctly? 'What did you say his name was again?'

'Santini. Domenico Santini. Why?'

Abby shook her head slightly. *It couldn't be...*

'I knew a Domenico Santini once,' she said lightly. 'I went to school with his sister. But it can't be him. He'd be too young.'

'Oh, this guy is young,' Greg told her, a trace of bitterness in his voice. 'I used to think my career was going well until I read his CV. His rise to stardom had been positively meteoric. The guy is a genius by all accounts. His nickname in the theatre is ''Iceberg'' because he's the coolest surgeon anyone has ever seen.'

Abby felt her heart thud uncomfortably in her chest. *Could it be him?* Lucia's brother?

As an impressionable young teenager she'd been thoroughly in awe of her friend's older brother. She was well aware that he was considered the ultimate catch by all the other girls in the school but on the few occasions that she'd met him she'd found him monumentally intimidating.

Fortunately he'd never even known that she existed.

She gave a slight smile at her own expense.

And why should he have noticed her? She'd been an awkward, leggy, painfully shy teenager with a brace on her teeth, glasses and hair that never behaved itself. There had been absolutely nothing about her that had been memorable. Especially compared to her peers.

The exclusive Swiss school which had been her home from the age of sixteen had attracted the children of the rich and famous from all over the world. Appeasing their consciences by selecting what they'd seen as the best, her parents had somehow found the money to send her there without considering whether Abby would fit in socially.

For the first term she'd been utterly miserable and painfully conscious of the differences in circumstances between her and the other girls.

She'd tried to shrink into the background to avoid attention and if it hadn't been for the flamboyant and boisterous Lucia Santini, her schooldays would have been a nightmare. As it was, the Italian girl had befriended her and made her life just about bearable.

Shocked that Abby's parents never visited, Lucia frequently invited Abby to stay with her own family but Abby declined, too awkward and embarrassed to accept hospitality which she knew she could never repay.

She also refused Lucia's invitations to join her on trips out with her older brother, knowing that such an outing would have been social torture. She never knew what to say to men anyway, let alone a man like Lucia's dark and dangerous brother. She must have been the only girl in the school that didn't try to attract his attention. Totally overwhelmed by his aggressive masculinity and cool self-confidence, Nico Santini made her thoroughly nervous. Carlo, the younger of the two brothers, seemed slightly more approachable, which was why she agreed to go to him for help so many years later.

She gave a sudden frown as an uncomfortable thought occurred to her.

Would the Santini family have discussed Rosa? Could Nico be aware of Rosa's history?

Greg cast her an odd look. 'Are you all right? You've gone really pale.'

'I'm fine,' she muttered, flashing him a wan smile and giving herself a sharp talking-to.

There was no way he could know. Everything that happened at the clinic was confidential, she assured herself. And even if Lucia had been so indiscreet as to mention it to her older brother, there was no reason why he should be in the slightest bit interested in her life.

It was highly unlikely that he'd even remember who she was.

Applying logic and reason but still feeling uneasy, she gave a start as the ward doors opened again and Dr Gibbs, the paediatric cardiologist, walked briskly down the corridor, accompanied by the rest of the team and a tall, powerfully built stranger.

Abby recognised him immediately and against her will her stomach flipped over as her eyes skimmed over the broad shoulders and long, muscular legs. Nico Santini had always been breathtakingly good-looking, but maturity had given his looks a lethal masculine quality which had a critical effect on her pulse rate.

Which just proved that, despite her protestations to the contrary, she was as shallow as the next woman, she thought with a resigned sigh.

But maybe it wasn't entirely her fault.

The man was devastating.

There were five male doctors in the group but he drew

the eye, not just because of his impressive physique but because of the air of cool command which he wore with the same effortless ease as his impeccably cut grey suit.

Nico Santini was more of a man than any other male she'd ever met and Abby felt her face flush slightly as she scanned his handsome features.

Iceberg.

The description suited him, she thought wryly, remembering just how cool and in control the man had been even in his twenties. Lucia had adored her older brother but she'd also been more than a little afraid of him.

Observing from a safe distance, Abby had always believed that he was very hard on Lucia who could certainly be a bit silly sometimes but had a very kind heart.

She hadn't seen him for at least six years.

Would he recognise her? Should she say something?

She almost laughed aloud at the thought. He absolutely would not recognise her and there was no way she was going to say anything. The mere thought was laughable.

Hello, remember me? I was the shy little mouse at school with your sister who never said a word whenever you were around....

Jack Gibbs was introducing him to everyone and finally it was Abby's turn and she lifted her chin and met that penetrating dark gaze head on, determined not to be intimidated.

Reminding herself that she was now a grown woman with a child, she forced herself to look composed, at least on the outside, and held out a hand.

It was a mistake.

Just touching those long, strong fingers was like connecting with a powerful electric force field and she felt her insides tumble unexpectedly.

'Abby is one of our best paediatric nurses,' Jack was saying, his expression warm, 'and we're very lucky to have her. When everyone else is in a panic you can rely on Abby to be the voice of calm. She has an amazing way with the children and the parents. We doctors fight over her. If we have something difficult to say to a family then we make sure we have Abby with us.'

Startled by the praise and unsettled by Nico Santini's unrelenting grip on her hand, Abby gave Jack a fleeting smile and took a step backwards, deliberately removing her hand from the pressure of those long fingers.

'I'll remember that.' He spoke in a deep, masculine purr that held just a hint of an Italian accent. Not enough to cloud his enunciation but just enough to make his voice unbearably sexy. 'Are you the nurse who is looking after the Wood family?'

Abby nodded, wishing that he didn't have such a powerful effect on her. She hated the fact that she was as vulnerable to his particular brand of scorching masculinity as the rest of her sex. She would have given anything to have been indifferent to him.

Not wanting to dwell on the effect he had on her, Abby quickly turned to the subject of work.

'His mother is very worried and has lots of questions, but she's afraid to ask them. I think it would be helpful if you could find time to talk to her.' The expression in her blue eyes was slightly challenging as they met his. From the little she knew of him it was highly unlikely that he would have the time or the skills to show much sensitivity to parents.

'Why is she afraid to ask them?'

His brusque question took her by surprise. 'She thinks you're very busy and doesn't want to disturb you.'

'Does she now?' He held her gaze for a long moment, his lush, dark lashes shielding his expression. 'Then we must make sure that she has all the time she needs.'

Against her will, Abby's eyes dropped to his firm mouth and she found herself remembering the rumour that had spread among the girls when she'd been at school.

That Nico Santini was a spectacular lover.

Shaken by her own thoughts, she looked away from him, her colour rising.

It was just the way that all women reacted to Nico Santini, she assured herself silently. He was much too powerful a personality to leave anyone feeling indifferent. At least she had more sense than to fall for him. She could admire him from a distance, but any more than that would have sent her running for cover.

Finally Nico's eyes left her and he turned to the rest of the doctors. 'I will see the baby and the parents straight away.'

Jack Gibbs, frowned slightly, clearly put out by that decision and by the fact that Nico had taken control. As paediatric cardiologist, all the children were referred to him initially and he very much considered it to be 'his' ward.

'But the teaching round… We were assuming…'

'If the mother has questions then I deal with those as a priority,' Nico said immediately, his tone discouraging any argument from those around him. 'In my experience it is counter-productive and cruel to leave the family worrying unnecessarily. It is important that they feel that we are all part of the same team. I'll do the teaching round when I have answered her questions and, of course, everyone is welcome. Until then I will see the family with just the nurse who cares for them.'

He looked expectantly at Abby who was having trouble hiding her surprise. Agreeing to see the family so quickly suggested a sensitivity that she hadn't thought him capable of.

'They're in the side ward,' she said quietly, and he gave a brief nod.

'Then let's go and talk to them. Has she signed a consent form or do I need to go through that with her?'

'Mr Forster did it before he left but I think she'd appreciate the chance to discuss the operation again,' she said tactfully, as she tapped on the door and walked into the room.

Nico Santini walked straight over to the parents and introduced himself.

'I will be your baby's doctor for the operation. Once you are discharged you will see Dr Gibbs again. With your permission I would like to examine Thomas, and then we will talk. I am sure you have many questions for me.'

'Well, yes, I suppose…' Lorna gave a nervous smile and clasped her hands in her lap. 'But I'm sure you're too busy for questions—'

'Not at all.' Nico gave her a warm smile which softened the harsh planes of his handsome face. 'At the moment I have nothing important to do,' he lied smoothly, 'and I am very happy to spend as long as you need in order to set your mind at rest. It's important to me that you don't worry. A worried mother means a worried baby and…' he raised his hands expressively '…I don't want either on my ward. Please, ask me anything you wish as many times as you need to. I understand that it can take a while to understand some of the things that we talk about. Hearts are complex things.'

Abby's jaw dropped and she struggled to hide her surprise as she listened to him talk. She'd always thought that Nico Santini was one hundred per cent alpha male. She hadn't imagined that there was a caring side to him.

But clearly there was.

She watched in fascination as he picked up Thomas with easy confidence, his hands swift and gentle as he examined the child. And all the time he spoke softly in Italian and the baby gazed up at him, his attention caught.

Even the baby can't look away from the man, Abby thought wryly, standing quietly in the background as Nico finally returned the baby to the cot and sat down next to Lorna.

'Please, feel free to ask me anything you wish.'

He inclined his dark head towards the young mother, listening closely as she blurted out all her worries. He was totally relaxed and attentive, nothing in his body language suggesting that there was a crowd of doctors waiting impatiently for him to finish so that he could do a teaching round.

'Tell me why you feel guilty.'

'He seems so well. I feel like a bad mother, deciding to make him have an operation that might—might…' Tears bloomed in Lorna Woods's eyes and Nico reached out and closed long fingers around her hand.

'It is clear to me that you haven't understood the explanations that you've been given so far and this is understandable. When a mother is told that her child is seriously ill, it is normal that she hears nothing more.' He shrugged a broad shoulder in a totally Latin gesture. 'I will explain, and you will ask me any questions you have. And then you will feel more reassured.'

Abby hid a smile. That was more like the Nico Santini she remembered. Accustomed to giving out orders.

You will be reassured or else…

Still, Lorna seemed to be hanging onto every word he said. And his hand.

'I just feel perhaps we should wait. I know he looks a bit blue but he doesn't seem that ill at the moment and I feel awful making him have this operation.'

Nico nodded, sympathy and understanding in his dark eyes. 'But you are not the one making the decision, Lorna. The doctors here have made the decision that Thomas needs this operation and you are being a good mother by agreeing to it.' He kept hold of her hand, his voice deep and level as he spoke. 'Thomas has something called Fallot's tetralogy, which basically means that there are a number of things wrong with his heart. Experience has shown us that if we delay the repair it puts a strain on one of the chambers of the heart. It can become enlarged and this may cause problems in later life. Also, repairing the fault early in life restores the oxygen saturation—the amount of oxygen in his blood. This is important for normal development.'

Lorna looked at her husband who shrugged his shoulders helplessly. 'So you really think it should be done now?'

'Definitely.' Nico didn't hesitate. 'I have reviewed all his tests and I am convinced that it is totally the right thing to do.'

Lorna nibbled her lip and looked at him shyly. 'Do you have children yourself?'

There was a long pause and Nico Santini glanced towards Abby, his dark lashes shielding his expression.

Confused by his sudden attention, she shifted slightly and felt herself colour.

Why was he looking at her?

He seemed to look at her for a long time and then finally he turned his attention back to Lorna. 'If you are asking if I would recommend this operation for my own child in the same situation, the answer is yes. I can assure you that if Thomas *were* my child, I would have no hesitation in letting the operation go ahead. Do you understand the actual mechanics of the operation? What I will be doing?'

Lorna blushed slightly and exchanged awkward glances with her husband. 'Sort of.'

Which meant no, Abby thought quickly, preparing to intervene. But Nico was ahead of her.

'Maybe I will explain it again,' he said smoothly, releasing Lorna's hand and reaching into his pocket for a pad and a pen. 'A drawing usually helps. Imagine the heart as four chambers…'

His pen moved quickly over the pad as he drew a diagram to illustrate his explanation.

'One of the problems with Thomas's heart is what we call a VSD—a ventricular septal defect. In other words, there is a hole between the two chambers here.…' He tapped his pen on the page to demonstrate what he meant more clearly. 'I will put a patch on that. Here the artery is narrowed and I need to sort that out, probably by opening up the valve that leads into it.'

Nico continued his explanation and finally Lorna's husband gave a weak smile. 'You make it sound like DIY.'

Nico gave a brief nod. 'In a way it is. I am a technician. Only I don't always know exactly what will need to be done until I have a look at the heart.' He gave another shrug. 'You just have to trust me.'

Lorna bit her lip and he lifted an eyebrow.

'There is something else you wish to ask me?'

'You say we must trust you....' Lorna hesitated and then took a deep breath. 'Are you good?'

Nico seemed momentarily taken aback by the question and then he gave a wry smile and touched her cheek briefly with a long finger.

'The best.'

Abby stayed silent as Lorna visibly relaxed and started to ask all the questions that had clearly been bothering her for some time.

Finally she seemed happier and Nico rose to his feet in a fluid movement and flashed her a smile.

'I hope you feel a little better now.'

Lorna nodded and gave him a weak smile. 'I do feel better, thank you, although I can't pretend I'm not worried.'

'Of course you will be worried.' Nico slipped his pen back into his pocket. 'You are a mother and it is a mother's role to worry. If there are any other questions that you wish to ask me then just ask one of the nurses to contact me and I will be happy to speak to you at any time. I will come and find you after the operation tomorrow so that I can tell you how it went.'

At the reminder of what lay ahead, Lorna swallowed and he reached out a hand and squeezed her shoulder.

'It will go well. Trust me.'

With that he strode out of the room, leaving Abby to follow in his wake, stunned by what she'd witnessed.

It wasn't at all what she'd expected.

She'd never seen a doctor take so much time with a family before and she was impressed by how skilfully he'd translated the technical aspects of the operation into language that the family could understand. She was also impressed by the way he'd picked up the signals that Lorna hadn't understood the previous explanations that she'd been given.

Maybe she'd misjudged him.

'Thank you for giving them so much time. I've never heard a doctor give such a clear explanation. You were amazing with them,' she admitted quietly, as she walked back along the corridor beside him.

He stopped dead and turned to face her, a frown touching his forehead, almost as though he'd forgotten she was there until she'd spoken.

His eyes locked with hers and suddenly she remembered the way he'd looked at her in the side room.

Accusingly.

Which was utterly ridiculous, she told herself firmly. What could he possibly be accusing her of?

Or maybe he'd recognised her but couldn't place her.

Maybe she should tell him that she used to go to school with Lucia?

His gaze was cool and assessing and something in those fabulous dark eyes chilled her to the bone.

'Are you staying for my teaching round?'

'I can't.' She was off duty at four and nothing was going to stop her seeing Rosa. She'd nipped down to the crèche in her lunch-break to check that the baby was all right, but she'd be happier when they were both at home.

'And will you be at home this evening?' His voice was silky smooth and she nodded, taken aback by the question.

Why would Nico Santini be remotely interested in her plans for the evening?

His eyes scanned her face with disconcerting thoroughness and then he turned on his heel and walked back onto the main ward, leaving her staring after him, thoroughly confused.

Nico completed his teaching round and glanced at his watch.

'Are you busy this evening?' Jack Gibbs was clearly about to extend a social invitation and Nico was quick to make his excuses.

There was only one place he intended to be that evening, and that was confronting Abby Harrington. Incredibly skilled at interpreting body language, he'd instantly recognised her nervousness when they'd been introduced.

His mouth twisted into a bitter smile. After all these years he didn't think that he made mistakes about women, but he'd certainly been way off the mark in her case.

He'd thought her extremely shy, but she'd also seemed to him to be sensible and intelligent and he'd hoped that she might be a favourable influence on his dizzy sister. She certainly wasn't the sort of person he would have credited with telling lies or choosing to become a single mother.

It was no wonder she'd looked nervous when he'd walked onto the ward.

She was afraid that he'd discovered her secret and at this very moment she was probably pacing the floor of the tiny flat that she was being forced to vacate, dreading his next move.

And she was right to dread it.

Perfect father material.

Wasn't that what Lucia had said when she'd persuaded him to be the donor? That they'd decided that he had all the qualities that a man should have. Looks and intellect. Unfortunately for them, they'd failed to realise that being perfect father material also included a sense of responsibility towards fatherhood and it was that same sense of duty that had driven him to check on the child that he'd fathered.

He wondered how Abby Harrington would react when he announced that he intended to claim his child.

For some reason she'd wanted a child of her own and had clearly been prepared to use any means to achieve her objective. Including persuading his sister to lie about her circumstances, he reminded himself grimly.

She'd played a dangerous game and lost.

And now she was going to pay the price.

CHAPTER TWO

ABBY tucked Rosa into her cot and stared down at her with a worried frown. Her cheeks were pink and she'd been unusually fretful again during the evening.

Abby kept trying to convince herself that it was probably just teething, but all her instincts were telling her that the child was coming down with something.

She gave a sigh and stroked the little girl's hair as she slept.

She loved her so much...

The sound of the doorbell disturbed her and she glanced at the clock, her heart accelerating like a roller-coaster.

Was it the landlord?

He'd given her two more weeks to find somewhere else to live but so far she hadn't found the time to start hunting.

Remembering what had happened during their last encounter, her breathing grew more rapid and she glanced at the phone.

Should she call the police?

Surely it was illegal to double the rent just because the tenant had refused sex with the landlord!

The bell went again, more insistent this time, and she walked purposefully towards the door, sparks in her blue eyes.

She didn't need the police. This time she'd handle him herself. She didn't even care about the flat any more. It wasn't anything special and in the winter it was freezing. But she needed time to find somewhere else that she could afford and that was impossible in London. She already had to take two buses to get to work and if she moved further out then it would make the journey even worse and that wasn't fair on Rosa.

But if he tried what he'd tried last time…

Determined to ask for a bit more time, Abby jerked open the front door and gasped in surprise as she saw who was standing there.

It was Nico Santini.

What did he want?

And how had he known where to find her?

For a moment she didn't speak, too taken aback to think of anything sensible to say, then finally she found her voice.

'Well—this is a surprise…'

Instead of answering, he stepped past her and strode into her flat, ducking his dark head slightly to avoid banging his head on the doorway.

Abby's jaw dropped. The arrogance of the man!

Closing the front door behind her, she followed him into the shabby sitting room and paused in the doorway. He was standing with his back to her, his powerful shoulders tense as he examined a photograph.

A photograph of Rosa.

Abby bristled, outrage overwhelming her usual shyness. 'Did you want something?'

He didn't even look up, his dark eyes intent on the photograph.

Abby tensed. 'That's my daughter.'

He looked up then, his gaze lifting slowly from the photograph to meet her eyes. 'I know exactly who she is, Abby. I know everything about her.'

Everything?

What exactly did he mean, he knew *everything*?

She hid her dismay. What was he saying? That Lucia had told him about her treatment at Carlo's clinic?

She watched, struggling to think logically as he returned the photograph to the shelf with the others, his lean brown hand totally steady.

Why was Nico even interested? she wondered frantically. Why would her daughter be of interest to him? He'd never even passed the time of day with her before.

He took a final look at the photograph and then turned, supremely confident, every inch the arrogant, dominant male as he faced her across the sitting room.

Abby fought the instinct to take a step backwards. This was her sitting room, for goodness' sake.

But his self-assured masculinity stifled her powers of speech and she dug her fingers into her palms and took a deep breath. There was something about this man that punctured her confidence levels.

'Secrets have a way of coming out, Abby.' He spoke slowly, his voice loaded with meaning, and she started to shake.

He definitely knew.

'Let's not play games. It isn't my style. I assume you're referring to Rosa's conception,' she said flatly, deciding that pretence was clearly a waste of time. 'That should have been confidential but I suppose between siblings anything goes. What I don't understand is why you could possibly be interested.'

'No?' His black eyes glinted slightly and he tossed a file onto the small writing desk by the French doors that led into the tiny garden.

Abby glanced at it, startled, realising that she hadn't even noticed until now that he'd been carrying a file.

She stared at it now with trepidation, instinct telling her that the contents would be unpleasant.

'Wh-what is that?'

'Take a look,' he suggested, his tone lethally smooth, and she looked at him with a total lack of comprehension.

What was this all about?

Staring at the file as though it were a deadly animal which might strike at any moment, she forced herself to cross the room. It had a plain brown cover which revealed nothing of its contents.

Pausing momentarily, she lifted a hand and flipped it open and then jerked her hand away as if it had been scalded.

The file was about *her*!

Her and Rosa.

Her whole body trembling, she flicked through the pages, nausea rising in her throat as she read intimate details about herself and her daughter. Intimate and exhaustive details.

Details that no one should know.

An intensely private person, she felt painfully exposed, flayed by the knowledge that this man was in possession of such detailed facts about her.

Appalled, she lifted her eyes to his. 'H-how did you get this information?'

Nico lifted a broad shoulder dismissively. 'That isn't important.'

It was important to her. She'd always hidden the truth about Rosa's conception from those around her. And here it was staring up at her, taunting her from the page of a file delivered by a virtual stranger.

The fact that he knew about Rosa's history was bad enough, but to know every detail of her life...

She stared at him, seeking some clue as to the game he was playing, but he was everything that his reputation suggested. *Iceberg.* If he was feeling anything at all, it certainly didn't show. There was no doubt as to who had the upper hand, and it wasn't her.

'Why? Why are you interested in us?' Her words were barely a whisper, almost a plea, but there wasn't a glimmer of sympathy in those hard black eyes.

'*Dio*, you really ask me that? Are you still pretending that you don't know why I am here?' He walked purposefully towards her and when he finally came to a halt he was standing so close to her that she could feel the warmth from his powerful body. 'Did you really think I wouldn't find out the truth, Abby?'

'The truth about what?' She swallowed, her breathing shallow as she struggled to understand what was happening. She was obviously missing something. And whatever it was that she was missing, it was clearly something very serious.

'Are you really pretending that you don't know who I am?'

Her chin jerked up and she met his gaze. 'I know who you are.' Clearly she should have confessed straight away, but it just hadn't seemed that important and she'd thought it unlikely that he even would have remembered her. 'You're Lucia's brother. I met you a few times when we were at school.'

'And?' he prompted her softly, and she felt her heart hammering uncomfortably in her chest.

He hadn't even raised his voice but somehow his tone had filled her with dread.

'And nothing.' She looked at him helplessly, her fingers curled into her damp palms. 'I haven't seen you since we left school. I truly don't know what this is all about.'

'But you're not denying that you had treatment at my brother's clinic?' His tone was silky smooth, challenging her to dispute the truth.

'No.' She swallowed painfully, accepting the fact that he obviously had all the facts at his disposal. The file was nauseatingly comprehensive. 'What would be the point of that when you've gone to so much trouble to find out every last detail about me? But that information should have been confidential.'

His mouth tightened. 'And you were doubtless depending on that fact when you lied to us all. You were confident that you wouldn't be caught.'

'Lied?' Abby's eyes widened and she shook her head, totally confused by the conversation. It was like taking the lead part in a play when she hadn't read the script. 'I didn't lie to anyone.'

'Maybe not directly, but you were happy for Lucia to do it for you,' he said harshly. 'She lied about your age and your marital status.'

Abby blinked. 'No, I—'

He made an impatient sound. 'I have been intimately acquainted with your sex since I was fifteen years old and I can assure you that I am no longer taken in by a pair of wide blue eyes and an innocent expression. I know everything there is to know about female manipulation.'

Abby grabbed the back of a chair, shell-shocked. Nico was accusing her of something, but she still didn't understand what. He was making no sense at all.

'What am I supposed to have lied about?' She let go of the chair and hugged her arms around herself. 'I really don't know what this conversation is about.'

He stared at her, his black eyes merciless. 'No? Then let me spell it out.' He paced across her small sitting room and she couldn't help comparing him with a caged tiger. Only maybe a tiger would have been safer, she thought weakly. Nico in a rage was a lethal force. 'You played a dangerous game and you have lost.'

She stared at him stupidly, her powers of speech temporarily suspended by shock.

He barely seemed to notice her lack of communication. As far as he was concerned, she'd been tried and found guilty. The only problem was, she had absolutely no idea what crime she'd supposedly committed.

'I was willing to help you only because I believed your circumstances to be worthy of intervention. I have now found out otherwise and this changes everything.'

Was the man mad? When had he helped her?

She struggled to find her voice. 'Perhaps you should be more specific,' she croaked. 'What exactly does it change?'

'Everything. I no longer consider you a fit mother,' he

delivered in a cool tone. 'I agreed to father your child because I believed you to be a woman in your late thirties in a stable relationship with a limited chance of producing a child naturally. That was what you and Lucia led me to believe. The truth was very different, as we both know. I never would have agreed to be the donor had I known that you were so young and on your own.'

She stared at him blankly, her brain slower than her hearing. 'Donor?'

He ignored her croaked response.

'You are clearly not able to give her the type of care I would wish for a child of mine, so I intend to apply for custody myself. I want my child.'

His child?

Donor?

The world stopped dead and Abby stared at him in mute horror.

Nico Santini thought that he was Rosa's father?

She opened her mouth and then closed it again, unable to voice the words aloud because that might have given credence to his absurd claim. And it *was* absurd, of that she was sure.

'Don't bother denying it,' Nico drawled, but Abby wasn't listening. Her mind was locked on something he'd said a few sentences earlier.

Something about Lucia...

A hideous suspicion formed inside her mind and Abby lifted a hand to her head as she tried to clear the humming in her ears.

It was possible, just possible that...

Nausea rose in her throat and she reached out and grasped the bookshelves for support, but it made no difference. The room suddenly started to spin and she heard Nico swear softly in Italian.

'*Dio*, fainting will not attract my sympathy.'

Sympathy? She didn't want his sympathy. She just

wanted him to be lying!! And she wanted him out of her house.

'Sit down and put your head between your knees.' His voice was rough and before she could protest he'd scooped her up into his arms and dumped her unceremoniously into a chair. Then she felt his long fingers biting into the soft flesh at the back of her neck as he forced her head between her knees.

She gulped in air, trying desperately to control the nausea that threatened to engulf her.

Finally the blackness receded and she gingerly tried to sit up. 'You can move your hand now,' she muttered sickly, 'I'm fine.'

The pressure at the back of her neck eased and she sat up slowly, one palm placed across her chest. She needed to check that her heart was still beating.

Nico stood in front of her, his legs placed firmly apart in an aggressive stance, his expression brutally unsympathetic.

'I always thought Lucia took the prize when it came to drama, but it seems I was wrong. I hate to disappoint you but I'm never impressed by female hysterics,' he informed her. 'Even less so in your case since you've always known that I might find out the truth.'

Abby was forcing herself to breathe normally in an attempt to get oxygen to her fuddled brain.

Finally she felt well enough to speak. 'Are you really telling me that you think you're the father of my baby?'

Her voice sounded thick, clogged with emotion. Totally unlike her own.

'I don't *think*.' He spoke the words with dangerous emphasis. 'I *know*.'

Her voice was little more than a whisper. 'You were the donor?'

Please, let it be a mistake....

His black eyes flashed with impatience. 'You know very

well that I was. And we also know that you and Lucia fed me false information so that I'd agree. She knew that I would never agree to father a child for a woman in your circumstances. Family is something that I feel very strongly about. The two of you concocted the sort of story that you knew I would respond to.'

Abby licked dry lips. Was he telling the truth? Could Nico Santini be the father of her child?

She and Lucia had discussed the qualities that would make the ideal donor, but she'd never asked for any details.

What would have been the point? She'd assumed that the man in question would have been a stranger to her.

Had Lucia really persuaded her own brother to be the donor? Surely she never would have done that.

But if she had…

Abby sank her teeth into her lower lip, refusing to face the awful possibility that Nico might be Rosa's father.

It was too shocking even to contemplate. She could see instantly that a man like Nico, an Italian who'd had the sanctity of the family injected into his veins from the cradle, wasn't going to sit back and allow his child to be brought up by a single mother. What had Lucia been thinking of?

And he'd said something about taking Rosa from her.

The colour drained from her face and she lifted a hand to her mouth. She was going to be ill.

Muttering an apology, she stood up hastily and sprinted to the toilet where she was violently sick. For endless moments she hung over the bowl and then finally she sank onto the floor of the bathroom, her eyes closed, every muscle in her body aching from her body's physical reaction to Nico's shocking announcement.

She had no idea of how long she sat there. Time was of no consequence. All she could think of was the fact that he just might be Rosa's father. And if he was then he was going to claim her.

Her baby.

Panic swamped her like a tidal wave and she wrapped her arms around her body, trying to settle her churning stomach. She had to stay calm, she told herself, clutching her shaking knees to her tummy and gulping in a lungful of air. Nico was exceptionally clever and so emotionally controlled that if she didn't get a grip and concentrate, he'd run rings around her.

She was still wrestling for control when Rosa suddenly cried out.

Struggling to her feet, she splashed her face quickly and ran down the hall as fast as her shaking legs would allow.

Pushing open the door of Rosa's nursery, she stopped dead. Nico was standing there, speaking softly in Italian, Rosa held firmly against his shoulder. The little girl lifted a chubby hand and patted his blue-black jaw, gurgling with laughter and blowing bubbles.

Abby watched in dismay.

Did her daughter have no sense of self-preservation? She should have been behaving like the child from hell so that there was no way on this planet he'd want to take her away. Instead of which, Rosa was being her usual sweet-natured self and she could see that Nico was totally enchanted by the little girl.

He held her against his broad chest with one large hand while he used the other to tease the baby gently.

Abby shook her head in disbelief as she watched them together. What a contrast. There was no sign of the hard, ruthless, male who had been prowling around her sitting room only moments earlier. With the baby Nico was a different person—incredibly gentle, tolerant and mildly amused by her antics.

Looking at the two of them together, Abby felt her heart sink into her boots.

How had she not noticed it before?

Rosa was the spitting image of Nico. They had the same

jet-black hair, the same incredible dark eyes. Only the mouth was different. Rosa's mouth was a small rosebud whereas—Abby glanced at him and then glanced away quickly, her face suddenly hot—Nico's was tough and sensual, and it wasn't something that she wanted to focus on. Whichever way you looked at it, physically Rosa resembled Nico closely.

Which meant that he was probably telling the truth.

The realisation hit her in the pit of her stomach and she sank against the doorframe for support. Even if she'd been thinking of contesting his claim to be the child's natural father, one look at the two of them together would have been enough to make her realise the futility of such an exercise.

Suddenly Rosa noticed her mother and squirmed in Nico's hold, reaching out her chubby arms towards Abby.

Distraught and not thinking clearly, Abby pulled herself together enough to cross the room and take her daughter from him.

Just feeling the familiar warmth of Rosa's little body made her feel better. There was something so comforting about her innocent hug and the smell of her skin and hair.

'She's mine.' Not wanting to upset Rosa, she spoke quietly, but her voice quivered with passion and sincerity. 'She's always been mine. It doesn't matter if you're the biological father. You can't take her away from me.'

Her words were sheer bravado and she met his cool gaze, hopelessly out of her depth. She had no idea about the legalities of the situation and she couldn't afford to pay anyone to tell her, not with the present state of her finances. Surely no one would give him custody? But, then again, they probably would, she reflected miserably, hugging her daughter even closer. The Santini family was loaded. When Lucia had been at school it had been bodyguards and helicopters all the way. They had enough money to buy the entire legal system if necessary. Whereas she—she closed her eyes briefly as she faced the painful truth—didn't even have the money for one consultation with a lawyer. If she had then she probably would have already seen one about her unscrupulous landlord.

Rosa squirmed slightly in her hold and Nico looked at her, the expression in his eyes hidden by sinfully long thick black lashes. 'I refuse to discuss this in front of the child. Put her back in the cot and settle her.'

Knowing that he was right and feeling guilty that she was upsetting Rosa, Abby had no choice but to comply. She settled the little girl in the cot, tucking her favourite teddy in next to her.

Then, with a last look at her precious child, she left the bedroom door ajar and walked into the tiny sitting room.

Nico walked in behind her and closed the door behind him with an ominous click.

'Now we can talk.'

If only it was that easy.

Painfully shy and a pacifist by nature, she'd always hated confrontation of any sort and in this case who could blame her? There was surely no one on the planet that would willingly choose Nico Santini as an adversary.

Even Lucia had been wary and nervous of her older brother and, facing him across the room, Abby could understand why. Nico just exuded masculine power and he clearly wasn't used to hearing the word 'no'.

But he was going to hear it now.

Abby folded her arms across her stomach and tried not to focus on just how anxious he made her feel. She'd never been comfortable with his raw, animal sexuality and nothing had changed over time. She was just a normal, everyday sort of girl and a complete novice when it came to handling men, whereas he—she swallowed as she risked a glance at his impressive male physique—was in a different league entirely.

Sophisticated, vastly experienced with women and used

to getting his own way in everything, he was just about as different from her as it was possible to be.

She tightened her fists by her side and lifted her chin. She might be nervous of him, but this was Rosa they were talking about.

Her baby.

Rosa was all she had in the world and he wanted to take her away.

Well, she wasn't going to allow that to happen, which meant standing up to him—whatever that took.

Maybe if she didn't look at him directly, he would seem less intimidating.

'I accept that you might be her father,' she conceded, proud by how steady her voice sounded. 'She certainly looks like you, but you have to believe that I knew nothing about it. I never would have wanted you to be the father!'

In fact, the mere thought that they'd been so intimately connected, albeit in such a clinical and detached way, made her feel hot inside.

Faint colour touched her cheek and she dipped her head forward, concentrating on the threadbare carpet. This whole situation was a total nightmare!

'You expect me to believe that?' His incredulous tone mocked her and she realised, helplessly, how utterly implausible she sounded.

She knew from Lucia that her brother had been chased by almost every female on the planet. Why should he possibly believe that there might be one who *didn't* see him as the perfect mate?

Nico Santini had everything. Intelligence, wealth, looks and power. He was the oldest son of one of the most powerful families in Italy, but he'd chosen not to enter the family business and instead had forged a staggeringly successful career as a heart surgeon. By all accounts the man was nothing short of a genius in the operating theatre. Who wouldn't want him to father her child? He was perfect father material for most women.

But she wasn't most women, she thought miserably, lacing her fingers in front of her in a nervous gesture.

She didn't respond to his full-on, testosterone-driven masculinity—it made her feel shivery and uncomfortable and strange inside. But, most importantly, for all his sense of family and responsibility, Nico Santini was a workaholic like her father and she knew only too well what it felt like to be the child of someone like that. A man like Nico would never have time for fatherhood.

She was still trying to find a tactful and convincing way to tell him that when he made an impatient sound.

'All right—let's leave that to one side for a moment and move on to the other issue. Your age. Lucia told me that you were in your late thirties, which was why I agreed to help.'

Abby shook her head, stunned into silence by the news that Lucia had told such lies.

'What I want to know is why a woman of twenty-two with no emotional or financial support from anyone would choose to have a child on her own.'

Abby's heart twisted.

How could she possibly tell him the truth? Nico came from a big, loving Italian family. How could a man like him even begin to understand what it felt like to be totally alone in the world, to have absolutely no one to laugh and cry with? How could he possibly understand what it felt like to be so achingly lonely that her idea of winning the lottery was to find a long-lost relative.

They probably didn't even have a word for lonely in the Italian language.

And she certainly wasn't confessing the details of her humiliating experience with Ian—

What would have been the point?

Lucia had always complained that her brother never let emotion interfere with any decision he made.

How could he begin to understand what had driven her to have a child of her own at such a young age, and how would she convince him that she hadn't taken the decision lightly?

She'd questioned herself long and hard before she'd finally decided to have a child, and that questioning hadn't ended with Rosa's birth. She was painfully conscious that she'd become a single mother through choice and that her decision had deprived Rosa of certain things in life.

Like a father.

But apart from that one factor, which persistently nagged at her conscience, she refused to believe that Rosa was badly off. She had a mother who adored her, which was more than many children had.

It was certainly more than she'd ever had herself.

Aware that Nico was looking at her with ill-concealed impatience, she forced herself to answer.

'I just wanted a baby.' It sounded lame even to her, and his mouth tightened.

'So you had one, with no thought to her future.'

'No!' Stung by the contempt in his tone, Abby forgot to be intimidated and lifted her head to look at him, her blue eyes blazing. 'I thought long and hard before I had Rosa. And I give her everything I have!'

'Which isn't very much, is it, *cara mia*?'

His softly spoken words were so cruel that she gave a gasp of disbelief.

'A happy childhood doesn't have to be about money.'

'Agreed.' He was ice cool, completely unfazed by her heated defence. 'But, correct me if I'm wrong, generally speaking a baby does need a stable home in which to live.'

Her heart started to beat faster. 'Rosa has a home!'

His dismissive glance round her tiny flat spoke volumes. 'One which you are being forced to leave.'

She stared at him, eyes wide. She hadn't told anyone about her accommodation problems.

'H-how do you know that?'

'I have impressive contacts.' He met her stunned gaze without a flicker of emotion. 'I'm intrigued as to how you are planning to give Rosa this "happy childhood" that you talk about when you don't have anywhere for her to live.'

Abby lifted her small chin. 'I'll find somewhere.'

'You wouldn't be leaving this place had you managed to keep up with the rental payments,' Nico pointed out smoothly, and she gasped.

He must have spoken to the landlord, and he'd obviously told him that she couldn't afford the rent.

She closed her eyes briefly and gritted her teeth. She'd done nothing wrong. The truth was that the landlord was totally corrupt. Unfortunately she had absolutely no experience in dealing with his type. He'd been pestering her for months and when she'd refused to give him what he wanted he'd increased her rent, knowing that she was already stretched to the limit on her modest nurse's salary. So now she was being forced to move out.

Pride prevented her from communicating the facts to Nico. It clearly suited his purposes to believe that she was a useless mother.

'You can't seriously want to take Rosa from me,' she said, her voice choked as she tried to reason with him. 'You're not even married. Why would you want a baby?'

He stilled, his powerful shoulders visibly tense. Abby watched him, intrigued in spite of her inner panic, her attention caught by the subtle change in him. So Nico Santini wasn't always an iceberg, she mused silently.

'I am in a position to give her a good life—'

'By whose definition?' Abby shot back, her shyness buried under the threat of losing Rosa. 'You're a workaholic. When do you have time for a child? Or are you planning to get married...?' Her voice trailed off at that awful thought. If he *was* getting married, he'd be a more appealing prospect for a judge, wouldn't he?

His dark eyes were veiled, any hint of emotion carefully concealed. Whatever had caused the tension moments earlier was now firmly buried again. 'I am not getting married.'

Belatedly Abby recalled conversations with Lucia. His sister had clearly said that her brother had never been emotionally attached to a woman in his life.

'He's never met a woman who didn't have an ulterior motive,' Lucia had told her once. 'They're either after his money or the status of being seen with him. It's the same with Carlo. Neither of them trust women an inch and frankly I don't really blame them.'

'Well, if you're not getting married, you're not in a position to give her a better home than I can,' Abby said, her voice shaking with passion. 'She's my baby and I won't let you take her!'

She had the satisfaction of seeing him look taken aback. In all probability no one had ever said 'no' to the man before. Well, tough, she thought. He'd better get used to the idea.

He opened his mouth to speak but then cursed softly as his mobile phone rang.

He reached into his pocket and flipped it open. 'Santini.' His voice was clipped, his face expressionless as he listened to the person on the other end. Then he issued some complex instructions and glanced at his watch. 'I will be there in ten minutes.'

He slipped the phone back into his pocket and a ghost of a smile played around his firm mouth.

'It looks like the rest of this conversation will have to wait until another time. One of the babies that was operated on yesterday has started to haemorrhage. I may need to take her back to Theatre.'

For a brief moment Abby forgot about her own problems. 'Which baby?'

'Katherine Parker.'

Abby gave a gasp and covered her mouth with her hand. 'No—not Katherine. That baby is so precious. They tried for ten years to have her—ten years…'

'Every baby is precious,' Nico said as he reached for the doorhandle. 'Which is why they deserve the security of a stable family. But we'll talk about that another time.'

Abby wasn't even thinking of her own problems any more. She was thinking about little Katherine and how devastated her parents would be. The operation had seemed to go so well.

'I hope you can save her,' she muttered, and he gave a cool shrug.

'I certainly intend to try.'

With that he tugged open the door and left her staring after him, trembling from the aftershock of the confrontation.

Crossing Nico Santini was like being caught in the eye of a hurricane. And it was far from over.

CHAPTER THREE

ALL the talk on the ward the next morning was about Katherine and the fact that Nico Santini had saved her.

'No wonder they call him "Iceberg". He opened her chest on CICU, cool as a cucumber,' Fiona said in an awed tone. 'I mean, can you imagine that? Apparently they wanted to take her to Theatre but he took one look at her and opened her up there and then.'

'Did he?' Abby was thrilled that the little girl was once again out of the woods, but all this hero-worship of Nico was making her feel slightly ill. Remembering the cool way in which he'd delivered his threats the night before, she wasn't exactly able to join the others in their adulation of the visiting consultant.

He might be a god in the operating theatre, but as far as she was concerned as a human being he left a great deal to be desired.

He seemed incapable of understanding normal human emotions.

Like the love of a mother for her child.

Fiona was looking at her closely. 'Are you all right? You're very pale. Did Rosa keep you up last night?'

Abby shook her head. After Nico had left, Rosa had slept right through the night, but she hadn't even attempted to sleep she'd been so anxious about the future.

Could he do as he'd threatened?

Could he take Rosa away from her?

She really ought to consult a lawyer but she wouldn't know whom to contact and it would mean admitting that Rosa had been conceived by donor insemination.

'I just feel a bit tired.' She managed a wan smile and

glanced at the clock on the wall. 'Little Thomas will be going down to Theatre in an hour—I'm going to check they're all right.'

Fiona walked along the corridor with her. 'Did you take them around CICU yesterday?'

Abby nodded, stroking a wild strand of pale blonde hair behind her ear. 'But you know how hard it is to make CICU seem anything less than scary. All those tubes and bleeping machines are enough to scare anyone.'

'Well, at least it's Nico Santini doing the operation. If it were my baby, there isn't anyone else I'd rather have after seeing what he did for Katherine,' Fiona said fervently, and Abby gave a half-smile, mildly amused by the other girl's attitude.

It was just as well she didn't know what he was really like.

'He's just a man, Fiona.'

Her colleague gave a cheeky grin. 'Oh, believe me, I've noticed. In fact, Heather has said I can go into Theatre this morning to watch him operate. I'm hoping that I don't faint.'

'Since when did you faint at the sight of blood?'

'It's not the sight of blood that's going to make me faint,' Fiona breathed, 'it's the sight of the surgeon. He's devastating.'

Abby looked at Fiona as if she'd grown horns. It was true that Nico was very good-looking, but he was also a control freak who had the emotional sensitivity of a wounded tiger.

She certainly wouldn't contemplate a relationship with a man like that that. But, then, her track record with relationships hadn't been exactly impressive, she reminded herself sadly.

Which was why she'd resorted to such extreme means to have a child of her own.

'Are you seriously telling me you don't find him attractive?' Fiona shot her a look of disbelief and Abby forced another smile.

'I can see that some women might find him handsome,' she said through stiff lips, 'but he isn't really my type.'

'Well, in that case don't ever introduce me to your type,' Fiona commented as they reached the door to the side ward. 'I'm off to see the man in action now. See you later.'

Abby watched her go and then walked quietly into the room. Thomas was lying in his cot, chuckling and playing with a rattle. His parents were sitting next to him, white-faced and clearly stressed. At the sight of Abby, Lorna shot to her feet.

'Are they ready for him?'

Abby gave her a gentle smile and shook her head. 'Not yet. Did you manage to get any sleep at all?'

'Not much.' Lorna bit her lip and twisted her hands together anxiously. 'I know that Nico said I could go with him to the operating theatre and stay with him until he'd had the anaesthetic, but I just don't think I can do that.'

Her voice was little more than a whisper and Abby gave her a hug. 'Lots of mothers find it too stressful, don't worry about it. Either your husband can go or I'll go with him.'

Lorna sniffed. 'He does know you and he likes you. Would you do it? Would you stay with him? I've given him a cuddle and said everything I need to say. If I go with him I know I won't be able to control myself and I don't want to upset him.'

'Of course I'll go.'

At that moment Heather put her head round the door to say that they were ready for Thomas in Theatre.

Lorna and her husband gave him a last cuddle and Abby felt her eyes fill with tears as she imagined the worry they must be feeling. At that particular moment she didn't care how arrogant Nico Santini was as long as he was able to operate successfully on Thomas.

In the anaesthetic room the anaesthetist chatted away to

her, but she barely heard him, her heart in her mouth as the doors through to Theatre swung open and Nico strolled through. He seemed impossibly broad-shouldered, his dark hair obscured by a cap and a hint of curling dark chest hair showing at the neck of his blue theatre pyjamas.

He walked up to the baby and touched his face gently, murmuring gently in Italian.

'For crying out loud, Nico, speak in English,' the anaesthetist complained cheerfully as he reached for a syringe. 'We're going to have communication problems here if you conduct this operation in Italian. The most I can do in your language is order a pizza.'

Nico laughed and his lean face was transformed from arrogant to devastatingly attractive. Suddenly Abby found herself thinking about the fact that they'd made a baby together.

Not in the traditional sense, of course, but still...

It was a strange thought that left her feeling hot inside and out.

She blushed slightly and at that moment he lifted his eyes and saw her. Their gazes locked and her breathing was suspended. An almost unbearable tension shimmered between them and she was unable to look away, unable to break the connection until finally he seemed to shake himself and turned back to the baby.

'If everything's all right here, I'll go and scrub.'

The anaesthetist nodded. 'Everything's fine.'

'*Bene.*'

With a last searing look at Abby Nico left the room, and she felt the tension drain out of her body.

The anaesthetist glanced up at her. 'Are you going into Theatre?'

Abby shook her head and smiled weakly. 'No.' *Her nerves couldn't stand it.* 'One of the other nurses from the ward is watching. I need to get back.'

The anaesthetist nodded as he concentrated on Thomas.

'Well, he's well and truly under, so you can go whenever you like.'

Abby made her way back to the ward and spent some time with Thomas's parents, who were beside themselves with worry. Then she busied herself on the ward, helping Heather with the drugs, feeding two of the babies who'd been in for investigation and changing a nasogastric tube.

Finally a call came through from Theatre, telling them that Thomas was off bypass and doing well.

Lorna stared at her, frantic with worry. 'What exactly does that mean—"off bypass"?'

'Thomas has had open heart surgery,' Abby reminded her, 'which means that in order to operate, they had to divert the blood flow away from his heart—basically a machine does the work of the heart for the duration of the operation.'

'So his heart stops?'

'Well, technically, yes. Once the surgeon has finished the operation, they start the heart again.'

Lorna rubbed a hand over her face and exchanged looks with her husband. 'So if he's off bypass, does that mean that Thomas is all right?'

'Well, it sounds positive, but we really have to wait to talk to Mr Santini to find out exactly how the operation went,' Abby said, knowing that it would be wrong of her to comment on the success of the operation without some knowledge of what had transpired in Theatre.

Lorna gave a wan smile. 'He's an amazing man. Fancy having the confidence to operate on a baby that small. My hands would be shaking too much.'

'I think I can guarantee that Mr Santini's hands don't shake,' Abby said lightly. In fact, she doubted whether Domenico Santini had ever had a single crisis of confidence in his life.

'He popped in to see us yesterday evening and again this

morning. He told us to call him Nico,' Lorna told her. 'He was really very informal and very kind.'

It was a shame he didn't seem to extend the same kindness to his personal life, Abby thought dully.

But all that mattered at the moment was that he did a good job on Thomas, she reminded herself firmly. Her personal problems could wait.

'His pressures are good.' Nico stared at the monitor and gave the anaesthetist a nod. 'How is he doing at your end?'

'He's doing all right but I'll be more relaxed once you're finished,' the anaesthetist said lightly.

'I'm going to close the chest.' Totally focused on the task in hand, Nico worked quickly, pausing occasionally to make an observation to his ever-increasing audience or ask a question of his assistant, Greg.

Finally, five hours after he'd started, he was finished. He stripped off his sterile gown and ran a hand over the back of his neck to relieve the tension.

His shoulders ached from standing in one position for so long and he walked through to the changing rooms, stripped off his clothes and stepped under the shower.

Then he grabbed a sandwich and a cup of coffee, knowing that by the time he'd finished Thomas would be settled in CICU.

He needed to check on Katherine Parker and speak to Thomas's parents.

Although there had been some complications that he hadn't anticipated, generally speaking he was pleased with the way the operation had gone.

Changing quickly, he checked his watch and strode down the corridor that linked the operating theatre to CICU.

The first person he saw was Abby and he stopped dead, his expert eye automatically running over the womanly curve of her hips and down her perfect legs. He frowned slightly. He hadn't ever thought of Abby as sexy until Carlo had mentioned it. In fact, he hadn't really given her any thought at all as a woman.

She was just someone who'd deceived him and given birth to his child.

Lowering his thick dark lashes, he surveyed her carefully, mentally stripping off the nurse's uniform and loosening her blonde hair from the childish ponytail.

The resulting image made him suck in his breath. There was no doubt in his mind that he'd been distracted by the events of the past few days or he would have noticed her sooner.

No red-blooded Italian male could miss those lush curves or the slight fullness of her lower lip.

As always in his judgement of women, Carlo was absolutely right.

Abby Harrington was gorgeous.

And after their encounter the previous night, Nico suspected that she was every bit as shy as he'd once thought.

He'd been totally aware of just how much effort and courage it had taken on her part to stand up to him and, despite his anger towards her, part of him was impressed. She'd defended her child like a tigress and he liked that about her.

She'd also clearly never expected him to find out that he was Rosa's father. Her shocked response to his announcement had been so genuine, so physical that despite his initial scepticism there was no way an experienced doctor like himself could dismiss it as feigned.

And it was now obvious to him that he was going to have a fight on his hands if he wanted the child.

And he did.

Nothing had prepared him for the raw emotion he'd felt when he'd held his child for the first time. The soft baby smell, her gurgle of delight when he'd held her close, her trusting acceptance of him had suddenly exposed a gaping hole in his life which he'd stubbornly refused to acknowledge before now.

Maybe Carlo was right. Maybe his reasons for wanting his daughter were more complicated than he'd claimed.

But as far as he was concerned, that didn't make any difference to the outcome.

He'd already contacted his lawyers and set the wheels in motion. One way or another he was going to make sure that he gained custody of Rosa.

Abby glanced up and her heart rate increased as she saw Nico approaching.

He'd obviously come straight from the shower and his dark hair was sleek and damp, his jaw dark with the beginnings of stubble.

He shot her a lingering glance and then checked the monitors, talked to the CICU nurse and the anaesthetist who ran the unit and then concentrated his attention on the parents.

She had to hand it to him, he was good with worried parents. He explained everything in simple language without being patronizing and by the time he left the unit Thomas's parents were looking much happier and had fallen over themselves to thank Nico.

'They need you back on the ward, Abby,' the sister on CICU called over to her, and Abby made her excuses, took a last look at little Thomas and made her way back to the ward.

'Sorry to call you back.' Heather was looking harassed and waved an arm towards the main part of the ward. 'We seem to be swamped all of a sudden and Mr Santini is going to do a teaching round, which, frankly, I need like a hole in the head. Would you mind feeding baby Hubbard? No one else can get her to take that bottle and you're a genius with babies. It's going to take ages because she gets

breathless. When you've done that we've got a toddler from
Paeds who needs admitting.'

At least feeding baby Hubbard would mean that she
could hide away from Nico Santini, Abby thought, as she
wandered through to the kitchen to collect the baby's feed.

She lifted the baby out of her cot and cuddled her close,
talking gently to her as she coaxed her to take the bottle.

'There, sweetheart,' she crooned softly. 'I know this is a
struggle for you so we'll take it slowly....'

Babies with heart problems often became breathless and
had trouble feeding.

Once she'd encouraged the little one to take the teat,
Abby settled down with a soft smile of satisfaction as the
baby started to suck.

A noise in the doorway made her glance up and she
stiffened as she saw Nico standing there.

'I gather they couldn't get her to take the bottle?' His
dark eyes were concerned and he moved closer and squat-
ted down next to her so that he could take a look at the
baby.

'She's taking it now.' Abby flushed beneath the intensity
of his gaze, uncomfortably aware of just how close he was.
She had an enviable view of his sinfully long black lashes
and just one move of her hand would have put her within
touching distance of that glossy black hair. 'She gets very
breathless so I suppose that doesn't help. She just needed
a bit of persuasion.'

He nodded, those dark eyes thoughtful as they rested on
her face. 'You are very good with her.'

The unexpected praise startled her and she looked up,
flustered, as the door opened and the rest of the team of
doctors and Heather entered the room.

Abby dropped her head and concentrated her attention
on the baby, trying to work out what was happening. How
could Nico behave as if nothing was wrong? As if they
were just colleagues working side by side with no other

interest? He'd made no reference to the night before, no mention of his plans for Rosa, and the anxiety was threatening to choke her.

'Thank goodness you've persuaded her to take that bottle,' Heather said, relief visible on her face. 'I might need you to sleep here if the night staff get stuck.'

Abby smiled, knowing that Heather wasn't serious. Everyone knew that she didn't work nights.

Once she'd finished feeding, Nico gently lifted the baby's fingers and examined them then uncoiled the stethoscope from his pocket.

Abby tried not to look at the dark hairs on his wrists or the way those skilled hands moved over the tiny baby. Having him so close unsettled her.

Finally he finished his examination and straightened. 'How is her weight?'

'She's losing weight,' Abby said flatly, watching as Heather handed him the chart. Nico's eyes flickered over it and he nodded and turned to Greg who was standing next to him, visibly tense in the presence of the consultant.

'Tell me about her.'

Greg cleared his throat. 'She's two days old and she was transferred from the postnatal ward late last night because one of the midwives thought she looked blue,' he said, shuffling through the notes to find what he wanted. 'The paediatrician suspects that she has congenital heart disease but he couldn't find a murmur and she has good pulses.'

Abby stared at the baby, noticing the blue tinge around her lips. 'Blue' or cyanotic babies didn't have enough oxygen in their blood.

Nico looked at him steadily. 'So what defects will I be considering in a cyanotic infant?'

Greg flushed slightly. 'Simple defects or complex defects—'

'Complex being?'

'Tetralogy of Fallot, transposition of the great arteries...'
Greg continued to list them and Nico nodded approvingly.

'And what tests has she had?'

'She's had a chest X-ray and an echocardiogram,' Greg
told him, flicking through the notes. 'Should we book her
in for a cardiac catheterisation?'

Cardiac catheterisation meant passing a tiny tube into the
baby's heart so that the doctor could get a close look at the
defect and measure the pressures in the heart chambers, but
Nico was shaking his head.

'Usually the diagnosis can be made with the echocardiogram and colour Doppler—we will see. If not then, yes,
Jack can do a catheter.'

They talked for ages and Nico turned his attention to the
other doctors, testing their knowledge and fielding their
endless questions.

Abby had to hand it to him, he was good. There seemed
to be no question he couldn't answer, discussing various
options with the same supreme confidence with which he
tackled everything in life.

Including taking her baby.

'This baby has transposition of the great arteries—TGA,'
Nico said finally, after they'd reviewed all the tests together.

Greg stared at him. 'So she must have another defect or
she'd be dead. TGA isn't compatible with life, is it? There
is no communication between the systemic and the pulmonary circulation.'

'She has a PDA,' Nico said briefly, and Greg blinked.

'A patent ductus? But I didn't hear it when I listened to
her chest.'

'But I did,' Nico said smoothly, folding his stethoscope
and slipping it back inside his pocket, his eyes on the baby.
'She has a murmur that is characteristic of a patent ductus
and that is why she is still alive. The blood vessel is connecting her aorta and pulmonary artery.'

'So what happens now?' Greg was looking distinctly uncomfortable that he hadn't detected the murmur and Abby almost felt sorry for him. He was a good doctor and everyone had to learn. Surely even Nico had been unsure early in his career?

She stole a glance at his glossy black hair, noting the arrogant tilt of his jaw and the sharp intelligence in his eyes.

Maybe not.

Nico Santini was super-bright and it was hard to imagine him ever having been unsure of anything.

'We give her Prostin and we check her oxygen saturation. If necessary, Jack can do a balloon atrial septostomy which will keep the blood mixing until we can do the repair,' Nico said immediately, taking a pen out of his pocket and writing something in the notes. 'We will do an arterial switch operation in the next couple of weeks. Where are the parents?'

'There's only the mother,' Abby told him quietly, supporting the little girl upright to help her breathing. 'This is her fourth child and the father left when he discovered she was pregnant again. She has very little help so she's had to go home to look after the other three. According to the postnatal ward she was distraught when the baby was kept in. She was expecting a six-hour discharge.'

'She is on her own? That is a dilemma,' Nico said quietly, a slightly frown touching his forehead. 'Are you sure she can't arrange child care so that she can be with the baby?'

'Not immediately.' Abby shook her head. 'She's doing her best to sort something out but for now she's just muddling along and visiting when she can.'

'I need to see her to explain the operation,' Nico said, and looked up at Greg. 'You are on call tonight—I want you to make yourself available to talk to her should she come in.'

Greg nodded. 'Of course. Will you be around if she wants to talk to you?'

Nico's dark eyes rested on Abby. 'I have plans for this evening,' he said evenly, 'but I will have my mobile with me. You can call me if it's urgent. Otherwise I will be in first thing tomorrow and I will be happy to speak to the mother then. This sort of news is always hard for parents to grasp. Speak slowly and clearly and check that they have understood you. Most people cannot even remember what a normal heart looks like so I find drawings helpful.'

He closed the notes and handed them to Greg then took a final look at the baby who was breathing rapidly and struggling to take the bottle from Abby.

'I will talk to Jack in the morning. If there is any change in her condition during the night, you can call me. Let's move on to the next patient.'

Heather rolled the notes trolley out of the room and Abby waited until the door clicked shut behind them then returned the baby to her cot with a sigh.

'I suppose you're lucky that he's going to operate on you,' she muttered, tucking the blankets around the dozing child. 'But somehow that doesn't make me feel much better. He might be a brilliant surgeon but he's very scary as a human being.'

What was she going to do?

How was she going to protect Rosa from him?

Nico was waiting for Abby when she came off duty, leaning casually against a low black sports car that shrieked of money.

'No limo?' Her voice was tart and she derived a certain satisfaction from the flash of surprise she saw in his dark eyes.

He obviously didn't expect her to talk back to him.

'I don't expect my chauffeur to wait around for me and

I was at the hospital last night,' he said smoothly, opening the door and jerking his head. 'Get in.'

Which meant that he did have a limo. And a chauffeur. *Ask a silly question...*

'I don't need a lift,' she said stiffly. 'I already have transport.'

And she wasn't ready to talk to him yet. She needed more time to work out her strategy. She also needed legal advice but she knew she couldn't afford that. Maybe she could persuade the bank to lend her some money.

'Transport?' He was frowning. 'You have a car?'

'Not exactly.' She avoided his gaze because looking at him affected her so dramatically. 'We take the bus.'

There was an ominous silence. 'You go home on a *bus*?'

'Well, two buses actually,' she told him, shifting Rosa more comfortably on her hip.

He was staring at her incredulously and it occurred to her that Nico Santini had probably never been on a bus in his life.

'I will give you a lift home.'

She clutched Rosa tightly, her reaction an instinctive rejection of his offer. 'I don't want a lift home. I'm fine on the bus.'

The skin over those incredible cheekbones was taut. '*Porca miseria*, my daughter is not travelling on a *bus*.'

If circumstances had been different she would have laughed at the look of horror on his face.

'It's a perfectly acceptable form of transport for most people,' Abby said defensively, and his eyes narrowed.

'But my daughter is not most people,' he said, his voice as smooth as silk. 'She will not travel on public transport—it is too risky.'

Abby blinked. Risky? For crying out loud, this was London in the rush-hour!

Then she remembered that Lucia had never been without a bodyguard at school.

To the Santinis it was a way of life.

'Look…' She kept her tone steady, more for her own benefit than his. She was trying to stay rational. 'No one knows Rosa is your daughter so she isn't at risk.'

'*I* know she's my daughter,' he pointed out immediately, 'and if I can get that information then so can others.'

Her heart gave a flutter and she stared at him. 'Are you seriously telling me that you think Rosa is at risk?'

'I don't want my daughter using public transport,' Nico said flatly. 'Now, get in the car. We have much to talk about.'

She shook her head. 'We have nothing to talk about. Nothing at all.'

He straightened with a fluid grace that reminded her of a lethal predator moving in for the kill. 'Then you should know that I have already contacted my lawyers and set in motion custody proceedings,' he said smoothly, and she felt her heart jump into her throat.

His lawyers?

'No judge is going to take a child away from a mother who loves her,' she said shakily, praying that she was right. She didn't have his ready access to endless funds so she had no way of obtaining her own legal advice. But surely the law wasn't that unfair?

Nico raised a dark eyebrow. 'You wish to discuss this in the hospital car park in front of an audience?'

Abby glanced around self-consciously and flushed as she intercepted several curious glances. 'I don't want to discuss it at all.'

Totally unperturbed, he gave a shrug and turned back to his car. 'In that case, I will see you in court.'

'No!' Her frantic protest made him stop and turn and he looked at her expectantly.

'You are ready to talk?'

She nodded, too upset to trust herself to speak. If she

opened her mouth she'd sob. And she'd rather swallow nails than lose control in front of Nico Santini again.

She clutched Rosa tighter and the little girl whimpered in protest.

'Let's go. She can go in the back,' Nico instructed, and she shook her head.

'I won't let her travel without a baby seat.'

Nico shot her a look of pure male exasperation. '*Dio*, you think I would be reckless with my own daughter? I purchased a seat today—take a look yourself if you don't believe me.'

Slight colour touching her cheeks, Abby peered into the back seat and saw the brand-new, top-of-the-range car seat strapped securely in the car. If she hadn't been in such a panic she would have laughed. She was willing to bet that he'd never put anything like that in his precious sports car before.

He drove fast but carefully, glancing into the back seat periodically to check on Rosa who was now fast asleep.

By the time they finally arrived at the tiny flat, Abby was shaking so much she wondered if her legs would hold her. Nico gathered the sleeping child against him and carried her into the house and laid her carefully on the sofa.

'Does she always sleep at this time?'

Abby bit her lip. 'Yes. It's the journey,' she muttered. 'It lulls her to sleep.'

His gaze was hard. 'In other words, she is tired from being left in a crèche all day.'

'She likes the crèche and I have to work!'

'Because you are a single parent,' he returned, his blue-black jaw tight and uncompromising.

'Plenty of people are single parents these days,' she said shakily, and he shot her a look of pure contempt.

'But rarely through choice. You made a conscious decision to have a baby without any financial or emotional support, and with that decision you chose to deprive her of all the things that a child has a right to. Most importantly, a father.'

Abby felt as though he'd stabbed her in the heart. It was true, of course. She *had* deprived Rosa of a father. But Rosa had a mother who adored her and that was worth a great deal.

Was Rosa really so badly off?

'I love her,' she choked, hanging onto her dignity by a thread. Never before in her life had she had to fight so hard not to cry. 'She's all I have in the world and if you take her...'

He frowned slightly, his dark eyes raking the pallor of her face. 'I no longer question your affection for her, but that doesn't alter the fact that she will have a better life with me.'

'How?' She gave up battling with tears and let them trickle down her face. So what if he thought she was a wimp? 'You're a complete workaholic, just like my father. When do you have time for a child? I can't see you giving up your job to look after her.'

'I have close family who would take on that responsibility,' he murmured, tension visible in his broad shoulders. 'Now that I'm convinced of your love for her, you will be allowed to see her.'

She scrubbed the tears away like a child and stared at him, appalled. 'And that's supposed to make it all right? I can see my own daughter *occasionally*?' He clearly believed that he was making an enormous concession and she gaped at him in disbelief. 'Why are you doing this? Why? If you want a child so badly, why not get married and have one of your own?'

There was a long silence and when he finally spoke his voice was flat, totally devoid of emotion. 'That isn't an option.'

'Getting married?' She stared at him stupidly, aware that

most of the members of her sex would have fallen over themselves to marry Nico Santini.

'Having more children.'

Abby was suddenly still, her attention caught by the tension in his shoulders. This had happened the last time she'd mentioned him having children of his own. 'But Rosa—'

'I developed testicular cancer almost two years ago.' He made the announcement with no emotion, in the same tone he might have used for reading the phone book. It was a statement of fact and no more. 'I had intensive chemotherapy. The cancer has gone but it is highly unlikely that I can father any more children.'

There was a shimmering silence while Abby digested that piece of information.

Nico Santini couldn't have more children?

With a stab of sympathy she reached out a hand and then let it drop to her side in sudden confusion. What was she thinking of? Her instinctive reaction had been to comfort him. Had she forgotten that he was the enemy? But, enemy or not, she felt sad for him.

She knew at first hand what it was like to be desperate for a family and suddenly it all fell into place.

'So that's why you want my child,' she whispered, and his dark gaze clashed with hers.

'She's my child, too. I tracked you down because I wanted to check that the child I fathered was happy and well cared for. Had Rosa been part of a loving family with two parents I never would have intervened, but in the circumstances I believe that she would be better off with me.'

Abby stared at him, her chest rising and falling as she breathed rapidly. 'I'm sorry that you can't have more children, I really am,' she croaked, her voice shaking with passion, 'but you can't take my Rosa. If you don't care about my feelings, at least think about her. I'm her mother. She needs me.'

'And she also needs her father.' His tone was devoid of

emotion. 'With me she will be part of a large and loving family who can give her everything.'

Abby's mouth was dry and the panic inside overwhelmed her. 'I'll get a lawyer.'

An ebony brow lifted. 'With what? Face it, there is no way you are in a position to contest my claim. One way or another, I will gain custody of Rosa.'

CHAPTER FOUR

'Don't let anyone take her but me, will you?' Abby handed
Rosa over to Karen who gave her a puzzled look.

'What on earth are you talking about? Who else is going
to want to take her?'

Abby bit her lip. It was an impossible situation. She
didn't want to tell Karen what was happening but she
wanted to protect Rosa. How could she be sure that Nico
wouldn't just take her?

'Just promise me,' she said urgently, scraping an escaped
strand of blonde hair behind her ear.

'All right, I promise, but I think you've gone mad.'
Karen gave Rosa a hug and smiled at Abby. 'How's
Thomas Wood?'

'Doing all right yesterday,' Abby's eyes were still on her
daughter. 'Might be back on the ward today. Depends how
it goes.'

'So the guy was as good as his reputation, then.' Karen's
tone was casual and Abby suppressed a sigh.

She didn't want to talk about Nico.

'He's a brilliant surgeon,' she said grudgingly, stooping
to pick up her bag. 'I'm off now. Call me if you need me.'

She leaned forward to kiss Rosa and then forced herself
to make her way to the ward, assuring herself that there
was no way Karen would let the baby go with Nico Santini.

Heather was already on the ward and clearly harassed.
'They're having a JCC this morning. Do you want to attend? It would be a good learning experience for you.'

The JCC—the joint cardiac conference—was a meeting
where everyone, including CICU staff, surgeons and car-

diologist, got together to discuss each child and decide on the best plan of management.

'Are you sure you're not too busy to spare me?' Abby had mixed feelings. Part of her was interested in sitting in on the conference, but she knew that it would mean coming into close contact with Nico and she wasn't sure that she could handle that.

'No, but I want you to go,' Heather said generously. 'They're transferring Thomas Wood back from CICU later on this morning so as long as you're back for that, we should manage fine. Do you know what happens at one of those meetings?'

'Not really.' Abby shook her head briefly. 'I always assumed everyone just pooled information and discussed the best way forward.'

'Well, that's right. Basically they discuss each child,' Heather explained. 'They look at the catheter and the echo and decide what type of operation is needed and how quickly. Whether it's an emergency that needs to be done in the next twenty-four hours or whether it should be delayed for a couple of months. If it's an emergency, they have to arrange a theatre slot and check that there are beds in CICU. I think you should go.'

'All right, if you're sure.' Abby made her way along to the meeting room and slipped into a seat towards the back of the room.

Nico and Jack, the cardiologist, were already deep in conversation about baby Hubbard.

'I've scheduled her for balloon atrial septostomy this afternoon,' Jack was saying, and Nico nodded approval.

'So we can discontinue the prostaglandin. Good.'

Andrea, the cardiac case manager who was the link between the ward, doctors and parents, made a few notes on her pad. 'So she can go home while she waits for her op?'

Nico frowned and turned his gaze to Abby. 'You said

that she has three other children and is on her own. Can she manage the baby, do you think?'

Everyone in the room suddenly seemed to be looking at her, and Abby felt her face grow hot. 'I'll talk to her when she visits tonight.'

After their emotionally charged confrontation the night before, how could he be so relaxed?

'Let us know the outcome.' Nico gave a brief nod and Andrea glanced between him and Jack.

'So if the mother is happy, when will you send her home?'

'Jack needs to do the atrial septostomy and then we will monitor her oxygen saturation,' Nico told her. 'If she maintains it between 60 and 70 per cent, we will send her home. If not, then she stays in and we operate.'

'And if her sats are all right, when will you operate?'

Jack looked at Nico. 'Two weeks?'

Nico nodded and they reviewed the tests together and discussed the operation.

When they were satisfied with the plan of action they moved on to the next child.

By the end of the meeting Abby's head was reeling. Each child had been reviewed in detail, with everyone in the room contributing to the discussion.

Back on the ward the CICU nurse handed over Thomas Wood and briefed Abby in detail.

'He's doing well. We've taken out the chest drain and the catheter. We're restricting his fluid intake because we don't want to overload the heart so we've been keeping him fairly dry, but for the next twenty-four hours he can have 65 mls of fluid per kilo.'

Which meant calculating everything, including feed and drugs.

The nurse finished the handover and Abby glanced at the monitors, checking that the baby's oxygen saturation was satisfactory. Then she used the dinamap to check Thomas's blood pressure.

'Do you really need to check his chest?' Lorna was look-ing pale and exhausted. 'I hate seeing the scar on his little body.'

'It's hard, I know, but we're giving him drugs for the pain and you'll be amazed by how quickly it heals,' Abby told her, her voice sympathetic. 'I have to check it for signs of bleeding, but it will only take a second.'

Very carefully she lifted the dressing and checked the stenotomy wound, satisfying herself that all looked well.

As she was replacing the dressing Nico strolled into the room, followed by a team of more junior doctors.

'Lorna...' he put a lean brown hand on her shoulder '...how are you feeling?'

'I'm doing fine.' Lorna gave him a shaky smile and her eyes filled. 'I don't know how to thank you.'

'No thanks are necessary.' Nico walked towards the cot and checked the stenotomy wound himself. Then his eyes lifted to the monitors, checking the readings. 'That is all looking good. The operation went well.'

Lorna breathed out heavily. 'When do you think he might be able to go home?'

Nico smiled. 'Perhaps in another week. We will need to keep an eye on him and see how he goes.'

He took time to answer all Lorna's questions and when he finally left the room Abby stared after him helplessly, wondering how on earth she was going to fight him.

It was towards the end of her shift when the hospital crèche called to say that Rosa had developed a temperature.

Abby felt her heart lurch. She'd known that Rosa was slightly off colour but she'd been hoping that it was nothing more than a teething problem. Now it seemed as though it could be something more.

Feeling guilty for deserting the ward when they were

busy, she asked Heather's permission to finish early and
then she made her way down to the crèche.

Rosa was crying miserably, her cheeks pink and blotched
with tears.

'Oh, sweetheart…' Abby reached out for her and cuddled
her close, feeling just how hot she was.

'I gave her some Calpol half an hour ago,' Karen told
her, 'but so far it hasn't had any effect. You were obviously
right about her coming down with something. Mother's instinct, I suppose.'

'Maybe. Thanks, Karen.' Still trying to soothe a wailing
Rosa, Abby gathered up her bags and struggled down the
corridor. There was no way she could take the child on a
bus like this. She'd have to blow the last of her month's
pay cheque and take a taxi home.

As she reached the hospital entrance Rosa's wails increased and Abby felt more and more anxious.

Was it something serious or was it just a simple virus?

One of the most frightening things about being a single
parent was handling a sick child alone.

'How is Rosa doing?' Nico's smooth tones came from
right behind her and she turned in dismay.

Typical.

He was just about the last person that she wanted to
bump into at this precise moment. He'd probably find some
way of blaming her for Rosa's illness and use it against
her.

'She's not well and I need a taxi.'

'I know she isn't well,' he said calmly. 'I was standing
next to Heather when you asked if you could leave, but
you were in such a state that you didn't even notice me.
And you don't need to call a taxi. I'll take you home.'

She started to shake her head and then realised how foolish that was. She needed to get Rosa home as fast as possible, and as there was no sign of a taxi Nico was the only
option.

'All right.' She tried not to sound grudging. 'But I want to call at the surgery on the way home so that our GP can check her over.'

Nico unlocked the car and held the door open for her. 'Abby, I'm a doctor, remember? I'll check her over myself when we get her home.'

Abby gritted her teeth. 'You're a heart surgeon.'

'Well, believe it or not, I am vaguely familiar with other parts of the anatomy,' he said dryly, and she bit her lip.

'I just don't think you're the right person.'

She didn't want him near Rosa. She didn't trust him.

He was totally unmoved by her declaration. 'Just get in the car.'

She looked at him in helpless frustration. The man just didn't understand the word 'no'!

But she needed to get Rosa home.

'You must have been an awful toddler,' she muttered as she strapped Rosa carefully into the car seat.

One dark eyebrow rose. 'You wish to know about my childhood?'

'No.' She closed the passenger door and stalked round to the driver's side. 'I don't want to know anything about you. Frankly, I wouldn't care if I never saw you again.'

'Oh, you're going to see me again, Abby,' he said softly. 'You're going to see plenty of me, but now isn't the time to talk about that. Now, get in and let's get her home.'

Once inside, Nico immediately examined Rosa.

'I can't see anything obvious wrong with her.' Finally he put down his stethoscope and looked at the baby thoughtfully. 'Her chest is clear, her throat is slightly pink but nothing dramatic and her ears are fine. We'll just watch her for a few hours and see how she goes.'

'*We*?'

Every nerve in her body frayed with worry, Abby stared at him blankly. 'Does that mean that you're planning to stay here?'

'*Sì.*' His black eyes clashed with hers. 'I won't leave her while she is ill and it will give us a chance to talk further.'

'Oh, yippee,' Abby muttered, and his eyes narrowed.

'I haven't eaten yet. I'm very hungry.'

'You know where the kitchen is,' Abby said tartly. 'Help yourself to anything you find.'

If he was expecting her to cook for him, he could think again.

For a brief moment she thought she saw surprise in his dark eyes. Well, tough, she thought, cuddling Rosa on her lap. Doubtless he was used to women falling over themselves to service his every need. She had no intention of joining them.

'You should get something to eat yourself.'

'I'm not hungry.' Distracted, she put her hand on Rosa's chest to check her temperature again. 'She's so hot....'

Nico's phone rang and as he entered into a detailed discussion with one of the doctors at the hospital, he strode out of the room and closed the door quietly behind him. Abby kicked off her shoes and curled up more comfortably in the old rocking chair that she'd found in a junk shop and lovingly restored. She knew that she ought to have followed him and asked him about his intentions but she was too much of a coward. And, anyway, Rosa needed her. The toddler was clinging to her like a limpet and there was no way she was letting her go.

About twenty minutes later something about the way Rosa was breathing made her suddenly anxious.

Reaching out a hand, she touched the baby's chest again and felt a dart of panic as she realised how hot she was.

'Oh, sweetheart, you're burning up again.' She checked her watch but it was too soon to give her any more medicine.

Rosa barely reacted to her touch, lying listlessly on her lap, showing no interest in anything. Really worried, Abby stood up and put the little girl in her cot, thinking that cuddling her so close must be raising her temperature. She was too hot and needed to be cooled down fast.

Rosa protested feebly as Abby put her down but within seconds of being placed in the cot the little girl went rigid and started to fit. Abby felt panic slam through her body.

'Nico!'

Frantic with worry, she shouted his name, anxiety about Rosa overriding all other considerations. Whatever else he might be, she knew he was a superb doctor.

He was beside her in an instant.

'What's the matter?'

'She got hotter and hotter and now she's fitting.' Abby felt sick and watched helplessly while Nico swiftly cleared the child's airway and adjusted her position.

'Call an ambulance,' he instructed calmly. 'If she doesn't stop fitting she'll need diazepam and I don't have any with me.'

Her whole body trembling, Abby sprinted along to the sitting room and dialled with a shaking hand.

By the time she returned to the bedroom Rosa had stopped fitting but her lips were blue and she didn't respond as Nico swiftly stripped her of the rest of her clothes.

'We need to bring her temperature down. Do you have a fan?'

Abby shook her head, gulping in air as she stared at her limp daughter. 'No.'

'Well, let's start by opening the window.' Nico dropped the clothes on the floor and left just the nappy on. 'We'll cover her in just a cotton sheet. What time did she have paracetamol?'

'Just two hours ago,' Abby told him, feeling utterly helpless as she looked at her daughter. 'She can't have any more yet.'

'But we can give her ibuprofen when she gets to hospital. She's still too drowsy to take it from us anyway. Her pulse is a bit fast and so is her breathing but she seems OK.'

Nico was checking the child's ears and throat again. 'Her pharynx is still slightly red. But that is all I can find wrong with her. Her temperature is very high, so I'm sure this is a febrile seizure and nothing more than that.'

Abby stared at him, desperately hoping that he was right. She was well aware that young children with very high temperatures could fit, but she was also aware that some of those went on to have epilepsy.

Nico looked at her and frowned. 'It is not epilepsy,' he said shortly, clearly reading her mind. 'I am as sure as I can be of that. She is the right age for a febrile seizure and her temperature is impossibly high.'

Abby voiced the other fear that had been nagging at her. 'Could she have meningitis?'

He hesitated. 'It's possible,' he said finally, 'but I think it unlikely. However, they might well want to do a lumbar puncture to be sure.'

At that moment Abby heard the ambulance arrive and ran to the door to let them in.

Nico spoke to them and within minutes Rosa was loaded into the ambulance.

Abby hesitated by the doors of the ambulance. 'Will you follow us?'

A glimmer of surprise showed in his dark eyes before he masked the reaction and nodded. 'Of course. I'll be right behind you.' He hesitated for a moment and then put a hand on her shoulder. 'Try not to worry. I'm sure it is just a virus that will settle in time. You know that it is common for children of this age to fit. They are not always able to control their temperatures like adults. It doesn't mean that she'll have long-term problems.'

She nodded, her lower lip caught between her teeth. She felt as though she was going crazy. She knew she ought to hate him and yet she was hugely relieved that he'd been there to deal with Rosa. For once she was grateful that he was a control freak. She'd needed someone to take over.

Once at the hospital, Nico didn't leave Rosa's side.

'We need to do a lumbar puncture,' the paediatrician said, and the colour drained from Abby's face.

'You think she has meningitis?'

Nico frowned at her. 'It's a routine check—they are trying to find the source of the infection. She has a high temperature and she's had a fit. We must check for meningitis. Go and get a coffee.'

Abby shook her head, knowing that someone had to hold the child while the doctor performed the test.

'No,' she said shakily. 'I'll do it. I want to be there for her. I'm her mother.'

Nico took her to one side so that no one could hear her. 'You're also so stressed that you will be doing her no favours,' he said quietly. 'Don't be stubborn. You are in no fit state to hold the child. I will do it.'

Abby pulled away from him, shaking her head. 'No. She needs her mother.' She walked quickly back to the paediatrician who was preparing for the test.

In the end it wasn't as bad as she'd feared. Rosa was so poorly that she barely flinched when the doctor put the needle in her back to draw off some of the spinal fluid.

'It's clear,' he said as he let the fluid drop into the bottle. 'It looks fine but I'll get this off to the lab. I suspect that this is just a virus that we won't be able to identify. We'll keep her in and see how she goes. One of you is welcome to stay with her.'

The paediatric ward was well designed, with beds next to the cots so that a parent could stay with the child.

Embarrassed that the paediatrician had assumed that they were in some way connected, Abby waited for Nico to correct him but he didn't.

Instead he questioned the other doctor minutely, checking that all the necessary tests had been performed and that every possibility had been covered.

For once Abby was thoroughly relieved that he was there.

'We've given her more Calpol and ibuprofen so we'll just keep an eye on her temperature and see what happens,' the paediatrician said, peeling off his sterile gloves and tossing them in the bin. 'I think you'll find that she settles during the night.'

He left the room and Nico turned to Abby.

'You aren't prepared for a stay in hospital. Do you need me to go home and fetch you something?'

She blushed. It sounded ridiculously intimate, and yet only a few hours earlier this man had been voicing his intention to take her child away from her.

'I don't need anything,' she muttered, all her attention focused on Rosa who was breathing noisily in the cot.

'In that case, I'm going to pop back down to the ward,' he told her. 'I want to check on a couple of patients so I'll see you later.' He hesitated briefly and then looked at her, his gaze disturbingly direct. 'You were brave to hold her for that lumbar puncture when you were so upset.'

Without waiting for a reply, he left the room and Abby stared after him, trying to work out the implications of what he'd just said. Was he praising her? Was he finally acknowledging that Rosa needed her?

And if that was the case, surely he would see that it wouldn't be fair to take Rosa away?

Rosa awoke at three in the morning, fretful and crying for her mother. A nurse was standing over her, checking her temperature.

'Is it OK to hold her?' Abby struggled to sit up and looked at the nurse anxiously in the dim light. 'I don't want to send her temperature skyward again. I know she needs to be kept cool.'

The nurse smiled softly as she checked the thermometer. 'Don't worry about that. Her temperature has come down a lot and I think what she really needs is a cuddle with her mother.'

As Rosa snuggled contentedly into her chest, Abby looked up and saw Nico standing in the doorway.

His dark eyes were watchful, his expression impossible to read as he studied the two of them.

'I-is something the matter?' Abby stammered slightly, and held Rosa closer. 'Do you think I should put her back in the cot?'

Whatever she felt about him as a man, she respected his opinion as a doctor.

'No, the nurse is right.' His voice was gruff. 'She needs her mother.'

For a tense moment their eyes met and Abby knew that they were both thinking the same thing—*that if he carried out his threat, he was going to be taking Rosa from her mother for ever.*

Vulnerable from lack of sleep and worry, Abby felt her eyes fill.

'Nico—'

'Not now.' His voice was low and gruff. 'We'll talk about it later.'

So he knew exactly what she was thinking.

Seeing her tears and misinterpreting the cause, the nurse slipped an arm around her shoulder.

'There, pet, don't upset yourself. She's going to be fine.'

Abby struggled to pull herself together but when she finally looked up there was no sign of Nico.

He reappeared the following morning, his expression grim. 'We have a new problem, which I'm afraid I didn't anticipate.'

Abby looked up from sponging Rosa. 'What's wrong?'

'I underestimated my importance to the British tabloid

press.' His tone bitter, he flung several newspapers down on the bed next to her.

She blanched as she saw the photo and read the story.

ITALIAN BILLIONAIRE IN PATERNITY CLAIM
Sources have revealed that top heart surgeon Domenico Santini, heir to the Santini fortune, has recently discovered that he is the father of a baby daughter. Nurse Abigail Harrington is known to be close friends with Santini's sister and has never revealed the identity of the father of her child. However, friends confirm that she was in Italy two years ago and there is speculation that the pair might have had a relationship. Santini has refused to comment on the rumours, but a spokesman for the hospital has confirmed that he will be working there for the foreseeable future.

Abby dropped the paper and stared at him, appalled. 'Where did they get this information?'

'That isn't important. What is important now is protecting Rosa.'

She looked at him blankly. 'Wh-what do you mean?'

Why would Rosa need protection?

He muttered under his breath in Italian and raked long fingers through his glossy dark hair. 'I can't believe that you are that naïve. The press are now camped outside the hospital entrance,' he said through gritted teeth, his eyes midnight black with anger. 'Given the opportunity, they will slip past Security and find their way up here.'

'But why are they so interested?'

'Because my sex life has always interested the media,' he said bitterly. 'I forgot just how bad your press is over here.'

Abby stared at the paper again and her cheeks flushed. 'They think we've had a relationship....'

He gave a short laugh. 'And maybe we should be thankful for that.'

Abby looked up at him, knowing that he was right. If the press ever found out the truth, they would have a field day.

'Could they find out?' she whispered, and his jaw tightened.

'I don't know. I suppose it is possible,' he said finally, lines of strain showing around his handsome features. 'We need to be prepared for that.'

As he finished speaking a burly man appeared in the doorway and spoke to Nico in Italian.

Nico replied and then looked at Abby. 'This is Matteo Parini. He is on my father's security team. He will stay with you until Rosa is allowed out of hospital. You'll both be safe with him.'

Security team?

Abby's jaw dropped. He'd arranged for her to have a *bodyguard*? Just what exactly was he afraid of?

'S-surely we're s-safe enough in here,' she stammered, but Nico ignored her, speaking to the other man in rapid Italian and then turning back to her, his expression cold and unsmiling.

'I have a ward round in ten minutes and then a theatre list. I'll try and pop up at lunchtime. In the meantime, don't leave the ward and if you need anything at all, ask Matt. He'll arrange it for you.'

With that he turned on his heel and left her staring after him with a stunned expression on her face.

Matt gave her a sympathetic smile. 'He has a tendency to dominate but take it from me—he has your best interests at heart.'

Which confirmed that Matt didn't have the slightest clue what was going on, she thought dully. Of course Nico didn't have her interests at heart. He had his own interests at heart, which was why he was protecting Rosa.

'I don't understand any of this—' She broke off, and

looked at him doubtfully. 'Are you going to spend the whole day here?'

Matt nodded. 'There are a herd of journalists outside the hospital and now the story is out, goodness knows who else might be lurking.'

Lurking? Her heart missed a beat. 'Are you talking about kidnap?'

Matt gave her a reassuring smile. 'It's only a precaution.' He glanced into the cot and his hard expression softened. 'She's the spitting image of her father.'

Which meant that there was no point in denying her paternity, Abby thought helplessly. Why couldn't Rosa have looked more like her?

'How did they find out about Rosa?'

Matt let out a long breath. 'We don't know that yet, but you can be sure that Nico will find out and I certainly wouldn't want to be in the culprit's shoes when he does. He's not a man to cross.'

He looked up as a cleaner tapped on the door.

'Can I come in and do the room?'

Matt straightened and his shoulders virtually filled the doorway. 'Sorry, no. Only medical staff.'

The cleaner scowled. 'I've got a job to do.'

'And so have I,' Matt replied calmly. 'If there's a problem I'll clear it with your supervisor.'

His tone was civil but the cleaner looked him in the eye and clearly saw something that made her back away.

Matt watched her go and then relaxed against the doorframe again.

'Why wouldn't you let her in?' Abby asked hesitantly, totally out of her depth. 'She was just a cleaner.'

'Was she?' Matt gave her a gentle smile. 'You really are an innocent, aren't you? She could be press. Or someone else. No one comes in this room that isn't essential. Nico's orders, I'm afraid.'

'I don't understand any of this. How did you get here so quickly? The papers only came out this morning.'

'They were printed last night,' Matt explained patiently, 'and we had warning that the story was going to break yesterday. And I was already here.'

'Already here? You mean Nico has a bodyguard in England?'

Matt gave a rueful smile. 'Not exactly, although strictly speaking he ought to. He always says that he can't operate with me hanging over his shoulder. And the honest truth is he can handle himself as well as I can. He's an expert in martial arts and he can use a gun with a precision that makes me green with envy. But basically the guy just wants to be a doctor and he can't stand the fuss that goes with being a Santini.'

'So why were you already in England?'

'It was a compromise. The boss wanted me close by in case anything happened, and as it turns out he was right.'

'The boss?'

'Nico's father. He owns and runs Santini Medical Supplies.' Matt looked at her curiously. 'You really don't know any of this, do you?'

No, but she'd heard of Santini Medical Supplies. Who hadn't? They were one of the biggest medical equipment companies in the world.

Abby realised that if Matt had read the papers, he probably thought that she and Nico had been involved in some sort of steamy relationship in the past, which meant that she should have known all these details about him.

At that moment Rosa woke up and Abby lifted her out of her cot and gave her a cuddle, relieved to find that she was much cooler.

The rest of the morning past quickly and the doctors came back to look at Rosa just before lunchtime.

'She seems much better.' The paediatrician nodded with satisfaction as he finished examining her. 'You can take her home this afternoon if you're happy with that. If you were on your own with her I'd suggest you stayed another night just for your peace of mind, but as her father is a doctor I'm sure you'll be fine at home.'

'Oh, but—' Abby started to correct him but Nico's voice interrupted her.

'That will be fine,' he said smoothly. 'I've arranged it so that I'm not on call tonight. I will be able to watch her.'

'Fine.' The paediatrician nodded, went through the test results with Nico and then made for the door. 'Oh, by the way…' He gave a rueful smile. 'You've attracted quite a lot of attention outside. If you need any help making your exit, I can call hospital security.'

Matt glanced at Nico who shook his head briefly. 'I have my own staff who are well used to dealing with this sort of thing, but thank you for your help.'

The doctor left and Abby glanced at Nico, wondering what he had planned. He was speaking to Matt in rapid Italian and the other man nodded and left the room at a brisk walk. Nico turned to Abby, his expression calm.

'Gather her things together and we'll take her home.'

Abby didn't even question how he planned to achieve a discreet exit with half the British press camped outside the hospital entrance. He clearly had it all covered.

As soon as she'd stuffed the last of her possessions into her bag, Nico took her arm and led her into the corridor and into the lift. They went down to the basement and emerged into one of the underground corridors which mapped their way beneath the hospital.

Matt was waiting, a mobile phone in his hand and a look of anticipation on his face.

Abby felt her heart lurch. They were obviously expecting trouble.

Together they flanked her as they walked briskly up the corridor, taking various turns that left her completely con-fused.

'I have no idea where we are,' she confessed to Matt at one point, 'and I work in this hospital. How do you know where to go?'

'It's my job,' he answered lightly, taking her arm and steering her into a small corridor.

He spoke in a low tone and for the first time Abby noticed the tiny earpiece. She glanced at Nico.

'It's like being with James Bond,' she muttered, and he gave a wry smile.

'The technology my father uses is probably more advanced.' He put a hand on her arm and looked questioningly at Matt who gave a brief nod.

'You follow Matt,' Nico instructed. 'I will take Rosa.'

Without arguing she did as he ordered, handing over her daughter and staying close to the bodyguard. He led her up a narrow flight of steps and she emerged into the daylight to find a limousine waiting.

She stopped dead but Nico gave her a sharp push from behind and she stumbled into the car without further question, aware that it had pulled away from the kerb before the door had even closed behind them.

Nico strapped Rosa into a child seat and spoke quickly to the driver.

Abby glanced over her shoulder but there was no sign of anyone following them.

'Where is this entrance?' She worked in the hospital and didn't recognise it at all.

'It's the psychiatric unit,' Matt told her. 'We arranged for a blonde woman to walk out of the paediatric entrance with a dark-haired toddler to keep the press busy. They should have realised by now that it wasn't us, but hopefully it will have distracted them sufficiently for us to get away.'

Abby blinked. It was a completely different world.

Rosa started to fret slightly and Abby slid across the seat and gave her a kiss.

'It's OK, sweetheart,' she murmured gently, 'we'll soon be home.'

She glanced out of the window to see where they were and realised that they weren't anywhere near her flat. They were driving away from the East End, through the centre of London and past the Serpentine.

'Where are we going?'

'Somewhere safe.' Nico leaned back against the seat and exchanged a glance with Matt.

She looked at him anxiously. 'But—'

'We'll discuss it later.'

Obviously he didn't want to talk about it in front of Matt and his driver, and she slunk closer to Rosa, feeling horribly out of her depth.

This couldn't be happening to her. She led a totally normal life, boring by some standards, but that was the way she liked it. She liked the predictability, the security of her existence. Since Nico Santini had strode into her life, all that had been turned upside down.

They drove for about twenty minutes and then the car plunged into an underground car park and came to a halt by a bank of lifts.

Matt was out of the car in a second, holding the door open for Abby. Nico took Rosa and they stepped into the lift.

It purred up to the top of the building and when the doors opened Abby gave a gasp of surprise.

A glass atrium spilled light onto a marble hallway complete with a fountain which gushed water over carefully placed rocks.

Rosa squealed with delight and reached out both hands.

Nico smiled indulgently. Understanding what she wanted, he immediately walked his daughter over to the fountain and let her hold her hand under the water, his smile broadening as she splashed him with a delicious giggle.

Matt grinned at his employer. 'Nice to know that someone likes it, boss.'

Nico gave a wry smile and turned to look at Abby. 'When this apartment was built, the designer was given free rein,' he explained. 'We all thought she'd gone overboard with the fountain. Maybe we were wrong.'

'Rosa loves water.' Abby was watching him in amazed fascination. He was so visibly smitten with his daughter. She tried to imagine another human being splashing him with water and being rewarded with a smile, and failed dismally. If she'd had any doubts about his feelings for his daughter, they vanished in an instant. 'If this is your apartment, surely the press know about it?'

'Not yet.' Nico shifted Rosa in his arms and walked towards a large living room. 'We've used various means of keeping it a secret, but I have no doubt that it will take them very little time to find us.'

Abby looked at him in dismay. 'And then what happens?'

'Even if they locate the building, this apartment is totally secure.' Nico turned to the other two men and spoke in Italian. They both swiftly melted into the background, leaving Abby and Nico alone.

'I apologise for bringing you here with no warning, but I didn't want to discuss our situation in front of my staff.'

Well, of course he didn't. Threatening to take her daughter hardly did him credit, did it?

'Why didn't you just drop us at home?'

His mouth tightened. 'Your flat would not have been safe.'

'But if they find out that we're together here, it just confirms the rumours.'

'I think we need to accept that this is one story that is going to be impossible to deny.' His gaze was steady. 'Unfortunately they are already convinced that Rosa is my daughter, and one only has to look at her to see the resemblance. Also, you have always concealed the identity of her father from everyone. Such secrecy will inevitably fuel the speculation that she is my daughter.'

Colour flooded her cheeks and she sank into the nearest chair with a thump.

'So…' She worked hard to keep the tremor out of her voice. 'We need to decide what we're going to do.'

'I've already decided.' Nico turned towards her, broad-shouldered and handsome, arrogantly sure of himself and totally in control. 'We will get married as soon as it can be arranged.'

CHAPTER FIVE

ABBY stared at him stupidly.

'*Married?*' Her voice was little more than a squeak. 'You have to be joking.'

'If you knew me better, you would know that I never joke about anything as serious as marriage,' Nico drawled, his eyes holding a hint of humour. 'Come through to the kitchen. You haven't eaten anything since yesterday lunchtime and we need to see if we can tempt Rosa with some food.'

Food?

'But—'

'Abby…' He dragged long fingers through his black hair, his voice weary and heavily accented. 'I have been up all night and I had a long theatre list this morning. Then I had to dodge the press in order to return to my home. I'm not exactly at my best. We'll sort out Rosa and discuss the details later.'

Details?

Her slim fingers dug into damp palms. 'You're the last man in the world I'd want to marry. I don't want to marry you and you can't possibly want to marry me.' She blurted the words out impulsively and then clamped her teeth on her lip and braced herself for the full force of his anger.

Instead he smiled, clearly amused by her passionate declaration. 'Actually, I'm becoming more taken with the idea by the minute. You're the first woman I've ever met who doesn't have designs on me. In fact, you don't seem to want a single thing from me, and I find that completely novel.'

Abby stared at him in mystified fascination. He just

didn't get it, did he? She'd just refused him but he hadn't even heard her.

He truly didn't understand the meaning of the word 'no'.

Maybe she needed to be blunt. 'You barged into my life without warning and threatened to take my child from me. You have the sensitivity of a sledgehammer. Give me one reason why I would even consider marrying you.'

'Well, most women start with my wallet,' he drawled softly, and she gave an incredulous laugh.

In her opinion, all the money in the world wouldn't compensate for being in a loveless marriage. 'I'm not interested in your money. Money doesn't make a family happy,' she said, working hard to hang onto her composure. 'It's love and attention from parents that does that.'

Something that she'd never had.

'I agree,' he said confidently, his dark eyes fixed on her face. 'And Rosa will have that. You cannot possibly be pretending that she won't benefit from also living with her father.'

She could barely hide her frustration. 'But we don't love each other.'

He frowned impatiently. 'I admire you professionally and I appreciate your deep love for Rosa. The rest is irrelevant. Marriages based on love frequently come unstuck. Mutual understanding is all we need. I don't need you to love me.'

He admired her professionally? He appreciated her love for Rosa? He certainly didn't win any awards for romantic proposals of marriage.

She looked at him helplessly. 'And if I say no?'

'Then you lose Rosa.'

His flat statement made the colour drain out of her face and she forced herself to face the facts.

For all his faults, Nico had struck up a warm relationship with his daughter in the short time they'd known each other. Seeing them together just sharpened the guilt she felt at depriving Rosa of the chance to grow up with a father.

Marrying Nico Santini would undoubtedly benefit Rosa, but what about the price for her personally?

Every time he walked into a room her stomach tied itself in knots and her body shook with nervous tension. How could she contemplate marrying him?

'There must be another way,' she said helplessly, and he shrugged.

'There isn't,' he said calmly, walking towards the kitchen without a backward glance.

She followed him almost at a run, outrage mingling with panic.

He settled Rosa in a high chair and started opening cupboards. 'What does she eat?'

'Anything. Everything.' Abby felt as though her head was bursting. He seemed to think that the conversation was finished. 'She isn't fussy.'

'*Bene*. She can have pasta.' Nico removed a packet from the cupboard.

'But you can't possibly—' She broke off in mid-sentence, suddenly distracted by the fact that he was reading the back of the packet. 'What are you doing?'

'Reading the instructions.'

'Instructions?' She looked at him incredulously. 'It's just dried pasta. You cook it in boiling water. What do you normally do with it?'

'Normally I have a chef,' he announced, emptying the contents into a large saucepan. 'But I wanted to have privacy while we sort out details so he has gone with Matt and my driver.'

Chef?

'You're cooking too much,' she said automatically as she saw the volume of pasta he'd poured into the pan. 'That's enough to feed an army.'

She got to her feet and walked across to him, taking matters into her own hands.

'I can't believe that you can do a complex heart operation but you can't cook pasta.' She poured half the pasta back into the packet and flicked the switch on the kettle.

'Abby,' his voice was patient. 'I spend eighteen hours a day at the hospital, sometimes more. I certainly don't want to return home and start cooking a meal. Fortunately, I don't have to. If you open the fridge you'll find a variety of sauces that my chef prepared earlier. Help yourself to whatever you think she'd like.'

Abby found a Bolognese sauce and emptied it into a pan.

Nico looked over her shoulder. 'Will she need that puréed? There's a gadget somewhere in the kitchen…'

'She's a year old,' Abby reminded him, giving him an odd look. 'She eats everything that you and I eat in exactly the same format.'

He lifted his eyebrows. 'She doesn't mind lumps?'

'She loves lumps. Toast, roast potatoes—you name it, she eats it.' Abby glanced at him and took a deep breath. 'How do you plan to be a good father when you can't even cook for her and you don't know what she eats?'

'I'm learning as fast as I can, but I came to that same conclusion myself,' he confessed calmly, watching as she stirred the source. 'Last night when I saw you with her in the hospital I realised that Rosa is very attached to you.'

Her heart lifted. 'But if you can see that, surely you can't threaten to take her from me.'

'I also believe that she needs her father.' His tone was cool. 'Which is why we will get married. It is the perfect solution.'

He really was serious.

Abby's whole body felt hot and strange. The mere thought of being married to Nico Santini made her shake with nerves. On the other hand, he just meant it as a business arrangement, she assured herself. He certainly didn't have any feelings for her personally. He wasn't suggesting that they become intimate.

Even so, the whole idea was ridiculous. He was a billionaire from one of the oldest and wealthiest families in Italy, whereas she...

The irony of the situation wasn't lost on her and she almost laughed aloud. There were probably thousands of women out there who would have done anything to be in her position.

'You can't possibly marry a penniless nurse,' she muttered, concentrating all her attention on the sauce as she attempted to reason with him. 'Your family would have a fit.'

'The opinion of my family is totally irrelevant, but I can assure you that my mother would be totally indifferent to your financial situation. She doesn't care about things like that. She would just be delighted to see me married,' he said wryly. 'Especially as you are the mother of my child.'

'But I'm *not*. I mean, not in *that* way. I mean we never— But if you marry me they'll think we did...' She broke off, painfully embarrassed. She'd never had this sort of conversation with anyone in her life before. 'They'll think we—'

'Were lovers?' Nico's tone was blunt. 'And that's exactly what we want them to think, *angelo*. The truth would undoubtedly sell more papers but I, for one, would rather not have the details of Rosa's paternity splashed across the press for all to read.' He shrugged off his jacket and removed his tie. 'If you marry me, we will be able to tell people that we had a relationship when you were on holiday in Italy, that I was unaware that you had become pregnant until recently. We are now reunited and deeply in love.'

Deeply in love?

Abby gaped at him. 'But why would you say that?'

'To please my mother and keep the press happy,' he said calmly, undoing his top button with lean, brown fingers.

'And because I don't want a breath of gossip attached to Rosa.'

'But people in the clinic know—'

'My brother will handle them. As a family we are very close.'

Abby sucked air into her lungs and tried to think logically. 'It doesn't make sense.'

'It makes perfect sense.' He contradicted her smoothly. 'I cannot have more children so I am determined to have Rosa, but I can see now that she also needs her mother. We will be a family.'

'But not a real family.'

He gave a careless shrug. 'This is the twenty-first century. The word "family" has achieved rather a broad definition.'

'And what do I get from marrying you?'

One dark eyebrow lifted mockingly. 'You get Rosa, and a lifestyle beyond your wildest dreams.'

'I don't have dreams about lifestyle,' Abby said flatly. 'There's more to life than money.'

Her time at school had taught her that. She'd been surrounded by the daughters of the rich and famous and she'd seen at first hand the problems that they'd often had to deal with. Nico's extreme wealth was one of the reasons they were currently hiding out in his apartment.

'If you don't want it for yourself, then think about what it would mean to Rosa. At the moment she is living in a damp, cramped little flat and soon you won't have anywhere to live at all. I still don't understand why you chose to have Rosa in such an unconventional way but, whatever your reasons, can you really deny that she'd be better off with two parents?'

Abby stared at the floor and blinked back tears. He was clever, she had to hand it to him. He'd discovered her weaknesses and was using the one argument that he knew would win her over. She'd never been hung up on the lack of money, knowing that such things weren't important to a child. But she'd always felt guilty that Rosa didn't have any family other than her. Most especially she didn't have a father.

And that was her fault.

She was painfully conscious of the fact that she'd taken the decision to go ahead and have a child on her own, but now she was being offered the chance to give her daughter a normal family life.

She almost laughed at her own thoughts. As if she had a choice! Nico had made it clear that he was taking Rosa anyway. The only choice she was being given was whether to go with her daughter. As his wife.

So what was her problem?

She should have hated him for threatening to take Rosa, but the truth was that she didn't. Part of her could even understand why he'd behaved the way he had. The knowledge that he was unable to father a child must have been almost unbearable for such a proud Italian male. It was hardly surprising that he'd gone after Rosa. He wanted a child and she knew all about wanting children.

And there was no doubting his love for his daughter. Even offering to marry her was driven by his love for Rosa. He genuinely believed that the child would be better off with two parents and was willing to sacrifice himself for that belief.

Abby bit her lip.

And that was the problem, of course. He was sacrificing himself. There was no love or affection involved. It would be a marriage of convenience.

Abby glanced at him surreptitiously, taking in the tangle of dark curls visible at the neck of his shirt. He was one hundred per cent virile male and the thought of being married to him, of spending time with him on a regular basis, made her struggle for breath.

But it wasn't going to be a physical relationship, she

reminded herself. It was purely a business arrangement. A marriage for the benefit of Rosa. And although she was suspicious of wealth, could she really deny Rosa the chances that money could buy her or the opportunity to have a loving, extended family?

Totally distracted, she watched while Rosa fed herself the pasta, using a mixture of fingers and spoon, spreading some of it on her face and some of it on the table.

If she'd expected Nico to be fazed by a messy toddler, she was disappointed.

He watched with quiet amusement as Rosa attacked the food with chortles of delight, and then finally fetched a cloth to clean her up.

She had to hand it to him, he was impressive. Even the antics of a mischievous toddler didn't threaten that legendary cool.

'I'm sorry about your kitchen floor,' Abby muttered, suddenly realising just what a mess her daughter had made of his pristine, hand-painted kitchen. There seemed to be splodges of Bolognese sauce everywhere.

'I'm delighted that she enjoys pasta so much,' came his calm reply as he lifted the little girl out of the chair and carefully wiped her face and hands. 'She is clearly more Italian than English. My mother will adore her.'

She studied him curiously, thinking how human he could be at times.

'Are you due back at the hospital?'

'Tomorrow.'

'Have the staff seen the papers?'

She hated the thought of the staff gossiping.

'Of course. Which is why we need to make a decision about the future.'

'If I married you—what would happen?' She bit her lip nervously, hardly able to believe she'd even asked the question.

'You and Rosa would come and live with me here,' he

said immediately. 'I would finish my contract with the hospital and then we would move back to Italy.'

'You want us to live in Italy?'

'*Sì*—of course.' Nico nodded, clearly surprised by her question. 'It is my home. I travel for my work, but my base is Italy. I have homes in Milan and Rome, a ski lodge in Cortina and my family owns a villa in Sardinia. All my family are in Italy. Rosa's family. I want her to be near them and I want her to speak Italian.'

'But if I married you—if we pretended that we—' She broke off, finding the conversation impossibly difficult. 'I mean, Lucia would know the truth. And Carlo. They both know that we never had a relationship. That Rosa was—'

'You can safely leave them both to me.'

'And there's another thing.' She flushed deeply and he lifted an eyebrow.

'Go on.'

'I just don't think we could be convincing. No one in their right mind would believe that you'd fallen for me.' She hugged herself with her arms, hideously self-conscious. 'I mean, look at me! I'm just a nurse, Nico. I'm not exactly the sort of girl that you usually wear on your arm.'

He frowned at her as if the thought hadn't occurred to him before, and then he reached forward and jerked the elastic band out of her ponytail, letting her blonde hair fall softly over her shoulders.

'What are you doing?' She clutched at it, painfully aware that she'd been up all night with Rosa and hadn't had time even to comb her hair. She must look an absolute fright.

'I would certainly never date a woman with her hair in an elastic band,' Nico said dryly, his aim perfect as he tossed the offending article into the bin. 'As for the rest—although you seem totally unaware of the fact, you have a stunning face and figure, *cara mia*. No red-blooded male, seeing you on my arm, will have any trouble seeing why I married you.'

A stunning face and figure?

Abby gaped at him. Nico Santini thought she was *stunning*?

Something shifted inside her and she looked at him closely, but he merely returned her gaze steadily, nothing in those fabulous dark eyes giving the slightest clue as to what he was thinking.

Abby stared at him helplessly, feeling completely trapped. If she said yes, it meant spending the rest of her life in close proximity to someone who drove her to a permanent state of nervous tension, but Rosa would gain a family. If she said no, she would lose Rosa.

And that just wasn't an option that she could ever contemplate.

'All right,' she said in a small voice, not meeting his eyes. 'I'll marry you if it means that I can stay with Rosa. But it's a business arrangement only.'

'Agreed.'

Without a flicker of emotion he rose to his feet in a fluid movement and picked up the phone. 'I'll make arrangements for us to be married here in the next couple of weeks and then we'll go home to Italy for our honeymoon.'

Honeymoon.

The kitchen suddenly felt hot and airless and Abby took a gulp of air and concentrated on cleaning up Rosa.

It wouldn't be a real honeymoon, she reminded herself quickly.

He was just taking her to meet his family.

It was a holiday really. Something that she and Rosa had never had together because such an option was well outside her tight budget. She should be looking forward to it.

So why did she feel as though she was entering the lion's den?

Abby stayed at Nico's apartment for another three days until she was sure that Rosa had recovered sufficiently to go back to the crèche. During that time she rarely saw Nico, although his staff were incredibly attentive.

Giovanni, the chef, took the time to discover her favourite foods and Rosa adored him from the first moment, eating everything he put in front of her with a messy enthusiasm that clearly delighted him.

Matt, the bodyguard, was always nearby, his broad-shouldered bulk a constant reminder of the life she was taking on.

It was he who vetoed her plan to take the bus to work on her first day back.

'Are you trying to get me fired? I have worked for the Santini family since I left the army,' he told her, 'and they are excellent employers. I have no wish to put my job at risk.'

'Surely the press won't be looking for me on a bus,' she reasoned, and he gave her a pitying look that answered her question.

'No bus,' he told her firmly, his eyes sympathetic. 'Nico's orders. If you want to go anywhere, you go in the limo.'

'The limo!' She gaped at him. 'But that's ridiculous! I can't turn up at work in a limo! I'm just a nurse.'

'You're also Domenico Santini's fiancée,' Matt reminded her dryly. 'And Rosa is his daughter. There's no way she's going anywhere without protection.'

'Well, what happens when we get to work? Am I allowed to put her in the crèche?'

He nodded. '*Sì*. We have run a thorough security check on the staff and Nico is satisfied that she is as safe there as anywhere. And she clearly enjoys the company. And, anyway, I will be around.'

Abby looked at him. 'Around?'

'Yes, I'll be around the hospital,' he said evasively. Abby wondered how on earth she was going to get any work done with all this going on around her.

'Does this often happen to Nico? The press chasing him?' How did he even begin to live a normal life?

Matt gave a wry smile. 'Only when he is seen with a new woman. The female hearts of Europe flutter briefly, hoping that it will be fleeting. I expect there'll be some serious disappointment when they read about you.'

And surprise, too, Abby thought wryly. She was hardly his type of woman.

'But I need to go to the flat to pick up more of Rosa's things,' she said lamely, and Matt held out his hand.

'Give me a list and the keys. I'll sort it.'

Abby sighed and reached for some paper and a pen. She'd known Nico long enough to know that it wasn't worth arguing.

They arrived at the hospital in comfort and Abby had to admit that it was bliss not to have to wrestle with bus queues and toddlers first thing in the morning. She slipped self-consciously out of the limo and slid into work as discreetly as possible.

Heather waylaid her as soon as she arrived on the ward.

'Is it true?' Her eyes were alight with curiosity and excitement. 'Are the papers correct? You had a fling with Nico Santini?'

Abby gave a wan smile. 'I…er…yes, it's true that Rosa is his child.'

She couldn't quite bring herself to say they'd had a relationship. Despite what Nico thought of her, she was extremely truthful by nature.

Hopefully everyone would still draw the right conclusions if she admitted that Rosa was his child.

'You are such a dark horse!' Heather looked stunned. 'You didn't even tell us that you knew him.'

'I was at school with his sister.'

'But you never told him you had his baby.' Heather was looking at her dreamily. 'But he came to find you and now you're getting married. That's *so* romantic.'

Romantic?

Abby pinned a smile to her face and wondered how on earth she was going to keep this up. She glanced around the ward, which was humming with activity. 'I can see we're busy. Where do you want me? I'm really sorry I've been off for the past few days.'

'No problem. We were worried about Rosa, but Nico kept us informed. He's been remarkably human to the staff since he announced that he was marrying you. You obviously bring out the softer side to him.'

No. It was Rosa that did that, Abby thought regretfully. She had no effect on him whatsoever.

'OK, what's been happening since you were here last?' Heather checked her notepad. 'Thomas Wood is still doing well, his wound is clean, his sats are good and he's on free fluids. You look after him as you've got such a good relationship with them. If he carries on like this, he'll be going home in another few days.'

'What happened to baby Hubbard?'

'I spoke to his mother that night Rosa was sick and she was happy to take the baby home. Jack did the balloon atrial septostomy and that improved her oxygen saturation so she's gone home and she's being readmitted in two weeks for her op.' Heather broke off as the ward doors opened and a medical team pushed a cot towards her. 'Oh, this is my new admission. Little boy born by Caesarean section in the night. He was very breathless and can't feed and the paediatrician was worried that he has a congenital heart defect, although he couldn't hear a murmur. Jack arranged for him to be transferred and he and Nico are going to review him together.'

She walked towards the team. 'You can put him in room six for now. Abby, can you bleep Jack and Nico and tell them that baby Hopcroft has arrived? Where's the mother?'

'Still on the ward,' the nurse told her. 'She's having her drip and her catheter out and then they've told her she can come up in a wheelchair. I ought to warn you, she's totally devastated that something is wrong. The sooner someone tells her what's going on the better.'

'Of course.' Heather listened while they finished the handover and then turned to Abby. 'If the mother is distraught, this is a good one for you. You're always brilliant with worried parents. You're so calm.'

Calm?

Abby gave a wan smile. After everything that had happened to her in the past week she didn't think that she would ever be calm again. She certainly didn't feel calm. She felt as though her insides were hosting a major hurricane.

She and Heather had only just finished settling the baby when Jack, Nico and a large number of junior doctors walked onto the ward. The group included the paediatrician who had referred the child.

'I was called to Theatre because it was a section,' he told the other doctors, briefing them on the history. 'The child was full term and there were signs of foetal distress but the baby was breathing hard from the moment he was born and in my opinion he was blue.'

Nico was watching the baby. 'Did the mother have ultrasound during her pregnancy?'

The paediatrician nodded. 'Yes. Two, but there was no evidence of a problem.'

Nico frowned. 'Any family history of congenital heart disease?'

'Not that I could discover, but I had some trouble getting any sense from her. The mother was distraught.'

'Understandably so.' Nico began to examine the tiny baby. 'His respiratory rate and effort are increased,' he murmured, moving the cot sheet down so that he could feel the pulses in the baby's feet. 'And his pulses are diminished.' He turned to Abby and for a brief moment she thought she saw something flicker in that dark gaze. Then it was gone and he was totally professional again. 'Could you do a four-limb blood pressure, please?'

Abby nodded, aware that a lower blood pressure in the legs was indicative of a congenital heart defect.

She pressed the button on the dinamap and recorded the pressures.

Nico nodded as he looked at the results. 'He has a lower blood pressure in the legs and weak femoral pulses. Also, his liver is enlarged and his lungs are congested. What is his oxygen saturation?'

Abby checked the monitor quickly. 'Eighty per cent.'

'Which is consistent with cyanosis.'

The paediatrician moved closer. 'I thought I detected a systolic murmur, but I could have been wrong.'

'You weren't wrong,' Nico said smoothly as he finished his examination. 'Well done. It isn't always easy to hear.'

The paediatrician looked stunned at the praise and then grinned as if he'd won the lottery.

Abby looked at Nico with helpless fascination. Until she'd started working with him she'd seen him as Mr Cool, so totally in control of his emotions that even a smile didn't see the light of day unless he'd planned it. But she couldn't have been more wrong.

She'd seen the warmth that he was capable of showing with worried parents, with Rosa and now with a colleague, and she was rapidly coming to the conclusion that there wasn't a person in the world that he couldn't charm if he wanted to. She was beginning to understand how Lucia could have adored her brother so much. The combination of masculine strength and human kindness was a potent cocktail that was devastatingly attractive. No wonder women went crazy about him.

The paediatrician was still looking at Nico. 'So what's your diagnosis?'

Nico didn't hesitate. 'I will want to see a chest X-ray

and an echo, but in my opinion he has a coarctation of the aorta.'

Abby listened carefully, knowing that a coarctation of the aorta was when the main artery taking blood around the body was narrowed, hence the lower blood pressure in the legs.

The paediatrician let out a breath. 'The mother's going to be distraught. She was hoping it was nothing.'

'Of course she was,' Nico said coolly. 'This is her baby—naturally she wants him to be completely healthy. I will speak to her when she arrives on the ward.'

'So what will happen now?'

Nico answered without hesitation. 'We will give him Prostin to reopen the ductus and that will improve the oxygen saturation. At the same time we will stabilise the circulation with fluids and dopamine. Once he is stable we will operate.'

'And what does that involve?' The paediatrician was losing no opportunity to question Nico but he didn't seem to mind.

He described the operation in detail and even invited the other doctor into Theatre to watch.

Abby watched him work, her mind only half on what he was saying. The other half was trying to get to grips with the fact that she was going to marry this man.

She'd been aware of a few curious glances from members of the medical team but Nico had behaved in his usual cool, detached manner, nothing in his behaviour indicating that they had anything other than a professional relationship.

'Stop drooling over him,' Heather murmured in an undertone as she walked past, and Abby gave her a shocked look.

Drooling?

Was that what people thought?

She certainly wasn't drooling. She was wondering what on earth she'd agreed to.

It was almost the end of her shift when Nico strode up to her, an ominous expression on his handsome face.

'Matt has just returned from your flat.'

She stared at him blankly, wondering why that would cause him to look so angry. 'And?'

'And he had the pleasure of meeting your landlord.'

Abby swallowed. 'Oh.'

'Yes, oh.' Nico's tone was low so that they couldn't be overheard. 'Why didn't you tell me that he was threatening you?'

'I— He wasn't— I didn't—'

'Abby, I know the truth,' Nico said flatly, a frown touching his dark brows. 'Matt pretended he was renting you a flat and the guy warned him not to expect any favours from you. He boasted to Matt that he'd put the rent up to get you out after you refused to sleep with him.'

Abby winced. It sounded so sordid, put like that. 'It wasn't that great a flat anyway,' she said lamely, and Nico gave a groan and raked his fingers through his dark hair in a gesture of pure male frustration.

'Why the hell didn't you tell me the truth? You let me think that you'd got behind with the rent, that you couldn't manage your finances, instead of which—' He broke off and took a deep breath.

'It really doesn't matter,' she mumbled, and he gritted his teeth.

'Abby, it does matter. You should have said something.'

'You wouldn't have believed me,' she pointed out, astonished that he should be so bothered by it. 'You were determined to take Rosa from me and you'd made up your mind that I was a bad mother and terrible with money.'

'Instead of which, you were being bullied and exploited,' he growled. He closed his eyes for a moment and exhaled sharply. 'I misjudged you and I apologise. If it is any consolation, I regret it immensely and I truly wish you had tried to tell me the truth. I like to think I would have listened.'

She stared at him, stunned.

Nico Santini was *apologising* for having misjudged her?

And that wasn't the only thing he'd misjudged her on, of course, but she knew better than to touch on the subject of Rosa's paternity again. Instead, she gave him a faltering smile.

'It doesn't matter.'

'*Dio*, it does matter. You are a single mother, struggling on her own. You were vulnerable and he took advantage.' Anger and distaste burned in the depths of his dark eyes. 'If it is any consolation, I doubt that he'll be doing the same thing to anyone else.'

Abby's eyes widened as she digested the implications of his last sentence. 'What did Matt…?'

Nico's mouth tightened. 'Matt seems to have grown quite fond of you over the past few days. He was furious and he can be quite intimidating when he's crossed.'

A pacifist by nature, Abby flinched at the thought of Matt so angry but then she remembered just how badly the landlord had frightened her and decided that Matt had probably done everyone a favour.

Suddenly a thought occurred to her.

'So I presume that's the end of my flat?'

'Of course.' He spoke with complete certainty, his tone autocratic. 'There is no way I would allow you to return there and, anyway, you have no need for a flat any more. We're a family now and your home is with me.'

Their eyes locked and her heart suddenly bolted.

Her home *was* with him.

But losing the flat made it seem even more final.

She no longer had anywhere to run if things didn't work out between them.

CHAPTER SIX

AT THE hospital Thomas Wood was finally discharged home and Lorna gave Abby a big hug.

'I really, really don't think I would have survived it if you hadn't been here. I can never thank you enough.'

Abby returned the hug. 'It was nothing—I'm just glad he's all right. Now, are you sure that you're happy about everything?'

Lorna nodded. 'I've got an appointment with the cardiologist in two weeks.'

'But if you're worried about anything at all in the meantime, you know you can call us.'

Lorna cuddled Thomas closer. 'When will his chest heal?'

'It takes about six weeks,' Abby told her. 'Try and avoid lifting him under the arms because that can make it sore.'

'OK.' Lorna glanced around the ward. 'Is Nico around? I really wanted to thank him again before we left.'

'He's in Theatre, but I'll pass on your thanks.'

Lorna gave an awed smile. 'I read in the papers about the two of you. Wow! You are one very lucky girl.'

Abby forced a smile.

Was she?

Lorna was obviously determined not to let the subject drop. 'The papers said that you were getting married—is that true?'

Abby nodded, resigned to the fact that everyone in Britain seemed to know everything about her life in minute detail.

'We're getting married soon,' she said vaguely, not liking to admit that Nico hadn't given her a date. All he'd said was that it would happen quickly.

In the meantime she was living in his apartment, being cooked for by Giovanni and chauffeured everywhere by his driver, while Nico spent most of his time at the hospital.

'I wasn't expecting to have to take time off while I did this job,' he'd explained to her on the first evening. 'I will arrange cover for us to have a week in Italy so that you can meet my family, but in the meantime I have a ridiculous workload to get through. I apologise for not being able to spend more time with you and Rosa.'

It was true that his schedule was punishing and it was a tribute to his stamina that he managed to keep up with the volume of work without any visible evidence of strain or pressure.

Abby didn't mind the fact that she only ever saw him on the ward. It made her life easier and more relaxed.

What worried her was what was going to happen when they had to spend a week in each other's company.

Ten days after Abby had moved into his apartment, Nico's driver and Matt collected her for the journey to work but drove in the opposite direction from the hospital.

'Where are we going?'

Matt kept glancing out of the rear window. 'To meet Nico.'

'But the ward—'

'Nico's arranged it all.'

Abby felt her stomach turn over and almost laughed at her own reaction. How on earth was she going to cope with being married to the man when the mere mention of his name had her reacting like a cat on hot bricks?

They drove through the centre of London and then the chauffeur pulled up on a double yellow line and Matt opened the door.

'Go straight inside without looking left or right,' he ordered. 'I think we've managed to fool the press but you can never be sure.'

'But…' Abby glanced at the elegant building and then at her daughter who was fast asleep, her dark lashes a perfect half-moon against her pale cheeks.

'I'll take care of her,' Matt said immediately, placing a reassuring hand on her shoulder.

Abby hurried up the steps and into the building, stopping on the threshold as she saw Nico standing there, dauntingly male and impossibly broad-shouldered in a dark grey suit.

'Rosa?'

'Asleep in the car. Matt said he'd take care of her.'

Nico gave a brief nod of approval. 'She has a tiring journey ahead of her. The sleep will be good for her.'

Abby looked at him. 'Journey?'

'We're getting married,' he said briefly, his footsteps echoing as he led her across the marble hallway.

She stopped dead and gaped at him. 'Getting married? Now?'

He lifted an eyebrow. 'You have changed your mind?'

'N-no,' she stammered, trying not to notice just how much her legs were shaking. 'Can I at least comb my hair?'

'Of course.' His smile was amused. 'I have also bought something for you to change into.'

He strode with casual assurance along an elegant corridor and flung open a set of double doors.

'Where is this place?' She glanced around her in confusion, noticing the comfortable sofas and the magazines stacked on the low table. 'It looks like someone's house.'

'It's a hotel.'

'A hotel?' She stared at him blankly. How could it be a hotel? From the outside the building had nothing to draw attention to it and she'd seen no staff.

'It's a very exclusive hotel,' he murmured, clearly reading her mind. 'People come here when they wish to be assured of discretion. You have twenty minutes before the ceremony.'

She glanced around the room and for the first time noticed the white silk dress hanging from a rail by the window.

'You bought me a dress? What if it doesn't fit?'

'It will fit.' His eyes ran over her in a totally masculine scrutiny which left her skin burning and her pulse racing. 'The rest of your wardrobe will be sent to the villa. I'll check on Rosa.'

The rest of her wardrobe? Without giving her a chance to question him further he strolled out of the room and left her staring after him.

Realising that she had very little time, she glanced at her watch in dismay and then reached for the dress.

It was fabulous and when she glanced at the label she almost dropped it. Knowing that it must have cost a small fortune, she hardly dared to put it on. But, then, Nico Santini was in possession of a very large fortune, she reminded herself dryly. Even a dress like this wasn't going to make a dent in his bank balance.

Two minutes later she was staring at herself, open-mouthed in amazement.

The dress fitted perfectly. In fact, a bit too perfectly.

It skimmed every contour of her body, showing her tiny waist and the womanly curve of her breast and hips.

He hadn't even laid a finger on her and yet he'd guessed her size exactly. But, then, he'd had plenty of experience with women, she reflected wryly.

Why did that thought give her butterflies in her stomach?

Abby bit her lip as she looked in the mirror. If Nico thought he was marrying a stick insect, he was in for a severe disappointment.

Scooping up her wild, wavy hair, she fastened it to the top of her head with a silver pin.

She'd just finished applying make-up when Nico and Matt strolled back into the room with Rosa.

'Wow!' Matt gave her an approving smile and then caught Nico's frosty gaze and subsided with a murmur of apology.

Nico released Rosa's hand and walked across to her, releasing her hair from the pin and nodding approval as blonde curls cascaded down her back.

'Much better,' he drawled, his eyes sliding with disconcerting thoroughness over her silk-clad body. 'And now we should be getting on. We have a schedule to keep.'

Abby sat on the plane and tried to get a grip on her emotions which were fast spiralling out of control.

The simple ceremony had gone smoothly, witnessed by Matt, one of the staff of the hotel and Rosa, who had sat on the floor with her thumb in her mouth throughout.

Nico had repeated his vows in his usual clear, cool voice, whereas her voice had been barely audible.

And all the time she'd been aware that the wedding was merely been a tool for Nico to take possession of Rosa.

And take possession he had, she thought miserably as she stared out of the window of the private jet. Rosa was asleep again and Nico was working on his laptop, the jacket from his suit slung over the back of his seat and the top button of his shirt undone.

He looked thoroughly male and wickedly handsome and she wondered how on earth they were going to convince his family that they were a couple. He hadn't so much as touched her hand since the registrar had proclaimed them married.

And she should be grateful for that, she told herself firmly.

Fortunately, at that moment Rosa awoke and needed attention, which prevented Abby from dwelling on the evening to come.

By the time they arrived in Sardinia, Abby was exhausted and Rosa was fractious and difficult, crying persistently as they were hustled into the car.

'We are nearly there,' Nico murmured, reaching into his pocket and producing a small toy for Rosa, which stemmed the tears for a short time. 'She must be very tired, poor thing.'

Abby gave a faltering smile, relieved and touched that he'd understood that Rosa's behaviour was the result of tiredness.

All the same, she was grateful when they finally arrived at their destination, pulling up outside a beautiful villa on the edge of a golden sandy beach. The sea shimmered temptingly in the late afternoon sunlight and in the distance a flotilla of boats sailed across the bay.

Abby gasped in delight, her own tiredness temporarily forgotten. 'What a beautiful place!'

'I'm glad you approve.' Nico's light drawl held a hint of amusement. 'It is our retreat from the smog of Milan and it's certainly a pleasant change from the East End of London.'

It certainly was.

Abby stared at the sand longingly and had to fight the urge to slip off her shoes and run into the sea.

'It looks deserted. There's no one on the beach at all.'

'That's because it's private,' he informed her dryly, and she blushed, embarrassed by her own naïvety.

Of course it was private.

The Santini family would hardly share a beach with tourists, would they?

The next half-hour was a whirl of introductions and shrieks and incomprehensible Italian as Nico's mother and extended family welcomed him home.

Where did Nico get his ice-cool approach to life? Abby wondered in amazement as she watched his warm and affectionate mother fussing over Rosa and his grandmother smiling benignly from a comfortable rocking chair.

She'd been expecting his family to be reserved and undemonstrative, instead of which they couldn't have been more welcoming.

'You will call me Francesca. And you should know that this is the happiest day of my life,' Nico's mother told her, enveloping Abby in a warm hug which brought a lump to her throat. 'You have done what I thought no woman could do. You have captured my Domenico's heart.'

Abby closed her eyes briefly, wondering what on earth Nico had told them all. She felt a stab of guilt that they were deceiving this woman.

'Two years ago, his life was so black,' Francesca told her in a low voice, aware that Nico was within earshot. 'He had that terrible illness...' She broke off with a shudder. 'But he was lucky and they cured him. But he thought he would never have children, until he found out about you....'

No. He'd found out about Rosa.

Abby smiled weakly. 'Yes...'

'And you should have told him you were pregnant,' Francesca scolded lightly, taking Abby's hand and patting it gently. 'My Domenico is an honourable boy. He would have done the right thing straight away and then you wouldn't have been apart for two years. You would have been there for him when he was ill, instead of which he shut us all out—'

Nico said something sharp which Abby didn't understand, but his mother subsided instantly and took Abby's arm.

'Nico tells me I'm interfering so I will be quiet now. Why don't I show you to your room and you can get washed and changed for dinner? You must be exhausted after the flight.'

'Is my father joining us?' Nico loosened his tie and poured himself a drink.

Francesca shook her head. 'He intended to, but he had to fly to Paris last night.'

Nico's eyes narrowed. 'He works too hard.'

'It is a family trait,' his mother replied quietly, giving him a meaningful look which he accepted with a grudging smile.

'And Carlo?'

'Carlo is already here and Lucia is planning a brief visit, too. Now, enough of that. Poor Abby must be overwhelmed by meeting all these new people. I've put you in the Beach Room.' Francesca turned to Abby with a smile. 'You'll love it. We had it decorated quite recently. There is a wonderful balcony which opens up onto the deck and the little one can sleep in her own room just down the corridor. I've employed a nanny to take care of her so that you can have a complete rest. If there's anything else you need, you only have to ask.'

Abby returned the smile, completely charmed by Nico's mother. Lucky Lucia, she thought wistfully as she followed her upstairs to her room. No wonder she'd always longed for the holidays.

She frowned slightly, wondering whether Lucia had been told about their wedding. Did she even know that Nico had tracked her down?

Hoping that the meeting wasn't going to be awkward, Abby took a shower and changed for dinner then checked on Rosa, who was tucked up fast asleep in the pretty nursery. A uniformed nanny was folding her clothes in a neat pile.

'Good evening, *Signora*.' Fortunately she spoke good English. 'I'm Chiara. I will be Rosa's nanny while you are here—it will give you a chance for some rest.'

Her eyes gleamed slightly and Abby gritted her teeth. There was no mistaking the implication and it wasn't anything to do with rest.

As it was, she knew that she was going to have plenty

of time to spend with her daughter but she didn't think it was sensible to argue that fact at this point. Instead, she checked Rosa quickly, thanked the nanny politely and made her way to her room.

A maid was unpacking two suitcases full of clothes that Abby didn't recognise.

'Signor Santini asked me to unpack,' the maid said respectfully, and Abby opened her mouth and closed it again. Clearly this was what Nico had been referring to when he'd said that he'd bought her a wardrobe.

She should have protested, but part of her felt like a child in a sweet shop confronted by such a variety of tempting outfits. Whoever had done the shopping had chosen well.

She selected a pretty dress, left her hair loose and made her way downstairs for dinner.

Nico was standing by the fireplace, looking relaxed and impossibly handsome, the sleeves of his dark linen shirt rolled back to reveal tanned forearms. His jet-black hair was still wet from the shower and Abby found herself wondering where his room was. Obviously nowhere near hers, which was all that mattered.

His gaze skimmed over the dress and there was no mistaking the masculine appreciation in those stunning dark eyes. 'You look wonderful, *bella mia*.'

Blushing frantically, she accepted a drink and shook hands with Carlo, whom she'd never met before but warmed to instantly.

Although physically there was a strong resemblance between the two brothers, Carlo had none of Nico's cool reserve, his gaze warm and welcoming as he introduced himself to Abby.

Although they'd never met in person, he had been instrumental in arranging for her treatment at the clinic but not by a flicker of an eyelid did he betray that he knew who she was.

It was clear that the two brothers were close and the conversation around the table was lively and interesting.

Halfway through dinner her eyelids started to droop and Nico frowned at her across the table.

'You are exhausted, *cara mia*,' he said quietly, his dark eyes narrowed as they scanned her pale face. 'No one will mind if you want to go upstairs.'

She smiled at him gratefully, surprised by his perceptiveness.

She *was* tired. All in all it had been a pretty stressful day.

Deciding to follow his suggestion, she excused herself and made her way up to the bedroom, took a leisurely bath and then changed into one of her new nightgowns.

It was ridiculously glamorous and revealing, but fortunately no one was going to see it except her, she reflected as she adjusted the thin silk spaghetti straps.

This nightie was designed for sin and passion, not warmth and comfort. It was fortunate that the nights were going to be extremely warm in Sardinia.

She snuggled down into bed, feeling instantly drowsy, but then she heard the click of the door and sat bolt upright, her heart thumping as Nico strolled in, his jacket slung carelessly over one shoulder.

Abby clutched the sheet to her chest, her eyes wide. 'Wh-what are you doing in here?'

'What do you think I'm doing?' He tossed the jacket onto a chair and started undoing the buttons on his shirt, his expression faintly amused. 'I'm going to bed with my wife.'

Abby stared at him, appalled. 'You have to be joking.'

One ebony brow lifted. 'Why would I be joking?' The shirt landed next to the jacket and her mouth dried as her eyes caught a glimpse of broad male chest covered in curling dark hairs.

Dear God, he was undressing in her bedroom....

'Wait a minute.' She looked at a point just behind him so that she didn't have to look at his body. 'We don't have that sort of marriage....'

He frowned. 'What other sort of marriage is there?'

'You know what I mean!' She clutched the sheet tighter. 'Ours is a business arrangement. Security for Rosa.'

'Precisely.' He stepped out of his trousers, revealing a pair of black silk boxer shorts. 'Security for Rosa means a happy marriage. And as far as I'm concerned, a happy marriage means plenty of sex.'

Sex?

She had a brief glimpse of hard, muscular thighs before dragging her gaze away.

'But I don't even really know you....' Her voice was strangled and a smile slashed across his male features.

'After tonight you will know every inch of me, *cara mia*.'

She shook her head, unable to grasp that he was serious. 'I— This isn't what I...' Inspiration struck. 'You can see other women! I wouldn't mind.'

'*I* would mind,' he said smoothly, his tone mildly amused. 'Anyway, I have too high a profile to be able to be seen with different women. It would cause gossip. Especially among my own family. We are newly married, *cara mia*, they expect us to share a room.'

Abby looked around the room, her heart tumbling in her chest. 'Well, in that case you could sleep on the sofa.'

'I'm six feet three,' he reminded her in a low, masculine drawl. 'If I sleep on a sofa, I'll never walk again.'

'Then *I'll* sleep on the sofa.'

The amusement vanished from Nico's eyes. 'You'll sleep in the bed.' There was no mistaking the command in his tone. 'With me. You married me. Sex is part of marriage.'

'We don't have to have sex just because we're married— plenty of couples don't have sex.'

He looked at her with blatant incredulity. 'If you are

suggesting that I can do without sex, you certainly have a great deal to learn about me. I'm Italian, *tesoro*. I have a high sex drive.'

The tip of Abby's tongue sneaked out and moistened her lower lip. She didn't even want to think about his sex drive. 'But you—we—don't love each other.'

He threw back his head and laughed in genuine amusement. 'I have never loved anyone, *cara mia*. Fortunately for you, my performance in bed isn't affected by the lack of that fabled emotion.'

She stared at him, heart pounding. 'You really think you're the ultimate lover, don't you?'

A smile slashed across his handsome face. 'I'm Italian, *angelo*. Making love is the one thing we know how to do really, *really* well. But first we need to—what's that phrase you have in English—set a few ground rules?' He lifted a hand and smoothed a finger down her cheek. 'Firstly you need to start looking at me. It is hard to build a relationship with someone who won't look at me. You look at the floor, or the ceiling, or my tie when I wear one—just about anywhere except my eyes.'

Nico lifted her chin firmly and gave a slight smile as she lifted her eyes to his. 'Better. Much better. Secondly, you need to stop being so jumpy when I walk into the same room as you. I want you to relax when you are with me.'

Relax?

Her heart was beating so fast she thought it might burst through her chest. She could no more relax with him than she could with an escaped tiger.

His dark eyes were lazily amused. 'This is the first time in my life I've had a woman asking me to sleep on the sofa rather than in her bed. This is a totally new experience, *tesoro*,' he drawled softly, 'and a not altogether flattering one.'

'—I'm not interested in flattering you,' she stammered. 'I married you because I wanted Rosa and because we agreed that two parents would be better for her than one. We don't have a relationship. We both know that I'm not your usual type of woman.'

'That is partly true...' His eyes narrowed and he looked at Abby speculatively as if he'd just realised something. 'Which makes it all the more interesting that the chemistry between us is so powerful.'

Chemistry?

She gaped at him in astonishment and then shook her head. 'I don't know what you mean. There's no chemistry.'

'Are you really so naïve that you can't see it?' He looked at her, stunning dark eyes raking her pale features. 'Why do you think I make you so nervous?'

'Because you're an autocratic bully,' she said immediately, too shaken by the direction of the conversation to be shy with him. 'You scare me.'

'That's not true. It is your feelings that scare you,' he said softly, his husky male voice torturing her nerve endings. 'There is a strong sexual charge between us. Go on, Abby, admit it,' he murmured thickly. 'You have often looked at me and wondered how I make love.'

Heat pooled in her belly and she shook her head in frantic denial, shaken by her body's reaction to his explicit statement.

'You're just so impossibly arrogant that you can't believe that there's a woman out there that doesn't want you.'

He sat down on the bed next to her and his male scent teased her nostrils.

Looking everywhere except at his powerful body, she tried to scoot across the bed but he stopped her with one lean, brown hand, leaning across her so that her means of escape was blocked.

Her heart was pounding. 'Don't you understand ''no''?'

'Perfectly. But you haven't said it,' he said huskily. 'When you do, I'll stop.'

She opened her mouth to say it and then froze with shock

as Nico's mouth descended on hers. The touch of his lips against hers was nothing like she'd expected. Instead of hard, he gave her soft, instead of rough, he gave her gentle, using every ounce of expertise to tease a response from her.

Fire burned deep in her stomach and she placed a hand against his muscular chest, intending to push him away. But instead she felt his weight pressing her back onto the bed as he came down on top of her, his mouth never breaking contact with hers.

He lifted a hand to her face, stroking her cheek gently as he used his tongue to trace the seam of her lips and dip seductively inside.

Suddenly she was surrounded by Nico—his scent, his taste, his weight, and his incredibly skilled touch.

His mouth still on hers, he slipped the straps of her nightie down her arms, and she felt the hair on his chest graze her exposed nipples. Then he lifted his head and looked down at her, his breathing not quite steady.

Instinctively Abby lifted a hand to cover herself, but he caught her wrists in his hands and she felt her cheeks burn with embarrassment under his heated scrutiny.

'You are impossibly shy,' he murmured gently, his Italian accent suddenly pronounced, 'and yet you have a stunning figure, *angelo*. You are full of surprises. Who would have thought that hidden under that nurse's uniform is the body of a goddess?'

A goddess?

Totally thrown by his comment, Abby lay still, barely breathing, fascinated by the expression in his eyes. He couldn't stop looking at her, his eyes dark with a primitive need as his eyes fastened on her pink nipples.

'You have the most incredible breasts....' he groaned, sliding down the bed so that his head was level with that part of her. For endless moments he hesitated, staring down at the soft roundness without trying to conceal his hunger.

Then he lowered his head and drew one nipple into the heat of his mouth and Abby gasped as sensation shot through her. She forgot about the fact that she barely knew him, she forgot about being nervous or shy. Instead, she arched towards him, instinctively seeking more.

When he finally lifted his dark head his breathing was decidedly unsteady, and he looked at her nipple, now glossy and wet from the touch of his mouth. Then he lifted his eyes to hers.

'Are you saying no?' His voice was husky and heavily accented and she shook her head, mute, her body a mass of sensation.

With a satisfied smile that was pure, conquering male, he lowered his head to her other breast and subjected it to the same treatment while he tortured the other with the tips of his fingers.

She writhed and arched underneath him, trying to free her body of the almost intolerable pressure he was creating inside her.

He continued his relentless assault on her breasts, his free hand sliding up her back and teasing the soft silk down her body. Suddenly she was naked except for a pair of silk panties and he slid further down the bed, kissing his way down her body until he reached the most private part of her.

'Nico!' She tensed with shock as she felt his mouth touching her through the flimsy silk and she tried to push him away but he gave a soft laugh and held her thighs apart. 'I want to know every part of you Abby. Every single part…'

'Nico, please…' She gave a sob of embarrassment which turned to a gasp of disbelief as he swiftly dispensed with her panties and used his tongue to caress her most intimate place.

Embarrassment was replaced by a sensation so exquisite that she thought she'd explode.

He used his mouth until she was writhing and shaking and then he lifted his head and slid up the bed to cover her with his powerful body.

She stared up at him, dazed, her blue eyes feverish. 'Nico...'

She couldn't believe what she'd just let him do.

'No more shyness, *cara mia*,' he purred softly, his dark eyes burning into hers as he used his fingers where his mouth had been. 'Soon there will be no part of you that I don't know intimately.'

The ache between her thighs was intolerable and suddenly she was desperate to have him there, where she needed him most. Frantically she pushed at his silk boxer shorts, sliding them down the hard muscle of his thighs so that he was left as naked as her.

'*Io voglio te...*' he groaned in Italian, and she looked at him dizzily, her body totally outside her own control.

'I said that I want you,' he muttered huskily, and she shivered underneath him as she felt him take her hand and guide her towards him, encouraging her to touch him with the same intimacy that he'd touched her. Her fingers stroked him gently and she just had time to register his size and power before he was parting her thighs and positioning her under him.

She stared up at him, her breath coming in shallow pants as she waited for the touch that she craved so desperately.

The tension between them had built to such an intolerable level that she didn't expect him to pause, but he did, lifting a hand and stroking blonde curls away from her face with fingers that weren't quite steady.

'I'll try and take it slowly but I'm not promising. You excite the hell out of me, *cara mia*,' he groaned huskily. 'You are so full of surprises. All shyness on the surface and passion underneath.'

Abby arched against him, begging with her body.

She didn't want slowly.

She just wanted *him*. And she didn't care if he hurt her.

Even so, his first thrust stretched her beyond her expectation and she gasped and tensed, her fingers curling into his back.

Nico paused and spoke softly to her in Italian and although she didn't understand, she felt herself relax.

His dark eyes hot with passion, he slid a strong arm under her hips and then entered her fully, thrusting deep into the heart of her.

She could hardly breathe, all rational thought suspended by the excitement which exploded inside her body. He controlled her utterly, building the rhythm until he created a sensation so exquisite and extreme that she cried out his name and moved against him in a frantic attempt to ease the almost intolerable tension that he'd created within her body.

His love-making was fierce and possessive and he drove them both to a state of fevered ecstasy until finally she crashed over the edge in a climax so intense that she cried out in disbelief, holding tightly to him as she felt the powerful thrusts of his completion.

Held securely in his arms, Abby closed her eyes, savouring the incredible closeness and the weight of his powerful body on hers. She never wanted the feeling to end. She wanted him to hold her for ever.

But he didn't.

Instead, he shifted his weight and looked down at her, a strange expression in his dark eyes.

Abby lay still, her eyes locked with his, totally shocked by the feelings that had erupted inside her.

What was he thinking?

What had it meant to him?

Afraid to speak in case she severed the incredible connection between them, she lay quiet, waiting for him to make the next move.

And move he did.

Muttering a soft curse in Italian, he lowered his mouth to hers again and Abby ceased to worry about what was on his mind.

CHAPTER SEVEN

ABBY awoke the next morning to find the sun blazing through the window and no sign of Nico.

Glancing at the clock, she gave a gasp of horror. How had she slept so late?

Hot colour burned her cheeks as she remembered the night before. It was hardly any wonder she'd slept so late. Nico had made love to her for most of the night and when eventually she'd fallen asleep, she'd been physically and emotionally exhausted by the intensity of the experience. For the first time in her life she'd felt truly close to someone. Remembering how she'd snuggled into his arms in the aftermath of their love-making, she gave a groan of embarrassment and covered her face with her hands.

How could she have even pretended to herself that she didn't find him attractive? The man was devastating and one flash of that electric smile had sent her into a tailspin from which she'd never recovered.

And now she had to face him.

Shrinking with shyness after the way she'd responded to him, she dressed quickly and made her way down to the terrace where the family seemed to take their meals.

They were all sitting around the table, talking and laughing as they enjoyed breakfast, and Rosa was in a high chair, beaming happily at her grandmother, her uncle and her father.

'Good morning.' Nico rose to his feet as she hesitated on the edge of the terrace, and Abby wished she could vanish into the background.

Her whole body tensed as he strolled towards her, her

cheeks flaming pink as she remembered the liberties he'd taken with her body the night before.

'If you don't look me in the eyes, everyone will guess what we spent the whole night doing,' he said softly, his voice husky and slightly amused. 'You have no reason to be embarrassed, *angelo*.'

Warily her eyes lifted to his and she saw speculation flicker on those dark depths. He must have had virtually no sleep and yet he looked totally rested. The man's strength and stamina were awesome.

'Come and have some breakfast.' He took her arm and guided her back to the table, pulling out a chair and seating her between Rosa and himself.

'She is a wonderful child, Abby, and a credit to you,' Francesca said warmly as she handed Rosa another piece of bread to eat. 'She is so happy and friendly. Nico tells me she goes to a crèche.'

Nico frowned slightly and Abby braced herself to defend her decision, but surprisingly enough Carlo spoke up, his voice calm and measured.

'And a good thing, too. That's probably why she's so sociable.' He threw an amused glance at his brother. 'And we all know that the more germs children pick up early on the healthier they are as they grow older.'

Nico gave a grudging smile and Abby looked at Carlo gratefully. 'My friend runs it,' she said quickly, 'and she's known Rosa since she was born, so she isn't with strangers.'

Francesca tutted. 'You must have struggled so much, trying to manage with a child on a nurse's salary. You should have contacted my Nico straight away to tell him you were pregnant.'

Abby coloured but before she could think what to say Nico had spoken to his mother in rapid Italian, his expression forbidding.

His mother pulled an apologetic face and looked at

Abby. 'I'm so sorry. Nico tells me off for interfering and he's right. Now, then, what are you going to do with your day?'

Abby glanced longingly at the beach which seemed to start at the bottom of the garden.

'I'd love to take Rosa to the beach,' she said shyly. 'She's never seen the sea before.'

'Perfect!' Francesca beamed approvingly. 'The three of you will spend the morning on the beach and when the sun gets too hot you'll come back up here for lunch and a siesta.'

Siesta.

Abby caught Nico's eye briefly and then looked away in embarrassment as she read the amusement and something else in his gaze. There was no doubting what he planned to do during the siesta and it certainly wasn't sleeping.

'Do you have everything you need?' Francesca poured herself more coffee. 'A bikini? A costume for Rosa? You must wear a hat. You are so fair you'll burn badly in our heat if you don't cover yourself up.'

Abby smiled at her, touched and warmed by her consideration. 'I have a hat, thank you,' she said, lifting a napkin and wiping the jam from Rosa's face.

'You must make sure you rest on the beach,' Nico's mother said firmly, handing Rosa another piece of bread to chew. 'You must be so tired after everything that happened yesterday. I cannot believe my Nico whisked you away and married you with no warning. He can be very overbearing at times. And none of us were able to be there.'

Nico was glowering at his mother but she continued regardless. 'Nico does not know how to be romantic. He is too impatient with such things.'

Carlo glanced at his mother. 'Stop stirring,' he warned gently, and she pulled a face.

'I just cannot believe he got married without inviting us.'

She turned to Abby again. 'What about your family—were they there?'

'That's enough.' Nico's tone was sharp but Abby put out a hand and smiled at his mother.

'My parents are both dead,' she said quietly, and Francesca closed her eyes briefly, clearly mortified.

'You poor thing—I didn't know.' She glared at Nico and then looked back at Abby with concern. 'But family is not just about parents—you must have aunts, uncles, grandparents?'

Abby gave a self-conscious shake of her head. 'I—I don't have anybody except Rosa,' she stammered quietly, and everyone around the table fell silent, all eyes fixed on her.

Nico was suddenly still, an odd expression in his eyes.

Finally Francesca spoke, her voice troubled. 'Nobody?'

'Nobody.' Remembering the years of loneliness, Abby gave a shaky smile and felt a lump building in her throat.

Did Nico have any idea how lucky he was, having such a fabulous family?

Francesca was staring at her in dismay. 'My poor girl…' She rose from the table and enveloped Abby in an enormous hug. 'Then it is doubly wonderful that you met my Domenico because you can no longer say that you have nobody. You have him and all of us.'

Did she?

Abby returned the hug and then risked a glance at Nico, but his expression was unfathomable, his dark eyes hooded as he surveyed her across the table.

She stared back at him in helpless fascination, appalled at the intensity of her own feelings.

One night.

That was all it had taken. One night in his bed and she was totally lost.

What a complete idiot!

She'd done the one thing he'd said that he didn't want from her. She'd fallen in love with him.

She dropped her eyes to her plate, afraid that he'd read the truth in her gaze.

How could it have happened?

How could she have fallen in love with a man who'd threatened to take her daughter from her?

Because she understood now what had driven him to such extreme lengths, and she sympathised with those emotions. And if his macho, controlling personality had shocked her to begin with, he'd more than redeemed himself since with his behaviour towards their daughter. He didn't seem bothered if she was fractious or tired, he still enjoyed her company.

Abby closed her eyes and faced the inevitable. She'd seen Nico Santini at his worst and she'd still fallen in love with him. She loved his strength and his ferocious intellect, she understood that his emotional detachment concealed an ability to feel deeply, but most of all she loved the vulnerability that she sensed was there but which pride prevented him from acknowledging.

Which meant that she was in trouble because he certainly didn't love *her*. She wasn't fooled by the closeness they'd shared in the bedroom. To a man like Nico, sex was something completely separate from love.

Nico had married her to gain possession of Rosa and for no other reason.

Why would he fall in love with her? No other woman had been able to hook him and if she thought that one night of enjoyable sex would be enough to make her different then she was fooling herself.

So what was she going to do?

Living in a marriage of convenience was one thing, but what happened when one of them broke the rules and fell madly in love? Abby swallowed hard and stared down at her hands.

Clearly thinking that she was upset about her past, Carlo reached over the table and touched her hand. 'We're all delighted that you're now part of our family,' he said quietly, the concern in his eyes visible evidence that he was all too aware just how close she was to tears. 'And now perhaps you two should get on the beach before it's too hot for Rosa.'

With a brief nod of gratitude to his brother, Nico rose to his feet and lifted Rosa out of her high chair and into his arms.

'I asked the nanny to put her things together,' he told Abby as they strolled back into the villa. 'You just need to change yourself and then we can go.'

He looked down at her with a slight frown. 'You're very pale, *angelo*. Are you feeling all right? My mother can be very tactless sometimes. If she upset you—'

'She didn't upset me,' Abby interrupted him quickly, keen to change the subject in case he guessed the real reason for her misery. Nico was the cleverest man she'd ever met. She had no illusions about his ability to work out just exactly what was wrong with her, given enough time.

'You are sure?' Still looking at her, he suddenly lifted a hand and freed her hair from the clip she'd used to restrain it.

'Nico…'

'You have stunning hair,' he breathed, the heat in his vibrant dark eyes a reminder of the intimacies they'd shared the night before. 'Don't wear it up again unless you are at work.'

With that parting shot he strolled back towards their room, leaving her staring after him, wondering what was happening to her. She was so affected by him, so starving for every morsel of attention, that she was ignoring the fact that he was behaving like a caveman.

By rights she ought to twist her hair into the tightest knot possible just to annoy him, but she knew that she wasn't going to do that. More likely she was going to wear her hair loose for the next fifty years.

You're pathetic, she told herself hopelessly as she followed him back to their room. One night in his bed and you're falling over yourself to please him.

But the incredible intimacy they'd shared the night before had unlocked something inside her that she'd kept buried since childhood. Fear of rejection and her mammoth insecurity had kept her from forming relationships and trusting another human being. Making love with Nico had changed all that.

Now she could think of nothing that she wanted more than to be intimate with Nico Santini for the rest of her life.

Chiara met her outside their room, carrying a bag stuffed with Rosa's belongings.

'I think I have remembered everything.' She smiled. I even found a bucket and spade.'

Abby thanked her, took the bag and slipped into their room to get changed, grateful that Nico was in the bathroom so that she could do it without an audience.

She pulled a pretty blue cotton sundress over a bikini that left virtually nothing to the imagination and remembered to pack a hat in the bag.

'Ready?' Nico strolled out of the bathroom, wearing shorts and a loose T-shirt which fell softly over the muscles of his broad shoulders.

Treating herself to a glance at his incredible body, Abby felt her whole body heat and quickly bent down to pick up the bag.

'Shy again, Abby?' His deep voice teased her and she glanced up with a wry smile.

'It's you,' she muttered, her eyes sliding towards the door. 'You turn me into a nervous wreck....'

'But at least we're joking about it, which is a start.' He

traced the line of her jaw with a strong finger and looked at her thoughtfully. 'Come on. Time to go.'

They settled themselves on the sand a few minutes later and Rosa plopped down on her bottom, delighted by her new environment.

'Now, bang the bottom of the bucket, like that. Good girl.' Abby laughed as Rosa beat the bucket with the spade and the sand plopped out in a perfect shape. 'There you are—castle.'

Rosa chuckled and bashed the sand with the spade until it was totally flattened.

'She likes the beach,' Nico said smiling indulgently, as Rosa stabbed the sand with the spade.

'Do you think she's all right?' Abby looked at him anxiously. 'Not too hot?'

Nico shook his head, his dark eyes narrowing as he looked at her. 'The reason you are finding it hot, *tesoro*, is because you refuse to remove your dress,' he drawled, and she hugged her knees self-consciously.

'That's because the clothes you arranged for me only include bikinis that aren't designed for swimming,' she muttered, and his eyes gleamed.

'Did you like them?'

She gave him a shy smile. 'You were very generous. Thank you.'

'*Prego.* As we've established that you like the clothes, there really is no logical reason for you to keep your dress on. I saw every single inch of your body last night,' he reminded her in husky tones, his eyes amused, 'so, in the circumstances, your shyness is misplaced. And if you are worried that I will be unable to control my baser urges, I assure you that I am not in the habit of making love to a woman with my entire family watching from the villa.'

Abby glanced behind them, realising that the beach was clearly visible from the terrace.

'I'm taking Rosa for a swim.' Nico rose to his feet and

dragged off his shirt and then bent to scoop Rosa into his arms.

Abby stared after them as they walked across the sand. The sea sparkled in the burning sunlight as though someone had thrown a million diamonds into the waves.

It looked thoroughly inviting and suddenly she decided that he was right. She was being ridiculous. Pulling the dress over the head, she applied sun cream liberally and then walked gingerly across the hot sand to the water's edge.

Nico was up to his waist in the water, dipping a giggling Rosa into the sea and then lifting her high into the air.

Abby watched them with a smile and then suddenly Rosa noticed her and babbled excitedly, straining towards her mother.

Nico turned and saw her, his eyes wandering thoroughly over her body as she paused with her toes in the water.

'It's a good job the water's cold,' he said dryly, a slight smile touching his mouth as his eyes rested on the tempting curve of her cleavage. 'You have a fabulous figure, *angelo*. Now, come into the water and have some fun.'

And they did have fun.

They played in the waves with the toddler and when Nico thought that Rosa had been in the sun for long enough, they retreated back to the sand where umbrellas shaded their towels.

'This is so wonderful...' Abby turned to him with a smile to find him watching her intently.

'You like my home? After the inquisition from my mother at breakfast, I was afraid you might be wishing for privacy,' he drawled, adjusting Rosa's hat so that she wasn't in the sun.

Abby shook her head. 'I love your family,' she said quietly, 'and I think you're very lucky.'

Nico gave a wry smile. 'Well, I apologise again for my mother. She interferes terribly.'

'She didn't upset me, and I think it's great that she interferes,' Abby said wistfully. She would have given anything for parents who loved her so much that they'd want
to involve themselves in her life.

'I knew your parents were dead but I didn't realise that
you had no other family,' Nico said gruffly, settling himself
on the towel next to her and leaning back on his elbows.
His dark chest hair glistened with sea-water. 'I am beginning to understand why you went ahead and had Rosa, even
though you were so young.'

Abby remembered the searing emptiness of her life before Rosa and stared bleakly into the distance.

'I always envied Lucia,' she said quietly. 'Not because
of the money but because of her family. Whenever something happened at school, one of you turned up to support
her. School plays, sports days—whatever it was, she always
had someone there cheering her on. And it was often you.'

Nico shrugged. 'Our father was often too busy running
the business.'

'But one of the family was always there for her.'

Nico gave a wry smile. 'I'm not sure that she was always
as grateful for my presence as you seem to think she should
have been. She thinks I'm overbearing.'

'I think you love her,' Abby muttered. 'I would have
given anything for someone to care enough about me to
tell me off.'

'Would you?' Nico's voice was disturbingly gentle. 'Tell
me about your parents.'

Abby hesitated. She wasn't used to confiding in anyone.
All her life she'd been on her own and it didn't come naturally to broadcast her feelings.

'It's pretty boring really,' she muttered, and he reached
out a hand and lifted her chin, forcing her to meet his disturbingly direct gaze.

'Not boring. We are married now, *angelo*,' he said softly.
'I told you last night that I wanted to know every single

part of you. That includes what is inside your head. No secrets, Abby.'

She swallowed. 'My parents both had big careers. They were appalled when they had me but fortunately for them boarding schools provided the answer. They seemed to think that as long as they put me in the best school, they could forget about me. So that's basically what they did.'

Nico frowned ominously, his disapproval evident. 'You must have been unbelievably lonely. I understand why you were determined to have Rosa.'

Abby stared at the sand. 'I *was* lonely. In fact, there was never a single moment in my childhood when I didn't feel lonely,' she admitted, wondering why she was telling him things she'd never even admitted to herself before. 'I always hoped that once I became a nurse my parents would be proud of me, but nothing changed and they died within six months of each other before I finished training.'

'And that was when you decided to have Rosa?'

She stared across the sparkling sea. 'I was always desperately maternal and I wanted a child so badly I was willing to contemplate anything. Whatever you may think, I didn't go into it lightly. I was worried that I was depriving her of a father but I managed to convince myself that one good parent was better than two indifferent ones.'

'I'm surprised that you didn't just rush into marriage with the first guy who asked you,' Nico drawled, his gaze disturbingly intense. 'What happened to Ian?'

Her head jerked towards him and she stared at him, eyes wide. 'How did you—?' She broke off and her slim shoulders sagged slightly. 'Oh, of course, I'd forgotten you hired a detective. You know everything about me.'

Sea-water clung to his thick, dark lashes and his jaw was dark with stubble. He looked sinfully handsome and she felt her stomach lurch in response to the lazy look in his eyes.

'Not everything,' he said smoothly. 'Detectives can give

you the facts but not the reasons. Why did you get engaged so quickly? Were you trying to create a family?'

She hesitated and then nodded, curling her toes into the sand and making patterns with her feet. 'Yes, I was,' she said honestly. 'I met Ian and he seemed really keen on me...' She broke off with a wry smile and his eyes narrowed.

'But?'

'A month before our wedding I discovered that he was already married. He never intended to marry me. Apparently I was just one of many.'

Nico's eyes narrowed. 'That must have hurt.'

'Well, the worst of it was, it didn't really,' she admitted. 'When I found out about his wife, apart from feeling very sorry for her I was just hugely relieved that I'd found out what a louse he was in time. I suppose I didn't really love him. I was just hideously lonely and loneliness makes you do stupid things.'

'Perhaps you confused lust with love, *tesoro*,' Nico drawled softly, and she gave an emphatic shake of her head.

'No. It definitely wasn't that. We hardly ever— I mean, I didn't really— I assumed I wasn't that keen on sex, but after last night I know—' She broke off, her face scarlet with embarrassment at the confession that he'd just managed to drag out of her.

He reached out a lean hand and tilted her face to his in a gesture of pure male possession. 'After last night you know differently.'

His husky voice and the look in his eyes scorched her flesh and for a long moment she stared at him, memories of shared intimacy pulsing between them. Then she jerked her chin away from his fingers.

'You are still so incredibly shy with me, *cara mia*,' he murmured, his tone amused. 'And if he was your first and only boyfriend, I'm beginning to understand why. You have a lot to learn about being relaxed with a man.'

'You don't help,' she blurted out, hating the way he made her feel. Hot, panicky—desperate for him to kiss her again. 'You're always so cool....'

'Not cool,' he murmured, leaning towards her, his breath warm on her heated flesh. 'Definitely not cool.'

'They can see us from the house,' she breathed, mesmerised by the look in his stunning dark eyes.

'I'm not touching you,' he drawled softly, his eyes dropping to her full mouth. 'I'm just cranking up the heat, ready for our siesta. I haven't finished talking to you yet. There is much, much more I want to know about you.'

'Oh.' She looked at him dizzily. He had a voracious appetite for sex and the knowledge of what he could make her feel had a devastating effect on her concentration.

'So you weren't upset over Ian?'

Running her tongue over her lips, she dragged her eyes away from his tanned, muscular shoulders and tried to drag an answer from her drugged brain.

'I—I was upset because it meant that I couldn't have children straight away.'

Nico looked at her quizzically. 'And that had been your plan?'

She nodded. 'I wanted an instant family. If I could have gone to a shop and bought one, I would have done it.' She gave a long sigh. 'And I suppose that's what I did in effect. I confided in Lucia and she suggested I talk to Carlo. At first it all seemed completely ridiculous, but then I started thinking, Why not? I convinced myself that plenty of children grow up in single-parent households with estranged parents sharing them and fighting over them. Would a child born to one parent who loved her deeply be so badly off?'

Nico frowned. 'You didn't just think of waiting a few years until you found a man you fell in love with?'

'I suppose I didn't have any faith that it would happen.' *But it had.* She was in love with Nico. And now they were married with a baby. The irony of the situation wasn't lost on her but, of course, that was one observation she could never share with him.

'So that's when you decided to have Rosa?'

'Well, it wasn't quite as easy as that, but basically, yes.' Abby reached for her dress and pulled it over her head, freeing her blonde hair with her hand so that it tumbled down her back. 'Lucia made all the arrangements for me. She was a real friend.'

Nico was watching her through veiled eyes and she wondered what he was thinking.

'Rosa's getting pink cheeks,' she said suddenly, kneeling up to gather their things together. 'I'm going to take her back to the villa.'

Without waiting for him to reply, she swept Rosa into her arms and started to make her way back up the beach.

She really didn't want to talk about Rosa's conception.

It just reminded her of the precarious nature of their marriage.

CHAPTER EIGHT

BACK in their room Abby showered quickly before joining the family for lunch on the terrace.

The table was laden with delicious food, bowls of shiny black olives, freshly grilled fish, salads and interesting breads.

Wine flowed as freely as the conversation, and by the time lunch ended Abby felt her eyelids drooping. She'd had virtually no sleep the night before and was feeling drowsy in the hot sunshine.

Noticing her predicament, Nico stood up and stretched out a hand, glancing round the table as he pulled her to her feet. 'If you will excuse us, we are going for a siesta.'

Abby smothered a yawn. 'But Rosa—'

'Chiara will take her for a nap,' Francesca said immediately, waving a hand towards the cool villa. 'Go, and we don't expect to see you until dinner, and not even then if you're too tired to join us.'

Once in their room, Nico pulled her deliberately in his arms and lowered his head. His kiss was hot and demanding and her insides felt scorched by the sensation that he aroused in her. Her lips parted and he cupped her face in his strong hands, exploring every inch of her mouth with his.

She felt the cool brush of soft cotton against her bare legs and back and then he had swiftly removed the dress, leaving her clad only in her bra and silk panties.

He backed her towards the bed with his powerful body, supporting her as she tumbled onto her back, a look of totally male satisfaction simmering in his dark eyes.

'I have been wanting to do this all morning,' he murmured huskily, removing her underwear with a speed that made her gasp with shock.

'Nico, it's broad daylight.'

'So?' Amusement slashed across his handsome face as he looked down at her body with an earthy groan. 'You are absolutely stunning, *cara mia*. It would be such a waste to only make love to you in the dark. I want to see every inch of you.'

Totally in control, he bent his dark head, taking one of her peaked nipples in his mouth and caressing it with maddening skill.

Burning between her thighs, she arched towards him and he lifted his head and rolled onto his back, taking her with him.

Her blonde hair trailed onto his chest and he lifted a strand with a hand that wasn't quite steady.

'I love the way you tremble when I touch you and I love the fact that you honestly have no idea how sexy you are,' he groaned, dragging her head down and kissing her deeply.

Abby felt the thickness of his erection against her own wet heat and she gasped as he lifted her with strong hands and positioned her to take him inside her.

'Nico…' Her cry of shock turned to a sob of ecstasy as he entered her in a smooth thrust, his body stretching and dominating hers even though she was supposedly in the position of control.

'You are mine now,' he murmured against her mouth, his touch fiercely possessive. 'You belong totally to me.'

Flushed and gasping for air, she felt her body move automatically to follow his lead, felt herself surrender to his powerful demands until the tension exploded inside her and she fell against him, her hot cheek resting on the tangled hair of his chest.

Briefly she felt his hand stroke her hair away from her

face and then he rolled her onto her back and slid down her body.

'Nico...' Her voice was an embarrassed squeak as he parted her thighs, his intention clear. 'You can't. It's the middle of the day....'

'Which makes it all the more exciting, *angelo*,' he breathed.

By the time the seduction was complete, Abby was too stunned to move. Nico had made love to her in positions that she'd never even imagined and done things that had brought hot colour to her already permanently flushed cheeks.

A look of intensely male satisfaction on his stunningly handsome face, Nico leaned across and kissed her swiftly before coming to his feet and prowling over to the bathroom.

'Sleep well, *tesoro*,' he murmured, the expression in his dark eyes lazily amused as they slid over her drained and sated body.

Through a haze of sex-induced stupor, it occurred to her that he should have been tired, too, but he certainly didn't look it. But that was Nico all over, she thought sleepily, her eyelids drifting closed even before he'd strolled into the bathroom. He had more stamina than the rest of the world put together.

The week passed in a haze of sociable meals, trips to the beach and wild love-making. Nico had a remarkable knack of getting her to open up to him and she found herself telling him things that she'd never told anyone before in her life and the closeness she felt from those confessions just fuelled her deepening love for him.

'What about you?' she said one day, after she'd finished telling him another secret of her life. 'I want to know you, too.'

He gave her a wolfish smile that was pure, predatory male. 'You are beginning to know me extremely well, *cara mia.*'

Abby blushed hotly at his husky implication. It was certainly true that he made very sure that she knew exactly what he needed in bed. 'You know I didn't mean that. I mean you never talk to me about how you feel....'

'I feel extremely content,' he said lazily, lying back in the sun and closing his eyes. Thick black lashes rested on his incredible cheek-bones and she looked at him shyly.

'Did you never think of getting married before?'

He gave a slow smile, his eyes still firmly closed. 'I never had a reason to.'

Abby's own smile faded and she felt as though she'd been showered with cold water. Of course he hadn't. The reminder that he'd only married her to gain possession of Rosa and give his daughter a family left her feeling miserably depressed.

'But did you plan to have children?'

'Of course. I'm Italian.' His voice was rough and he kept his eyes closed. 'All Italian males want a family. I just assumed I'd be able to have them whenever I was ready.'

'And then you were diagnosed with cancer?' She faltered slightly, bracing herself for rejection. His mother had made it obvious that he'd never talked about his illness with anyone. Why did she think he might talk to her? Just because she'd trusted and confided in him endlessly over the past few days, it didn't mean that he was obliged to do the same.

There was a long silence and then he gave a sigh and covered his face with a tanned forearm. 'That diagnosis was the biggest shock of my life. At first my fertility was the last thing on my mind. I just wanted them to treat it as aggressively as possible, but then once they were convinced that they'd done everything they needed to do I was suddenly faced with the reality of not being able to have children.'

'That must have been awful.' Her voice was soft. 'I can understand why you came after Rosa.'

His eyes flew open and he propped himself up on his elbows, looking at her through wickedly thick lashes the colour of dark chocolate.

'For a few very bleak months I thought I would never have a child of my own.' He gave a humourless laugh. 'That knowledge is not easy for any man to cope with, but for an Italian male it is particularly hard on the ego.'

Abby held her breath, aware that such an admission from him was an amazing step forward.

'Did you talk to anyone about it?'

Nico shook his head. 'Of course not. It was something I had to come to terms with myself and I have to admit I had a few very low months. I worked myself to the bone as a means of distraction and there wasn't a day that I didn't think about the child that I'd fathered. I told myself that I couldn't interfere but it nagged at me so badly that I thought I'd at least check what had happened to the child.'

Abby bit her lip and felt suddenly sick. 'Nico, about—'

'I don't want to talk about that,' he interjected smoothly, as he pulled her towards him. 'It's history now and I really couldn't care less about what happened at the clinic. At one point in my life I had given up on ever being a father in the real sense of the word. To find myself living with my daughter is a miracle that I would have paid any price to achieve.'

'Even marriage,' she joked shakily, and he dealt her a lingering smile that made her toes curl.

'Being married to you definitely has its compensations, *cara mia*,' he said in a husky voice, and then the talking stopped and he rolled her over and pushed her down onto the blanket.

Nico glanced down at Abby's sleeping form, shaken to the core by the unfamiliar feelings that swamped his normally logical brain.

When he'd embarked on this relationship, he'd been prepared to pay any price to gain possession of his daughter, even marriage.

It had never occurred to him that making love to Abby would turn his world inside out.

It was just sex, he told himself firmly, standing up in a fluid movement and pulling on a robe. And what he needed was fresh air to clear his head.

Without waking her, he opened the French doors that led to the terrace and strolled noiselessly out into the night air.

Just sex.

Glancing back into the dimly lit bedroom, his eyes narrowed at the sight of her blonde hair tangled over the pillow and wandered appreciatively over the pale curve of her hip.

Sucking in his breath he dragged his gaze away and faced the truth.

It wasn't *just sex* at all.

With her warmth and her generosity, Abby had curled her way around his heart. She'd even persuaded him to talk about the subject that he avoided with everyone else. *His infertility.*

And somewhere between meeting her and making love to her he'd even ceased to care that she'd deceived him. With a childhood like hers, who could blame her for grabbing any opportunity that had come her way?

He rubbed a hand over the back of his neck to relieve the tension, grimly aware of the irony of the situation.

He'd never fallen in love with a woman before and when it had finally happened it had to be with someone who didn't love him and was never likely to.

Nico swallowed a groan of frustration. He was only too aware that she'd married him for her daughter's sake.

Was there any way he could persuade her to fall in love with him?

*   *   *

Abby was curled up asleep on his chest that night when she heard Rosa crying.

Still half-asleep, she went to move but he stopped her, tucking the sheet around her and dropping a kiss on her head.

'You are exhausted, *tesoro*. Go back to sleep. I will see to her.'

Thinking that sharing parenthood very definitely had its advantages, Abby went back to sleep and enjoyed a completely undisturbed night.

When she awoke the next morning there was no sign of Nico and she padded next door to Rosa's room, astonished to see him trying to change a nappy.

Rosa was twisting and wriggling and refusing to co-operate, and he was muttering something in Italian as the tapes of the nappy stuck to his arm.

He glanced up and saw her in the doorway, frustration written all over his handsome face.

'*Dio mio*, how do you get a nappy near her?' He looked at her with naked incredulity. 'She won't keep still.'

Abby grinned and walked across the room. 'She thinks it's a game.'

'Some game,' Nico growled, admitting defeat and handing her the clean nappy. 'This is the second one I've wrecked. I am prepared to be a very hands-on father, but even I have my limits.'

Abby was hiding her amazement. She never, ever would have thought that a man like Nico, the original macho male, would have even contemplated changing a nappy.

'What's happened to Chiara?' Abby smoothed the nappy out, grabbed Rosa's ankles and snapped the tapes together before the toddler had time to squirm.

'I sent her away, but I won't make that mistake again,' Nico murmured, amusement simmering in his eyes as he watched the efficient way she completed the task that he'd struggled with. 'You do that with amazing speed and effi-ciency. I'm totally floored with admiration, *cara mia*.'

'You sent her away?' Abby scooped Rosa up into her arms and looked at him questioningly.

Colour touched his cheek-bones and for the first time she noticed the heavy stubble on his jaw and the lines of tired-ness around his eyes.

'Rosa had a very disturbed night,' he said through gritted teeth. 'I think she's teething.'

Abby frowned. 'I remember hearing her cry and you get-ting out of bed to see to her. I don't remember you coming back.'

'That's because I didn't,' Nico said dryly. 'I never would have thought that someone so small could cause so many problems. She refused to go to sleep unless I was holding her, and as soon as she drifted off and I tried to put her back in the cot, she woke up again.'

Abby smothered a smile. 'You should have called me or let Chiara take over.'

Something flickered in those dark eyes and he looked away from her, concentrating his attention on his daughter. 'I couldn't sleep,' he muttered, his Italian accent more pro-nounced than usual. 'Just remind me never to do the night shift if I'm operating the next day. I can survive on very little sleep but I have just discovered that it does have to be in one go. Last night I had about three hours in snatches of eight minutes at a time.'

Abby laughed. 'It's torture, isn't it? They always say that the person who invented the phrase "sleep like a baby" had never actually had one.' Her smile faded and she touched his arm gently. 'You're a brilliant father,' she said softly, 'and Rosa is a very lucky girl.'

There was an electric silence and an odd expression flick-ered across his face, but before she had time to interpret the look Nico gave a groan and took her mouth in a dev-astating kiss. His tongue explored the interior of her mouth in a kiss so explicit and intimate that she moaned in protest when he finally lifted his head. If she hadn't been holding Rosa she knew that he would have made love to her there and then in the nursery.

'Give Rosa to Chiara,' he instructed, his breathing unsteady as he looked at her with flattering appreciation. 'I might be prepared to forfeit sleep for my child, but I've decided that a whole night away from my wife is asking too much.'

Two hours later Abby sat at the breakfast table, totally dazed by the intensity of Nico's love-making. For a man who'd been up all night, he certainly didn't suffer on the energy front, she thought, feeling her cheeks grow pink as he strolled across the terrace to join the family.

Considering he didn't love her, she couldn't fault him. He was totally attentive to her every need, he listened and confided and as for their love-making... She breathed in unsteadily. Well, maybe it was just sex to him, but when they were in bed together she had no trouble pretending that what they shared was real. He might not love her but she knew how much he wanted a family. Surely that should be enough for her?

'I hear the little one had a bad night,' Francesca fussed over Rosa and the little girl beamed at her happily, banging the table with her cup and threatening everyone with jammy fingers.

They'd almost finished breakfast when there was a sudden bustle inside the villa and Lucia breezed out onto the terrace in a waft of dark hair and expensive perfume.

'Surprise! I'm a day early.' She stopped dead when she saw Abby, her eyes widening in amazement. 'Abby? What are you...?'

Her gaze flickered to Rosa and then Nico, and suddenly her smile faded and her face lost its colour.

'You told me you'd met someone,' she whispered, her

eyes fixed on Nico's face. 'You told me you wanted to introduce me to your wife.'

'And so I do,' Nico replied calmly. 'But I don't suppose you need much in the way of introductions. You already know Abby.'

Lucia looked at her friend in confusion and Abby immediately got to her feet and gave her friend a hug.

'It's really great to see you,' she murmured, and Lucia returned the hug, her eyes flickering to Carlo and then to their mother.

'You should have told us you were coming early,' Francesca reproved. 'You shouldn't be taking taxis. Tell her, Nico.'

Nico's eyes rested on his sister, noting her pallor. 'I think Lucia is old enough to make her own decisions on such things,' he drawled softly. 'She's more than able to think through the consequences of her actions.'

Abby gave a start, wondering if there was a hidden meaning behind his words.

Lucia obviously thought so, too, because she suddenly looked distinctly nervous.

Francesca rose to her feet, oblivious to the tension simmering around the table. 'I'll go and tell Maria that we're one extra for breakfast.'

She vanished into the villa and Lucia turned on her brother, visibly nervous. 'How did you—? I mean—'

'How did I discover your little deception?' Nico's tone was chilly. 'Simple really. I decided to follow up the child I fathered. Remember the one, Lucia? The child of your thirty-eight-year-old friend and her infertile husband?'

Lucia winced and threw a pleading glance at Carlo who sighed and rubbed a hand across his jaw.

'Nico—'

'It's fortunate for you that this story has a happy ending,' Nico said evenly, his eyes still fixed on his sister. 'I now have the family I wanted. What you and Abby did is history. I don't want it mentioned again.'

'But Abby didn't do anything,' Lucia said shakily. 'I was the one who persuaded you to be the donor. Abby didn't know anything about it.'

There was a frozen silence around the table, and even Carlo seemed beyond speech.

Groaning inwardly, Abby stared down at her plate, waiting for the inevitable explosion.

It was a long time in coming. The silence built and built until Lucia's discomfort and anxiety were felt by everyone.

When Nico finally spoke his voice was deceptively calm. 'Are you telling me,' he said softly, 'that Abby had no knowledge that I was the father?'

Abby held her breath and put the fork she was holding back down on her plate.

'Look, it really doesn't—'

Nico lifted a hand to silence her, his dark eyes fixed on his sister's flushed face.

'Well, of course she didn't.' Lucia threw her brother a look of disbelief. 'She never would have chosen you. That's why I didn't tell her. Abby was about the only girl in school who *didn't* fancy you. She's always been terrified of you, that's why I'm so amazed that she agreed to marry you and—'

'That's enough, Lucia,' Abby said shakily, interrupting her friend quickly before her indiscretion could create any further damage. 'As Nico says, it's all history now. Let's forget it.'

Nico's eyes were still on his sister, his tension pronounced. 'I assumed she knew.'

'Oh, my God…' Lucia paled visibly as the truth hit her. 'You bullied her into marrying her, didn't you? You thought she'd *wanted* you as the father of your child.'

His handsome face ashen, Nico rose to his feet. 'Are you seriously telling me that this was all your idea?'

'Yes.' Lucia's confession was little more than a whisper and Nico switched languages, his eyes fixed coldly on his sister's crumpling face as he spoke in rapid Italian.

Abby couldn't understand a word of it but Lucia burst into tears and there was a sudden tension in Carlo's broad shoulders.

'Nico, please…' She put out a hand and touched his arm gently and he broke off and drew in a shaky breath, clearly battling to regain control of his temper.

'Why?' He glared at his sister. 'What made you do it?'

'Because I thought you were the greatest,' Lucia sobbed. 'I adored you, Nico. You were the very best big brother a girl could have, and when Abby said she wanted a baby, I couldn't think of a single person in the whole world who'd be better than you.'

Nico closed his eyes and let out a long breath. '*Dio*, I don't believe this.'

'I knew you wouldn't agree to father the child of a young girl so I lied to you. I didn't mean any harm. I didn't think you'd ever find out.' Tears poured down her cheeks and she lifted a shaking hand to her mouth. 'I certainly didn't think you'd bully Abby into marrying you. I can't believe you did that. She's terrified of you.'

She was crying so hard now that Abby stood up and went to her, instinctively wanting to comfort her friend.

'No one bullied anyone. Please, don't cry. It really doesn't matter,' she said softly, slipping her arms around the other girl and holding her close.

'Of course it matters.' Lucia rubbed away the tears with the back of her hand and gulped. She glared at her brother, her eyes filling again. 'I always thought you were the cleverest person I knew but obviously you're not. Anyone can see that Abby isn't the sort of girl who lies. She's gentle and good and horribly shy with men. How could you even *think*—?'

'Because that's what you led me to think,' Nico interjected, his tone harsh. 'You told me that you drew up a list of qualities you were looking for in a father—'

'We did,' sobbed Lucia, 'and then *I* decided that you were the best match. *Me*, Nico. Not Abby. I never told Abby. She was totally innocent. You have to let her go. You can't do this!'

Nico's face was a mask, his features expressionless as he faced his sister across the table.

Then he said fired something at her in Italian and she gave another sob and ran into the villa.

Abby made a move to follow her but Carlo put a hand on her arm. 'I'll go to her and I'll deal with Mamma,' he said quietly, consternation in his eyes as he looked at Nico. 'You two have things to discuss.'

He left the table and Abby stared down at her hands, totally at a loss. What should she say?

Unable to bear the tension any longer, she stood up quickly and excused herself, hurrying to their bedroom, her heart sinking as she realised that Nico was close behind her.

He closed the door behind him with an ominous click.

For a long moment he just stared at her, visibly tense, and then he paced across the room to the French windows, clearly at a loss for words.

Finally he stopped dead and faced her, a muscle working in his darkened jaw.

'Again I've misjudged you.'

'It doesn't matter.'

'It *does* matter!' He raked a hand through his dark hair and gave a short laugh. 'I thought that you had chosen me to be her father—'

'Can we just forget it?'

'No. I have been wrong about you so many times. I doubted your love for Rosa but then when she was ill I saw just how deeply you care for her. I assumed that you were hopeless with money but it turned out that you were totally innocent of that crime, too.' His mouth set in a grim line as he ticked off his crimes on his long, strong fingers. 'And if that wasn't enough I then accuse you of conspiring with my sister because you wanted me to father your child. I remember you telling me repeatedly that you weren't lying. I wasn't willing to listen to you then, but I'm listening now.'

'Nico, please…'

Did any of it really matter now? They were married and it was all in the past.

And she loved him.

'I want the truth,' he growled, turning away from her and pacing across their room like a caged tiger. 'And this time I'm listening to every word.'

Abby clasped her hands in front of her and took a deep breath. 'When she found out about Ian, it was Lucia who suggested that I had a baby on my own,' she told him. 'In a way it was my fault that she chose you. I told her that I wanted someone that—'

'Please, don't defend my sister,' he breathed, interrupting her with a lift of his hand. 'I am fast becoming aware that you are every bit as good and kind as you seem. I suspect you wouldn't see bad in anyone.'

'But Lucia—'

'The truth, Abby!'

'She arranged for me to speak to Carlo and then have tests and some counselling. To be honest, I never knew anything about the donor. Then Lucia arranged for me to go to the clinic. I saw a young doctor that I didn't know.…' She frowned as she remembered that day, 'I was surprised because I'd been expecting to see Carlo.'

Nico sighed. 'Lucia made sure that you didn't. He knew that I'd agreed to be a donor to a couple in their late thirties.'

Abby didn't know what to say to him. 'I'm sorry.'

'I had never agreed to be a donor for Carlo before,' Nico

continued, 'and she knew it. She knew that if she'd told me the truth, that you were young and single, I never would have agreed.'

'But she meant well.' Abby glanced at him helplessly, daunted by the simmering anger she saw in the depths of his dark eyes. 'She did it because you're her hero. You always were, Nico.'

His mouth twisted into a wry smile. 'You told me that you hadn't chosen me to be the father but I was too arrogant to accept it.'

Abby dipped her head. The whole situation was too embarrassing. 'It isn't your fault,' she mumbled. 'In the circumstances it was a reasonable assumption. Most women think you're the answer to their prayers.'

'But as I am fast discovering, *you* are not most women,' he said dryly, 'and it would have been better for both of us had I realised that a little sooner.'

He was saying that he wished he'd never married her.

She struggled to hide her dismay. 'I don't see that anything has changed,' she said, staring hard at the tiled floor of their bedroom. 'We are still Rosa's parents, and we both still want to be with her.'

'You're staring at the floor again! *Dio*, look at me!' he ordered, exasperation in his deep voice. 'How do you think I feel, knowing that you were frightened of me? Shyness is one thing but the thought that you're scared of me…'

'I'm not scared of you.' Horrified at the mere suggestion, she lifted her head and their eyes met in a clash of fierce awareness.

'But you *were*.'

'Well, it's true that you made me nervous,' she admitted, butterflies coming to life in her stomach as she looked into his incredibly sexy eyes. 'But you were right when you said that it was chemistry. I just didn't recognize it at the time.'

He sucked in a long breath. 'I'm ashamed of the way I

treated you. You were totally innocent and yet I threatened to take your child—'

'Because you thought you couldn't have a family any other way,' Abby said softly, and he rubbed a hand over the back of his neck, his tension pronounced.

'Can you forgive me?'

'What is there to forgive?' She gave a gentle smile. 'Wanting to have your child with you is something to be proud of.'

'But I wanted to punish you.' The honesty of his rough admission made her smile.

'Remind me never to cross you.'

'And remind me always to believe everything you say in the future,' he groaned, dragging her against him and taking control again as always. 'We both love Rosa and that will be enough to make this marriage work.'

Abby swallowed, wishing desperately that he hadn't voiced that last statement.

Although his opinion of her may have altered, his reasons for marrying her hadn't. He'd married her to gain possession of his daughter and nothing was ever going to change that fact.

As the limo moved swiftly through the darkened streets, Abby could hardly believe she was back in London.

And in many ways she didn't want to believe it.

Sardinia had been amazing.

Apart from one afternoon when Nico had gone out with Carlo, they'd spent the entire week in each other's company.

She still felt nervous when he entered the room but it was a different type of nerves. This time she was well aware that it had nothing to do with intimidation and everything to do with sexual awareness.

Awareness of just what he could make her feel in bed.

Not that she had any illusions about Nico. He clearly

enjoyed making love to her because he had spent virtually the whole week doing little else, but she knew that there was no emotion involved.

Such incredible and intimate sex was obviously perfectly normal for him.

'You are very quiet, *cara mia*,' he said suddenly, a frown touching his dark brows as the limo pulled up outside his apartment. 'Are you feeling ill?'

'No.' She gave him a wan smile and reached to undo the straps of Rosa's car seat. 'I—I just enjoyed my time in Italy.'

There was a tense silence and her face heated under his watchful gaze. For a fleeting second she had the impression that he was going to say something else but then Matt opened the door and the moment passed.

Fortunately there was no sign of the press and everything in the apartment was as cool and elegant as ever.

Abby glanced around her, hardly able to believe that only a week had passed since she'd last been here.

Nico was talking into his mobile phone, a frown on his face as he listened to whoever was on the other end.

When he finally flipped it closed his expression was grim. 'I'm sorry to abandon you on our first night back, but I have to go to the hospital.' He raised his hands in a gesture of apology. 'Baby Hubbard has been readmitted and they want me to take a look at her. She might need to have surgery sooner than we'd planned.'

Abby tried to hide her disappointment. 'Will you be back later?'

He was already walking towards the bedroom, preparing to change. 'I hope so, but if not I will see you in the hospital tomorrow and we will have dinner tomorrow night. In the meantime, Matt will be around if you have any problems and Giovanni will cook for you.'

She didn't care about the cooking. She wanted Nico's company.

Which was completely ridiculous, of course. They didn't have that sort of relationship.

No ties. Wasn't that what he'd promised when he'd married her?

They had married for Rosa, not for each other.

She watched as he emerged from the bedroom dressed in a suit that emphasised his height and the width of his shoulders. He was every inch the successful surgeon and she thought regretfully of the way he'd relaxed with her at his home in Sardinia. She'd had a glimpse of part of him that he usually kept hidden from the world. But now the holiday was over and the 'Iceberg' was back.

So what did that mean for their relationship?

'You look fantastic. You obviously had a wonderful week,' Heather said as they watched the night staff leave the ward.

Abby smiled. She *had* had a wonderful week.

In fact, it had been a week like no other.

'And now you're Mrs Santini.' Heather looked at her with awe and Abby shrugged self-consciously.

'I'm still the same person, Heather,' she said awkwardly, but Heather shook her head.

'There are subtle differences. You've got this luminous glow, but I suppose that's just love,' Heather said wistfully.

Abby blushed.

Was it really that obvious?

If it was, she needed to be careful around Nico. The last think she wanted was for him to find out her true feelings for him.

'Well, you're one lucky girl,' Heather said firmly, 'and I don't suppose you're going to be working with us for much longer so I'm making the most of you while I can. I suppose Nico told you that baby Hubbard was readmitted last night?'

Abby nodded and Heather rolled her eyes. 'Well, of course he did. How stupid of me. You live with the man so you ought to know when he's not at home. Anyway, her oxygen saturation has dropped so they're going to operate tomorrow. They're checking that there's a bed in CICU and arranging a theatre slot.'

'And has the mother managed to find anyone to take care of the other children?'

'She has, but she's in a bit of a state.' Heather smiled sheepishly at Abby. 'And that's where you come in, of course. I need you to try and calm her down as she's making the baby stressed. You're always so amazing with the patients.'

'I'll talk to her,' Abby said immediately, and Heather nodded.

'Good. Nico checked her last night for us and he's running a few more tests today, but basically he intends to operate tomorrow. He said he'd be up later to talk to the mother again and get the consent form signed. By the way, baby Hubbard has a name now—Suzy.'

Abby finished updating herself on the changes on the ward and then made her way to the side room to find Suzy and her mother.

Vanessa Hubbard was a thin, stressed-looking woman whose clothes looked slightly too big for her.

The moment Abby walked into the room she looked up with worried eyes.

'Hello, Vanessa, I'm Abby Har— Santini,' Abby corrected herself quickly, shaking the other woman's hand and peeping into the cot at the sleeping baby. 'I'm going to be your nurse. I can imagine just how worried you are so, please, feel that you can ask me anything you want to.'

'Santini?' Vanessa looked startled. 'That's the same name as the surgeon.'

'He's my husband,' Abby said quietly, and Vanessa gave a weak smile.

'You must be very proud of him.'

Abby nodded. She was proud.

Very proud.

'My GP checked him out for me,' Vanessa confessed ruefully, 'and he said that he's one of the best. Not that that is much consolation. I just wish Suzy was OK....'

'Well, of course you do.'

'I thought we were going to have a few weeks at home together but then she started breathing quickly and I couldn't get her to take her bottle.'

'That's because her oxygen saturation dropped,' Abby told her, her eyes flicking to the monitor to reassure herself that the readings were now within normal limits. 'When did she last feed?'

'She had a bottle at six,' Vanessa told her, watching the baby with tears in her eyes. 'I just can't believe this is happening....'

The tears rolled down her cheeks and Abby felt her heart twist for the poor woman.

'It must be awful for you, but try not to upset yourself.' She slipped her arms around the other woman and gave her a hug. 'Isn't there anyone who can be with you?'

Vanessa blew her nose and shook her head. 'No. My parents died a long time ago and Suzy's father left us when I told him I was pregnant again. He said we just couldn't afford another child.'

Tears spilled down her cheeks again and at that moment Nico walked into the room dressed in blue theatre scrubs.

He frowned as he saw that Vanessa was crying. 'Has something happened?'

'She's just very upset and worried about little Suzy,' Abby told him quietly, her arms still round the other woman who was finding it hard to control herself.

'Of course.' His voice was rich and masculine. 'That is understandable. Perhaps it would help if I sat down and went through the operation with you, Vanessa?'

Vanessa sniffed and made a visible effort to pull herself together. 'Thank you. I'd like that. My GP has been great but he said that you were the best person to explain everything.'

Nico glanced at Abby. 'Can we arrange some coffee?'

She nodded, understanding that he wanted to be left alone with Vanessa for a few moments.

By the time she shouldered her way back into the room with two cups of coffee, Vanessa was looking more relaxed. She didn't know what Nico had said, but whatever it was had obviously done the trick.

Abby handed Vanessa a cup of coffee and placed Nico's next to him.

'You understand that the main vessels coming out of your daughter's heart are the wrong way round—we call this transposition of the great arteries. I will show you with a diagram.' Out came the pad and Nico's pen moved smoothly over the paper as he drew the heart. 'This artery takes blood from the heart around the body, this artery takes blood to the lungs, but with Suzy they are in the wrong place.'

Vanessa stared at the diagram and nodded. 'So how is she getting her oxygen?'

'She survived at the beginning because she had what we call a PDA—that stands for patent ductus arteriosus—but you don't need to worry about that bit.' He waved a hand dismissively. 'The PDA connects the two arteries and therefore allows the blood to mix.'

'But she still wasn't getting the oxygen she needed, which was why she was blue?' Vanessa looked at him keenly and Nico nodded, evidently surprised.

'You grasp the problem astonishingly quickly,' he observed, and she blushed at the praise.

'I loved biology at school. I would have loved to have been a doctor but I got pregnant and—' She broke off and gave a shrug. 'Anyway, you don't want to know about that. Carry on.'

'If you remember your biology, you will recall that in a

normal heart blood flows in a series.' He used a fresh piece of paper to demonstrate what he meant and then glanced up at her. 'In TGA there are two separate circulatory patterns.'

'So the two sides don't connect?'

Nico nodded. 'Exactly.'

'So that P— PDA…?' Vanessa glanced at Nico to check she'd got it right '…was the only connection?'

Nico nodded. 'That's right.'

'So how does the operation help?'

'I will basically move the arteries to the correct anatomical position.' Again Nico's pen flew over the page. 'I move this to here, and this to here.…'

'And what is the risk of the operation? What are the chances that I might lose her?'

'We quote a risk of five per cent for all our major heart operations,' Nico said quietly, and Vanessa closed her eyes.

'But I don't have a choice, do I? Without the operation she won't survive.'

'That's correct,' Nico's voice was gentle and Vanessa took a deep breath.

'Well, if someone told me I had a five per cent chance of winning the lottery, I'd know that I wouldn't.'

Nico smiled, admiration evident in his dark eyes. 'That is a positive way of looking at it. Today we will need to do a few more tests and get her ready for Theatre tomorrow. The anaesthetist will pop up and see her and Abby will take you for a visit to CICU. It is important to see where she will be taken after the operation or it can be very daunting.'

He answered more of Vanessa's questions and then he examined Suzy.

Finally he moved towards the door. 'We will operate tomorrow. If you have any questions in the meantime, Abby will be able to get hold of me.'

Abby followed him out of the room and he smiled down

at her apologetically. 'I'm sorry about last night. I had intended to come home but things were rather hectic here—'

'It doesn't matter,' she said immediately, trying not to be distracted by the heat in his eyes. 'I was wondering—could I watch you operate on Suzy? I've never seen an arterial switch.'

He nodded immediately. 'Of course. If Heather can spare you, I don't have a problem with that. I will warn the theatre sister. There are quite a few other people watching, too, so you won't be alone.' He checked his watch and pulled a face. 'I have to go. I need to see a patient on CICU.'

Suddenly he seemed miles away from the man she'd spent the last week with. He was driven and focused and thinking about nothing but work. Which was what made him such an exceptional surgeon, of course, she reminded herself. He had incredible self-discipline.

'I'll see you later, then....' Her voice tailed off feebly. She was dying to ask him if he would be coming home, but there was something forbidding about those broad shoulders and the grim set of his mouth. With the gravity of the operations he had to perform, the last thing he needed was her asking him to come home.

He started to walk down the corridor and then turned to face her, a ghost of a smile playing around his mouth.

'By the way, *tesoro*, your coffee is disgusting—remind me to give you lessons.'

Nico didn't come home again that night and Abby lay alone in the enormous bed, a seething mass of frustration.

Before last week she'd never really thought about sex. Her few brief encounters with Ian had been completely unmemorable but since her week with Nico she seemed to have turned into a sex addict.

All she could think about was the way she felt when he made love to her.

Unfortunately he obviously didn't feel the same way, she

thought miserably as she dressed for work next morning and lifted Rosa out of her cot. Since they'd returned home, his entire focus had been his work.

She was under no illusions that he'd married her to get Rosa, but after last week she'd also consoled herself that he enjoyed their love-making.

But maybe she was wrong.

The ward was humming with activity when she arrived and Heather caught her immediately.

'Suzy Hubbard is already prepped for Theatre and ready to go. They rang two minutes ago so if you can grab a porter we can take her down. Her mum is determined to go with her so expect some tears. Once Suzy's under the anaesthetic, you can go into Theatre.'

Abby looked around the bustling ward doubtfully. 'Are you sure that's all right—that we're not too busy?'

Heather shook her head. 'We're fine actually. I've got a brilliant agency nurse on today, which helps, and it's really important for you to see a switch. It's easier to understand the relevance of post-operative care if you've seen what the operation involves.'

Abby phoned for a porter and together they wheeled the cot down the corridor towards the theatre.

Vanessa was pale but in control.

In the anaesthetic room she held the baby in her arms until the anaesthetist had put her under and then she kissed the child gently and left the room with the porter.

One of the theatre nurses stuck her head round the door and looked at Abby. 'Are you watching? Come with me and I'll show you where to scrub.'

Abby followed her instructions to the letter, changing into theatre scrubs and wearing a sterile gown and gloves.

She walked into Theatre, her knees trembling slightly. What would it feel like, seeing Nico operate? She wasn't sure she'd be able to concentrate.

But she was wrong.

She was so mesmerised by the speed and skill of his fingers that all she could think of was what an outstanding surgeon he was.

'This is a standard arterial switch operation,' he told the paediatrician, who was also watching. 'I move the aorta to the left ventricle, and the pulmonary artery to the right ventricle and the coronary arteries to the aorta.'

The paediatrician lifted his eyebrows. 'So basically you're restoring normal anatomy?'

'Precisely. More light, please.'

The theatre nurse adjusted the light and the paediatrician watched, clearly fascinated.

'So how long has this been the operation of choice?'

'In my hospital in Italy, we moved from a Senning to a switch policy some time ago,' Nico told him. 'The Senning procedure was more of a physiological repair—they didn't change the anatomy, but they helped the blood get to the right places. Initially the mortality rate was lower than for the arterial switch.'

'So why did surgeons adopt the switch?'

Nico glanced at the monitors and then at the anaesthetist, assuring himself that everything was all right before he continued. 'It was found that various problems developed 10 to 15 years after the operation. The right and left ventricles have different abilities to cope with pressure and volume work. In patients who've had the Senning operation, the right ventricle has to do the work usually done by the left ventricle and in some patients it was just too much and the heart failed.'

'And what happens then?'

Nico gave a shrug. 'That is a very serious problem. The only real option is to refer the patient for a heart transplant.'

The paediatrician leaned forward to get a closer look at what Nico was doing. 'Could you do a switch operation on them later on?'

'It has been done.' Nico held out his gloved hand and

the nurse immediately gave him the instrument he wanted. 'But it is experimental at this stage.'

'So the switch operation is pretty much used everywhere?'

'Surgical technique has improved in the years since it was first introduced,' Nico murmured, his dark eyes fixed on his tiny patient. 'It's recognised as being the operation of choice for this condition.'

The operation took almost five hours from beginning to end and Abby was starting to get backache and leg-ache when the anaesthetist gave a frown.

'Her pressure is dropping slightly—are you going to be long?'

'I've finished.' Nico glanced at his registrar. 'I'm sending her to CICU with her chest open. It makes it easier to see what is going on and monitor any bleeding,' he told the paediatrician. 'We will close the chest on CICU in twenty-four hours if everything is well. Thank you, everyone.'

He stepped back from the operating table and stripped off his gloves. 'I'm going to shower and check on my patients in CICU then I have a ward round.' He looked at his registrar. 'You have time for a cup of coffee. I'll meet you on the ward in twenty minutes.'

Abby blinked as she watched him stride out of the room, the doors swinging closed behind him.

He was giving his registrar a short break but she was willing to bet that he wasn't taking one himself. His schedule was punishing and yet there was no visible evidence that he was tired.

She made her way up to the ward and Heather immediately asked her to feed a baby who was waiting to go for a cardiac catheterisation.

Abby walked into the kitchen, fetched the correct formula and then returned to the cot to feed the child.

She'd just finished when Nico strolled onto the ward.

He looked impossibly handsome and she felt her heart stumble in her chest.

She wanted him so badly.

It was funny really, she mused. She'd expected marriage to Nico to be torture, but not for this reason. *Not because she'd fallen in love with him.* What an utterly stupid thing to do, she thought helplessly. She was no different from all those other women who'd thrown themselves at him since he'd been a teenager.

As soon as he saw her he walked across the ward and bent down to look at the baby.

'One of Jack's?'

Abby nodded. 'She's going for a catheter tomorrow.'

'Did you find the operation interesting?'

She glanced up shyly, unable to keep the admiration out of her gaze. 'I thought you were amazing,' she said quietly, and he looked amused.

'I wasn't fishing for compliments.'

Of course he wasn't. A man like him didn't have the need for strokes from others. His self-confidence was total.

'It was interesting and I still think you were amazing,' she said simply, and his eyes locked on hers.

Tension simmered between them and Abby felt her body grow warm.

'Will you be home tonight?'

He tensed slightly and his dark eyes narrowed. 'Abby…'

He hadn't slept with her since Sardinia and she was afraid that he was still feeling guilty about what happened with Lucia.

An awful thought struck her.

Maybe he thought that she didn't *want* to sleep with him.

In which case it was up to her to show him that she did.

Taking a deep breath, she returned the baby to the cot and then looked him in the eye, her hands and knees suddenly weak.

She'd never propositioned a man in her life before. What if he rejected her?

'I—I really need to talk to you,' she stammered, glancing over her shoulder to make sure that none of the other staff were nearby.

He frowned slightly. 'Abby, I—'

'Please...' Her voice was urgent and she licked her lower lip in a provocative gesture. Or at least she hoped it was provocative.

Judging from the sudden tension in his shoulders, it had the desired effect.

'I'll try and get home tonight,' he said cautiously, and she shook her head and jerked her head towards the linen cupboard.

If she waited until tonight something would prevent it happening. She'd have lost her nerve or he'd get called back to the hospital.

'Not tonight—*now*! I need to get a clean sheet. Come with me?'

She walked into the tiny linen room and after a few moments he walked in behind her. His eyes never leaving hers, he closed the door firmly behind him, keeping his back to it so that no one else could enter.

'Abby—'

'I want you, Nico,' she breathed huskily, her heart thudding heavily against her chest. If he rejected her she'd die of embarrassment. Trying to forget that they were in a semi-public place, she lifted a hand to the buttons of her uniform and started to undo them one by one.

Nico stood frozen to the spot, visibly stunned by her performance. He seemed incapable of moving, his shocked dark eyes raking over her with blatant incredulity.

She reached the last button and paused, doubt suddenly showing in her huge eyes.

Finally he moved, dragging her against him with a harsh groan, his kiss hard and urgent.

Without lifting his mouth from hers, he slid her uniform up her thighs and gave a groan of satisfaction as he curved his hands over her bottom.

'*Dio mio*, I've missed you so much,' he growled against her mouth. 'If the other doctors knew that you were wearing stockings under this uniform, I'd have to do heart surgery on all of them.'

Swamped by the intense relief that he still wanted her, Abby kissed him back, happy for him to take over the dominant role.

'I really, really can't believe we're doing this *here*,' he said thickly, reaching down and dealing with his zip in a swift movement.

'Well, there didn't seem much choice. You haven't been home for days and I couldn't wait any longer.' Abby was breathing heavily, her body aching with need for him.

'That makes two of us. I want you *so* badly, *cara mia*,' he muttered, turning her swiftly so that she was the one against the door. In a smooth movement he slid his hands up her bare thighs and Abby's breath came in shallow pants as she felt his strong fingers sliding inside her panties and touching her intimately.

'Nico…' She forgot where they were and what the risks were if they were caught. Her brain was swamped by the explosive feelings inside her trembling body.

'You are so wet for me,' he groaned, lifting her so that she straddled him and entering her with a fierce thrust that brought a gasp of ecstasy to her lips.

The feeling was so exquisite, so unbearably exciting that she completely lost control, allowing her body to be totally dominated by his powerful thrusts.

Their mouths locked together as they climaxed violently, both of them stunned into silence by the intensity of what they'd shared.

Nico dropped his forehead to hers and looked deep into

her eyes, his breathing decidedly unsteady. 'That was fantastic, *cara mia*.'

Letting her out of his grasp, he adjusted her uniform so that she was decent.

Abby felt totally shell-shocked.

What was happening to her?

She was a shy, law-abiding person and here she was making wild passionate love in a tiny linen cupboard where they could have been caught at any minute.

Nico zipped his fly in one swift movement and threw her a dizzying smile. 'Now I feel much more relaxed.'

Abby stared at him weakly. She felt as though she'd never walk again.

He touched her cheek gently and suddenly seemed to hesitate. 'There are things I need to tell you—things we need to talk about...' He seemed about to say more but then his bleeper went off and he rolled his eyes. 'But now is clearly not the time. I will *definitely* be home tonight. I will see you there.'

With that he jerked open the door of the linen cupboard and walked out with his usual confidence, not even trying to be discreet.

But it was that very confidence that would probably save them, Abby reassured herself. There was nothing furtive about the way Nico behaved. Looking at him, no one would ever imagine that moments ago he'd been making love.

Which was probably more than could be said for her.

She smoothed her blonde hair, wriggled her hips to adjust her uniform and then made her way back onto the ward, thinking about what Nico had said.

He wanted to talk to her. And it was obviously something serious.

What was he going to say?

CHAPTER NINE

THE phone was ringing when Abby arrived home so after putting Rosa on the floor to play with some toys, she answered the call.

She was still dazed and in shock from her breathlessly exciting encounter with Nico and she fully expected it to be him on the phone.

'Hello?'

But it wasn't Nico, it was Carlo, calling from Italy, and Abby smiled as they exchanged small talk.

'Nico isn't home yet,' she said finally, stooping to remove a shoe from Rosa's mouth. 'Do you want me to give him a message?'

Carlo's voice was warm and friendly. 'No message. I just rang for a chat. I spoke to him last night when I gave him the news, but he was in a rush so we didn't really have time to talk properly. You must be thrilled about it, Abby.'

Thrilled about what?

What news?

'Well—' Abby was about to confess that she'd barely seen Nico since they'd returned from their honeymoon, and the time they *had* spent together had been at the hospital, but Carlo was still talking.

'I told him a year ago to take the test, and that it would probably be all right, but he was too stubborn. All that worry over nothing. At least now he knows that he'll be able to give you as many babies as the two of you can cope with.'

Babies?

Abby froze to the spot. Rosa had the shoe in her mouth

again but this time Abby didn't even bother removing it. She just clutched the phone tighter.

'Abby?' Carlo's voice sounded puzzled. 'Abby, are you there?'

'Yes, I'm here.' Abby plopped down onto the nearest chair, her palms sweaty. 'So—so everything's fine for him, then? He isn't infertile?'

'No way. I did the test for him when you were in Sardinia, but I suppose he told you that.'

No, he hadn't. But that was obviously where he'd been when he'd vanished with Carlo for the afternoon. He hadn't told her anything about what he'd been doing, and why should he? She was nothing but his key to Rosa. He had never wanted to marry her at all. He'd done it to gain custody of his one and only child. But now he could have more children....

Suddenly Abby felt physically sick.

'I have to go, Carlo,' she said quickly. 'I'll get him to call you back.'

She hung up, her fingers shaking, scooped Rosa into her arms and walked in a daze back to the bedroom.

Nico had married her because he'd wanted a family. But now he had discovered that he could have a family of his own. As many children as he liked, with the woman of his choice.

He didn't need to be with her any more.

And that was obviously what he'd been trying to tell her earlier. Which meant that she knew exactly what the conversation would be when he arrived home later.

He already believed that she hadn't wanted to marry him and now he'd discovered that *he* hadn't needed to marry *her* either. Their marriage had been a compromise for both of them, but he no longer needed to make that compromise.

Which meant that the marriage was over.

* * *

An hour later Abby was packed and pacing nervously around the huge living room.

Why on earth hadn't she just left Nico a note?

What was she hoping to achieve by staying to face him?

Was she hoping that he'd beg her to stay?

No, of course not. She knew he wasn't going to beg her to stay, but somehow, even knowing that he didn't love her, she couldn't bring herself to say goodbye on a piece of paper.

Not after everything they'd shared.

She was still wondering whether she should write a note when Nico strolled out of the lift, deep in conversation with someone on his mobile.

Still talking, he tossed his briefcase onto the nearest sofa and then paused, his black eyes narrowing as they homed in on her suitcase.

He ended the conversation abruptly and slipped the phone back into his pocket.

'What are you doing?'

His voice was deceptively calm and Abby felt her heart beat faster.

'I'm making things easy for both of us. I know what you wanted to talk to me about,' she blurted out, wishing that she didn't love him so much. Leaving him was the hardest thing she'd ever had to do in her life. 'I've spoken to Carlo.'

Nico was suddenly still, his lean, handsome face expressionless. 'About what, precisely?'

'I *know*, Nico,' she said softly, trying to hide the pain she felt inside. 'I know that you can have more children. You can have as many children as you like with whoever you like. You don't need me any more.'

Nico said nothing and Abby started to chatter nervously, filling in the gaps herself.

'You can still see Rosa and I'll always talk about you and let her know that she has a father she can be proud of,' she said hoarsely, knowing that if she didn't get away soon she was going to make a total fool of herself, and that was the last thing she wanted. She didn't want to join the ranks of women who'd made fools of themselves over him. She was going to hang onto her dignity if it killed her.

The silence seemed to stretch to infinity. When he finally spoke, his expression gave nothing away. 'So where are you planning to go?'

'I've found a bedsit that's available immediately—'

'A *bedsit*?' Finally he reacted and she couldn't help smiling at his horrified tone. Bedsits obviously rated down there with buses for Nico Santini. His black brows met in an ominous frown. 'Are you seriously telling me that you'd rather live in a *bedsit* than my apartment?'

She swallowed hard. 'I'd rather live anywhere than stay in a loveless marriage. It isn't going to work, Nico. We both know that. In Sardinia you gave me the option to end the marriage. I'm taking that option for both our sakes.'

He looked at her for a long moment and then paced over to the window.

Abby stared at his back helplessly. Wasn't he going to say anything at all about their time together? What was the matter with him?

She'd never known him short of words before.

'We'll be fine,' she muttered finally, stooping to pick up Rosa and her small bag. 'I've taken a few of the clothes. I hope you don't mind, but if you do then obviously I can—'

'I don't care about the clothes,' he grated, tension visible in his powerful shoulders as he turned to face her.

This was agony.

'I really have to go,' she said quickly, picking up Rosa and her bag and giving him a bright smile. 'I'll be in touch so that we can arrange when you want to see Rosa. That's if you want to, of course.'

Without waiting for him to reply, she hurried to the lift

and stepped inside, thumping the button for the foyer and praying for the doors to close quickly.

If she spent any more time in the same room as him, she was going to lose all self-control and throw herself at the man. Walking away from him without confessing just how much she loved him was the hardest thing she'd ever done.

Tears threatened but she refused to let them fall until she was safely away from his building.

She absolutely would not make an exhibition of herself.

As the lift doors opened on the ground floor she hoisted her bag further onto her shoulder and walked across the marbled foyer, stopping as she saw her exit blocked by Matt.

'Wait a moment.' He put one powerful arm across the door and gave her a rueful smile. 'I can't let you go, I'm afraid.'

'It's OK, Matt.' Touched that he was still keeping an eye on her, she gave him a shaky smile. 'Mr Santini knows I'm going.'

But Matt wasn't listening to her. He was staring across at the other lift, relief in his eyes as his boss came striding towards him.

'Just caught her,' he said quietly, and Nico nodded and spoke briefly in Italian.

Without question Matt melted into the background, hovering just out of earshot.

Abby looked at Nico, waiting for him to speak, her heart thundering in her chest so violently that she was amazed he couldn't see it.

'Please, come back upstairs,' he said finally, his dark eyes wary and his shoulders rigid with tension. 'There are things I need to say to you.'

Abby shook her head. She absolutely wasn't capable of a drawn out confrontation.

'I can't, Nico,' she muttered, clutching Rosa more tightly and turning towards the door.

'Abby, wait!' His voice had a rough edge and he caught her arm, preventing her escape. 'Wait—please. Just five minutes, that's all I ask. And then you can go.'

Five more minutes of torture....

She glanced up at him and her attention was caught by the look in his eyes. She'd never seen Nico nervous before, but this time he definitely looked nervous.

Why?

'I've never begged in my life,' he said, a wry smile touching his firm mouth. 'And I would rather that my first experience wasn't in front of my staff.'

Begged?

His staff?

Abby frowned and glanced round the foyer, noticing the doorman and a few other people watching discreetly.

They were his staff?

'I own this building,' he said gently, and she gave a weary smile.

Well, of course he did. That explained why the press had never been near his flat. He was totally protected on the top floor.

'I have had plenty of first experiences since I met you,' he said, his tone slightly bitter, 'but I would prefer that making a spectacle of myself in public wasn't one of them. Would you at least come back up to the apartment with me so that we can talk in private?'

His restrained courtesy was so unlike his usual arrogant, controlling style that her eyes widened.

'You're *asking* me, Nico, not telling me?' She couldn't resist teasing him and he gave a wry smile, the expression on his handsome features a visible admission that he was aware of his own faults.

'As I said, I have had plenty of first experiences with you,' he drawled, 'and asking instead of telling is probably another example.' His smile faded. 'Please, Abby.'

She hesitated and then nodded.

Instantly Nico was back in control, indicating with a snap of his fingers that Matt should take Rosa.

He ushered her into the lift and back into the apartment, not speaking until she was standing in his elegant living room with its amazing view across Hyde Park.

Abby stood there, waiting for the inevitable. He was going to discuss divorce. She knew he was. He'd decided that there was no point in delaying.

'Would you like a drink?'

She shook her head, twisting her hands in front of her and trying to look composed. She hated all this restrained courtesy. She'd actually grown accustomed to his volatile Italian temperament. She liked it. It was part of Nico. Part of who he was.

Nico paced over to the window and then turned to face her, his gaze disturbingly direct. 'I have acted in an unbelievably selfish way since the first day I met you, so I see no reason to change now.' His sensual mouth tightened and he took a deep breath. 'At least hear me out and then if you still want to go I won't stand in your way.'

Abby's heart lurched and her eyes widened. But surely he wanted her to go. She'd expected him to grab the chance to be rid of her with both hands.

'I know what you think of me,' he said roughly, raking a hand through his dark hair, 'and frankly I don't blame you. I've treated you very badly indeed. I bullied you and threatened you and behaved appallingly. I never once listened to your side of a story or considered your situation. I forced you into a marriage that you must have found totally abhorrent and yet you haven't complained. All you have done is shown unstinting love for our daughter and kindness to my family, especially my sister who is extremely fortunate to have such a loyal and forgiving friend.'

Stunned by his admission of guilt, Abby stared at the floor, thoroughly embarrassed by his gruffly spoken words. He made her sound like some sort of saint.

'Nico, I—'

'If you're about to say that none of it matters, please, don't,' he ground out, pacing across the carpet with such restrained violence that she blinked in surprise. 'I'm only too aware that I've been a lousy husband to you.'

Lousy husband?

She opened her mouth to deny it but he was still in full flow.

'My only defence is that I wasn't thinking rationally. When I had the cancer diagnosis I was devastated.' He paced over to the window, staring out across the park. 'Like most people, I had always believed myself to be immortal. It came as a shock to realise that I wasn't. Until then I'd always believed that I was totally in control of my life.'

She walked over to him and put a hand on his arm, her touch gentle. 'It must have been terrible for you.'

He shrugged dismissively. 'They did what they needed to do and I was lucky. The disease hadn't spread and they are confident that there will be no recurrence. But I was told at the time that it was very likely that I would be infertile. I was given the opportunity to freeze sperm before my treatment but I just wanted the disease treated as soon as possible.'

'But you never actually had a test until Carlo did one last week?'

He gave a short laugh and shook his head. 'No.'

'You just assumed you'd never be able to have children.'

'Which was why I decided to find out how the one baby I had fathered was doing.' His jaw tightened and he didn't look at her. 'That was when I discovered the deception.'

'It must have been very painful for you to see your child with a young single mother,' she said quietly. 'I can totally understand your frustration. You had so much to offer a child and yet were unable to have one of your own.'

He turned to look at her, his expression incredulous. 'How can you be so generous? I stormed into your house that night and threatened to take your daughter away from you.'

'But you believed that I'd lied to you,' she said, easily able to understand how he must have felt in the circumstances and willing to defend him. 'You believed that she would have been better off with you.'

'I was arrogant and unforgivably rude.' He sighed and rubbed a hand over the back of his neck in a visible effort to relieve the tension. 'I pretended that I was concerned for Rosa's welfare but the truth was I was just being selfish. I thought that she represented my only chance to be a father and I was determined to take that chance, no matter what. I searched around for reasons to justify taking her and I'm ashamed for having intimidated you. I remember how hard it was for you to look me in the eye that night. It was a testament to just how much you loved Rosa that you stood up to me.'

Her eyes teased him gently, her hand still on his arm. 'Apologising, Nico?'

He gave a wry smile. 'Yet another first.' He turned slightly and covered her hand in his. 'You are the only woman I have ever met who showed absolutely no interest in me or my money, and you were the first woman to say no to me.'

Abby couldn't resist smiling. 'Not that you listened.'

'That's because I haven't heard it that often in my life,' he confessed ruefully. 'I was so stunned when you told me that I was the last man on earth you'd want to marry that I didn't even believe that you meant it.'

Abby's smile faltered. Had she really said that? She must have been totally deluded.

'And this brings me to the hardest part of all.' He cupped her face in his hands and forced her to look at him. 'I know you didn't want to marry me, but I want you to stay. Please.'

She stared at him, unable to believe what she was hearing. 'You want me to still be your wife?' She must have sounded as incredulous as she felt because his hands dropped from her face and his dark eyes were shuttered.

'It is too much to contemplate, clearly.' He moved away from her but she moved after him, hardly daring to ask the question that needed to be asked.

'Why do you want me to stay, Nico?'

He turned slowly, his eyes wary. 'Why do you think?'

'I don't know.' Suddenly she was aware of every beat of her heart. 'I assumed that you didn't, which was why I was leaving.'

His eyes were suddenly sharp. 'You were leaving because you thought I wanted you to?'

She nodded. 'That's right. Now that you can have babies, you can have them with any woman you choose.'

His gaze burned into hers. 'And what if I choose you?'

There was an electrified silence. 'Me…?'

'Yes, you.'

'But you married me because you wanted Rosa.…' Her voice faltered and he moved towards her and took her hands in his.

'That's true. But I want to *stay* married to you because I love you,' he said quietly. 'I have never said those words to another human being in my life. I didn't believe love existed, but I was wrong about that, too.'

He loved her?

Dazed with shock, Abby stared at him. 'How—? I didn't know—'

'I didn't know myself until I saw the lift doors close,' he confessed, stroking a long finger down her flushed cheek. 'Then I suddenly realised that if I let you walk out of my life I would have lost everything that mattered to me.'

He loved her.

Abby stared at him. 'You're asking me to stay?'

He frowned. 'Not exactly asking. I'm not great at asking, as you know by now.' His dark eyes gleamed with wry amusement. 'I'm actually *telling* you to stay. I've had enough firsts for one day. From now on I'm back to my autocratic, controlling self.'

She felt light-headed with happiness. 'And what if I don't want to?'

'You do want to, Abby.' He was arrogantly sure of himself and the expression in his eyes was so sexy that she felt the heat curl deep in her stomach. 'I know you love me....'

Her eyes widened in consternation. 'How do you know?'

'Dragging me off for rampant sex in the linen cupboard was a slight clue,' he drawled, amusement in his dark eyes as she blushed scarlet.

She gave a groan of embarrassment and buried her face in his broad chest. 'Don't remind me.'

'On the contrary, I intend to remind you frequently, *tesoro*,' he teased gently. 'If I needed any more evidence that you loved me, that was it. You are naturally reserved and I am well aware that displaying your desire for me in a public place said a great deal about the way you feel about me.'

She wasn't willing to let him have the upper hand just yet. 'Maybe I don't love you. Maybe I just enjoy good sex....' She smiled.

'*Sì*, that is undoubtedly true, thank goodness.' He hauled her hard against him so that she felt the heat of his arousal pressing through the fabric of her dress. 'But the reason it was so good was the strong love we both feel for each other.'

He lowered his head and took her mouth in a drugging kiss that left them both dazed.

Eventually she lifted her eyes to his. 'So you're really asking me to stay married to you?'

He shook his head and claimed another kiss. 'Not asking. Telling.'

Her eyes teased him. 'And if I agree to stay married, you promise you won't intimidate me?'

'I'll try not to.' He kissed his way down her neck and she gasped.

'And when I say no, will you listen?'

He paused and then lifted his head, his expression wicked. 'That depends on when you say it.' He flashed her a smile that made her insides tumble over. 'If we are making love then I'm afraid I can't promise to listen.'

Despite the teasing note in his voice, she knew there was an element of truth in what he said. There probably would be occasions when he'd be controlling and overbearing, but she also knew that it was just one of the many things that she loved about him.

'I'm not saying no at the moment,' she said huskily, and his dark eyes gleamed and he swept her up in his arms and walked towards the bedroom.

'I love you.' He laid her gently on the bed and came down on top of her, all dominant, virile male.

'And I love you.' Her breathing rapid, she reached up and touched his face. 'So what am I going to do about my bedsit?'

He laughed and rolled onto his back, hauling her with him. 'Is this a good time to confess that I don't actually know what a bedsit is?'

Pressed against his powerful body, Abby was having trouble concentrating. 'You don't?' She broke off as he slid her skirt up her thighs and positioned her to take him. 'Nico!'

This time the excitement of his love-making was almost unbearable and when she finally collapsed against him she felt tears on her cheeks.

'Don't cry, *tesoro*.' He brushed them away with a gentle finger. 'No more tears, ever. My sole purpose in life is to make you and Rosa happy and keep you both safe. And you have to promise no more bedsits—whatever they are— and no more buses. From now on you are mine.'

He said it with such a smug note of possession in his voice that she should have objected, but how could she when she wanted nothing more than to be his?

'Agreed.' She looked him in the eye and dropped a kiss on his mouth. 'But will you do something for me?'

He smiled at her indulgently. 'Anything.'

'I want you to forgive Lucia and make your peace.'

He groaned and closed his eyes briefly. 'That girl is a minx.'

'If it weren't for her, we wouldn't be together,' Abby pointed out softly, and his eyes flew open, passion burning in the dark depths.

'Don't even remind me of that,' he growled, holding her so tightly that she could barely breathe. 'All right, I'll call her later tonight.'

'She did us a favour, Nico,' Abby reminded him as she snuggled against his powerful frame, and she felt him laugh.

'Well, for goodness' sake, don't tell her that or she'll be matchmaking for Carlo next.'

Abby lifted her head, suddenly interested. 'I love your brother.' She saw the ominous look in his dark eyes and bent to kiss him. 'Not in the way that I love you—but he's such a nice person. I can't believe he doesn't have a woman....'

'He has plenty of women,' Nico drawled, trailing a hand gently up her spine. 'But when you're wealthy it becomes very hard to trust people. What he needs is a woman like you who would choose a—a *bedsit* instead of life with a man who she believed didn't love her.'

'I'll tell you a secret.' Abby smiled. 'I would have *hated* it.'

'Good,' Nico said arrogantly, rolling her until she was underneath him. 'From now on the only place you're going to live is with me.'

'And that suits me just fine, Signor Santini,' she whispered, her heart thumping as he lowered his head again. 'That suits me just fine.'

THE ITALIAN DOCTOR'S PROPOSAL

by

Kate Hardy

Kate Hardy lives in Norwich, in the east of England, with her husband, two young children, one bouncy spaniel, and too many books to count! When she's not busy writing romance or researching local history, she helps out at her children's schools; she's a school governor and chair of the PTA. She also loves cooking – see if you can spot the recipes sneaked into her books! (They're also on her website, along with extracts and stories behind the books.)

Writing for Mills & Boon has been a dream come true for Kate – something she wanted to do ever since she was twelve. She's been writing Medical Romances for nearly five years now, and also writes for Modern Extra. She says it's the best of both worlds because she gets to learn lots of new things when she's researching the background to a book: add a touch of passion, drama and danger, a new gorgeous hero every time, and it's the perfect job!

Kate's always delighted to hear from readers, so do drop in to her website at www.katehardy.com

Don't miss Kate Hardy's exciting new novel
The Consultant's New-Found Family
**out in April 2007 from Mills & Boon
Medical Romance™**

For Richard and Chrissy –
the best uncle and aunt in the world

PROLOGUE

'YOUR money or your life?'

Lucy whirled round and stared at the highwayman. She didn't recognise the voice or the lower half of his face not hidden by the domino mask. Or the dark hazel eyes, a curious mix of brown and grey that somehow managed to be soft and piercing at the same time.

Dangerous eyes.

Your money or your life?

Without giving her a chance to answer, he smiled at her. A smile that was even more dangerous than his eyes. A smile that started a small, slow smoulder in the pit of her stomach.

He was a walking definition of gorgeous. Dark hair that curled beneath a flat-crowned black hat; smooth olive skin; a loose white silk shirt, laced half-open to reveal a sprinkling of dark hair on his chest; tight black trousers leading down to highly polished black boots; and a silky black cloak.

Every woman's dream highwayman.

Including Lucy's.

'A kiss would do,' he said huskily, and leaned forward to claim it.

As kisses went, it was fairly chaste. And in the middle of a very public arena: the staff charity fancy-dress ball at Treverro Hospital. But the touch of his mouth against hers did something to her. Lucy's knees actually buckled. If he hadn't been supporting both her elbows, she would have fallen flat on her face.

5

And it got worse.

Because when he broke the kiss and pulled back just far enough to see her face, she saw it in his eyes. He *knew* what effect he'd had on her. He knew he'd blown just about every fuse in her body. And his eyes said that if she'd let him, he'd blow the ones she didn't even know she had.

'Catch you later, princess,' he said, then tipped his hat briefly, gave her a broad wink and spun on his heel as he wrapped his black cloak back round him.

It was completely theatrical and over the top. She should have laughed. Except she felt too sick when she realised what had just happened. Whoever the highwayman was, that kiss had been a set-up. A very public one. She could guess just who'd put him up to it, too—even what he'd said. 'Lucy's an ice maiden. It's about time someone proved she melts.'

She gritted her teeth. If she ever—*ever*—came across the highwayman again, she'd roast him alive.

And as for her SHO…Malcolm Hobart had better hope she was in a better mood when she was back on duty tomorrow morning.

CHAPTER ONE

'Hard luck, Luce.'

Lucy forced herself not to make the response that rose instantly to her lips—a snarl of 'don't call me Luce'—knowing that Mal just wanted to get a rise out of her. She wasn't going to give him the satisfaction of knowing he'd managed to rattle her. Though once she'd done the ward rounds, she was going to have a private word with him about practical jokes.

One practical joke in particular.

'You know, that job really should've been yours,' Mal continued.

'Obviously the powers that be thought differently.' She gave what she hoped looked like a philosophical shrug. 'Was there something specific you wanted to ask me about, Malcy, dearest, or can we do the ward round now?'

He whistled. 'You're really sore about it, aren't you? Losing out to Nic Alberici like that, when everyone thought the job had your name on it.'

'I am *not* sore,' Lucy said through gritted teeth.

'Lucy Williams, obstetric consultant. Sounds good.' Mal gave her a mischievous look. 'Maybe if you'd been *Luke* Williams, you'd have been in with a better chance.'

Lucy knew better than to listen to Mal—and better still than to let him wind her up. And far better than to say what he clearly believed she was thinking. So why did she have to open her mouth and say it? 'Jobs for the boys, isn't it, Mal? And as I'm not intending to have a sex change and

7

become an Italian playboy to suit the hospital bigwigs, I'll just have to lump it, won't I?'

Too late, she saw Rosemary, the senior midwife, shaking her head, grimacing and holding her hands up flat and crossed, moving them slightly but very fast: the age-old signal for 'stop right there'.

Too late, she heard a sultry voice behind her say, 'It's *half*-Italian, actually. My mother's English.'

Please, earth, open up and swallow me right now.

It didn't.

Please? she tried again.

Not even a tiny dent in the tiles, let alone the huge pit she needed.

So there was only one thing for it. Face her embarrassment head-on. She stopped holding her breath and spun round on her heel, ready to apologise to Nic Alberici for her rudeness and reassure him that she was looking forward to working with him...

And then she saw his eyes. Dark hazel eyes, a curious mixture of brown and grey. Eyes she'd seen before. Except this time they weren't warm and smiling and sexy and knowing. This time, they were cold and absolutely furious.

Can today get any worse? she thought. The man who'd embarrassed her at the fancy-dress ball was her new boss. So she couldn't bawl him out, the way she'd promised herself she would.

She also couldn't give in to the feelings that threatened to make her knees buckle again. He was her *boss*, for goodness' sake.

So there was only one thing she could do. Be professional.

She lifted her chin. 'I'm sorry. You must be Mr Alberici,' she said politely, extending her hand. 'Lucy Williams, special reg. Welcome to River Ward.'

He didn't take it. 'Jobs for the boys—an Italian play-boy, hmm?'

Uh-oh. Raw nerve. She shrugged. 'Figure of speech. It wasn't personal.'

'I think, Dr Williams—' his emphasis of her title made it clear he wasn't going to be easily mollified '—that you and I need a little chat. Sooner rather than later. Perhaps we could go to my office?'

She could see Mal's smirk out of the corner of her eye and could have kicked herself. But it was her own fault. She knew what Mal was like: he put everyone else out of the running for the wooden spoon award. He'd probably spotted Nic Alberici coming their way when he'd started needling her about the fact she hadn't got the consultant's post. She should have second-guessed Mal and avoided the subject. Now she and Nic Alberici had got off on the wrong foot. Just what she didn't need.

Meekly, she followed Nic to his office. The office *she'd* been using for the last month or so as acting consultant.

He gestured to her to sit down opposite him.

'I'm sorry you overheard that,' she said quietly.

'Clearly I wasn't meant to.' If anything, his eyes had grown even colder.

And she'd always thought brown eyes were warm. Lucy swallowed. 'I shouldn't have said it in the first place.'

'If you're going to have a problem working with me, Dr Williams, I'd prefer to be the first to know,' he said. 'It's important that patients—'

'Feel confident in the team working with them,' Lucy cut in. 'I agree. And I don't have a problem working with you, Mr Alberici. What you overheard…' She paused, wondering how to say it without making it sound as if she was blaming Mal, too gutless to take responsibility for her own mistakes. 'It's not the way *I* think. It's the way some of the other staff believe I think.'

'Ever heard the saying, "Perception is reality"?'

'Yes, but not in this case. I admit I thought I'd get the consultant's job; I've been standing in as acting consultant ever since Mike left. But you're older than I am, you're more experienced and you've a good reputation.' And he was better qualified. 'So you were the better candidate and I'm sure I can learn something from you.'

He didn't look convinced. 'So why...?'

'Why did I say that to Mal?' She shrugged. 'You know Mal.' Of course he did. Hadn't Mal been the one to talk him into kissing her at the charity ball? She ignored the tiny niggle of doubt, and continued, 'Work it out for yourself.'

There was a long, very awkward pause.

Finally, he spoke. 'So what now?'

'I apologise again, I reassure you that I'm a professional, you accept it—' Lucy ticked off the points on her fingers '—and we do the ward round before our pregnant mums get discharged with their three-day-old babies.'

His lips quirked at that. So he had a sense of humour. Well, that was a start.

'Apology accepted, Dr Williams.' The warmth she'd seen when he'd kissed her was slowly seeping back into his eyes. Not to mention the warmth in the pit of her stomach. Why did he have to have a smile like that? Why couldn't he have been...well, middle-aged and dull and not the slightest bit sexy?

Not to mention that voice. The slight accent that made her wonder what his voice would sound like in passion...

No. She was *not* going to start thinking like that about anyone, let alone her new boss. She was a professional. And she was completely focused on her career.

'Though I prefer to work on first-name terms,' he said. 'Call me Nic.'

The slight hint of a long 'i', a sensual Italian 'Nic' rather than a diffident English 'Nick'.

She had to get her libido back under control. Fast. Hadn't she already learned the hard way that it was stupid to follow her hormones instead of her head?

'Lucy.' She made it sound as cool and English as she could. Ice maiden. To match her reputation. She held her hand out. 'And I meant what I said. I'm looking forward to working with you.'

His handshake was firm and cool and professional. So why was her blood fizzing where he'd touched her? And if a handshake did this to her, what would a more intimate…? No. She forced the thought to the back of her mind. 'Shall we?'

He nodded and they went to join Rosemary and Mal. Just as Rosemary was about to update them on the first patient, Lucy's bleeper went.

'Sorry,' she mouthed, headed for the phone and dialled the number on her bleeper.

'Lucy Williams—you paged me?'

'Thanks for ringing back,' the A and E nurse said. 'We have a patient with a suspected placental abruption.' Placental abruption was where part of the placenta became detached from the uterus. It could be dangerous, possibly even fatal to both the mother and the baby. If the bleeding was severe, they'd need to do an emergency delivery.

'Have you done an ultrasound?' Lucy asked.

'A machine's on its way. Could you take a look at her?' the nurse asked.

'I'll be right down.' Though it was only courtesy to let her new boss know where she was going. She hated interrupting colleagues when they were with patients, but the only other choice was leaving a message with one of the midwives, and he'd probably think she was sulking and using any excuse to avoid him. She pulled back the curtain just enough to put her head through the gap. 'Mr Alberici, I'm sorry to interrupt. Could I have a quick word, please?'

'Of course. Please, excuse me,' he said to the patient, then came to join Lucy in the middle of the ward. 'What's up?'

'We've got a patient with a suspected placental abruption in A and E. They've asked me to see her.'

'I'll come with you—if it *is* that, we'll need her in Theatre pronto. You'll assist?'

Yeah, he *would* be a qualified obstetric surgeon. He could have offered to assist *her*. But, no, he had to take charge. 'Sure,' she muttered.

'I'll brief Mal and I'll be right with you,' he said.

Efficient, courteous—to the patients, if not to her—and drop-dead gorgeous. It was a tempting combination. A dangerous combination.

Stop it, she warned herself. You are *not* going to think about Nic Alberici like that.

Though in her mind's eye he wasn't wearing a formal white silk shirt, teamed with a silk tie and an expensively cut dark grey suit and topped with a white coat. He was wearing that half-open white shirt, tight black trousers, a hat and a domino mask. Sexy as hell. With a smile that promised—

'Mal's going to carry on with the rounds and page us if there are any problems,' Nic said, breaking into her thoughts. 'I'll let him know if we go to Theatre.'

She flushed. 'Right.'

'I'm not checking up on the quality of your work,' he added, misinterpreting the reason for her high colour.

'I didn't for one moment think you were.'

He sighed. 'Oh, hell. Look, Lucy, we got off to a bad start. Let's just forget it and start again, shall we?'

Forget what? That kiss, or what he'd overheard, or the dressing-down he'd started to give her? The second two, she could do, but the memory of the kiss firmly refused to budge.

Even now, she could still feel his lips against hers. Worse, she wanted him to do it again. In a much more private situation…

She'd only just got herself back under control by the time they reached A and E. 'I'm Lucy Williams—you paged me to look at a patient with suspected placental abruption,' she said to the receptionist.

'Yes. Her name's Mrs Andrews—Liza Andrews. She's in room two,' the receptionist replied. 'Yvonne Roper's with her.'

'Thanks.' Lucy led the way to room two and knocked on the door.

Yvonne answered the knock. 'Thanks for coming, Dr Williams.'

'It's Lucy,' Lucy responded. 'Any time. This is Nic Alberici, the new consultant on River. Before we see the patient, what's the presentation?'

'She's in constant pain, her uterus is tender and tense, she's bleeding slightly—it's dark red and clotted—and she's starting to look shocky,' Yvonne said.

'Out of proportion to the loss?' Nic asked.

'Yes. Her blood pressure's low.'

He and Lucy exchanged a glance. There were other causes of bleeding in pregnancy, but the symptoms Yvonne had described sounded very like placental abruption.

'I'm not happy with the foetal heartbeat either,' Yvonne added. 'I think the baby's getting distressed.'

'Is the scanner here yet?' Nic asked.

'No. I'll chase it up.'

'Thanks. We'll go and see her,' Lucy said. She knocked on the door, walked in and introduced herself and Nic to Mrs Andrews. 'Yvonne tells me you're in pain and you're losing blood. Would you mind if we examined you?'

'Please. Anything. Just don't let me lose my baby,' Liza Andrews whispered brokenly. 'I'm forty-three. It's my first baby. We waited so long, and if I lose him…' She choked. 'I might not be able to have another.'

'We'll do our best,' Lucy reassured her. 'There are lots of reasons for bleeding in pregnancy so don't assume it's the worst.' Lucy glanced at the observation chart. 'Your baby's heartbeat is still pretty regular, though your blood pressure's a bit low so we'll get some blood into you to help. Yvonne, can you cross-match and get me four units of O-neg?' she asked as the nurse came back in.

'We're waiting for the portable scanner to arrive,' she told Liza, 'then we'll be able to check what's going on a bit better. It might be just that your placenta's low-lying, what we call placenta praevia, so I'm not going to give you a vaginal examination.' If it was placenta praevia rather than an abruption, a vaginal exam could cause a catastrophic bleed. 'But I will give you some oxygen to help you breathe more easily.' She unhooked the mask from the wall. 'Just breathe in through this and try to relax.' She set the output at fifteen litres a minute. 'OK?'

Liza nodded.

Lucy gently examined the woman's abdomen.

'That hurts,' Liza said, taking the mask off her face.

'I'm sorry,' Lucy said. 'The good news is that your baby's lying normally.' She mouthed to Nic, 'I'm almost certain it's an abruption.'

Nic nodded and took Liza's hand. 'It says here you're thirty-six weeks.'

Liza's face screwed up in anguish. 'And it's too early for the baby to come!'

'It's quite normal for babies to arrive at thirty-seven weeks—so a few days earlier really isn't as bad as it sounds,' Nic reassured her, smiling. 'You're in the right place.'

'So my baby's going to be all right?'

'We'll do our best,' Lucy said, gently settling the oxygen mask back in place. She listened to the baby's heartbeat and didn't like what she heard. Nic was watching her face and she gave him a very brief shake of her head to let him know.

Yvonne arrived with the scanner in tow and the units of blood. Lucy quickly set up an intravenous infusion while Nic put the scanner in place.

'Lucy,' he said quietly.

She took one look at the screen and her heart sank. The placenta wasn't low-lying. And as Liza Andrews hadn't been visibly losing that much blood, the chances were that most of the blood from the abruption was trapped, known as a 'concealed abruption'.

'Mrs Andrews, you have what we call placental abruption,' Lucy said. 'It means that your placenta's started to come away from the wall of your womb.'

Liza blenched. 'Am I going to lose the baby?'

'Not if we can help it. But it's too big for me to let you go home again,' Lucy said. 'And I don't want to take any risks with the baby.'

'I'd like to deliver the baby by Caesarean section,' Nic said.

'Now?' Liza asked, horrified.

'Now,' Nic said. They could have given Liza tocolytic

drugs to stop the contractions, then medication to help mature the baby's lungs, but from Liza's symptoms they knew the abruption was big. The baby needed at least half the placenta to be attached and functioning, so they couldn't take the risk of leaving it.

'But—why me? Why now?'

'We don't know the causes,' said Lucy, 'but it's more common if you've had high blood pressure, you're an older mum or you have twins or triplets, you're a smoker or you take cocaine.'

Liza smiled weakly. 'I've never smoked or done drugs. I haven't even have a glass of wine since I found out I was pregnant, let alone anything else!'

'That's good,' Lucy said, squeezing her hand.

'Have you been in a car accident or had a fall, or banged your stomach in any way?' Nic asked.

Liza shook her head. 'Not that I can remember.'

'We'll take some blood for tests to see why it's happened,' Lucy said, 'and to check that your blood's clotting properly.' If Liza Andrews had lost a lot of blood, she might have clotting problems after the birth, known as DIC or disseminated intravascular coagulation—around a third of cases did. And she had a much higher risk of a large bleed after delivery, so she might need a transfusion. 'We might need to give you some drugs to help your uterus contract after the birth.'

Liza nodded.

'And because your baby's early, we'll need to take him—or her—to the special care unit for a little while, to help him with his breathing and feeding. But you'll be able to see the baby any time you like,' Nic said.

'Is there anyone you'd like us to call?' Lucy asked.

'My husband's already on his way in. And my mum.' Liza's eyes filled with tears. 'He wanted to cut the cord.'

'I'm sorry,' Nic said. 'I'll need to give you a general anaesthetic, so he won't be allowed in for the delivery. But as soon as the baby arrives, he'll be able to have a cuddle.'

A tear slid down to pool on the mask. 'It was all supposed to be so different.'

'I know,' Lucy soothed. 'Though you're not alone. This happens in around one in fifty pregnancies.' Not all abruptions were as severe as this one—if the baby wasn't in distress and the bleed was minor, the mum could often go home if she chose. 'But you'll have your baby very soon.' She just hoped the abruption wasn't so severe that the baby wasn't getting enough oxygen—it could suffer brain death or even die.

'I'd like you to sign a consent form, please,' Nic said.

'I'll call the anaesthetist and get Theatre to prep,' Lucy said.

On their way up to Theatre, Nic said, 'You handled that well. It's a rough situation.'

'Let's just hope she doesn't get renal failure or a bad PPH,' Lucy said, referring to postpartum haemorrhage, a major bleed after delivery. She couldn't bring herself to talk about the risks to the baby.

Before she knew it, they were in Theatre and Nic was making the first incision. Lucy couldn't believe how fast he worked, but she was relieved when she was finally able to lift the baby out. 'It's a girl,' she said.

'Welcome, *bellissima*,' Nic said softly. His eyes crinkled at the corners, betraying the smile behind his surgeon's mask, and he handed her to Lucy. 'What's the Apgar score, Lucy?' he asked as he delivered the placenta and started stitching—the Apgar score was a check on the baby's pulse, breathing, whether the skin was pink or blue and the baby's reaction to suction.

'First Apgar score of five,' Lucy said, checking the baby.

She gave the baby gentle suction to clear her airways. Her skin wasn't pink enough either for Lucy's liking.

'Second score of seven,' she reported four minutes later.

The ten-minute score had improved to nine. 'But this little scrap's going to up to SCBU—' the special care baby unit '—to warm up for a bit,' Lucy said.

Nic finished closing. 'We'll leave Liza in the recovery team's capable hands and baby Andrews to SBCU.' He glanced at the clock. 'And we're going to have some lunch.'

Lunch? He wanted to have lunch with her? Her stomach fluttered at the idea of it. Lunch. Sitting opposite him on one of the small cafeteria tables, close enough for their knees to touch...

Way, way too dangerous. 'Thanks for the offer, but I'd better get back to the ward,' she said. 'Finish the rounds—it's not fair on Mal. One of us ought to go back and you did all the tough work in Theatre, so you deserve the break. I don't think I've ever seen a scalpel move that fast.'

Coward, his eyes said. 'Maybe Mal needs to feel you trust him enough to finish the rounds on his own.'

And maybe Nic ought to get to know the staff properly before he started throwing his weight about. Just because he'd got the consultant's job, it didn't mean he knew everything. She knew Mal far better than he did. She lifted her chin. 'Maybe I don't feel he's ready.'

'Lunch first,' Nic said.

'I really need to get back.' *Liar*, a voice in her head taunted. *You'd love to have lunch with him. And more.*

Given her track record at judging the men in her life, that'd be a very bad move. Anyway, she doubted if he meant *that* sort of lunch. He was her boss, not her lover.

Despite that kiss.

'I want to get to know all the team,' Nic said, 'and I thought I might as well start with you.'

So he *was* thinking of her as a doctor, nothing else. Just part of the team. He was going to ask everyone else to lunch, too. He hadn't singled her out as special. But she still couldn't help thinking about that kiss. He hadn't mentioned it, but was he remembering the way it had been between them, that unlooked-for spark at the ball when their mouths had touched?

'So, shall we?'

Before Lucy could open her mouth to refuse—or, worse, accept—her pager bleeped. She glanced at the display.

'Sorry. I'm needed back on the ward. Catch you later,' she said, hoping she sounded as casual as he had when he'd told her he wanted to get to know the team. And without giving him the chance to answer, she strode swiftly away.

CHAPTER TWO

COOL, calm, very English—and clearly as mad as hell at him.

And Nic couldn't blame her, in the circumstances. He'd taken her job and he'd embarrassed her at the ball in front of all her colleagues...and friends? Nic wasn't sure, yet, if Lucy Williams believed in friends.

She certainly didn't believe in lovers. The shock on her face when he'd kissed her had told him that.

What he couldn't work out was why. Why a woman who was clever and talented—enough to take on the role of acting consultant at the very young age of thirty—and beautiful wasn't already spoken for. No, scratch the beautiful—she was more than that. She looked like an angel, with that alabaster skin and those clear blue eyes and the ice-blonde hair pulled back severely from her face—hair he wanted to see tumbling down over her shoulders or, better still, over his pillow. Her mouth was a perfect rosebud and he just hadn't been able to resist kissing her at the ball.

And then she'd vanished. He'd looked for her immediately after the next dance, but she'd gone.

And then, when she'd faced him on the ward...

He took a swig of coffee. Leave her alone. That would be the sensible thing to do. Anything else would be breaking all his rules, professional and private.

Except...he couldn't.

'Down, boy,' he said softly to his libido.

It didn't take the slightest bit of notice.

* * *

20

Lucy somehow managed to avoid Nic for the rest of her shift. Usually she stayed later than she needed to, because the team on River was overstretched and she didn't mind giving up her free time. She loved her job. But today she needed to get as far away from Nic Alberici as she could. Until she'd managed to get her hormones under control and could treat him with detached professionalism.

The next day, she thought she'd managed it.

Until Nic walked into the side-room where she was talking to Liza Andrews.

'Mr Alberici.' Liza was beaming. 'Thanks so much for what you did for us yesterday—you and Dr Williams. You saved our lives.'

'Pleasure,' Nic said. 'How are you both today?'

'Tired, but fine. Lucy sleeps all the time.'

Nic cast a quizzical look at his senior reg.

'This Lucy,' Lucy explained, still holding the sleeping baby.

'We called her after you both—Lucy Nicola,' Liza told him.

'Thank you. It's an honour,' he said quietly. He stroked the baby's cheek. 'She's beautiful.'

'And Rosemary says the white stuff on her skin—vernix—will wash off in a couple of days.'

'When they're overdue it goes the other way—they're like little, wrinkled old men with very dry skin and you go through tons of moisturiser,' Nic said.

To Lucy's horror, he actually sat down on the arm of the chair she was using. Not quite close enough to touch—but close enough for her to feel his body heat. Why couldn't he have sat in the chair on the other side of the bed? Why did he have to invade her space like this?

'My turn for a cuddle,' he said, holding his arms out.

For one heart-stopping moment, she thought he meant a cuddle with *her*. But, of course, he meant baby Lucy.

'You're worse than the midwives—want to keep the babies all to yourselves,' he teased.

'I'd better get on anyway,' she said, gently transferring her tiny bundle into his arms and making sure that the baby's head was supported.

You're avoiding me, his eyes accused.

Tough, hers said back. 'Bye, Liza. Catch you later, Nic,' she said a lot more casually than she felt, and left the little room. Why did he have to look so—so *sexy*, holding baby Lucy?

'Get a grip,' she warned herself, and went to check the file of her next patient.

But her avoidance strategy didn't last long. She'd seen two more patients when Mal met her in the corridor. 'Boss wants a word with you,' he said.

'What about?'

'Dunno. He did say as soon as you could manage it.' He gave her a wicked grin. 'What have you been up to, Luce?'

'Working, Malcolm,' she said, clearly a shade too defensively because his grin broadened.

'I'll believe you, Luce.'

Lucy decided not to dignify him with a reply and went down the corridor to Nic's office. She rapped on the door.

'Come in.'

She put her head round the door. 'You wanted a word?'

He nodded. 'Come in and close the door, please.'

Her heart sank. What was she supposed to have done now?

He waited for her to sit down, and the knot in her stomach tightened. She hadn't done anything wrong. So why did she feel as if she were about to be carpeted for some stupid mistake? The tension in the room grew until she wanted to scream.

And then he smiled at her. 'I wanted to apologise,' he said, 'for embarrassing you at the ball the other night.'

She stared at him in disbelief. He was *apologising*?

'If you want to slap my face, feel free—any time,' he said, shocking her further. Did this mean that kiss *hadn't* been a set-up? But, given what she now knew about him, thanks to an old friend she'd trained with, he could be teasing her again.

There was only one way to find out. 'Why did you do it?'

'Kiss you?' He gave her a wry smile. 'Why do you think?'

'You always have to rise to a challenge.' The words were out before she could stop them.

'Something like that.'

So it *had* been a set-up. She lifted her chin. 'Then you're very easily manipulated. And you'll find certain junior staff more than willing to take advantage of that.'

He frowned. 'I'm not with you.'

'If someone dares you to do something, you'll just do it?' She rolled her eyes.

'Dares me to do what?'

It was her turn to frown. Weren't they talking about the same thing? 'You were dared to kiss me at the ball.'

Lucy thought someone had set him up him to kiss her? Nic just about managed to stop his jaw dropping. She really had that low an opinion of herself? But why? Didn't she know how gorgeous she was? 'Lucy…it wasn't like that,' he said carefully.

'Wasn't it?'

'No.'

'So why did you kiss me, then?'

'Because I wanted to.' He tipped his head on one side. 'Why do you think I was *dared* to do it?'

'Because…'

The words clearly stuck in her throat. Though he could guess what she was going to say. His brief getting-to-know-the-team conversation with Rosemary had told him an awful lot more than the senior midwife realised. Especially about Lucy. Which meant he had to handle this carefully.

'You looked as if you wanted to be a thousand miles away,' he said. 'I wanted to…' He lapsed into Italian.

'Sorry. Latin, yes, as long as it's medical—Italian, no,' Lucy said.

He smiled wryly. 'I said I wanted make you smile. It was all meant to be a bit of fun. Theatrical.'

'It was that all right,' she said drily.

Until their mouths had actually touched. Then it had become a whole new ballgame. A much, much more serious thing. He couldn't help looking at her mouth now. Big mistake. It reminded him how she'd tasted. And he wanted to do it again. And again. Somewhere they wouldn't be disturbed.

Here, a little voice said inside his head. *Here and now. Your office door is closed…*

He should be detached and professional. He was her colleague—a colleague who'd taken the job she'd been doing for weeks. So he was supposed to be treading on eggshells. He was supposed to keep his distance. He knew all that. And in spite of it, he found himself walking round to her side of the desk. Taking her hand. Turning it palm uppermost… And she didn't pull away.

'I wanted to kiss you, Lucy,' he said. 'I wanted to…' The touch of her skin was too much for him. All his good intentions went straight out of the window. Unable to help

himself, he bent his head and kissed the inside of her wrist.
'I wanted to do this,' he said huskily.

Nic's Italian. A showman. A flirt. For goodness' sake, you
know what Pauline told you yesterday—the corridors at
Plymouth hospital are littered with broken hearts. *He's a
brilliant doctor and great to work with—but don't be stupid
enough to go out with him. He never dates anyone more
than three times.*

What's he's doing to you doesn't mean a thing, Lucy
warned herself frantically. That smouldering smile's just a
performance. As soon as you let him sweep you off your
feet, you'll have two more dates and then he'll be off to
the next challenge.

Her body wasn't buying it. It went completely un-doctor-
like. Her pulse quickened, her pupils expanded and she
could feel her face growing bright red. 'I...'

'And this,' he said, touching his tongue to the pulse that
had started to beat crazily against her skin.

'And—' The harsh sound of his bleeper cut across his
words.

'Saved by the bleep,' he said wryly, taking his pager
from his pocket and glancing at the display. 'But I think
we need to talk, Lucia *mia*.'

Lucy stayed sitting exactly where she was as he left the
room. What on earth was going on? She was the sensible
one in the family—apart from the one huge mistake in her
life that nobody ever talked about, she'd always been sensible and studious and never let anything get in the way of
her work. She hardly knew Nic Alberici, only what she'd
heard about him from her friend Pauline in Nic's old hospital—that professionally he was wonderful and personally
he was a walking disaster area.

So why was her body reacting to him like this? Why did

her pulse race when she heard his voice or saw his smile? Why did her body go up in flames every time he touched her?

Why had he kissed the inside of her wrist like that?

And as for the way he'd Italianised her name—well, she wasn't a glamorous and sexy Lu-chee-ah. She was sensible Lucy Williams, senior registrar. She wore sensible, comfortable shoes and tailored trousers to work; she kept her hair pinned back severely, never wore nail-varnish and her make-up was non-existent. Lucia, on the other hand, would be tall and elegant. She'd wear a little black skirt and kitten heels, with her dark pre-Raphaelite curls tumbling down her back, her dark eyes outlined with sexily smudged kohl and her lips with kiss-me-now red lipstick.

Lucy Williams wasn't the sort of woman Nic Alberici wanted, and she wasn't going to forget that. She wasn't going to have some wild fling with him that would last no more than three dates anyway; she wasn't stupid enough to think she was the one who could change him. She'd learned at a very young age that happy-ever-after didn't exist. The one time she'd been tempted to take a risk had taught her only too painfully that she'd been right all along—and her judgement in men was rotten.

Lucia mia. The words made her heart miss a beat. And a second.

Don't be stupid, she reminded herself. You're not his. Nothing's going to come of it. Next time you see him, you're going to tell him to leave you alone.

'You haven't had a break for five hours.'

A shiver ran down her spine; Nic's voice was like a caress on her skin.

Don't be ridiculous, Lucy, she told herself crossly. 'I'm fine,' she snapped.

'You need a break. So do I. And you know the hospital better than I do—you can show me where to find some decent coffee instead of the stewed stuff I had at lunchtime.'

'I can tell you where to go.'

He grinned, deliberately misinterpreting her. 'I'll bet.'

'I don't need a break, Mr Alberici.'

'OK—then I'll pull rank, Dr Williams. Coffee. With me. Now.'

She walked in silence with him out of the ward, aware of the speculative looks cast their way and determined not to give anyone the excuse to gossip about her. She remained silent until they were well out of earshot of the ward.

'I'd like you to leave me alone in future,' she said. 'What you did in your office—' *made my knees go weak again* '—was sexual harassment,' she finished stiffly. 'I'd prefer you not to repeat it.'

He nodded and his face became impassive. 'In future, Lucy, I'll make sure I have your permission before I touch you.'

It was what she wanted. So why did his words make her feel as if the sun had stopped shining?

And why was he going to drag her through the torment of having coffee with him?

'Though I prefer to be on friendly terms with my colleagues,' he said.

Yeah, right. Three dates and you're out.

'So perhaps we should put all this behind us.'

'As you wish.' Lucy gave him a cool nod.

'So, where are we having this coffee?'

She seized the chance to change the subject, turn it to something more neutral. 'Pat's Place, on the second floor. The mochaccino's to die for. Not to mention the blueberry muffins—Pat makes them herself. Pat's the one with the dangly earrings.'

Shut up *now*, Lucy. You're babbling, she told herself.

Not that Nic seemed to mind. There wasn't a trace of impatience in his tone. 'Blueberry muffins, hmm? A woman after my own heart,' he said.

She wasn't anything of the sort. The man was a born flirt. And anyway, he was just trying to find common ground with a member of his new team, she reminded herself.

The walk to the coffee-bar was torture. With every step, she remembered the way he'd touched her. The way her skin had heated as he'd turned her palm over. The way his lips had brushed her skin, sending tingles down her spine. The way he'd licked her pulse point…

She glanced down quickly, relieved that her white coat was thick enough to hide the obvious signs of her arousal. Hell. She couldn't let this happen. Not again. And she absolutely refused to let herself believe that Nic was different. She'd leave that line to her mother and her three sisters. Susie, Allie, Mum and Rach—every time they convinced themselves that 'this one's different' and he never was.

As for Nic Alberici, Pauline had told her he was a heartbreaker—and what reason would one of her best friends from med school have to lie to her? No, Nic Alberici was just the same as all the rest. Love 'em and leave 'em. She should stay well clear.

He's gorgeous, the voice in her head insisted.

That's irrelevant, she told herself. Looks don't come into it.

But you want to—

'Lucy?'

She'd been so intent on arguing with herself she hadn't heard a word he'd said. 'Sorry. I didn't catch what you said,' she mumbled, embarrassed at being caught wool-gathering.

'Mochaccino and a muffin?'

'Yes, please.'

'Grab us a table. These are on me.'

She was about to protest that she'd pay for her own, but his eyes warned her it'd be better to accept with good grace. 'Thanks,' she said.

She found a small table in the corner. He joined her with a tray of coffee and muffins.

This is his part-of-the-team chat, she reminded herself. So let's keep it work-related. 'Settled in OK to Treverro?' she asked.

He nodded. 'They're a nice bunch on River.'

'Yes.'

'Spit it out,' he said, surprising her.

'Spit what out?'

'You're obviously dying to take me to task.'

'I don't know what you mean.'

He grinned. 'Lucy, your eyes go all schoolmarmy when you're annoyed about something.'

Did they? She'd never realised she was so transparent.

'You are to me,' he said softly, and she realised she'd spoken aloud.

'Nonsense,' she said crisply.

'So what am I doing wrong?'

'Nothing.'

'Explain the schoolmarmy look, then.'

Well, he was asking for it... 'You're right about the staff on River. They're a nice bunch and I'd hate to see them hurt,' she informed him.

'You think *I'd* hurt them?' He frowned. 'Why?'

'You have a reputation.'

He rolled his eyes. 'Oh, not that Italian playboy stuff

again! Lucy, I'm not a stereotype. Yes, I like to have fun—
but I stick to the rules and no one gets hurt. Just take me
as I am.'

Her libido fluttered and she stamped on it hard. Don't
go getting any ideas, she warned it. 'Yes, boss.'

His lips thinned. 'If you don't believe me, ask yourself
if *your* reputation's deserved.'

She didn't need to ask him which reputation. She was
all too aware of it. 'My career's important to me.'

'But that doesn't make you a cold fish.'

She knew that. Her patients did, too. And as for the men
she'd turned down—they just needed to grow up enough
to realise they weren't irresistible and it didn't mean she
was a challenge to be conquered. Her reputation didn't
bother her.

'Or any less of a woman,' Nic added softly, and her
insides melted at the flash of sensuality in his eyes.

This conversation was definitely straying onto worrying
territory. She sat up straighter. 'My private life's just that.'

'And so is mine.'

'Good. Then we're agreed.'

He spread his hands. 'Lucy, why are we fighting?'

'Because...' Her voice faded. She didn't know why she
was fighting Nic. She couldn't even remember the last time
she'd rowed with a colleague. Bickering with Mal was different because it wasn't *personal* and the SHO reminded
her of one of her kid brothers, and she didn't find Mal
remotely attractive. Whereas Nic...

No. Focus. Career first, last and always, she reminded
herself.

'Because I kissed you?' His voice grew husky. 'It was
before I knew who you were. And, yes, I lost it a bit in
my office this afternoon. I shouldn't have done what I did
and I apologise. What can I do to make it up to you?'

Kiss me again.

Lucy prayed she hadn't said that out loud. She hadn't meant to think it either. And it had better not have shown on her face.

He took a sip of coffee, then broke off a piece of blueberry muffin.

Since when had eating cake been sexy? Lucy tried very hard to stop looking at his mouth. Or remembering what his lips had felt like against her skin.

'This is good,' he told her.

'Mmm.' She took refuge in her own coffee. Though she'd lost her appetite for her blueberry muffin. It was too dangerous. She'd already had to yank her thoughts away from the idea of Nic feeding her morsels of cake as he—

No!

'Why are you so anti-relationship?' Nic asked without warning.

Lucy almost choked on her coffee. 'I beg your pardon?'

'Being committed to your job doesn't mean you have to spend your life alone,' he said. 'So what's the real story?'

'You've got a nerve!'

'I just want to know what makes you tick. You're my number two in the department,' he reminded her. 'The most important member of my team.'

'All right, since you want to know.' She folded her arms. 'Both my parents are on their fourth marriages, all my brothers and sisters are divorced and I don't see the point of wasting all that emotion when I could use the energy much more effectively in my work.'

'Who says you'll go the same way?'

'Because there's a pattern.'

'You could be the one to change it.'

She wasn't. Jack Hammond was living proof. Not that she was going to tell Nic about *him*. Nobody at Treverro knew about Jack, and she wanted to keep it that way. 'I'm not. And you're in no position to lecture me, anyway.'

'No?'

'Has anyone lasted more than three dates with you?' She waited for a moment. 'If you have to think that hard about it, clearly not many have.'

'You know when you meet the right one,' he said.

Lucy scoffed. 'Come off it. Don't the statistics show that one in three marriages end in divorce?'

'Which leaves two in three that don't.'

'So you're telling me you believe in happy-ever-after?'

He nodded. 'Since you believe in patterns, there's one in my family. My parents had a holiday romance—they didn't even speak the same language when they first met—but my father followed my mother back to England and they've been married for more than forty years. And they're still in love. My sisters are both happily married—Gina for fifteen years and Sofia for twelve.'

'So why aren't you following their pattern?'

'Because I'm waiting for the right one.'

'And that's your excuse for a trail of broken hearts?'

'That's an exaggeration, Lucy. Do you expect your date to propose to you at the end of the first evening?'

'Of course not.'

'Exactly. If I go out with someone, it's to have a good time and we both know the rules right from the start. I'm not a heart-breaker—and you're not frozen.'

That look in his eyes was back. The one that made her insides smoulder. This really wasn't fair. 'What's Nic short for?' she asked, desperate to change the subject.

'Niccolo.'

'As in Machiavelli?'

He grinned. 'Yup. But I'm not manipulative.'

'No?'

'I didn't manipulate you into telling me things. Just as I'm not going to manipulate you into bed.'

That feeling flooding through her spine was *not* disappointment, she told herself. 'Good,' she said tightly. 'So we know where we stand.'

'I'm attracted to you, Lucy,' he said softly. 'Very. I'd like to get to know you better—a *lot* better—outside work. But you've made it clear you're not interested, and I'm not going to push you into something you're not comfortable with.'

'Good,' she said again, even though her heart was wailing *You idiot!* and doing the mental version of foot-stamping and hair-tearing.

'So we're colleagues. I'd like to think we can be friends, too.'

'Of course.'

'Good.' Nic finished his muffin. 'Aren't you going to eat yours?'

'I'm not hungry.'

'Would you mind if I…?'

She pushed the plate over to him. 'Help yourself.'

'It's my mum's fault. I have this weakness for cake,' he said.

'I'll remember that,' she said lightly.

He hadn't taken more than a mouthful before his bleeper sounded. He glanced down at the display and raised an eyebrow. 'What do you know about TOPS?'

'Twin oligohydramnios-polyhydramnios sequence—also known as twin-to-twin transfusion syndrome,' she said.

'Good. I prefer to call it twin-to-twin transfusion—it's more of a parent-friendly explanation. We're needed downstairs in the antenatal clinic,' he said. 'Now.'

CHAPTER THREE

THEY left their unfinished coffee and headed for the ground floor. Gemma Burton, one of the midwives, gave them the case notes and directed them to room two. Nic scanned them swiftly, gave them to Lucy to do the same, knocked on the door and introduced them both to Molly Drake.

'How have you been feeling?' he asked, sitting next to her and holding her hand.

'OK—but then last week I started to feel a bit breathless. And I look like a house—I'm only seventeen weeks and I look like I'm going to deliver any day,' she said. Her faced was pinched with anxiety. 'I know I'm having twins but I never expected to be this big. And my tummy's felt really tight in the last day or so.'

'Would you mind if I examined you?' Nic asked.

'No. I just want to know, are my babies all right? The midwife said she wanted the consultant to see me...'

'Hey, we always take extra special care of our mums having twins, so you'd get to see me a lot more often than mums of single babies anyway,' Nic said reassuringly. 'But, yes, I'm a bit concerned that you've put on weight very quickly and you're breathless. I'd like to do a scan to see what's going on, if I may?'

Molly nodded.

It didn't take long for Nic to do the scan and see that his worst fears were realised. One twin was much bigger than the other. It had a full bladder, whereas the other twin's bladder was empty, and the smaller twin seemed almost stuck to the wall of the placenta—which, he knew,

34

meant that it had much less amniotic fluid in the sac surrounding it.

'Is everything all right?' Molly asked.

Nic held her hand again. 'There's a bit of a problem, but the good news is that we can do something about it. You have something called TTTS or twin-to-twin transfusion syndrome.'

'What's that?'

Nic gestured at Lucy. 'Over to you, Lucy.'

'It's something that happens when identical twins share the same placenta,' Lucy said. 'Their blood vessels form a link in the placenta—most of the time that isn't a problem, but sometimes the link isn't balanced properly, so one twin ends up donating blood to the other. The babies are perfectly normal—the problem's in the placenta. We don't know exactly why it happens, but it might be to do with how late the fertilised egg splits to create two embryos. It happens in around one in a thousand pregnancies.'

'And that's what's wrong with my babies?' Molly asked.

Lucy nodded and turned the ultrasound screen so that Molly could see it. 'You can see on the scan here that one twin's a lot bigger than the other. If we measure their lengths, it looks as if this one's a week older than his twin, even though we know he's not. The bigger twin has too much blood going round his system, so his heart has to work harder, and he produces more amniotic fluid—that's the bag of fluid the baby lives in—so he wees more and his bladder's full. The smaller twin is anaemic and has less amniotic fluid surrounding him; he doesn't grow as well and his bladder's usually empty.'

'Are they going to be all right? What—what can do you do to stop it?'

'There are quite a few options,' Nic said. 'We can do something called amnioreduction—that means draining some of the fluid from around the bigger twin, which gives the smaller twin more space in the womb and will make you feel a lot more comfortable. It also reduces the chance of you going into premature labour. If we do that, it takes about an hour and we drain off two to three litres of fluid. I'd also like you to stay in hospital for a day or so, so we can monitor you, and then you can go back home, as long as you promise to stay in bed and take it easy for a few days.' He squeezed her hand. 'Though if you do take this option, we might need to repeat it later in your pregnancy, depending on how things go with the twins.'

'There's also something called a septostomy, where we make a little hole in the membrane that separates the twins and the fluid balances out between the sacs—we often do that at the same time as an amnioreduction,' Lucy said. 'Or we can send you to a hospital in London for laser treatment, which will break the joined blood vessels and stop the blood going from one twin to the other—it won't hurt them and they'll be able to grow normally. There's another new treatment being tested at the moment which involves high-frequency ultrasound therapy—the same sort that's used to treat kidney stones—though again if you choose this we'll have to send you to a centre in London, as we can't do it here.'

'And the babies will both be all right?'

'We've caught you relatively early, which is a good sign,' Nic said. 'If they both survive, the smaller twin should catch up on growth after the birth. But at this stage I can't guarantee they'll both be fine.'

'So they might die?'

'I know it's a horrible thing to have to consider, but there's a possibility you might lose one or both of them. I can't quote any odds at this stage, and we'll monitor you a lot more often than we'd usually plan and make sure we do everything we can to keep your babies safe,' Nic reassured her. 'There are two other options you need to think about, and I'm afraid they're not very pleasant, but you need to know all the facts before you can make a decision. Some parents opt to have a termination now, because they feel the odds are stacked too high against them. I know it's an unbearable thing to think about, but if you decide that's what you want, we're not going to judge you or criticise you.'

'We're here to give you the facts and to support you, whatever decision you make,' Lucy said. 'We're on your side.'

'I…' Molly was clearly close to tears and Lucy handed her a tissue.

'The other option, if we find that the procedures don't work and the twin-to-twin transfusion is getting worse, is that we might be able to save one twin at the expense of the other,' Nic said. 'I know it sounds callous, but it's a question of weighing up the risks.'

'But you and your partner really need to discuss it and decide what you want,' Lucy added.

'George isn't here,' Molly said. 'He's away in the States on business. He said he'd change his meetings if I needed him here today, but I thought this'd be just…well, a routine visit.'

'I know.' Lucy brought a chair to the other side of the bed and held Molly's other hand. 'And this must have come as a shock to you. Is there anyone we can call to be with you?'

Molly shook her head. 'I'm not on good terms with my parents, and George's mum panics at the least little thing—she's the last person I need fluttering round me. I just…' She bit her lip hard. 'Twins. When we found out, we never thought we'd cope. We'd just got used to the idea and started getting excited about it, and now this!'

'Take your time,' Nic said. 'I'd like to start treatment in the next twenty-four hours—but if you want to talk to your husband or a friend first, discuss it with them, that's fine.'

'Would you explain the options to my husband?' Molly asked Lucy.

'Of course,' Lucy said. 'There's no pressure. Take all the time you need. Can I get you some water or anything?'

'It's all right. It's just a shock. I need to think—I need to talk to George.' She swallowed. 'I can't use a mobile in here, can I?'

'No, it might interfere with the machines,' Lucy said. 'But I can take you somewhere where you can use it.'

'Thanks.'

She looked at Nic. 'See you back on the ward?'

'Yeah.' Nic smiled at Molly. 'We're here whenever you need us. If either of us isn't on duty, just ask someone to bleep us. We'll be straight here.'

Four hours later, Lucy was sitting in the rest room and trying very hard not to cry. She'd held Molly's hand throughout the difficult call to the States, and the even more difficult decision that had followed.

Molly had been admitted to the ward and Lucy was well past the time when she was supposed to finish her shift, but her vision was blurred with suppressed tears and she didn't feel quite up to cycling back to her cottage.

'Are you OK, Lucy?'

Lucy looked up and gave Nic a watery smile. 'I thought you were supposed to be off duty ages ago.'

'I'm not the only one.' He came to sit next to her. 'It's Molly Drake, isn't it?' he guessed.

She nodded. 'I know, I know, these cases are rare and

most of the time our mums have a healthy pregnancy and a healthy baby—but I hate to see the heartbreak some of our parents have to go through.'

'Me, too,' Nic said. 'But remember this—we can make a difference. We *do* make a difference.'

'Yes. Molly's having a septostomy tomorrow and we'll be monitoring her weekly. The twins stand a much better chance now.'

'Chin up.' He gave her an exaggerated wink, then sent her hormones into overdrive by gently touching her cheek. 'Go on. Home with you. And I'll see you tomorrow.'

Lucy slept badly that night; when she did drift off, her dreams were filled with Nic Alberici. And they were so graphic that she was actually blushing when her alarm went off.

When she got to work, she seemed to hear nothing but Nic's name. Every single patient beamed when they talked about him—all saying he was far dishier than any Hollywood star and acting as if they were half in love with him. The midwives were similarly smitten—the young and single ones virtually swooned when they heard his name, and the older ones clucked over him like a favourite son. 'He's lovely—a real gentleman,' Rosemary said dreamily. 'And those gorgeous eyes! If I were twenty years younger…'

'Oh, he's just another consultant,' Lucy said, aware how grumpy she sounded and hoping that no one would pick up on it.

No chance. Rosemary's eyes widened. 'Have you two had a fight or something?'

'No. It's just a bit wearing hearing how fantastic Mr Alberici is—almost as wearing as Mal's sense of humour. Even the mums who've had a difficult delivery say they'd like another baby right now, please, if it means they'll have Mr Alberici looking after them.'

Rosemary whistled. 'Someone got out on the wrong side of the bed this morning, didn't she?'

If she said anything else, it'd start the hospital rumour mill whirring. 'Yeah, probably,' Lucy said, and switched the topic back to work.

Though she couldn't get Nic out of her mind. She was aware of exactly when he walked onto the ward and exactly when he left. And she hated this out-of-control feeling. It's like you told Rosemary—he's just another consultant, she reminded herself.

Except she had a nasty feeling that he wasn't.

'I'm worried about this one,' Beth said, handing Lucy the notes of another patient. 'Judy Sutherland's diabetic and the baby's big. I think there's a high risk of shoulder dystocia.' Shoulder dystocia, also known as impacted shoulders, was where the baby's shoulders couldn't be delivered after the head had been delivered. It happened when the baby was large, overdue or had a short cord—babies of diabetic mothers had greater shoulder-to-chest ratios so they were particularly prone to it.

'Judy says she doesn't want a section under any circumstances,' Beth added.

'We might not have to give her a section. If you're right and the shoulders are impacted, we'll have to do the McRoberts manoeuvre,' Lucy said. That meant putting the mother into the lithotomy position with her buttocks supported on a pillow over the edge of the bed, then flexing her hips to make her pelvic outlet bigger, hopefully enough to deliver the baby. 'Then if we rotate the baby so his anterior shoulder is under the symphysis pubis, we should be OK. Though she'll need a large epidural and there's a possibility of problems with the baby—a fractured clavicle at the very least.' Erb's palsy, where the nerves in the arm were affected, was another possibility, and a third of babies affected by shoulder dystocia had permanent damage. She sighed. 'Do you want me to have a word with Judy and check she understands all the risks?'

'Or maybe we should ask Nic to do it,' Beth suggested. Lucy sighed inwardly as she saw the familiar glow in the midwife's face. Beth was clearly yet another member of the Niccolo Alberici fan club. 'He's so charming, she's bound to listen.'

'Yes, Nic's very charming, on the surface,' Lucy agreed, all sweetness and light and wanting to strangle the man.

'Nice of you to say so, Dr Williams.'

Lucy's eyes widened as she heard his voice. Her early warning system had just failed spectacularly, and again he'd caught her saying something outrageous. Gingerly, she turned to face Nic.

'There's a case I want to discuss with you in my office, Lucy,' he said. 'If you'd be so kind.'

'And then would you have a word with Mrs Sutherland for me, please, Nic?' Beth asked.

'Sure.' Nic gave her one of his trade-mark smiles, his eyes crinkling at the corners in a way that clearly made the midwife melt. 'Lucy?'

Sighing inwardly, she followed him into his office.

'Close the door, please,' he said.

Lucy did so.

'Take a seat.' He frowned. 'This is beginning to be a habit—me overhearing something you'd much rather I didn't.'

'Well, eavesdroppers never hear any good of themselves,' Lucy retorted.

'I thought we'd sorted out all the problems between us?'

She sighed. 'OK, OK, I'm sorry.'

He folded his arms. 'Not good enough.'

She couldn't read his expression. 'You'd prefer me to ask for a transfer?'

'No.'

'What, then?'

'Make it up to me.'

Her eyes narrowed with suspicion. 'What do you have in mind?'

'Spend the day with me tomorrow.'

'Spend the day with you tomorrow?' she echoed, surprised. That was the last thing she'd expected.

'Mmm-hmm. I'm a new boy in the area. I could do with a hand finding my feet. I want to explore the district and I'd like some company.'

Lucy scoffed. 'Why ask me? Talk to the midwives. And the nurses. And all the unattached female doctors. They're lining up in droves for you.'

He grinned. 'Oh, Lucia *mia*. You should know better than to believe the hospital rumour mill.'

She didn't dignify that with a reply.

'Lucy, I'm off duty tomorrow. So are you.'

How did he know? No, that was an easy one. All he had to do was look in the off-duty book.

'So spend the day with me, Lucy,' he coaxed. 'Show me the area.'

'You're perfectly capable of reading a map.'

'True. But it's not the same as playing tourist with someone who knows all the good spots.'

'Your idea of good spots might not be the same as mine.'

'On the other hand, they might be.'

Lucy shook her head. 'I don't think it's a good idea.'

'No strings, I promise.'

'Then two more dates and you'll leave me alone?' she asked hopefully.

Nic's eyes crinkled at the corners. 'We're not going on a date, Lucy.'

You couldn't get more crushing than that. She stared at the floor and wished herself a thousand miles away.

'We're merely spending the day together, as friends. Tell you what—I'll do you a deal. I'll talk your patient into being sensible over the shoulder dystocia issue and agreeing to a section if we find we have to do one for the baby's sake, and you can show me your favourite bits of north Cornwall.'

She opened her mouth to say no, but he didn't give her a chance to speak.

He laced his fingers together. 'I would suggest sealing the deal properly... But we're at work, and I promised I wouldn't touch you without your permission.' His eyes filled with mischief. 'It's a shame you're not a mind-reader. Then again, if you knew what I was thinking right now, you'd probably slap my face.'

'Don't tempt me.' Though her words were hollow. Just his mere existence tempted her. And she had a nasty feeling that she knew exactly what he was thinking. Sealing the deal with a kiss. Like the one at the fancy-dress ball—a kiss that might start out sweet and innocent but would heat up the minute their mouths met.

He said something in Italian and she folded her arms and glared at him.

'Translate.'

'I wouldn't dare.' He gave her a lazy grin. 'If you want to know what I said, you'll just have to learn Italian, won't you?'

It wasn't fair. Why did he have to have such a sensual mouth? And when he smiled like that, it made her want to act completely out of character. It made her want to reach over and kiss him. Passionately. And very, very improperly.

'Am I dismissed?' she asked.

'Are you going to spend tomorrow with me?'

'No,' she said crisply.

He clasped his hands theatrically to his heart. 'I tried.'

'You're very trying,' she snapped back.

He spread his hands. 'What can I say? The lady's always right.'

'I do have patients to see.'

'Then *arrivederci, Lucia mia*,' he said softly.

Corny, smarmy, pathetic... Oh, who was she trying to kid? That Italian accent was way, way too sexy for her peace of mind. Worse, she almost opened her mouth to say she'd changed her mind and, yes, she *would* spend the day with him.

Almost. Common sense prevailed. Just.

'You need your head tested, Lucy Williams,' she muttered to herself as she closed his office door.

Nic touched his mouth. No, it wasn't hot. And he hadn't kissed her, much as he'd wanted to. So why did he feel so scorched?

He smiled wryly. It was obvious: it had a lot to do with a certain Dr Williams and that beautiful rosebud mouth. It had taken all his self-control not to pull her into his arms and kiss her, make her feel that same blood-heating passion that zinged through his veins when he saw her.

Working with her was going to be torture.

Working with her was going to be heaven.

CHAPTER FOUR

THAT evening, Lucy found herself pacing her cottage, thinking about Nic.

'Stop it,' she told herself.

But she couldn't. Every time she closed her eyes, she could see his face. Smell his clean, masculine scent. Feel the sweetness of his mouth against hers.

Her day off was even worse. Supposing she hadn't been so stubborn—supposing she'd agreed to spend the day with him. It would have been a chance to get to know him better.

'You don't *want* to get to know him better,' she reminded herself. 'You want to be a top consultant. Your personal life's been a disaster zone for years. Stick to your career—it's safer.'

But what if? What if she'd gone to the beach with him? Supposing she'd taken him to Pentremain, her favourite place on earth, the tiny bay that was one of the best surfing sites in Europe and was spectacular in winter, with the waves crashing onto the rocks and the gulls wailing and the wind whipping roses into your cheeks... They'd have had lunch together in the tiny fishing port, at a secluded table overlooking the sea. Maybe another walk along the beach as the sun was setting.

And then a kiss...

Anyone would think she was a hormonal teenager, not a level-headed thirty-year-old! It was crazy, going weak at the knees at the thought of a kiss.

A kiss from a man who'd told her he felt the same attraction.

A kiss from a man who'd licked her pulse point and looked into her eyes and dared her not to believe how much he desired her.

If she didn't stop thinking about him, she'd go insane!

Well, there was one thing that would take her mind off him. Spring-cleaning. No matter that it was way out of season. Scrubbing every corner of her cottage would stop her thinking about him.

In theory. In practice, it didn't. So she chose the last resort. Cooking. Preferably something that would use up her energy and calm her down again. She didn't have any flour suitable for making bread, so that idea went out of the window...

Then she smiled. But she did have walnuts, honey and sesame seeds. Which meant she could knead out her frustration on a different sort of dough, still have that comforting breadmaking scent, and end up with something sweet to soothe her soul. *Kahk*, the recipe her Egyptian friend Noor had taught her when they'd shared a house in their second year of med school.

She ignored the fact that Nic had a thing about cake.

Or that the sweetness of the honeyed filling reminded her of his mouth.

'These are seriously good,' Nic said, taking a second sugar-dusted cake from the tin at the nurses' station the next morning. 'Icing sugar on the top. Not too sweet on the outside, but then you hit the inside... The mixture of textures and tastes is fabulous. Which mum do I need to thank—and beg to tell me where she bought them?'

'You don't,' Rosemary said.

'One of the staff brought them in?'

'Made by the fair hands of our own Lucy Williams.'

Rosemary winked. 'She's not just a pretty face and a good doctor, you know.'

You can say that again, Nic thought. I just wish she'd let me close enough to find out for myself.

'Hey, Lucy. You've got another convert to *kahk*,' Rosemary said.

Nic nearly choked on his cake. Since when had his radar stopped working and neglected to let him know that Lucy was in the same building, let alone a couple of feet away? He just about managed to retain his composure. 'Lucy, hi. These are very good. Unusual filling.'

'Walnuts, honey and sesame seeds,' she said.

And made by her. Was she still professional and orderly and neat when she cooked, or did she let her guard down? Did she push her hair out of her eyes and end up with a dusting of flour on the end of her nose? Did she filch bits of her favourite ingredients? Did those ice-blue eyes turn into the colour of sunny skies as she relaxed?

Nic had a vision of her in his kitchen, and himself removing her blue-and-white striped butcher's apron before—

'Are you all right, Nic?' Rosemary asked.

Hell. He'd actually moaned aloud at the thought of Lucy in very close proximity to him. He flushed and covered his confusion by taking a third piece. 'I have this thing about *dolci*—sweet things. And these are to die for. Oh-h-h,' he said, hamming it up and hoping that Rosemary hadn't guessed what he'd *really* been thinking about.

Making love with his registrar.

'You'll end up looking like our mums-to-be if you eat them at that rate—especially when it can't be more than half an hour since you had your breakfast,' Lucy informed him sweetly—then disappeared to see a patient before he could make an equally rude retort.

*   *   *

Well, I managed that OK, Lucy told herself. Cool, calm, even jokey.

But she still couldn't stop thinking about Nic. She was on autopilot when she answered the bleep from A and E asking her to see a pregnant holidaymaker who was bleeding, so she missed the patient's name. Until she saw the notes.

Nina Hammond.

Coincidence. It had to be. Hammond was hardly an uncommon surname, and Nina was a popular first name.

But the second she stepped into the cubicle and saw Nina's husband, she knew it wasn't a coincidence. It was the kind of nightmare that ripped open old wounds and then poured salt in them for good measure. Why, why, why hadn't she erred on the side of caution and let someone else deal with this?

But she was a professional. She wasn't going to let her ex see that she was affected by seeing him. Not in the slightest. 'Hello, Mr and Mrs Hammond,' she said, relieved that she was at least able to control the threatening tremor in her voice. 'I'm Lucy Williams, special registrar from the maternity unit.'

'Please, Dr Williams—don't let me lose my baby,' Nina Hammond said, clutching at Lucy's hand. 'Make it stop. Make the bleeding go away.'

'I'll do my best,' Lucy said, and took refuge in her clipboard as she took the patient history.

'We're on holiday,' Nina explained. 'We just wanted to spend some quiet time by the sea. We only got here yesterday. We were going for a drive round the coast—then I realised I was bleeding and Jack drove me straight here.'

'Someone's looking after your other children?' Lucy asked.

Nina shook her head. 'We don't have any.'

Shouldn't they have an older child—Lucy did a rapid mental calculation—one who was nearly four? Or maybe she'd got it wrong. She'd got a hell of a lot wrong where Jack was concerned.

'I've had three miscarriages,' Nina explained.

Lucy refused to meet Jack's eyes. 'I'm sorry to hear that. Has your GP sent you for any tests?'

'No. Should he have done?'

'If any of my patients lost three babies, I'd recommend further tests to see why,' Lucy said. 'It could be that your body's producing antibodies which make you miscarry, called antiphospholipid syndrome—if that's the case, we can give you something to help with that. Or maybe you have a problem with your cervix, and again that's something I can help with. But first of all, I'd like to examine you and do an ultrasound—a scan—to see what's going on. Are you losing much blood?'

'No—just spotting, really. I had cramps and I felt a bit of wetness and just panicked.' Nina bit her lip. 'I so want a baby. We've been trying for years. I've lost three babies already. If I lose this one, I…' She broke into sobs. 'I can't *bear* to go through all this again!'

'It's OK,' Lucy soothed. 'I'd like to take you up to my department—we can do a scan there and see what's going on, then maybe I'll admit you overnight so we can keep an eye on you and give things a chance to settle down.'

'Can my husband stay with me?'

Lucy took a deep breath. 'Let's cross that bridge when we come to it. I'll get a porter to bring you up to the ward and I'll meet you there—I'll have the equipment all set up to check you over. How many weeks are you, by the way?'

'Sixteen.'

Most women with antiphospholipid syndrome miscarried in the first trimester, so the most likely cause of Nina's miscarriages was either polycystic ovaries or an incompetent cervix, Lucy thought. 'Right, then, Mrs Hammond. I'll see you upstairs in a few minutes.'

She made a quick call to River to make sure a room was ready on the ward, then took the stairs back to the unit. The exercise helped calm her.

Jack Hammond. Tall, blond, blue-eyed and tanned. The kind of man who turned heads everywhere he walked. The kind of man women watched and sighed over. The kind of man who'd broken her heart into tiny, tiny shards that had taken her years to repair. She'd thought she'd never, ever see him again. After the messiest possible break-up, she'd moved down to Cornwall, where there'd be no memories to taunt her. She'd never, ever imagined that their paths would cross again.

She was back under control by the time she walked back into River Ward. Nina was waiting for her in one of the side rooms, still trembling and tearful.

'Can I get you a drink of water?' Lucy asked her.

'No, thanks. I think I'd be sick if I drank anything.' Nina clutched Jack's hand. 'My baby... Please, I need to know if my baby's all right.'

'Lift up your top and bare your tummy for me, and we'll see what's going on,' Lucy said gently. She set to work with the gel and the ultrasound scanner and soon had the picture she wanted on the screen.

She tilted the monitor so that Nina could see it. 'Can you see his heart beating there?' she said, pointing to the dark pulsating spot on the screen. 'It's nice and strong. He's given you a nasty scare but I'm pleased to say your baby's looking quite happy right now.'

'It's a boy?' Jack said.

'I can't tell from this angle. I don't like calling foetuses "it" so I call all the difficult ones "he",' Lucy said.

That one hit home, she thought with satisfaction as dark colour slid over Jack's cheekbones.

'Mrs Hammond, would it be all right if I examined you now?'

Nina nodded her consent, and Lucy examined her gently. 'I think you've got what's known as an incompetent cervix,' she said. 'It just means your cervix is shorter and thinner than it should be, so as the foetus gets bigger and heavier, the weight presses on your cervix, which opens earlier than it should do. The good news is, I can do something to help. I can put a stitch called a cerclage round your cervix to stop it opening too early; it acts almost like a purse-string and keeps your cervix closed. I'll need to do it under anaesthetic and keep you in on bed-rest for the next twenty-four hours, but it should hold your cervix closed for the rest of your pregnancy, and your doctor can remove it just before your due date.'

'So I won't lose my baby?'

'Hopefully not,' Lucy said. 'There are some side-effects with the procedure, such as bleeding or infection, but it'll give your baby more of a chance. You'll need to take it very easy for the rest of your pregnancy—your own doctor might even put you on full bed-rest until you have the baby—and I'm afraid you'll have to avoid vaginal intercourse for the rest of your pregnancy.'

'I see,' Jack said.

Lucy refused to look at him. Tough, she thought. You need to look after Nina, not think about your own selfish needs.

'If you feel anything like a contraction or you start leaking fluid, you should ring your midwife straight away,' she continued.

'I will,' Nina said. 'When can you put the stitch in?'

'Today,' Lucy said. 'When did you last have anything to eat?'

'Last night,' Nina told her. 'I couldn't face breakfast.'

'That's good. Don't eat or drink anything now, and I'll check when Theatre's free so I can take you up there. I've got a clinic to run, but I'll let the nursing staff know what's happened. If you need anything, just press your buzzer, OK?' Lucy showed her how the buzzer worked. 'I'll see you in a bit.'

'Can I have a word, Doctor?' Jack asked as Lucy reached the door.

She summoned every bit of her professional reserve and politeness. 'Yes, of course, Mr Hammond.'

He closed the door behind them and moved so that they were out of Nina's sight. 'Hello, Lucy. It's good to see you again.'

Did he honestly expect her to say the same? She simply remained unsmiling.

His gaze travelled the length of her body and back up to her face. 'You look fantastic.'

What was she supposed to say to that? Was he fishing for a compliment? Probably not. He'd always known his looks turned heads. Again, she remained silent.

'Thanks for what you did for Nina,' he said, trying to take her hand.

She shook him off. 'It's my job, Mr Hammond.'

'Though seeing you again today…it's made me realise what a fool I was,' he said. 'I know I hurt you and I wouldn't have done that for the world. Lord only knows what I was thinking at the time. I must have been mad.'

Yeah, right. There was no answer to that.

'I've never really been able to get you out of my head, you know.'

Lucy shrugged. 'That's not my problem.'

'I suppose what I'm trying to say is…' He tried to slide his arm round her. 'Seeing you again has made me realise how much I've missed you. How much I've wanted you. I'm still in love with you, Lucy.'

Lucy pushed him away. How could she ever, ever have been in love with a man like this? A man so shallow and fickle that he'd let his wife lie in a hospital bed, terrified that she was going to lose yet another baby, while he tried to chat up his ex? 'I don't think so, Jack. Your wife—' she placed extra emphasis on the words '—needs your support right now. The least you can do is give it to her.'

'Lucy…'

She shook her head. 'Whatever was between us, Jack, it was over four years ago. And it's staying that way. Now, excuse me. I have a theatre slot to book for your wife and an antenatal clinic to run.' With relief, she went to the nurses' station and rang Theatre, though her hands were less than steady as she dialled the extension.

Jack was here. After all these years. *Jack*. Jack, the man who'd…

She forced herself to concentrate and booked the slot, then gave Rosemary a quick update and left the ward.

As she walked down the stairs, her vision blurred, and she realised that she was actually crying. She rubbed her eyes hard and stiffened her spine. No way. She'd cried enough tears over Jack Hammond. More like an ocean than a river—and she wasn't going to do it again. Seeing him on her ward had brought it all back, the slicing pain she'd once thought would never end, but she was older and wiser now. She could handle this. She *could*.

By the time she reached the antenatal clinic, she was the cool, calm ice maiden she'd always been at Treverro General. Professional first, last and always. 'Holly about yet?' she asked.

'She called in sick,' Moira, the receptionist, told her. 'Food poisoning.'

Lucy grimaced. 'Poor thing.' She knew how awful food poisoning could be—she'd eaten a dodgy chicken korma once and it had made her ill for three days—but it was going to make life tough for her this morning. She needed a radiographer to help her with an amniocentesis, the procedure where she took a sample of the amniotic fluid surrounding the baby so the lab could culture the baby's skin cells from the fluid to check the chromosomes. 'Is anyone covering for her?' she asked hopefully.

Moira shook her head. 'I did try, the minute I got her message—but everyone else is fully booked up with scans. There are a couple off duty, but I haven't been able to contact them and see if they'd come in for a morning. I could try getting them to do one each with you and delay some of their own scans...'

But the ultrasound clinic always overran, and Lucy had already had some stroppy memos from the finance team about her budget. Not that it was her budget any more, she reminded herself. It was Nic's budget now. *His* problem. Though if she gave him a budgetary headache, she knew he'd carpet her for it. 'Not to worry. I can do it myself,' Lucy said. It just meant that she'd have to concentrate more on the procedure and wouldn't be able to give the parents as much reassurance as she wanted. Though maybe that was what she needed. Something to occupy her mind a hundred and ten per cent.

'Problems?' a voice said behind her.

A voice that only recently had been husky with desire, murmuring, *Lucia mia.*

Nic.

No, she didn't need this added complication right now. She didn't need Nic and she didn't need Jack. She was going to concentrate on her job. Behave yourselves, she told her knees, and spun round to face him. 'Sort of. Holly—one of the radiographers—is ill.'

'And she was working with you this morning on an amnio?' he guessed.

She shrugged. 'I'll manage.'

'I can help if you like,' he offered.

The devil and the deep blue sea, she thought. If she said yes, she'd be able to do her job properly, but she'd also be close to Nic all morning. Nic, who had already cost her more than one sleepless night. She hated this feeling of being out of control, and with Jack around as well to torture her with might-have-beens...

Work, she reminded herself. 'Thanks. Do you want to do the ultrasound or the needle?'

'Ultrasound.' He grinned. 'So *you* get to be the baddie.'

So that was how he was going to play it: light and cool. Just as well. Lucy didn't think she could cope with one of his intense looks. Not when she was all churned up inside as it was. 'OK.' She glanced at her watch. 'Now?'

'I'm all yours, Dr Williams.'

The picture that conjured up meant she didn't trust herself to respond in a similar light-hearted vein, so she ignored him and glanced through the notes for her first patient.

'Mr and Mrs Sanders?' she said to the tearful-looking woman sitting in Waiting Area Two and the silent man by her side.

'Yes.' The woman's voice was hoarse, clearly from crying.

'I'm Lucy Williams, senior registrar, and this is Nic Alberici, the consultant. Would you like to come with us?' She led them through to consulting room with its ultrasound unit.

'You get the special offer today—two for the price of one,' said Nic, 'so there's nothing to worry about.'

'He looks after the monitor and I can concentrate on you,' Lucy added. 'If there's anything you want to ask either of us at any time, just say, but I'll try to tell you exactly what I'm doing and why. Have you had a glass of water while you've been waiting?'

Kay Sanders nodded. 'The midwife said I needed a full bladder.'

'That's so we get a better picture on the screen. If you could lie down on the couch for me, Mrs Sanders, and bare your tummy, Nic will do an ultrasound scan to see how the baby's lying and show me where I can take a little bit of fluid. It won't hurt the baby at all, and the little one shouldn't even notice that I've pinched a bit.'

She smiled warmly at the couple. 'I know it's a horrible situation for you both, but I'll do my best to make this as quick and painless as possible for you. I'm only going to take about ten millilitres of fluid—that's a couple of teaspoonfuls—and then I'll send it off to the lab for culture. As soon as the results come back, we'll ring you to let you know. If it's bad news, your GP will ring you and ask you to go in to the surgery for a chat.'

'How long will it take?' John Sanders asked.

'Three weeks, I'm afraid. We need the time for the cells to grow,' Nic put in.

Lucy squeezed the woman's hand. Unfortunately, the hospital wasn't yet able to offer the 'fish' test, the chromosomal marker test which only took three days, but maybe Nic could start to influence that. 'This shouldn't hurt, Mrs Sanders—you'll feel a jab as the needle goes in, but I promise it's not as bad as having a tetanus shot.'

'That's one good thing, then.' Kay Sanders was clearly trying to be brave, and Lucy's heart went out to her. The

notes showed that the couple had been trying for two years
to conceive, and had even been on a waiting list for IVF
treatment when they'd discovered that Kay was pregnant.
Then the results of a routine screening test had shown that
the foetus had a higher-than-average risk of having Down
syndrome, so Kay and John had been offered an amniocentesis to clarify the situation.

Lucy put Nic and Jack out of her mind and concentrated
on the two worried parents-to-be in front of her.

'The triple test is a screening test, not a definite yes-or-
no result. You had higher than normal levels of protein in
your blood—what we call alpha-foetal protein or AFP—
and your midwife wanted to give you the option of checking the results,' Lucy continued. 'I know it's easy for me
to say, but most babies are completely normal, so try not
to worry too much.'

Kay nodded, clearly too choked to answer.

'The amniocentesis test carries a very small risk of miscarriage, around one per cent. Our record's actually better
than average here as it's less than half a per cent,' Lucy
reassured her, 'so we recommend that you take things easy
for the next couple of days. I'll give you a leaflet explaining
what you can expect to feel—the odd bit of stomach cramp,
a bit like period pain, is very common. Though if you get
any bleeding or feel any fluid leaking, call your midwife
or GP straight away.'

Gently, Nic squeezed gel onto Kay's skin. 'We warm the
gel here—not like your midwife in the GP's surgery—and
it just helps us get a better picture of the baby.' He passed
the ultrasound scanning head over Kay's abdomen, pressing
in gently to get the picture Lucy needed.

'If you look on the screen, you'll see your baby,' Lucy
said. 'Lying on his or her back with hands behind the
head—just like mum. They often do—sometimes I see

them crossing their legs and then I look at the mum, who's doing the same thing.'

Nic did some quick measurements. 'According to this, the baby's seventeen weeks.'

'And three days,' John Sanders added.

The triple test results—which showed the risk of spina bifida and Down syndrome—were often wrong if the gestation dates were inaccurate, but that wasn't the situation in this case. Lucy exchanged a glance with Nic and her heart went out to them. 'Well, I can see a nice patch here. I'll be able to keep the needle well away from the baby and he won't even notice. Mrs Sanders, would you mind watching the fish mobile above your head rather than the screen? It's just that it can be upsetting, seeing the needle go in—and if you're upset, the baby will start to fidget. If you could keep as still as possible, it'll be quicker for me to take the fluid.'

'All right.'

The couple were holding hands so tightly, their knuckles showed. 'Now, you'll feel a bit of a scratch.' Gently, Lucy inserted the needle, checking its position against the baby all the time on the ultrasound screen, then drew back the plunger on the syringe to take the fluid. 'All done,' she said, taking the woman's other hand and squeezing it. 'And you were brilliant—you didn't even flinch when I put the needle in. Well done.'

Kay gave her a wobbly smile.

'Have a rest outside for a while while I write up your notes, then if you're feeling OK in twenty minutes or so you can go home—but take it easy and make sure you get plenty of rest for the next day or so. We don't insist on complete bed-rest any more, but you need to be sensible and not overdo things.' She took a leaflet from her clipboard. 'This should answer your questions, but have a read through it while you're sitting in the waiting room. If there's anything you'd like to know that isn't on there, just grab me or one of the midwives and ask us. I know we all look as if we're rushing around, but don't feel you're being a nuisance—you're our patient, too, and we're never too busy to answer questions,' she said, giving the leaflet to Kay. 'If you feel any pain in your abdomen or lose any fluid, or you're worried about anything, ring your midwife straight away. We'll be in touch as soon as the results come back. And, if it helps at all, I can't see any major problems on the scan,' Lucy said.

'Thank you, Doctor,' Kay said gratefully, tears welling in her eyes again.

'And because the test checks the chromosomes of the baby, we can tell you for definite if your baby's a boy or a girl, if you'd like to know,' Lucy added.

Kay nodded. 'I'd like to know, please.'

'OK. I'll make sure it's in your notes. Though we won't be able to tell you that over the phone—we'll send you a letter to confirm it.'

The couple left the room. When Lucy had finished labelling the sample, Nic smiled at her. 'You've got a great way with patients, Lucy. You took them through it clearly without being patronising, and you put the mother at her ease.'

'As would any senior registrar worth his or her salt,' Lucy reminded him. 'They're in a horrible situation and it's my job to make it as easy for them as possible. If I can't do it by now, I shouldn't be in this job.'

And until last week, she *hadn't* been in this job—she'd been doing his job.

Nic held both hands up. 'Hey, I wasn't trying to patronise you.'

'Of course not.'

He smiled ruefully. 'We make a great team. We work on the same wavelength and I like that—I don't want to fight with you, Lucia *mia*.'

'Would you please stop calling me that?' she hissed. 'I'm not *your* Lucy.'

He didn't say anything. He didn't have to. His eyes said it all for him: *yet*. He brushed the backs of his fingers against his cheek and she shivered as if he'd touched *her*. 'It's a shame you didn't come out with me on our day off.'

Why had he had to say 'our'? Linking them together like that? They weren't an item. Not even *close*.

'I went for a long walk on the beach down the road, and tried a traditional Cornish pasty.' He gave her a sidelong look, one he'd probably calculated to melt her, she thought crossly. 'But it would have been even better if you'd been there to share it with me.'

'I'm sure you'd have plenty of offers of company if you asked.' Just like Jack had.

'I don't want just any company.' He rubbed the pad of his thumb against his lower lip and her knees buckled. Nic wasn't playing fair. OK, he'd kept his promise and he wasn't touching her—but she could imagine how it would feel if his fingers were touching her skin instead of his own. Worse, she *knew* what it felt like, and she wanted more.

Or was it just because she'd seen Jack again?

'I only want you,' Nic murmured, holding her gaze.

It would be so, so easy to say yes.

And then she'd spend a lifetime regretting it. Happy-ever-after didn't exist. She knew that. The proof of the pudding was sitting right upstairs, next to his wife.

She backed away and crossed her arms defensively. 'I've already told you, I'm not looking for a relationship.'

'You kissed me back at the ball, Lucia *mia*,' he reminded her softly.

She coughed. 'Everyone's entitled to their mistakes.'

'It wasn't a mistake.'

'Let's agree to differ. We have patients to see and a budget to stick to.'

He stared at her for a long, long moment, then nodded. 'As you wish.'

He kept out of her way for the rest of the clinic. Lucy wasn't sure whether to be relieved or disappointed. She'd half expected him to suggest having lunch together, and then she saw him talking to Beth, one of the midwives. He was smiling at her—the special smile Lucy had begun to think was reserved for *her*—and Beth was smiling back just as warmly.

Worse, they left the clinic together. It hadn't take Nic long to choose a replacement for her company—so much for his 'I only want you'.

Don't be such a dog in the manger, Lucy told herself. You don't want Nic. You've already told him as much. Don't begrudge Beth her chance of happiness.

Though she knew she was lying to herself. She *did* want Nic, and she was as jealous as hell of the young midwife. Which was precisely why she should stay well away from Nic Alberici. Just like her mother and her sisters, she had appalling judgement in men. And she wasn't ever going to let herself get hurt like that again. She'd already been there, done that and worn the T-shirt with Jack. And she was a fast learner. She didn't repeat her mistakes.

Ever.

CHAPTER FIVE

TRYING to ignore the twinge of misery in her heart, Lucy gathered her notes together and went to see her next patient. The woman sitting in the consulting room, supported by a nurse, was clutching a cardboard bowl and her face was very pale.

'Hello, Mrs Jacobs. I'm Lucy Williams, senior registrar.'

'Hello.' The woman's face tightened and she closed her eyes, as if willing herself not to be sick.

'You're sixteen weeks now?' Lucy asked gently, glancing at her notes.

She nodded.

'And you've been feeling like this since six weeks?'

'Yeah. This one's definitely going to be an only child,' Sonia Jacobs said, grimacing.

'Are you keeping much down?'

She shook her head. 'Hardly anything. I'm sick from the minute I get up to the minute I go to bed—and half the night, too. I've tried ginger and sniffing lemons and acupressure bands—nothing works.'

'Would you mind if I examined you?' Lucy asked.

Slowly, Sonia got up on the couch, and was promptly sick. Lucy immediately dampened a paper towel and handed it to her, together with a box of tissues.

'Sorry,' Sonia said, almost crying.

'Not to worry. We'll have you feeling better soon,' Lucy said comfortingly. Gently, she examined Sonia's abdomen. Her skin wasn't as elastic as it should have been and didn't spring back immediately when it was pinched: one of the first symptoms of dehydration. Given that Sonia was feeling sick all the time as well as being sick, she probably wasn't eating or drinking much in the first place.

'Some mums are unlucky with morning sickness—it lasts all day and seems to go on for ever,' Lucy said. 'It's what we call hyperemesis gravidarum—basically, it means you're vomiting a lot during pregnancy. Though I don't like prescribing anti-nausea drugs.' Not after the thalidomide problem—even though it had been decades before, doctors were still wary. 'I'm worried that you're not getting enough nutrients and you're a little dehydrated. I'd like to admit you for a couple of days to give you some fluids.'

'Can't I just try to drink a bit more at home?' Sonia asked.

'If you're not keeping anything down, you'll just be making life harder for yourself,' Lucy said. 'We'll put you on a drip—that is, we'll put a very fine needle in your hand and pass some fluids through it. It won't make you sick and you'll feel a lot better,' she said. 'Don't worry, the baby will be fine,' she added. 'Research shows that when your baby's growing well, you're more likely to suffer morning sickness.' She grinned. 'Though I think when your baby arrives, he's going to be a hungry one who'll scoff all day! Now, if you'd like to go home and pack whatever you need, I'll arrange for you to be admitted to the ward this afternoon. I'll be up to see you on my rounds, and we'll see how you're getting on in a couple of days—when you're feeling better and keeping a bit more down, you'll be able to go home again.'

Sonia nodded. 'Can my husband come in and visit me?'

'Of course,' Lucy said. 'And if you're worried about anything, just ask one of the midwives—they're a really nice bunch on River.'

'Thank you, Doctor,' Sonia said.

'I'll see you later on,' Lucy said with a smile.

She couldn't quite face lunch—the idea of seeing Nic and Beth together in the canteen was too much for her—so she headed back for the ward. Her Theatre slot had been put back by an emergency, so she got her paperwork out of the way.

She was just going to check on Nina when Jack came out of the side room.

'I've been waiting for you,' he said.

'Is Nina all right?' she asked, immediately assuming the worst.

'Yeah.' He shrugged. 'I'd have called one of the midwives if there was a problem. That's what you said, wasn't it?'

'Yes.'

'No, it's you I was looking for,' he said softly. 'Lucy. I've called myself all kinds of fools. I never should have let you go.'

'It's all water under the bridge,' she said crisply.

'It doesn't have to be.'

Did he really think she was the type to have an affair with a married man? Particularly one who'd already brought her world crashing down once? Did she have GULLIBLE tattooed on her forehead or something? 'Yes, it does. It's over, Jack.'

'Is it? Can you honestly say with your hand on your heart that you never think about me? That you don't miss what we had?'

'Yes.'

'Look me in the eye and say it.'

Her lip curled. 'I don't have to do anything, Jack. I certainly don't have to justify myself to you. Now, leave me alone.'

'It's not over, Lucy. It never really was. You and me.

We were good together; don't you remember? That day at the waterfall, when we—'

'Was a long time ago,' Lucy cut in. She definitely didn't want to think about that day. The day when she and Jack had made love for the first time. When she'd realised how much she'd loved him. 'It's in the past and it's staying that way. If Nina doesn't need me, other patients do.'

He caught her hand. 'But *I* need you, Lucy. I can't stop thinking about you. The way we used to be together. The way you felt against me.' He gave her a lazy smile and rubbed his thumb against her palm. 'The way we used to spend whole days in bed together. Do you remember? We'd only get up for long enough to make toast—and then we'd end up having to chuck it away because it got cold, because we hadn't been able to wait long enough for it to cook before making love again.' He lifted his other hand to stroke her face. 'It was so good between us.'

So why did you end it the way you did? Lucy asked silently. Why did you hurt me so badly?

'Meet me later,' he said. 'Tonight. We'll go for a meal, talk a bit. And maybe then…' He cupped her face, catching her off guard, and lowered his mouth to hers.

For one heart-stopping second, Lucy almost responded to the familiar pressure of his lips—and then she remembered where they were. And who was in the room just behind them. She shoved hard at his chest. 'Get off me!'

'You don't mean that. Come on, Lucy,' Jack wheedled. 'You know you feel the same way I do.'

'Is this man bothering you, Dr Williams?' an icy voice demanded.

'It's fine. I'm handling the situation,' Lucy said.

'If you're sure you don't need any help,' Nic said, giving Jack a ferocious stare.

Jack shrugged it off. 'Lucy and I go back a long, long way.'

'Then you should know that when she says no, she means it,' Nic informed him tartly. 'And there are rules in this hospital about abusing staff. If I catch you annoying one of my staff again—and Lucy in particular—I'll throw you out personally and warn Security that you're barred from the hospital. Understand?'

'You and whose army?' Jack sneered.

'Just me. And that's more than enough for your sort, believe me,' Nic said, his voice very quiet and very, very dangerous. 'Dr Williams—I need to discuss a case with you in my office. Now would be a good time.'

'Of course, Mr Alberici.' Lucy refused to look at Jack again and accompanied Nic to his office in silence.

'Take a seat,' Nic said, closing the door behind him.

Lucy did so.

'Care to tell me what all that was about?'

'Nothing important,' she said, lifting her chin. 'What's this case you wanted to discuss?'

'There wasn't one. I just thought you could do with an excuse to leave the ward. Fast.'

'Don't worry, I can handle the situation.'

'Lucy, I don't doubt your ability with patients,' Nic said, 'but it looked as if the guy was hassling you. Which makes it my problem, and *I'll* handle it, as your boss.'

She narrowed her eyes. 'Yeah, right. Pull rank, why don't you?'

He raked a hand through his hair. 'Lucy, you're as capable as I am of running this ward. You did it for weeks before I got the job. I know that and I'm trying to stay out of your hair and not interfere with the way you're doing your job.'

'What's wrong with the way I'm doing my job?' she demanded.

'Nothing!' He rolled his eyes. 'OK. Tell me this. If a patient or relative was hassling one of your staff, what would you do?'

'Step in, defuse the situation, make sure everyone knew the rules and that I'd enforce them if I had to,' she said.

'Precisely. And that's what I'm doing now. I'm doing exactly what you'd do in my shoes. So don't give me a hard time about it, OK?'

She flushed. 'I'm sorry. I suppose it must be as tough for you, having a second in command who was in charge until you came along.'

'So we'll make the best of it. Together. As a team.' Nic's voice softened. 'Are you all right, Lucy?'

'I'm fine,' she said through gritted teeth.

'You don't look it. He's upset you—you're shaking.'

'I'm not.' She whipped her hands behind her back before he could challenge her to prove it.

He smiled at her. 'Come on, I'll shout you a coffee at Pat's Place.'

'I said I'm *fine*, Nic.'

He looked as if he didn't believe her, but at least he didn't argue with her. 'I know you've got a slot in Theatre this afternoon, so you're due a break before you operate—coincidentally enough, I'm due a break right now, too. So let's get out of here before someone bleeps us.'

Lucy was about to snarl at him to leave her alone, but stopped herself. It wasn't Nic's fault that Jack had turned up—or that Jack had behaved the way he had. Jack the lad. Jack the selfish bastard, only thinking of himself and what he wanted. Jack, who actually thought she'd fall into his arms again. Jack, who'd had the nerve to remind her of the time they'd first made love, of the time they'd lived together… Jack, who'd never given her a real explanation for what he'd done, let alone a proper apology.

Though 'sorry' wouldn't be nearly enough.

Nic didn't press her for more details on their way to the café, but the silence between them wasn't awkward either. He was just giving her some much-needed space, and Lucy appreciated it. Right now, she could do with being several hundred miles away from Treverro. Preferably on some remote Scottish island where she'd be guaranteed never to see Jack Hammond again.

'If you find us a table, I'll get the coffees,' he said as they walked into the café. 'And before you insist on paying your share, Dr Independent Williams, you can buy me cake and coffee next time I have the day from hell. Deal?'

'Deal.' Though she didn't think that Nic would have this sort of day. Not ever. She hadn't expected it in a million years, being called to treat Jack's wife. She really, really should have walked out and let someone else deal with it. Yet Nina had looked so frightened, so desperate. How could Lucy, as a doctor, have refused to help the poor woman?

Nic put a mug of mochaccino and a muffin in front of her. 'Pat's trying a new recipe—toffee *crème* and pecan,' he said.

'Thanks.' Lucy took a swig of coffee. And the muffin was exactly what she needed—sweet, stodgy comfort food.

Nic waited until she'd finished before he spoke again. 'Better?' he asked.

'Yeah.' She forced a smile to her face. 'Thanks. I needed a breather.'

'So what's the story?'

A story she didn't want to talk about. To *think* about, even. She wanted to keep it buried so she never had to feel that kind of misery and disillusion again. 'There is no story.'

'Talk to me, Lucy,' he said softly. 'You'll feel better than if you keep it all locked up inside.'

'I wouldn't even know where to start.'

'Try the beginning.'

She sighed. 'OK. Though I trust you'll respect my confidence. No one here at Treverro knows about this.'

Nic's heart missed a beat. Lucy was going to trust him with something no one else knew? 'Of course. Lucy, I know what hospital grapevines are like. I won't breathe a word to anyone else.'

'It's my cerclage patient—Nina Hammond.'

He waited. If he asked a question now, he might push her back behind her defensive wall. He had to let her tell him in her own time.

'She's married to my ex. Jack. The one you saw...' She took a deep, shuddering breath and the look of pain on her face made Nic want to push Jack Hammond through a window.

'It was a bit of a messy break-up. Once I'd picked up the pieces, I left London and came here.'

To Cornwall. As far away from her ex as possible. Whatever had happened between them must have been really bad—from what he'd seen of Lucy, he didn't think she was the type to run away. It would have been easy for her to resign from her job here once he'd taken over—but she hadn't. She'd stayed to see it through. Lucy Williams was a fighter, not a coward.

'I never thought I'd see him again.' She shrugged. 'But Cornwall's a really popular holiday spot, so I should have anticipated running into him around here at some point. I just didn't expect it to be here, at work.'

'Do you want me to look after the Hammonds?' he asked.

She shook her head. 'It's OK. I'll manage.'

'Lucy, it's not a good idea. Apart from the fact that he's hassling you now, you know the patient so you're involved.'

Lucy shook her head. 'Actually, no. Nina and I never knew each other.'

'So he met her after you broke up?'

She smiled bitterly. 'You know, I didn't think Jack could sink any lower in my estimation. But the fact that he came on to me just now—while his wife was lying in my ward, terrified that she was going to lose her baby—how could I *ever* have got involved with someone like that? How could I have misjudged his character so badly?'

Nic's fists tightened and he made himself relax them deliberately. Being macho wasn't going to help Lucy. Right now, she needed understanding, not puffed-up male bravado. 'Hey, it's not your fault the guy turned out to be a low-life.'

'No?' Lucy made a face. 'I'm like the rest of my family. I've got rotten judgement when it comes to my life partner. We're all useless at this kind of thing.'

'Everyone makes mistakes, Lucy. Don't blame yourself.' He squeezed her hand. 'Look, if it'll make things easier for you, I'm happy to swap a case with you.'

She shook her head. 'Even if I don't do the cerclage on Nina, I know Jack'll seek me out again. I've told him I'm not interested, but once Jack gets an idea into his head... Let's just say he's persistent.'

'Oh, Lucy.' Sitting there, holding her hand, had probably blown his common sense into some far universe—it was the only explanation Nic could think of for the words that came out of his mouth next. 'There's one thing you could do to prove to him you're not interested.'

'What?'

'Show him you're off limits—you're someone else's girl.'

Lucy blinked hard. 'Someone else's girl?'

'If he knows you're still single, he'll think you're pining for him. Whereas if he sees you with someone…he'll know you're not. And then he'll leave you alone.'

She was silent for a long, long time, clearly thinking about Nic's suggestion. The volcano was about to explode at any minute, Nic thought. She was going to slap his face, throw the remains of his coffee over him, storm out.

Instead, she nodded. 'Good point.'

She was going to go ahead with it?

'So what's the plan?'

The plan? Nic didn't have one! He had to improvise—fast. 'We go back onto the ward. You go up to Theatre. I tell him he has to wait for his wife in the dayroom or in her room. He sees you arriving at the door after the operation—and he overhears you make a date with the man in your life.' This was the crunch. The bit where she'd say no. 'Me.'

'And you think it'd work?'

Yes! Yes! his heart screamed. 'It's worth a try,' he said, as casually as he could.

There was a long, long pause and Nic could feel his blood pressure rising. Was she going to knock him back?

'OK,' she said at last.

She'd agreed? Nic surreptitiously pinched himself. Yes, he was awake. 'Fine. I'd better get going. Bleep me when you get out of Theatre, and we'll put Plan A into action,' he said softly.

* * *

It was a crazy plan, Lucy thought, but she wanted Jack out of her life. Now and for ever. And Nic had a point: the only way Jack would leave her alone was if he thought she was involved with someone else.

No, not just someone else. *Nic.* Involved with Nic.

The idea terrified her and excited her at the same time. But it was just a smokescreen, she reminded herself. This wasn't the same as actually having a relationship with Nic. She wasn't his girlfriend, his lover—she wasn't *anyone's* girlfriend or lover. She was her own person, and she had a fulfilling career to concentrate on.

Even so, she was glad she had the operation to deal with so she had to give her full attention to her work, and even gladder that Mal was assisting. Her SHO hadn't seen a cerclage done before and it was a good opportunity to teach him; plus, she'd have to keep herself well under control in front of him. She couldn't risk him teasing her about all this.

In Theatre, Mal dropped his habitual clowning and assisted her well, asking intelligent questions—showing the side of him she liked best. Absorbed in her work, Lucy almost forgot about the turmoil in her life. But as soon as she'd finished the suturing, cleaned up and asked Mal to check on another patient, it came back to her with full force. She was going to have to face Jack again. And show him that she wasn't interested in him—now or ever.

She bleeped Nic, and he was waiting for her outside Nina Hammond's door when she came down to the ward.

'How did it go?' he asked.

'Fine. As long as she takes it easy…' Lucy shrugged. 'She's going to need a lot of support. Support I don't think Jack's going to give her.' No doubt when Nina had had her miscarriages, he'd been playing the field, dropping her off at hospital, letting the nurses look after her and going straight to the nearest club to exercise his pulling power.

'Talking of Jack, he's watching us,' Nic said very softly. 'As far as he's concerned, we're just two colleagues discussing a case. We need to prove you're off limits.'

'How?'

'Kiss me.'

'What?'

'Or let me kiss you. Like this.' He bent his head and touched his lips to hers. What started out as a gentle kiss suddenly turned explosive, and Lucy was kissing him back with abandon, caressing his face and revelling in the beginnings of stubble rubbing against her fingers.

A loud cough brought them both back to reality.

'How's my wife?' Jack demanded. The suppressed fury in his face told Lucy that Nic's idea had worked—and how!

'Everything was very straightforward, no complications. She should be fine,' Lucy said.

'Though we'll keep her on bed-rest here for the next twenty-four hours,' Nic said. 'I'm sorry that it's going to interrupt your holiday, but it's standard procedure and I'd prefer to err on the side of caution, especially as your wife's had several miscarriages already.' He held out his hand. 'I'm sorry, I didn't introduce myself earlier. Niccolo Alberici, obstetric consultant.'

Jack took his hand as if it was something the cat had dragged in. 'Jack Hammond.'

Nic slid his arm round Lucy's shoulders. 'I apologise if we embarrassed you just now, Mr Hammond. We try not to let our private life spill over into work, which is why I didn't explain to you earlier that Lucy's more than just a member of my staff. But when it comes to *amore*...' He smiled. 'When you're in love, sometimes you can't help yourself, don't you find?'

Jack shuffled on the spot, looking uncomfortable. Lucy just bet he was wondering how much she'd told Nic about him. Well, she wasn't going to enlighten him. Let him sweat a bit, for a change.

'I'm sure you must have questions for Lucy, so I'll leave you to it.' Nic dropped a kiss on top of Lucy's head, still playing his part to perfection. 'Bleep me when you're ready to go home, Lucia *mia*.'

It was working! Lucy thought gleefully. The disgruntlement on Jack's face was plain. 'Remember it's your turn to cook tonight, darling,' she said.

'Again? You're a tough woman,' Nic grumbled jokingly, winked and left them to it.

'So—you're seeing that smarmy Italian?' Jack asked when Nic was out of earshot.

'That's my business. And Nic isn't the slightest bit smarmy.' Which was true. He was infuriating, a flirt, drove her crazy…but never smarmy.

'But—' Jack began.

Lucy gave him a scornful look. 'What did you expect? That I'd eat my heart out over you and wait for you to change your mind again?'

Jack flushed dully.

'Now, do you have any questions about Nina's care?'

'I— No, I suppose not.'

'She's going to need you, Jack. She's going to feel as if everything's her fault. So your job's to reassure her and support her and tell her how much you love her. OK?'

'Yeah,' he muttered.

'Good. I'll probably see you *both* tomorrow, then.' She gave him a tight smile, gathered up her clipboard and a set of notes and swept off to see her next patient.

CHAPTER SIX

'YOU'RE a dark horse, Luce,' Malcolm said, grinning. 'How long have you and His Lordship been...you know?' He nudged her.

'I haven't the faintest idea what you're talking about, Malcolm,' Lucy said coolly, hoping that her SHO hadn't noticed the tremor running through her.

'Oh, come on! Beth saw the pair of you kissing outside one of the side rooms a few minutes ago. Quite a clinch, she said. A snog, not just a little peck on the cheek. And you both sneak off together on a regular basis. *Now* we know why,' he teased.

'We do not "sneak off", as you put it. We merely adjourn to Pat's Place. Where we discuss work in a civilised way,' Lucy said.

'You don't discuss work with *me* like that,' he retorted.

She ruffled his hair. 'Malcy, dearest, if you were a civilised human being, instead of being like my kid brothers at their most annoying, I'd have patient conferences over coffee with you, too. You did well in Theatre today. If you're a good boy tomorrow and keep it up, I might even buy you a mochaccino at Pat's.' She blew him a kiss and walked away, though inside she was shaking.

Why hadn't she seen this coming? Why had she agreed to Nic's stupid plan? Why hadn't she just swapped the Hammonds for one of his cases? Why?

She asked herself the same question several times in the next half-hour, when the midwives started quizzing her, too.

'So does our Italian sex god kiss as beautifully as he looks?' Beth asked.

'How should I know?' Lucy responded.

'Come on, Lucy. I *saw* you in the corridor. It was enough to steam up my glasses!'

'It's not what you think,' Lucy said, feeling her face grow hot. 'It's complicated.'

'You're a lucky cow, Lucy Williams. He's *gorgeous*.'

'Beth, I...' She sighed. 'He's my boss.'

'Who cares? He's the sexiest man ever to have walked into this hospital,' Beth said cheerfully. 'But at least now I know why he was polite but firm when I asked him out the other day.'

'You asked him out?' Lucy was shocked.

'I didn't know you were interested in him—I just thought he was young, free, single and gorgeous. But he turned me down, obviously because he had someone else in his sights. You.' Beth gave her a broad wink. 'Go for it, girl!'

Rosemary was even worse. 'Talk about the lady doth protest too much, Lucy Williams. Now we know your little secret!' she said.

Secret? Did she mean Lucy's supposed affair with Nic— or did she know all about Jack Hammond? No, she couldn't. Nobody knew the truth about Jack. Not the whole truth. Not even Nic.

'Don't look so worried,' Rosemary said with a grin. 'It couldn't happen to a nicer couple.'

'We are *not* a couple,' Lucy said through gritted teeth.

'Come off it. Look at the way you work together— you're a perfect double act on the ward. I've never seen such teamwork. You clicked right from the start, and I wondered how long it'd take you to get together in private as well as professionally.'

'There's nothing to talk about,' Lucy insisted.

'Oh, look! There goes another flying pig,' Rosemary teased, pointing to the ceiling.

Lucy realised her misery must have shown on her face, because Rosemary gave her a hug. 'Hey, I'm only teasing. Half of us are jealous because he's so gorgeous, and all of us think it's about time you stopped working so hard and had some fun.'

By the time her shift ended, Lucy was extremely glad to remove her white coat and hang it in her locker. But she didn't even make it out of the department. Nic was there in the corridor. Waiting for her, by the looks of it.

'You OK?' he asked.

'Fine,' she said, tight-lipped.

'Jack Hammond hasn't tried it on with you again?'

'No, he's left me alone. Unfortunately, I can't say the same about the hospital rumour machine.'

'Ah.' Nic had the grace to look penitent. 'I didn't think of that.'

'Neither did I.'—

'The way I see it, you've got three choices. Number one, tell them the truth.'

Her eyes widened. The truth? She hadn't even told Nic the full story! And if she did, she'd have to face a repeat of all the pitying looks she'd had in London... 'No way.'

'Number two, ignore them. It'll blow over.'

Eventually. He was right there. 'And number three?'

He took her hand, kissed her palm and curled her fingers over the imprint of his kiss. 'Not telling, Lucia *mia*. You'll slap my face.'

'Nic,' she said warningly.

'OK.' He launched into a stream of Italian.

'Funny guy,' she snarled.

'Come on. Let's get out of here.' He opened the door

and shepherded her out of the department. 'You've had the day from hell and right now you need a bit of TLC.'

'I'm perfectly fine,' Lucy said frostily.

He didn't argue with her, just smiled. 'You're going to pass on my bruschetta, then?'

'What bruschetta?'

'You told me it was my turn to cook tonight, did you not?'

'That was just to make Jack think I...' Her throat dried.

'And it's a great idea. I'll cook you dinner. As your *friend*,' he emphasised. 'Coming?'

'What about my bicycle?'

'It's secured, yes?' At her nod, he said, 'Pick it up later. And if you're worrying about people seeing us leaving together, it won't make a difference because they're already talking about us. Tomorrow morning, something else will have knocked you off the top gossip spot, and everything will go back to normal.'

Normal? Right then, Lucy wasn't sure that anything would ever be normal again.

'I'm hungry,' he said. 'And if you really, really hate my cooking then I have ice cream in the freezer. Luxury ice cream.' He grinned. 'And that's an offer you can't possibly refuse.'

Nic gave her a sidelong look as he held the passenger door of his car open for her. He'd seen her expression as she'd looked at his car—it was obvious she'd expected him to drive some macho sports car. 'Disappointed?'

'What?'

'That I drive a boring, mid-range Audi rather than a Ferrari?'

Lucy flushed. 'I'm trying not to stereotype you.'

Oh, wasn't she? 'Good. Because I never wanted a red

Italian sports car.' He chuckled. 'I wanted an Italian motor-bike. A big, fast one. I bought a Ducati.'

'So why the switch to the car?'

'My mother.' He climbed into the driver's seat. 'Her reaction was more Italian than my dad's when I came home with it. She yelled at me—in Italian—that I was going to kill myself and would I be so pleased with myself then, and she slammed every single door in the house, hard enough to knock a couple of pictures off the wall and break the glass in them. We didn't speak for three days, and then I did a stint in A and E. We lost a twenty-year-old who'd come off his bike—a much smaller bike than mine—and I had to break the news to his parents. I realised then I couldn't ever put my mother through the hell of learning her only son had died in an accident, and I sold the Duc the next morning.'

'And now you're Mr Predictable?'

'Oh, I wouldn't say *that*,' he told her, his voice soft and low. She flushed spectacularly, and he chuckled. 'Don't play with fire, Lucia *mia*. My self-control's good—but not that good.'

Neither was hers, she thought. This was a stupid idea, going home with Nic. Seeing Jack again had brought back all her old insecurities. If Nic paid her the slightest attention, she'd probably fall straight into his arms, be another notch on his bedpost and then have to cope with seeing him go after his next conquest. Hadn't he already admitted that he couldn't resist a challenge? And what more of a challenge could he have than the hospital's ice maiden?

She was silent as Nic drove them back to his flat, a conversion in the old priory at the edge of Treverro. 'Wow,' Lucy said as he ushered her inside and dropped his suit jacket over the back of a sofa. The Gothic-arched windows let light flood into the rooms, and everything screamed expensive luxury—white walls, honey-coloured wide wooden floorboards, a thick cream wool rug before a honey-coloured marble fire surround, dark gold sofas with huge plump cushions and matching curtains. Bookshelves ran along one wall, filled with well-thumbed medical textbooks and an array of paperbacks.

'I can't take credit for the décor. It's rented, though I might try persuading the owner to sell it to me,' Nic said. 'I did think about commuting from Plymouth every day, but I really didn't want an hour's drive each way as well as a full day at work.' He gestured to the windows. 'These almost make up for losing a view over Plymouth Sound.'

He had a place on the waterfront in Plymouth? They cost an arm and a leg. Maybe Nic had grown up rich—it suddenly struck her how little she knew about him. Just that his father was Italian, his mother was English, he had two older sisters and he'd once owned a very fast Italian motorbike.

The idea of Nic wearing leathers made a hundred butterflies start doing the salsa in her stomach. He'd look stunning. Black leather trousers, a loose black T-shirt, black leather boots, a fitted black leather jacket left casually undone. And carrying a single white rose as he sang a serenade outside her bedroom window…

She gasped. Where on earth had *that* come from?

He'd obviously heard her gasp or seen the panic in her face, because he smiled at her. 'Relax, Lucy. We both know the rules. I won't lay a finger on you without your permission.' He loosened his tie. 'Glass of wine?'

'I shouldn't. I'll be cycling later.'

'You don't have to.'

He was expecting her to spend the night with him? Her eyes widened in shock.

'I'll call you a taxi,' he said, beckoning to her. 'Come and talk to me while I'm cooking.'

So he *wasn't* expecting her just to fall into his bed. Lucy wasn't sure whether to be relieved or disappointed.

'The kitchen's this way.'

The kitchen was narrow, galley-style, but again it screamed luxury, all beech—real wood, not just veneer—and black granite. Most of the appliances were hidden away behind beech doors, but Lucy guessed that they'd be the same top brand as the cooker and hob.

'Red or white?' Nic asked as he took two plain narrow-stemmed glasses from a cupboard.

'What are you cooking?'

'Hmm… Do you like chicken?'

'Yes.'

'Then I'll cook chicken *cacciatore*,' he decided. 'So we should have white. Italian, of course.' He took a bottle from the built-in rack hidden at the side of a unit, opened it deftly and poured them both a glass of Soave. 'And Italian music. Well, French—sung by an Italian.' He had a micro-system hidden in an alcove; he flicked a switch and the kitchen was flooded with classical music.

She didn't recognise the haunting lament. Instead of being backed by a full orchestra, the tenor was backed simply by a classical guitar. 'This is lovely. What is it?'

'"*Elle est là*", from Bizet's *La Jolie Fille de Perth*,' he told her. 'I heard this piece on the radio once and it haunted me for days—in the end, I went into this little classical specialist shop in Plymouth and hummed it to the guy behind the counter. He recognised it and ordered it for me.'

Could Nic sing like this? she wondered, then was cross with herself. It wasn't a given that all Italian or Welsh men could sing like angels. He'd already told her not to stereotype him. And she really had to rid herself of that vision of him as the man in black, serenading her by moonlight. 'Anything I can do to help?' she asked.

'No. Just stay and chat to me. Or have a wander round the flat, if you like.'

It was tempting—a chance to learn more about Nic, his tastes in music and books and films. But right now she wanted to be with him. Watch him as he worked. As he cooked for her.

Her man.

Except he wasn't *really* hers. It was just a smokescreen they'd concocted so Jack would leave her alone.

Lucy leaned back against a worktop, sipped her wine and watched him as he deftly prepared first the bruschetta— ciabatta bread brushed with garlic, topped with dolcelatte, mushrooms, pancetta, off-the-vine tomatoes and a drizzle of olive oil—then whizzed up a sauce of white wine, to- matoes, onions and olives, throwing in extra garlic and a handful of mushrooms. And fresh herbs, she noted, from one of the little pots on his window-sill.

'I told you before, I enjoy cooking,' he said as he saw her glance. 'And I only use first-class ingredients. Fresh, rather than dried. Before you ask, yes, I do make my own pasta. I learned how in Tuscany, no less, from my *nonna*— my Italian grandmother.' He grinned. 'You'd like Nonna. She's like you—very direct, no nonsense. And she likes to have things her own way.'

Lucy was about to protest when she realised that he was teasing her. Flirting with her. It threw her off balance and she took refuge in her wine.

He prepared the chicken as the bruschetta was cooking, threw some vegetables in a steamer and two large potatoes in the microwave, then slid the bruschetta onto two plates and left the chicken simmering in the sauce. 'Bring the wine and our glasses,' he told her, gathering up the plates.

Lucy followed him to the small dining table set in an alcove with a view of the moors. 'You're overlooking the sunset,' she said.

'And I get the sunrise in my bedroom,' he told her. 'It's one of the things I like most about the flat. The light's perfect.'

Nic's bedroom. Excitement rippled at the base of her spine and she suppressed it ruthlessly. No. She wasn't going to start putting Nic and bed in the same thought. Too dangerous. 'The bruschetta's very good,' she said, changing the subject.

'Relax, Lucy,' he said softly, almost as if he'd read her mind. 'I've already told you I'm not going to do anything you don't want me to do, and I'm a man of my word. You're here as my friend, my colleague. I respect you.'

There was a lump in her throat the size of a rock. She didn't want Nic Alberici to be *kind* to her, like a stray puppy. But she was too scared to take their relationship in the direction he'd told her he wanted it to take.

She shouldn't have come here. She really, really shouldn't have come here. Especially with Jack in the background, reminding her what a disaster she was when it came to relationships. She didn't want a three-date affair. But she wasn't ready for a rest-of-our-lives moment either. Right now, she didn't know what she *did* want.

Except for Nic to kiss her.

Which she knew would be a very, very bad idea.

Miserably, she forced herself to eat the rest of her bruschetta. Nic topped up her glass.

'I'm cycling home,' she reminded him.

'No, you're not. I'm sending you home in a taxi. Your bike'll be fine at the hospital overnight,' he said. 'You've had a rough day, and you need to relax.'

But how could she, when she was so aware of his nearness? So aware of the possibilities? So aware of his beautiful mouth?

He saved her from having to make polite conversation by disappearing back into the kitchen and returning with their laden plates.

'This is very good,' she said after the first mouthful.

'Thank you. My father's hopeless in the kitchen and my mother was determined I wouldn't grow up the same—and when Dad told me being able to cook would put me in a better negotiating position to get me out of doing the washing-up, I leapt at the chance to learn.'

As he chatted on, keeping the subject light and harmless, Lucy found her tension easing. By the time they'd finished eating, she was surprised to realise she was actually enjoying herself.

'As you cooked, I should do the washing-up,' she said.

'No need. I have a dishwasher,' he said with a grin. And then his face grew serious. 'But you can do two things for me.'

'What's that?'

'Firstly, loosen your hair.' He swallowed hard. 'Lucy…I promised you I wouldn't touch you without your permission, and I keep my promises. But right now, what I want to do most in the world is to run my hands through your hair.'

'My hair?'

'Mmm-hmm. The way you wear it at work drives me crazy. I've been trying to imagine what it would be like all loose over your shoulders. It looks like sunlight. And I want to know whether it feels as soft and warm as I've been fantasising. Whether it smells like sunlight.'

His words sent a shiver through her. But they were just words, she reminded himself. He was Italian. Had a silver tongue. Could talk anyone round to his way of thinking. 'It's just hair, Nic.'

'It's beautiful,' he said simply. 'Like your mouth. And, believe me, your mouth's given me a lot of difficult moments lately.'

She flushed. He could have been talking for her, too. 'Nic…'

'I know, I know. I'm not supposed to be saying this sort of thing to you. I have all these good intentions,' he said ruefully, 'but they just melt whenever you're near me. I'm OK when I'm with a patient—but the second I'm not, all I can think about is you.'

That made two of them.

His voice deepened slightly, taking on a note of raw desire. 'You, and how much I want to touch you, how much I want to kiss you. Right now, it would be so easy to take your hand and kiss my way up to your shoulder. To touch my mouth to your pulse point. To hold you close to me. To tangle my hands in your hair and kiss you until neither of us can see straight.'

She wasn't sure which of them moved. Maybe both of them. But then she was in his arms and he was kissing her, his mouth dropping tiny butterfly kisses along her eyelids, her cheekbones, the line of her jaw, purposely teasing her mouth until she slid her hands behind his neck and pulled his mouth onto hers.

Nic's kisses were so different from Jack's. Asking, not demanding. Sweet. Seductive. Promising. Offering.

He teased her at first, keeping to those same tiny butterfly kisses, tracing the outline of her lips until she slid the tip of her tongue between his lips. And then he kissed her with abandon, his hands tangled in her hair, and she matched him kiss for kiss, hunger for hunger.

When he broke the kiss, they were both shaking. His

eyes were very, very dark, the pupils expanded with desire, and his mouth was reddened and slightly swollen. Lucy knew she must look the same, because her mouth was tingling. Worse, she wanted to do it all over again—but this time with fewer barriers between them.

'Lucia *mia*.' He took his hand and placed it over his heart, against the soft, warm silk of his shirt. 'Feel what you do to me.'

The same as what he did to her: his heart was beating so hard, so fast, she could feel it thudding against her palm. This was dangerous. Too dangerous. She pulled her hand back and moved out of reach. 'This isn't fair, Nic.'

'I know, and I'm sorry. I just...' He groaned. 'I don't know how to explain it. You've knocked me for six.'

Said the man who'd taken a different woman to lunch every day since he'd joined the hospital. Probably dinner, too. 'I bet you say that to all the girls.'

His gaze was steady as he looked at her. 'Yes, I date, but I'm not a notch-carver. I never have been. Forget all this nonsense about Italian men playing the field. This is about you and me.'

This was a conversation she definitely didn't want to have with him. She needed a diversion. Fast. 'Two things, you said. You wanted me to do two things. What was the second?'

'I'm not sure if I should ask you now.'

Her eyes narrowed. 'You might as well spit it out.'

He chuckled. 'That's my Lucy.'

'I'm not *your* Lucy.'

'No. You're your own woman and you're scared of nothing. Except, maybe, yourself,' he said thoughtfully.

She lifted her chin. 'I want to go home.'

'I'll call you a taxi.'

'Thank you.'

He walked over to the phone and paused with his hand on the receiver. 'The second thing, by the way—I wanted to dance with you.'

Her throat dried. 'Dance with me?'

'Mmm-hmm. By moonlight.' The sun had set and the dusk was deepening to the point where he really needed to switch a light on. Except he hadn't: he'd left the curtains open so that moonlight flooded the room. He moistened his lower lip with his tongue. 'And I'm a poor host, sending you home in a taxi before pudding.'

Oh, that mouth. She wished he hadn't done that thing with his mouth. It made her want him to kiss her again. Kiss her and touch her and take her to paradise. 'It doesn't matter.'

'It does, to me.' He looked at her, his eyes intense. 'If I promise to behave myself, Lucy, will you dance with me before I send you home?'

Say no, she told herself.

Her body had other ideas. Because she nodded. He held out his arms and she stepped into them. Maybe it was the wine, she thought—though she hadn't drunk that much. A glass and a half, tops. No, she was dancing with Nic because she *wanted* to dance with him.

At some point, she wasn't sure when, he'd changed the music. Instead of the haunting tenor serenades, Nic was playing blues with a soft, slow, mournful beat. A sensual beat. One that made her sway in time with him.

He was dancing with her. In the moonlight. Holding her close. Rubbing his cheek against her hair. And when the song changed, he held her closer and started singing along: *Need your love so bad.* He had a good voice, soft and deep and husky and perfectly in tune with the CD he was playing. And it was as if he was singing directly to her rather than crooning along to a favourite record, telling her just how much he wanted her and needed her. Just like that fantasy she'd had about him serenading her, except his voice was even better. It was irresistible. She reached up and touched her lips to his. Just once.

He stopped moving—stopped singing—and kissed her back.

Time came to a halt. The world ceased turning. There was nothing but Nic and the moonlight and the slow, soft music in the background and the way he was kissing her.

And then he broke the kiss. 'Lucy.' His voice was husky with suppressed desire. 'I promised you I wouldn't lay a finger on you. I can't keep that promise much longer, unless I put some distance between us.'

He was giving her the choice. Go home to her cottage and brood—or stay here and make love with him.

It was a choice Jack would never have given her.

It was a choice she couldn't make.

'Nic, I…'

He walked away from her, pulled the curtains and switched on the uplighter in the corner of the room. 'I want you, Lucia *mia*. Very badly. And I think you want me, too. But I'm a man of my word. I promised I wouldn't touch you and I'm not going to push you into something you'll regret later.' He came back to her as if she'd tugged some invisible cord between them, and brushed her cheek with the backs of his fingers. 'I'll call you that taxi.'

'No.'

She felt as shocked as he looked. Had she *really* said that?

'No?' he queried. 'Are you telling me you want to stay?'

'I…'

'Tell me, Lucy,' he pleaded. 'Tell me you want to stay with me. Tell me you want me to make you forget…' He paused, and for a horrible moment she thought he was going to say 'Jack', and then he smiled again. 'Tell me you want me to make you forget the world for a while.'

'Nic, I…' Her throat dried. 'I want you to…to…'

He refused to say it for her. Those dark, soulful eyes gave her their own message. *Say it, and I'll do it.*

'Kiss me. Make love to me,' she said.

CHAPTER SEVEN

Nic kissed her again, his mouth more demanding this time, and Lucy realised that he'd picked her up and was carrying her. Carrying her to his bedroom.

Her temperature rose a notch at the thought of Nic and bed.

He drew the curtains and switched on the bedside lamp. And then as he kissed her again, she stopped thinking altogether, just letting herself feel as he stroked away her clothing, discarding her formal black trousers and cream linen shirt. His own clothes ended in a crumpled heap beside hers—regardless of the fact that his suit trousers were expensively cut and his shirt was pure silk and both needed hanging up—and then she was lying on cool, cool cotton, with his heated, hair-roughened skin pressed against her.

His clever fingers stroked her to fever pitch, until she was writhing and begging him to take her. And then, shockingly, he stopped.

'Lucia *mia*.' The words came out as a husky groan. He picked up her hand and kissed her palm, curling her fingers over it. 'I wasn't intending to do this.'

Was he going to stop now? No. Surely he wasn't going to change his mind? She stared at him in shock. 'Don't—don't you want to?'

'Oh, I want to, all right. I've wanted to see your hair spread over my pillow like this since the first moment I met you. I've wanted to touch you and taste you—you have no idea how many times I've almost turned caveman at work, hoisted you over my shoulder and taken you off to my lair.' His eyes were tortured. 'But there's a small matter of responsibility.'

'Responsibility?' she echoed, dazed.

'Are you on the Pill?' he asked softly.

'No.'

'Then, *carissima*, I can't do what I very, very desperately want to do. I can't make you *mia innamorata*, my lover.'

She didn't understand. 'Why?'

'Because,' he told her, his face a mixture of torment and amusement, 'despite this reputation you seem to think I have, I don't sleep around. I don't keep a stock of condoms on the off-chance I'll find a beautiful woman in my bed. Much as I want to make love with you right now, I wasn't planning to seduce you when I brought you here tonight. I'm not prepared. And neither are you.'

Lucy was silent for a long, long moment. And then she began to laugh. She laughed until her stomach hurt and tears were running down her cheeks. Nic joined her. And when they stopped laughing, she rested her cheek against his chest. 'Oh, Nic. After all this.'

'*Lucia mia*,' he said softly. 'Yes, I've dated. A lot. But I don't sleep around, neither do you. So it's safe in that respect. But I don't think you're ready to carry my baby. We can't take that risk.'

'Of course not.' Carry his baby. No. Surely that wasn't *her* heart fluttering at the words? But—she didn't want children. She didn't want marriage and the inevitable divorce and emotional shrapnel. She wanted her career. She had her life all planned out, step by step—had done for years. Lucy Williams, consultant. Senior consultant. Professor.

Why did it all suddenly sound so empty?

And why was her body urging her to pull Nic's head down to hers again, make him lose control until their bodies were joined and they were both so far outside time and space nothing else mattered?

An urge that was so strong she couldn't deny it. She shifted so that her face was close to his.

'Lucy?'

His pupils were dilated, his voice hoarse. And *she* was the one who was making him lose control.

'Nic.'

He muttered something in Italian and her heart did a crazy somersault. Even the sound of his voice turned her on. And she was in his bed. Naked. With him. Skin to skin. She leaned forward and kissed the tip of his nose.

'Lucy, we—'

She stopped his words the quick way. By placing her mouth over his and sliding her tongue between his lips. She could feel his body tensing and smiled inwardly. This was what she wanted. Right here, right now. Niccolo Alberici. Her man.

Before she knew it, she was lying back against his pillows and Nic's clever fingers were caressing her body, coaxing a response from her. She arched against him and he murmured something against her skin—something Italian, so even if she'd caught the words she wouldn't have understood completely. Though as his fingers teased her, playing her body like some cherished instrument in the hands of a master, she found herself whimpering his name.

'Nic. Please.'

'Ah, Lucia *mia*.' And then he was off in Italian again, murmuring husky endearments against her skin. Teasing her nipples until she thought she'd die with longing. And finally kissing his way down over the slight swell of her abdomen.

Surely he wasn't intending to...?

He was. He did. And Lucy cried out as her climax hit

her, a climax stronger than anything she'd felt before in her life.

'Lucia *mia*.' He shifted to lie beside her and cradled her against him.

'Nic.' She held him close. 'What you just did... Thank you.'

'*Prego*. The pleasure was mine too,' he told her softly.

'Not quite. I should...repay the compliment,' she said, her voice shaking.

'You don't owe me anything, Lucia *mia*.' He kissed the tip of her nose. 'Though I wish to hell I lived up to my reputation and had something here so I could make love to you properly.'

'Me, too.'

'Ah, Lucy, if you knew what that just did to me...' He paused. 'There is a way.'

'How?'

'The supermarket across town's open all night. If I, um, take the car and buy...supplies...would you stay until I get back?'

Her eyes widened in surprise. He'd just brought her to the most stunning climax she'd ever had. So unselfishly. Not expecting anything in return—a million miles away from her experiences with Jack. And he thought she was going to disappear? 'Do you honestly think I'd run out on you now?'

'I don't know,' he said. 'Right now, you're here in my bed—exactly how I want you to be, your mouth red with my kisses and your eyes almost black with passion—but if I leave you alone, give you time to think...will you still be here when I get back? Or will you have turned back into my incredibly talented, incredibly sensible registrar and be buttoned back into your suit?'

'Nic.' She rubbed his lower lip with the pad of her

thumb, and he drew her thumb into his mouth and sucked it. 'Oh…I can't think straight when you're around.'

He released her thumb. 'You could come with me.'

'And buy…supplies?'

'No. I wouldn't ask you to do that.' He rubbed his nose against hers. 'There is another way I could keep you here.'

'Such as?'

'Give me thirty seconds.' He pulled on his shirt—now spectacularly crumpled—and a pair of jeans, then raced from the room. She heard crashing and banging. And then he was standing before her with a tub of blueberry Cornish ice cream and a teaspoon and a wide, wide smile.

She inspected the label. 'Not Italian ice cream?'

He grinned. 'I don't have *everything* Italian. Remember, I'm half-English as well.' He bent to kiss her briefly. 'Don't eat it all. I'll be back in ten minutes. Wait for me?'

She nodded. 'Yes. I'll wait for you.'

'Ten minutes, Lucia *mia*. And then…'

He didn't have to say it. She knew exactly what he meant. And her whole body thrilled at the idea.

Nic felt like a teenager as he drove to the supermarket. The feeling only intensified as the young girl at the checkout rang his purchase through and gave him a speculative look. Then he realised how rumpled he probably looked—he'd dragged on a pair of jeans and his shirt at record speed, the shirt wasn't buttoned in the right places, he wasn't wearing any socks and he hadn't bothered with a jacket, despite the coolness of the October night.

Given what he was buying, it was obvious to the whole world why he was in such a rush and what was going to happen in a few minutes' time. What had been happening only a few minutes before.

He could only thank his lucky stars that no one from the

hospital was there to see it. The hospital rumour machine had more than enough material to work on, without him adding to it. Lucy would never, ever live it down.

He gave the checkout girl his sweetest smile and headed for home.

Would Lucy still be there? She'd said she would wait for him. But now she'd had time to reflect on the situation, would she have changed her mind and called a taxi? Would she have left him a note? Something cool and precise, saying she was sorry but this really wasn't a good idea and she was sure they'd manage to work together as colleagues tomorrow?

No way could he be just her colleague on the ward. Not now. Not now he'd seen her eyes as she'd come. Not now she'd cried out his name as she'd climaxed. He wanted everything. The moon, the stars, the universe—and he'd trade the whole lot for that single moment with Lucy and still know he'd got the better bargain.

His pulse accelerated as he parked the car. He just about remembered to flick the button on the keypad to lock it, and rushed back to his flat.

'Lucy?' he called softly as he closed the front door behind him.

She appeared in the kitchen doorway, wearing his navy blue towelling dressing-gown, her hair still loose over her shoulders, and his heart missed a beat.

'Well, hello, there,' she said.

'You stayed.'

She nodded. 'I left you *some* of the ice cream—I put it back in the freezer. I hope you don't mind, but I took a quick shower while you were gone.'

His heart missed another beat as he thought about her in his shower. About joining her there.

She was still here.

'You're quite, quite sure about this, Lucy?' he asked carefully.

She nodded again. 'I'm sure.'

He smiled. 'I feel somewhat overdressed.'

She folded her arms and leaned against the doorjamb. 'So what are you going to do about it, sweetheart?' she drawled in her best Mae West impersonation.

For a long, long moment, they just looked at each other. And then Nic smiled again. 'Wait there.' Nic went over to the stereo, selected a CD then disappeared into his bedroom.

Lucy waited. What was he planning? As he emerged from his bedroom again, she stared in surprise and delight. He was wearing his highwayman's hat. Not the domino mask and the cloak—she felt a twinge of disappointment that he'd left them behind—but the jeans and silk shirt did very, very nicely. The old, faded denim was just as close-fitting as the black trousers he'd worn that night and the white shirt set off his dark complexion to perfection.

Even better, now she knew what he looked like underneath his clothes...

He pressed a switch on the remote control and the music began to play. Lucy almost laughed out loud as she recognised it—'You Can Leave Your Hat On'.

Nic kicked off his shoes and began to dance, his hips weaving sinuously. As he danced, he unbuttoned his shirt and turned his back to her. He turned his head and gave her a broad wink, then slowly eased the white silk over his shoulders.

Lucy really, really couldn't help licking her lips.

He was perfect. Utterly, utterly perfect. His muscles were beautifully toned and his back was beautiful—even more so than the Raphael drawing of Michaelangelo's *David* which her sister Allie had had pinned on their bedroom wall when they'd been teenagers.

He dropped the shirt on the floor, spun round to face her and slowly began to unbutton his jeans, still in time to the music.

Lucy's knees went weak and she was forced to lean back against the wall so she wouldn't fall over. The front view was every bit as good as the back—that beautiful olive skin, the dark sprinkling of hair on his chest, the perfect six-pack. And—her stomach tightened—the arrowing of hair that disappeared beneath the waistband of his jeans...

She grinned as again he turned his back to her and let his jeans fall to the floor.

And then he glanced over his shoulder and blew her a kiss.

'Lucia *mia*,' he said softly. 'Come to me.'

On legs that she thought for a moment would refuse to carry her, she made her way slowly towards him.

He turned to face her. 'Now you're the one who's over-dressed, *mia innamorata*.'

She folded her arms and repeated her earlier challenge. 'So what are you going to do about it?'

'*Permesso?*' he asked in that husky, sexy voice.

'Yes. Oh, yes,' she breathed. She'd wondered once if he made love in Italian or English. Now she knew. And she found the words unbelievably exciting; she didn't under-stand the words themselves, but their meaning was very plain.

'Oh, Lucia. Lucia *mia. Bellissima*,' he said as he untied the belt and slowly eased the robe over her shoulders. He bent his head and kissed the rounded curve of her shoul-ders, the dip of her collar-bones. She tipped her head back and he kissed her throat, his lips making tiny fires spring up in each nerve end.

The robe pooled on the floor. And then Nic picked her up, carrying her as easily as if she were a feather.

He was still wearing the hat. The hat that had started everything, when the highwayman had accosted her at the ball.

'My highwayman,' she said, dipping her head beneath the brim of his hat so she could kiss him.

'*Mia principessa*,' he murmured—my princess—and carried her back to his bed.

This time, when his mouth and hands had aroused her to fever pitch, they didn't have to stop. Or compromise. When he paused to protect her, it felt like a lifetime. She wanted him now, now, now. And when he entered her, Lucy felt as if her world was complete, for the very first time in her life.

'Ah, Nic.'

'*Ti piace?* You like that?' he asked softly as he moved.

'Oh, yes.'

'*Mi bacii*,' he said. 'Kiss me, Lucy.'

She shook her head. 'No.'

'No?' He stayed very, very still.

She gave him a lazy grin. 'No. *Mi bacii*, Nic,' she said huskily. 'Now.'

'We'll have to work on that accent, Dr Williams,' he said, nuzzling her mouth. 'I'll have to give you lessons. *Lots* of lessons.'

She gasped as he changed the tempo of his thrusts. 'Yes,' she hissed, arching up to meet him.

'Ah, Lucia *mia*. I've wanted this since the first moment I saw you. My princess...' He lapsed into Italian again.

She had no idea what he was saying, but it was as sexy as hell, hearing him murmuring against her skin. And then she stopped thinking as he kissed her again and changed the tempo again, taking it slowly until she was begging him to take her, take her over the edge.

And he did.

'We're going to have to renegotiate this no-touching rule,' Nic said, some time later, when Lucy was finally capable of rational thought.

'Oh?'

'Mmm-hmm. After that, I'd say you were definitely my girl. Wouldn't you?'

She gave him a playful punch. 'That sounded incredibly smug.'

'I *feel* incredibly smug,' he told her, leaning over to drop a kiss on her lips. 'What just happened between us... It's never happened to me before.'

She looked at him in disbelief. 'Are you trying to tell me you were a virgin?'

He chuckled. 'No. I haven't been a monk—but I haven't been a playboy either. I've always been very selective. I suppose what I'm trying to say is...' He lapsed into Italian.

'I'm still on Italian for beginners,' Lucy reminded him. 'Not advanced conversation. Just about all I know is "*mi bacii*".'

'If you insist.' He kissed her lingeringly.

She was shivering when he lifted his head again. 'Not fair. I can't think straight when you do that.'

He rubbed his thumb along her lower lip. 'You're the one who told me to kiss you. In Italian, no less. So now I know what to do when we have a fight.'

'When, not if?'

He shrugged. 'You're stubborn and opinionated. And don't try to protest, you know you are. And I'm half-Italian. We're bound to fight, at some point.' His eyes held a wicked gleam. 'But at least we'll enjoy making up.' He coiled a strand of her hair in his fingers. 'Why do you always pin this back at work?'

'Hygiene.'

'I bet you wear it pinned back out of work, too.'

She flushed. 'Habit.'

'Hmm. Perhaps, *mia innamorata*, I should teach you some new habits.' He lapsed into Italian again.

'I think you're lucky I didn't understand a word of that,' Lucy told him.

He stroked her cheek. 'My apologies, *mia principessa*. When I get emotional, the Italian side of me takes over.'

'Mmm, I had noticed,' she teased.

'For that, *you* make the coffee.'

She shook her head. 'Uh-uh. I'm the guest.'

'And I'm forgetting my manners.' His eyes crinkled at the corners. 'But I don't think I could bear to leave you in bed for long enough to make coffee. Not even instant coffee.'

'You have *instant* coffee in your flat?' Considering his scathing comments about the coffee at Treverro General—with the exception of the mochaccinos at Pat's Place—she couldn't quite believe that.

'No,' he admitted. 'The quickest thing I can offer is coffee ice cream.'

Lucy chuckled. 'You know all my weaknesses.'

'And you mine.' He lapsed into Italian again.

'Translate,' she demanded.

'Ice cream.'

'Even *I* know that's "*gelati*",' Lucy said.

He pressed a kiss into her palm and curled her fingers over it. 'Give me thirty seconds.'

He fetched the ice cream and a teaspoon, and fed her spoonful by spoonful, making her reach up for it and then 'accidentally' dripping ice cream on her so he had to lick it from her skin. She grabbed the spoon and retaliated, and the ice cream was quickly forgotten as teasing became caresses and caresses turned into love-making.

And afterwards, she let him lead her to the shower. Soap her all over. Wash her glorious hair—and make love with her again.

'I can't get enough of you, Lucy,' he said. And switched to Italian. '*Lucia del mio cuore*. Lucy of my heart. I want time to stop. I want this moment to last for ever, this perfection of being with you.'

This time, she didn't ask him to translate. She kissed him.

They ended up back in Nic's bed. 'Will you stay with me tonight, Lucy?' he asked.

She moved restlessly against him. 'I should go. My clothes are at home—I don't even have a toothbrush with me.'

He kissed her hair. 'I'll get up early tomorrow and buy you one from the supermarket.'

'I can't go to work in the clothes I was wearing today.'

'You don't have to. You're on a late tomorrow. I'm on early so I'll drive you home after breakfast,' he promised. 'Stay with me? Please?'

She was still for a long, long moment, and then relaxed against him. 'All right. I'll stay.'

'*Grazie*,' he said softly. '*Mia innamorata*.'

CHAPTER EIGHT

THE phone shrilled insistently. Lucy reached out automatically—and opened her eyes in shock when the phone wasn't where it should have been, on her bedside cabinet.

Because this wasn't her bed.

It was Nic Alberici's.

And her legs were still entwined with his, though his body was no longer cradled round hers. He was sitting upright. He'd grabbed the phone from his side of the bed and had thrust one hand through his rumpled hair. 'Maternal tachycardia—any shock? What about the contractions? Any sign of foetal distress? Right. Previous labour? Oh, hell. Yes, I'm coming in. Right now.'

Gently, he disentangled his body from Lucy's and got out of bed, still talking on the cordless phone. 'Give her oxygen at fifteen litres a minute—I want a tight-fitting mask with a reservoir—and cross-match six units of blood. If you see any signs of shock, get a transfusion in fast. Has she got an epidural in? Good. Get it topped up to the max. Get in touch with Theatre, tell them I'm going to do an emergency section and I'll need to do a laparotomy as well, so I can see how bad it is and whether I can repair it or if I'll have to do a hysterectomy. OK. Yes, I'll talk to her husband. I'll be there in ten minutes.'

'Uterine rupture?' Lucy guessed as Nic started to pull his clothes on. It was rare in the UK—around one in fifteen hundred deliveries—but she recognised the symptoms Nic had described.

'Yes. Caesarean scar dehiscence. Apparently the mum

102

had been upset by all this too-posh-to-push nonsense she'd read in the papers and decided she was going to have a vaginal delivery this time at any cost. She moved here before her second pregnancy and didn't tell us her full history in case we made her have another section. Somehow it was missed when she went into labour. And she only told the midwife when it was too late.' He raked a hand through his hair. 'I'm sorry, Lucy. I have to go in. I know I said I'd take you back to your place this morning. And I wanted to bring you breakfast in bed. I was going to get hot croissants from the local bakery, but—'

'Go,' she interrupted him gently. 'I can ring for a taxi home. It won't kill me if I don't clean my teeth until I get back to my place.'

'I'll see you when you get in. Have lunch with me?'

'If you're out of Theatre by then.'

Nic kissed her lightly. 'I don't want to leave you.'

'I know. But you're needed on the ward, and I know that, too. I ought to be there with you really.'

He shook his head. 'You're not on call. I am. Help yourself to breakfast, bath, shower—whatever you want. The fridge is full and there's plenty of hot water. The door's on a latch so you don't need to worry about a key—just close the door behind you. And I'll see you at lunchtime, *mia principessa*.' He kissed her again. '*Ciao*.'

'*Ciao*,' she echoed.

It felt strange, being in Nic's flat without him there. She definitely couldn't spend the morning lying in his bed, tempting though it was to roll over and get some sleep. They hadn't slept much last night—they'd dozed for a while and ended up making love again.

Lucy smiled at the memory. Nic was a generous lover. He'd been concerned for her pleasure, and he'd held her so close afterwards, cherishing her. If she closed her eyes now, she could almost imagine he was still beside her, the bed still warmed by his body heat and his clean male scent on the sheets.

But she really ought call a taxi and go home to change before her shift. Not to mention checking whether her bike was still safely at the hospital. And facing the Hammonds again.

Her heart skipped a beat. Jack. Would he leave her alone, now he thought she was with Nic?

And what about Nic himself? Last night had been incredible, but had it been the same for him? Or was she just a temporary diversion, another in his long line of three-dates-and-you're-out women? By the time she went on duty, would he have changed?

'You're just being paranoid, Lucy,' she told herself. 'Not all men are like Jack. Stop analysing and live for the moment, for once in your life. Everything's going to be fine.'

'So you finally melted the ice maiden, then.' Mal gave his boss a broad wink.

'Excuse me?'

Mal missed the warning note in Nic's voice. 'Just what she needed. Not that she'd ever have given any of us the chance to do it.' He grinned. 'So what was she—?'

'If you say anything remotely like that to her,' Nic cut in, 'and I find out about it—which, believe me, I will—you'll be out of this rotation straight away without a reference. Understand?'

'Hey, no need to be so touchy!'

'I just think your senior registrar deserves a little bit more respect. Don't you?' Nic asked.

Mal flushed dully and mumbled a response.

'Good. Now, I have an emergency in Theatre. I trust

you're not going to delay me any further.' Nic gave him a wintry look and strode off to Theatre.

Though Mal's words had brought home the reality of the situation. Nic had made love with Lucy. His closest colleague—his number two on the ward. Professionally, it was the most stupid thing he could have done, compromising their relationship at work. He'd never even dated a colleague from the same ward, let alone slept with one. Everyone knew it made life too complicated. So why, why, *why* had he done it? And with the most senior of his staff, too?

Personally, it was even more of a mess. Because of Lucy's ex. Supposing Jack hadn't been there on the ward, hadn't kissed her or tried to push her into something she'd said she didn't want…would Lucy still have slept with Nic last night? Or had she just got carried away in the heat of the moment and taken their smokescreen a bit too far?

Then a worse thought hit him. Had he just been a substitute for Jack, the man Lucy really wanted but couldn't have because he was married to someone else? When he himself had made love with her, she'd called out his name—but had she really been seeing Jack's face? And when she'd had time to think about what had happened between them, would she regret it?

Adrenalin tingled in his fingers. Facing her wasn't going to be easy, when he didn't know how she was going to react. Or how *he* was going to react, for that matter. They'd rushed into it, gone for what they'd both wanted right there and right then—but neither of them had thought of the consequences.

They hardly knew each other. Yes, Lucy was the most gorgeous woman he'd ever met and when they'd made love it had been better than he'd ever known—but it was still too soon to know if she was The One. Or for her to know if he was The One for her. They hadn't even been on a proper date—he'd simply cooked her a meal, danced with her and rushed her into his bed.

How stupid could he get?

He didn't even know where they could start trying to sort this out.

But he was needed in Theatre. He had to concentrate on his patient. For now, the situation between him and Lucy would have to wait. Maybe they should give each other some space to work out what they really wanted. He'd talk to her about it later.

Taking a deep breath, he went into the scrub room and started to get ready.

Nina was the first on Lucy's rounds. To Lucy's relief, Jack wasn't there. 'He's gone to have a cup of coffee and read the paper. I think he's a bit bored, hanging round the hospital,' Nina confided. 'And it's the second day of our holiday. He'd got so many things planned. It's such a shame that he's going to miss out on them. Can't you let me go a bit earlier?'

'How are you feeling?' Lucy asked.

'Fine. Really good.'

Lucy looked at the chart and didn't like what she saw. 'Your temperature's up a bit.'

'Only because it's hot in here.'

'Hmm.' Lucy took the thermometer from the holder by Nina's bed. 'Let me check this again.' She looked at the reading and shook her head. 'I'm sorry, Nina. Your temperature's up and I really don't want to discharge you just yet, just in case you've picked up an infection. It's quite common after a cerclage and you've come this far—why take risks now?'

'I suppose.' Nina's voice was thick with disappointment.

'Jack's not going to be happy about having to hang around here even longer.'

I'm not happy about him hanging around either, Lucy thought. But she was a doctor. She couldn't discharge a patient who might be at risk, just because the situation unsettled her. Nina clearly didn't know anything about Jack's past with Lucy and it wasn't her fault that her husband was a complete louse.

Lucy examined Nina carefully. 'I can't see any other obvious signs, but I'd rather not take the risk. I'm sorry, Nina. If you'd like a second opinion…'

Nina smiled. 'From that gorgeous Mr Alberici, by any chance?'

Lucy flushed, and Nina's smile broadened. 'I thought there was something going on. Jack said as much last night.'

'What?' Lucy blurted. Surely Jack hadn't told Nina about them? No, he couldn't have done. If Nina knew everything, she wouldn't be talking to Lucy so easily.

'He said you two were, well…snatching a bit of time together. It must be difficult, working together.'

'It is,' Lucy admitted. And it would be even harder now she'd actually slept with him.

'You're *so* lucky. He's even more handsome than my Jack,' Nina added in a whisper. 'And that voice! He could talk Italian to me any time.'

Lucy shifted uncomfortably. 'Well, I'll be back to see you later. But I think Nic will say the same as I do about your temperature.'

'I suppose it's better to lose another day of the holiday than to risk the baby,' Nina said. 'Maybe Jack can do a bit of sightseeing on his own.'

'I'm sure he'd rather be with you,' Lucy said.

Nina shook her head. 'He doesn't like hospitals. I think

he's scared of them, though he won't admit it,' she confided. 'My mum's going to be my birth partner. I think he'd pass out!'

'Men,' Lucy said, and took her leave before Jack could come back and demand a private discussion with her. Right now, Jack Hammond was the last person she wanted to see. Except possibly for Nic. Because if she'd made her usual mess of things, shown her usual hideous lack of judgement where men were concerned, Nic wouldn't want to have anything to do with her now she'd slept with him. And that was way too scary to contemplate.

Lucy was writing up her notes from the rounds at the nurses' station when Nic came out of Theatre and slumped on a chair beside her.

'I think today's *my* turn for the day from hell. I need cake,' he said.

'So how did it go in Theatre?' Rosemary asked, handing Nic the tin of chocolate biscuits she kept at the nurses' station.

'The baby's OK—we managed to deliver her before any real damage was done. But the mum… You know how more than two-thirds of scar ruptures are repairable. Hers wasn't. She had a tear right down to her cervix, so I had to give her a hysterectomy. And she's only twenty-six. She's not going to be able to have any more children—and her husband said they were planning four.' He swallowed hard and crumbled a biscuit between his fingers. 'I had to get her permission to do it while she was on the operating table. Her husband was holding her hand at the time—and he broke down.' He continued fidgeting with the crumbs. 'I'd like her in a side room, Rosemary, if you can manage it. She needs some space. There isn't any renal damage, thank God, so I've written up intravenous antibiotics.'

'How's she coping?' Lucy asked.

'Not well. She's going to need counselling. So's her husband. And it wouldn't surprise me if one or both of them ended up with depression after this.' Nic raked a hand through his hair. 'It's such a bloody *mess*. The sad thing is, it needn't have happened. If only she'd told us about it right at the start.'

'Do you want me to have a word with her health visitor and community midwife?' Lucy asked.

He shook his head. 'I'll do it. If only she'd talked to us about her fears, told us the truth about her last pregnancy. We could have reassured her that it's possible to have a vaginal birth after a section, depending on why she needed a section last time. If it had been for something that wouldn't necessarily happen in this pregnancy, too, we could have given her a trial of labour and kept more of a watchful eye on her.' He shook his head, clearly distressed and angry. 'Why the hell didn't anyone notice her scar before?'

'It's not your fault, Nic,' Rosemary said.

'It feels like it is. I'm the consultant. I should have made sure.' He sighed. 'I need someone to moan to. Come and have a late lunch with me, Lucy?'

'Go on,' Rosemary said, before Lucy could protest. 'We'll bleep you if we need you.'

'What a woman. Rosemary, *carissima*, if you weren't already married...' Nic teased.

Lucy's stomach tightened. After what had happened between them last night, he was flirting with Rosemary?

Lighten up, she told herself silently. It's the way he is. He doesn't mean anything by it. And he hasn't ignored you, has he?

Though he hadn't actually said much to her. Nothing that wasn't work-related.

On the other hand, he wouldn't have asked her to have lunch with him if he was going to avoid her...would he?

'You OK?' Nic asked as they headed for Pat's Place.

'Yes.'

'But?'

Lucy wasn't going to admit to her fears about him. She took refuge in work. 'I was hoping to discharge Nina Hammond today, but her temperature's up.'

'Infection?'

'Might be. There aren't any other signs right now, but I'd rather keep an eye on her, so if it is we can catch it early,' Lucy said.

'Though it means Jack's going to be around for a while longer.'

She nodded.

He shrugged. 'So be it.'

She couldn't read the look on his face, but she wasn't sure she wanted to know what he was thinking right now. Supposing he'd changed his mind about her? She couldn't ask him to keep the smokescreen going until Jack had left. She'd have the worst of both worlds—Jack refusing to leave her alone, and the most embarrassing kind of awkwardness between her and Nic at work.

Her stomach dived. All in all, yesterday might just have topped the league table headed 'Lucy's worst mistakes'...

No. She was being paranoid. Nic had had a rough morning in Theatre. That was why they were here now—he needed her to do the same thing he'd done for her yesterday. Provide coffee, cake and sympathy.

'Go and find us a table,' she said, 'and I'll get you some cake.'

She was choosing a selection of muffins when she heard a voice behind her in the queue. 'Off with loverboy again, are we?'

She stiffened. 'That's none of your business, Jack.'

'Oh, it is. Because we've got unfinished business, Lucy,' he whispered, his breath fanning her ear.

She gave a mirthless laugh and pulled back from him. 'I don't think so. Jack, your wife is in my ward, after nearly miscarrying your child. Doesn't that mean anything to you?'

His face twisted. 'Yes, of course it does—but Nina doesn't really want me. She just wants a baby. It's all she's thought about for years. That's what I've been trying to tell you. Nina'll be OK, just her and the baby. It's what she wants. Our marriage was virtually over anyway.'

Jack honestly expected her to believe that—when she'd seen with her own eyes how Nina looked adoringly at him, had heard his wife chattering about their plans for the future?

She went cold. How many times had he used that line before? How many times had he been unfaithful to *her*?

'Lucy, I know I've hurt you, but I'm going to make it up to you. We're going to be together and I'm going to make you happy.'

Lucy wasn't sure whether to laugh or throw something at him. 'Jack, stop being stupid and go back to your wife. She needs you.'

'But *I* need *you*,' Jack said.

Lucy shook her head. 'All you need,' she told him, 'is to grow up. Learn to deal with your responsibilities instead of running away and letting someone else pick up the pieces. I'm not interested in you, Jack. Not now, not ever. There is no you and me—and there isn't going to be either.'

'But, Lucy—'

'Tell me,' Lucy said, driven beyond her patience with him, 'what's so hard to understand about the word "no"?'

'You don't mean it.'

'Oh, but I do. I don't love you, Jack. I don't want you. I don't need you. You have no place in my life. And I'm looking you straight in the eye as I'm saying it. So believe it.'

'That smarmy Italian isn't right for you,' Jack burst out.

'It's *half*-Italian, actually,' Nic said, appearing beside them. 'And that's for Lucy to decide, not you.' He placed a hand on Lucy's shoulder. 'Everything OK, Lucia *mia*?'

'Yes. I think Mr Hammond here was asking for a second opinion.'

'I trust my registrar's judgement. From what Lucy's told me, she's right not to take any risks with your wife's condition.' Nic's smile didn't reach his eyes. 'And I've already asked you to leave my staff alone, Mr Hammond. Perhaps I didn't make myself clear.'

'My staff', Lucy noted. Not 'my girl'. Though Jack didn't seem to notice the difference. He simply shot Nic a poisonous look and left the café.

'I'll take a rain-check on the cake, Lucy. I'm really not in the mood,' Nic said, taking his hand from Lucy's shoulder. 'But don't feel you have to rush back to the ward. You're entitled to your break.'

And then he was gone. Just like that.

Lucy stared after him in disbelief. What was going on? Nic had virtually dragooned her into having lunch with him—why had he suddenly stomped off before he'd had anything to eat or drink?

Please, no, she begged silently. Please, don't let me have made the same mistake again. Please, don't let me have found myself another Jack, someone who's only interested in the thrill of the chase and gets bored in two seconds flat.

Three dates and you're out.

But she and Nic hadn't even had one proper date, really. Just sex.

What the hell had she done?

CHAPTER NINE

THE day got worse, because Nic seemed to be actively avoiding her.

You're overreacting. He's just playing it cool at work to stop us being the focus of gossip, Lucy told herself. He's being sensible about things.

But when he'd left at the end of his shift without saying a word to her or leaving her a message, a nasty, cold feeling squirmed its way down her spine. And when she left at the end of her own shift to find no message from him in her locker or on her answering-machine at home, the cold feeling spread to her stomach as she realised what was really going on.

Nic had slept with her and dumped her. He hadn't even had the courtesy to tell her to her face.

She had indeed found herself another Jack.

As nights went, Lucy rated it as one of the worst she'd spent—worse even than that terrible night four years ago. Every time she closed her eyes, she saw Nic. Remembered the passion in his eyes, the way he'd made love with her. The way he'd lied to her.

The worst thing was, she'd believed him. She'd allowed herself to think that there really was such a thing as happiness. That she and Nic maybe had a future. And now she knew the truth: the whole thing was a sham. She'd made a fool of herself in public again, because the whole ward was gossiping about the affair between them. Tomorrow, they'd be speculating about why it had blown over so quickly—why Lucy hadn't even lasted more than one date.

She was never, ever, ever going to put herself in that position again. From now on, her job would be her life. It would be enough.

It had to be.

She'd gone past the stage of tears, but she slept badly. The next morning, her eyes were sore and gritty from lack of sleep, her head hurt, no amount of teeth-cleaning could take the nasty taste from her mouth and the idea of going into work and facing everyone made her stomach heave. But her reputation as an ice maiden would stop the gossip soon enough. All she had to do was smile politely and be professional and pretend she didn't give a damn.

All.

But she'd forgotten about Mal, whose first comment to her was, 'Wow. Heavy night with His Lordship, was it?'

'I beg your pardon?' Lucy's eyes widened with anger.

'He doesn't look any better than you do! Maybe you two ought to have…' he gave her a salacious grin '…a night off.'

Anger ripped through Lucy. Normally, she'd have ignored him or made some cutting comment, but this…this, on top of the miserable night she'd spent wishing herself a million miles away, was too much! 'Sister's office. Now.'

'Luce—'

'Now,' she said, her voice low and measured, her control belying the depth of her fury.

'Luce, I was only—' he began as she closed the door to Rosemary's office behind them.

'Having a laugh?' she cut in. 'Malcolm, I've cut you a lot of slack in the past. I've put up with your jokes and your teasing and all the rest of it. But it's time you grew up. You're my SHO. By now, you're supposed to be past the student prank stage.'

'Hey, I didn't mean—'

'No, you never do. But you need to learn there's a time and a place for jokes. If you do it all the time, it's wearing. More than wearing. And working with you is starting to become like a long, tiring labour with no pain relief. It's not funny, it's not clever and I've had enough. You've got the potential to be a great doctor. Don't screw it up because you think you're a comedian.'

'Lucy, I...' He shifted uncomfortably. 'I don't know what to say.'

'Try nothing, for a change,' she told him. 'Try thinking of other people before you open your mouth.'

'I'm sorry.'

She put her hands on her hips and glared at him. 'And you can stop spreading rumours about me and Nic Alberici. I work with him, just as I work with you. End of story.'

'OK, boss.'

Her eyes narrowed. 'And less of the flippancy.'

This time, he didn't make a comment—simply flushed, nodded, and followed her meekly back out of Rosemary's office.

At least she didn't have to put up with Jack today. That was one small mercy. 'He's gone for a drive,' Nina said. 'I think he said something about finding a golf course, whacking a few balls across the fairway. He's fed up, being stuck here all the time.'

'And you're feeling just as stir-crazy, stuck in that bed,' Lucy said.

'Yes. But I know you're not going to let me move until my temperature comes down.' Nina smiled wryly. 'I thought about sticking ice in my mouth and across my fore-head.'

Lucy chuckled, despite her inner misery. 'Sneaky! But your temperature's down on what it was. Give it until to-morrow. Just to be on the safe side.'

'If it goes on much longer, I'll have to take up knitting,' Nina grumbled good-naturedly.

Nic reviewed the set of notes on his desk and frowned. This wasn't like Lucy. He was used to her neat, precise writing and short but detailed notes. He flicked through another set. And another. Her last lot of reports were slap-dash, to say the least. Even Mal's notes made more sense. He was going to have to have a word with her about it.

Yet another reason why he should never have got in-volved with Lucy. Having a chat about work standards with junior staff had never been his favourite task—he enjoyed teaching and the moments when his younger colleagues suddenly grasped the point and were illuminated, but hav-ing to tear strips off people for sloppy work was something he really, really hated doing. The fact that the member of staff in question had slept with him and could take his comments personally instead of professionally made it even worse.

Hell. He was trying to give Lucy space to work out what she wanted; he needed space to work out what *he* wanted, too. One more day, he decided. He'd give her one more day—and if her reports tomorrow were like these, instead of her usual high standard, he'd tackle the problem. In the meantime, he'd do an unobtrusive second round after her to make sure the patients were getting the care they needed.

Lucy and Nic exchanged polite nods when they came across each other, but neither said a thing that didn't involve a patient. Not even the pleasantries that most of the staff exchanged.

So this is how it's going to be, she thought miserably. Cold and just the right side of civil. But what other option did she have? To leave the hospital, find herself a job somewhere else? And she'd been happy here, until Nic. She loved her job and she loved Cornwall and she loved her cottage. She didn't want to give it all up and start again somewhere else.

She managed to avoid Nic for most of her shift—until what had started as a straightforward delivery suddenly became difficult, and Gemma called for her help.

'Lucy, I know you're just off home, but Nic's not answering his bleeper and—'

'That's what I'm here for,' Lucy said gently. She was aware that everyone in the unit had been treading very carefully around her all day—no doubt, Mal had regaled everyone with the story of how she'd suddenly become the scariest doctor in the hospital. Though Lucy liked to think they'd all worked with her for long enough to know she was perfectly approachable and she'd never, ever let a patient down. 'What's up?'

'I think I've got a mum here with a retained placenta—her name's Tracy Johnson. We agreed to do a managed third stage and I gave her oxytocin, but she's been in third stage for twenty minutes now.'

Lucy knew that in the third stage of labour—the delivery of the placenta—most placentas were delivered within ten minutes. If it hadn't been delivered within thirty minutes of a managed labour, it was likely to need manual removal. The main danger with a retained placenta was the potential risk of a large bleed, followed by an infection.

'I'm a bit worried about doing cord traction,' Gemma said.

Lucy nodded. 'Yes—we don't want the cord to snap or her uterus to invert. What kind of pain relief did she have?' She crossed her fingers. Please, please, don't let it have been a gas-and-air or pethidine delivery. Please, let it have been an epidural.

'Epidural.'

Lucy realised then that she'd been holding her breath. 'Well, that's one good thing—we won't need a general anaesthetic.' All they had to do was top up the epidural anaesthesia. 'But you'll need to bleep the anaesthetist, cross-match a couple of units of blood and get me a consent form, please.'

'Will do.'

Lucy went into the delivery room and introduced herself to Tracy. 'From what Gemma tells me, your placenta might not have separated properly, so I might need to give you a bit of extra help to finish off the last stage. Would you mind if I examined you?'

Tracy nodded. 'I'm just so tired—I just want it all over with and a cuddle with my baby.'

'You've done really well,' Lucy said, palpating Tracy's abdomen. It was still bulky, so Lucy knew the placenta hadn't separated. 'What I'm going to do now is try to get your body to do the last little bit of work. I'm going to rub up a contraction, and we'll get your baby to help out a bit, too—if he suckles, it'll stimulate your body to produce a hormone that'll help deliver your placenta.'

After three more minutes, by which time Lucy had helped Tracy latch her son onto her breast and Gemma had returned with Ray Edwards, the anaesthetist, there was no sign of the placenta moving. Lucy sighed inwardly. 'Tracy, it's not going to shift. I need to remove it manually. Can I have your consent, please?'

Gemma handed Lucy the form, and Tracy duly signed

it. Ray topped up the epidural, Gemma swaddled the baby and put him back in his crib and Lucy put Tracy in the lithotomy position. She placed one hand on the abdomen to stabilise the uterus, then gently inserted her other hand into the cervix, following the cord to find the placenta. If she couldn't work it free from the uterus—a condition known as placenta accreta, which was rare but every obstetrician's nightmare—Tracy would need a hysterectomy. 'Can you ask someone to bleep Nic and get him on standby?' she asked Gemma.

Gemma nodded and hurried off.

Lucy located the placenta and gently began to work it free, using the edge of her hand. 'You're doing really well here, Tracy,' she reassured her patient, though inwardly she was shaking. Please, please, let the placenta separate, she begged silently. If it didn't, it would mean another hysterectomy on another very young mother, and Nic had been upset enough about the last one he'd had to do.

Not that Nic's feelings made any difference to the situation. She didn't care about him any more, she reminded herself.

At last, the placenta separated, and Lucy was able to remove it by cord traction. She examined it carefully. 'It's all complete. Good news.' She smiled at Tracy. 'I'm going to give you some oxytocin now to help your uterus contract down properly, and some antibiotics to make sure you don't pick up an infection.' She wrote up the prescription on Tracy's notes. 'I'd like to keep you in overnight—and I'll be in to see you tomorrow morning, see how you're feeling and how this gorgeous little one's doing.' She stroked the baby's cheek. 'He's beautiful. You did really well.'

'Everything all right?' a voice asked as she left the room.

She looked up at Nic and stiffened her spine. 'Fortunately, yes. We won't need your surgical skills tonight.'

'Good.' He nodded abruptly. 'Ask the midwives for twenty-minute obs and tell them to bleep me if there's any sign of a bleed or her blood pressure dips.'

'Of course.' Lucy just managed to stop herself adding a sarcastic 'sir'. Did he think she wouldn't have already thought of that? She was a senior registrar, not a wet-behind-the-ears student doctor who needed someone to check on her work to make sure the patient was properly cared for.

For a moment, she thought he was going to say something else—and then he turned on his heel and left.

Even though she knew now what a louse he was, it was hard to watch him walk away. 'No might-have-beens, Lucy,' she reminded herself, and went to hang up her white coat before handing over to the next shift.

Even cycling home at top speed didn't improve her mood; she didn't get the usual rush she felt at zooming down the hill towards her cottage. And the red light wasn't blinking on her answering-machine—Nic clearly didn't want to get in touch with her.

She wasn't sure that she wanted to talk to him either. On impulse, she unplugged her phone. If he did ring her, she wouldn't hear it. And if there was an emergency at the hospital, they'd bleep her.

But the evening dragged. She couldn't concentrate on anything, even cooking. For the first time in years, she burned her omelette and had to scrape it into the bin. Not that she felt like eating. Comfort food was out—ice cream reminded her too much of Nic and making love at his flat. She associated chocolate, cake and sweet things with him, too. And she quickly discovered that pummelling a cushion didn't help in the slightest.

*   *   *

By the time she got to work the next day, Lucy felt like an overwound spring. Every muscle was tight with tension and she couldn't concentrate enough to use the relaxation techniques the midwives taught the doctors as well as the mums-to-be.

'Are you all right, Lucy?' Rosemary asked.

'I'm perfectly fine,' Lucy snapped. 'Why does everyone keep asking me that?'

'You just…' Rosemary stopped. 'Never mind. Give me a shout if you want anything.'

'Right.'

Lucy was aware that she was more brusque than normal with her patients on her morning round. And when she came to Nina Hammond and saw Jack's sly grin when she went to Nina's bedside, she only just suppressed her urge to pummel him in the same way she'd pummelled the cushion the previous evening.

Nina, after several days of bed-rest, was itching to be discharged.

'Will you let me out today?' Nina asked. 'Please?'

Lucy checked the observation charts and did a last run-through herself. 'Yes. Though I'd recommend taking it very, very easy for the next few days,' she said. 'How much longer were you planning to stay in Cornwall?'

'Three or four days—weren't we, Jack? We were going to go round the Eden Project. Jack's really into gardens,' Nina said.

He certainly hadn't been when Lucy had known him. People changed, she supposed. Though Jack had already proved he hadn't changed for the better. 'It's a big site and you'd be walking for hours. I really think you'd be better off leaving the Eden Project for your next trip to Cornwall,' Lucy said. 'Do you have a long way to go back home?'

'Five hours or so—depends on the traffic. We live in London,' Nina explained.

'Well, as long as you're not the one doing the driving,' Lucy said. 'Make sure you take plenty of breaks on the journey back.'

'We will.' Nina smiled at her. 'Thank you, Dr Williams. You've been so kind.'

'Just doing my job,' Lucy said.

'You've been fantastic,' Jack said, taking her hand.

She couldn't shake him off in front of Nina. Not without an explanation she didn't much want to give. She gave him her most wintry look and only just resisted the urge to kick him when he rubbed his thumb against her palm. Clearly he thought he was giving her some secret signal.

If only she had long, sharp nails so she could give him one back. A signal that would tell him very clearly to leave her alone.

'I'm sure you'll be only too pleased to get out of here, Nina,' she said. 'Good luck, anyway, and I hope the rest of your pregnancy's plain sailing.'

'Cheers. If it's a girl, we'll call her after you,' Nina said.

Lucy Hammond? Oh, no. Surely Jack wouldn't twist the knife that much? Lucy fervently hoped that the Hammonds had a boy. She gave them what she hoped was a professional smile and left the room.

She decided to take her break before Nic was due in. Maybe a walk in the hospital gardens would clear her mind and she'd be able to face him calmly and professionally. She paced up and down the path by the flower-beds, scowling at the pansies, but she could actually feel her blood pressure rising as she walked. Up and up and up until she was ready to explode.

'Hi, Lucy. I thought I saw you come this way.'

She spun round to face Jack. 'Oh, for heaven's sake! Not you again. Can't you leave me alone?'

'Not now I've seen you again. Not now I've realised what a fool I was. I haven't been able to stop thinking about you. I've tried to stay away, really I have. But we were meant to be together, Lucy. Can't you see it?'

'No, Jack, I can't.'

He grabbed her hands and held them tightly. 'I know I upset you—'

'Upset me?' she cut in. 'You have no idea, do you? I loved you, Jack. I was planning to spend the rest of my life with you.'

'I'm sorry.'

'Sorry isn't enough, Jack. You weren't there when it counted. Do you know what it feels like to stand there at the church in your wedding dress, waiting and hearing all the whispers going on behind you as the guests wonder what the hell is going on? To wonder if maybe there's been some terrible accident and your fiancé's lying in hospital somewhere, seriously hurt or even dead? And then for the vicar to say that he's really sorry, but he can't wait any longer for the groom as there's another couple due to be married and their wedding guests need to be seated if their wedding's to take place on time?'

Anger surged through her. She pulled her hands free and yelled at him, not caring any more if anyone overheard. 'You left me at the altar, Jack. You just didn't turn up. You didn't even leave me so much as a note to tell me why— I had to find out the hard way. You left me to sort out the whole bloody mess because you'd run off to Spain, like the spineless bastard you are! I had to face everyone and return all the wedding presents. I had to explain to everyone. I had to leave the job I loved because of you—it was unbearable, going into work and seeing all the pitying glances, hearing people stop their conversations every time I walked into the room.' She shook her head in disbelief. 'You ruined my life, Jack.'

Nic, who'd heard the last part of Lucy's speech as he made his way towards them, stopped dead.

So Jack wasn't just Lucy's ex, a persistent and trouble-some former boyfriend who wouldn't take no for an answer.

Jack had jilted her at the altar.

Jack was the man who'd wrecked her life and turned her into an ice maiden.

CHAPTER TEN

'I THINK you'd better go, Hammond,' Nic said coolly, coming to stand protectively next to Lucy. 'Your wife must be waiting in the car for you.'

'That's Lucy's decision, not yours.' Jack lifted his chin. 'Want to make something of it?'

'No. You're not worth it.' Nic put his arm round Lucy. She was shaking uncontrollably and he pulled her back into the strength of his body. 'Come on, Lucy. Let's go.'

For a moment she resisted him, but then she let him lead her away from Jack. The moment they were round the corner, she pulled away. 'I don't want you touching me either.'

Nic sighed. 'We need to talk.'

Said the man who'd barely spoken to her since he'd slept with her. 'I don't think so.'

'About work, among other things. I saw you come out here and I wanted to have a word with you about what's been happening on the ward. And then I saw Jack bothering you.'

'And you decided to come to my rescue. How very, very noble of you.' Her voice dripped scorn. 'What a perfect knight you are.'

Nic raked a hand through his hair. 'Lucy…'

'How much did you hear?' she demanded.

'Enough.'

'Don't you *dare* pity me,' she warned.

'I'm not pitying you. But I wish I'd known.'

'And that would have made a difference?'

'Yes. No. Oh, hell. This is difficult.'

'It's not a bed of roses for me either,' she snarled back.

'I don't want to discuss this in the middle of the hospital grounds. Let's go to the park—somewhere a bit quieter, where we won't be disturbed.'

She looked at him as if he'd just crawled out from under a stone. 'You seriously think I want to go anywhere with you?'

'We need to talk. The park, or my office—your choice. But I'd rather say what I've got to say away from the ward. The last thing either of us need is for someone to overhear this and start the rumour mill churning.'

So this was it. His 'dear Jane' speech. For a nasty moment, Lucy thought that she was going to be sick there and then—bile rose in her throat and she actually felt her stomach heave. She put a hand across her mouth and choked it back.

'Are you all right?'

Of course she wasn't! But she was used to pretending, used to maintaining her cool, calm façade. Years of practice made it easier. She swallowed hard. 'I'm fine,' she lied. 'Let's go to the park.'

They walked in silence across the road to the municipal park. Leaves crunched under their feet. In any other situation, Nic would have taken her hand, teased her into kicking up the leaves with him and reliving her childhood. Having a bit of fun. But what he'd overheard and what he had to say weighed too heavily on him.

He felt like the worst kind of louse, kicking her when she was already down. Pulling the straws from her reach while the current swept her on. But what choice did he have? He was responsible for the ward and right now she was putting the patients at risk. They had to come first.

The park was almost deserted. Nic strode over to a bench and gestured to her to sit down.

Lucy folded her arms. 'Spit it out, then.'

He bit his lip. 'I feel a complete bastard, saying this to you when you're already so upset—but I think you ought to take a few days' leave.'

'What?' Lucy stared at him, clearly not believing what she'd just heard. 'Are you suspending me?'

'Not formally. Just giving you some space.'

'But—I don't understand.'

'You're an A-1 doctor, Lucy. Or you have been, until the last couple of days.'

Lucy gave a short laugh. 'Oh, I get it. I'm supposed to be a good girl and resign meekly, not cause you any trouble or embarrassment about the fact you slept with me.'

'No! It's got nothing to do with that.' Nic shook his head emphatically. 'It's nothing to do with you and me. Look, you've been a bit...' He knew he had to choose his words carefully. 'You've been in a difficult situation, with Jack coming back on the scene, and you've been distracted lately. Understandably so. Yesterday, you wrote up the wrong drugs for a couple of patients—luckily the midwife concerned was experienced enough to spot it and double-checked it with me, so no harm was done.'

Her eyes narrowed. 'Are you saying I'm incompetent?'

'No, because you're not. You're a good doctor and I know you can run that ward as well as I can. I said that you'd just reverted to being a doctor like everyone else—one whose handwriting's atrocious and she just hadn't been able to read it properly,' Nic told her. 'But your reports were slapdash yesterday.'

'Is that why you gave me chapter and verse on Tracy Johnson's care?'

He sighed heavily and nodded. 'In normal circumstances, I wouldn't have dreamed of it because you know what to do as well as I do. But these aren't normal circumstances.

And you're not coping, Lucy. Your reports are just as bad today.'

'It's a blip. Temporary. It won't happen again.'

'So what you're saying is, now Nina's been discharged from the ward and you don't have to face Jack again or be reminded of what he did to you, you'll be fine?'

'Yes.'

Nic shook his head. 'I can't risk that, Lucy. It's not fair to the patients. Next time you make a mistake, it could be fatal—and I don't want you throwing your career away over a low-life like Jack Hammond.' Or me, he added silently. 'Take a few days off, get it out of your system. And then I want the Lucy Williams we all know back on the ward, the doctor who should have been a librarian, she's so neat and tidy and organised.'

'I'm fine. I don't need time off,' Lucy insisted. 'Jack's out of my system.'

'Lucy, I heard what you said to Jack just now. You said he'd ruined your life.' Nic's mouth felt as if he'd been eating sawdust. 'That he left you at the altar.'

'So?'

He could see the glimmer of tears in her eyes and hated himself for doing this to her. He wanted to take her in his arms, hold her close and soothe away the pain—but the set look on her face warned him she wouldn't let him touch her. If he tried, she'd only push him away. 'So you're obviously not over him. Or not over what he did to you, anyway.'

One tear started to trickle down her cheek and she scrubbed it away with her hand. 'And you're the man to help me, are you?' she asked nastily.

'I'm here if you want to talk about it, yes,' he said. As her boss? Her friend? His conscience pricked him—as her ex-lover? 'And it'll stay confidential, I promise you that. Anything you tell me is just between you and me.'

'I'm over Jack,' she insisted.

He shook his head. 'It didn't sound like it, just now.'

'And what would you know about it? Mr Dump-them-after-three-dates-if-they-last-that-long!'

He knew he deserved that. But it still stung. 'Lucy, we really need to talk about this.'

'I don't think so. It's none of your business, anyway.'

'Lucy, if your private life affects your work, then it *is* my business,' he said.

'My word, you've got a nerve! You're as bad as Jack!'

'I wouldn't leave my bride standing at the altar.'

'No?'

'No.'

'Then obviously there's something wrong with me,' Lucy said.

He frowned. 'How do you mean?'

'I loved Jack. I thought he loved me. Clearly he didn't.' Pain seared across her face. 'But what I can't work out is what I did wrong. What's so unlovable about me.'

'You're not unlovable.'

'So why didn't he turn up at the church? If he didn't think I was the one for him and wanted to call it off, why didn't he tell me before? Why did he make me wait for him at the church? I never wanted the frills and what have you—I'd have been happy with a quiet little civil wedding. He was the one who wanted the top hat and tails, the vintage car, the champagne and all the trimmings. So why did he make me go through with it when he had no intention of doing it himself? Or am I so slow on the uptake that the only way he could make me realise he didn't want me was to show me in front of all our friends and family?'

'You're not slow on the uptake, Lucy.'

'It was…a nightmare,' she said, her eyes glittering. 'I waited and waited. And all I could think was that he'd been in some terrible accident, that he was hurt or dying or even dead. It never even occurred to me he wouldn't turn up because he didn't want to marry me.

'My sister tried his mobile. It was switched off. And then we realised the best man was there—the best man who was supposed to be with Jack. He didn't know where Jack was either. Nobody knew. I could hear everyone talking, asking what was happening, where Jack was. And then the vicar said he couldn't wait any more, he had another wedding to do and the wedding guests were waiting outside. Everyone was staring as we walked out of the church. The bride, bridesmaids and no bridegroom. No confetti, no organ music, no bells. Trooping out as if it were a funeral, people saying how sorry they were.

'And then I had to face everyone at work. Everyone knew. The grapevine was working overtime. They all knew he'd just stood me up at the altar—and everyone was trying so hard to be kind, nobody actually wanted to talk to me. It's like when someone dies and people cross the road because they don't know what to say and they're too embarrassed to face you. All the whispers and the looks—conversations actually stopped when I came into the room, so I knew they'd been talking about me, speculating about why Jack hadn't wanted me. It went on for weeks. And in the end I couldn't stand it any more. I resigned before I'd even found another job, it was that bad. Luckily there was a position here. And it was far away from London—I wasn't going to have to face Jack again.'

'Don't blame yourself, Lucy. What Jack did was cruel, unfair and spiteful.'

'But *why* did he do it? I mean, I know now he'd met Nina and she was pregnant and he wanted to support her and the baby—at least, he told his mother he did—but why didn't he tell me before? Finding out in front of all our friends and family that he just didn't love me enough to make that commitment—it was just so humiliating. So horrible to have people pitying me and speculating about whether it was my fault or his. Am I so hard to talk to? What's so wrong with me?'

'There's nothing wrong with you, Lucy. And Jack's behaviour was…' Nic searched frantically for the right word but it wouldn't come. 'Vile,' he ended heavily. 'But not all men are like that.'

'Aren't they?' She gave a bitter laugh. 'They are with me. Let's face it, since I slept with you, you've barely spoken to me. Only as much as you had to, at work.'

Guilt balled in Nic's stomach. It was a fair point: he couldn't argue with that. He'd thought he was giving her space, but she thought he'd been avoiding her.

'So it's me, isn't it? The problem's basically…me.'

He shook his head. 'It's not you, Lucy. You're a lovely woman.'

'Oh, spare me the "dear Jane" bit!'

'Look, you're my number two on the ward. We rushed into it without thinking, and now I've had time to step back from the situation a bit. I'm attracted to you, Lucy—more than attracted. You're beautiful and talented and clever and fun to be with. But we have to work together, so we shouldn't get involved.'

'Why didn't you think about that before you touched me?'

'Because I can't think straight when you're around,' he admitted.

She laughed mirthlessly. 'But *I'm* the one who's distracted, according to you.'

'Enough to write up the wrong drugs, yes.'

'OK, so I made a mistake. I'm human. I'm not the first and I won't be the last.'

'You can't afford to make mistakes in our job.'

'I'll double-check in future. You won't be carrying dead weight on the ward.' Lucy folded her arms again. 'But why did you ignore me at work? Why didn't you just tell me you were having second thoughts? Why didn't you ring me at home—or even arrange to meet me someplace in the middle of nowhere so we could talk about it, if you were afraid people were going to gossip about us?'

'I…wanted to give us both some space. Space to decide what we both wanted.'

'What *you* wanted, more like.'

'All right. So tell me—what do you want, Lucy?'

She rubbed one hand across her eyes, dashing away another tear before it fell. 'I don't know now. I thought I knew—but you're not the man I thought you were.' Her mouth twisted. 'No, I stand corrected—you're *exactly* the man I first thought you were. An Italian playboy. Love 'em and leave 'em. What happened between us the other night—it didn't matter a bit to you, did it?'

'Of course it did.'

'So why are you backing off now?'

'I told you. Because we work together and it's too complicated,' Nic said.

'And I'm just supposed to forget that anything happened?' Her eyes darkened with pain. 'I hadn't slept with anybody since Jack. I hadn't even kissed another man until you kissed me at the ball. But you… I let you too close. I thought you liked me. Really, really liked me.'

'I did! I do.'

She continued as if she hadn't heard him. 'But I got burned again. You slept with me and dumped me. Maybe…maybe I'm just useless at sex. Maybe I ought to place a personal ad asking someone to teach me how to do it right,' she said bitterly. 'Someone who won't get involved with me so I won't get hurt this time.'

'That isn't true, Lucy. You're not...' Nic flushed. He was supposed to be giving them both space. Not telling her that sex with her had been mind-blowing and he could hardly keep his hands off her even now. Even now when he was trying to explain that they needed to work through the complications first—the ward, plus the Jack situation. 'Lucy, you're truly lovely. You're everything a man could want.'

'So why did Jack abandon me at the altar? Why did *you* dump me?'

'I can't speak for Jack, and I haven't dumped you.'

'No? When a man completely ignores a woman he's slept with, Nic, it means he's ditched her.'

'I just think...we need a little space, that's all.'

'Which is the nice guy's way of saying, "You're dumped." Give the woman a chance to say it's over first so she feels better about it.'

Had *he* made her this cynical? 'Lucy, I really, really didn't want things to happen like this. I'm sorry.'

'So am I. Because I'll never, ever let anyone get that close to me again. I don't want to go through this again. I don't want to spend all my time wondering what the hell's so wrong with me. Wondering how long it's going to be before the next man in my life decides I'm not what he wants and finish with me without bothering to let me know.' She turned away from him.

'Lucy...' He reached out to her.

She shook him off. 'Leave me alone, Nic. You've done enough. And you're right, I do need some time off. Make up whatever excuses you like for me on the ward. I don't care. Because nothing matters any more.' And before he could say another word, she stood up and walked off.

*   *   *

An hour later, Nic was still brooding in his office, with the door firmly closed. What had he done? He'd wanted Lucy. Wanted her very badly. Badly enough to let it cloud his judgement and make a mammoth mistake for both of them.

But if he'd had the slightest idea that Lucy had been so badly hurt…he'd have let her be. Because Lucy didn't need just a bit of fun, someone to get her out of her shell and let her relax. She needed someone she could rely on. Someone who'd never let her down.—

Could he be the one? Or was he what she thought he was, an Italian playboy who just flitted from one woman to the next?

He'd already let her down. Badly.

What now? Should he go after her and tell her that he'd been stupid, he'd dropped a major clanger but he'd never let her down again? That he'd teach her to trust?

Could anyone teach her to trust? Had she been so badly burned by Jack—and then by what she'd seen as his own betrayal, too—that she'd never be able to trust again?

What a mess. What a horrible, horrible mess.

And he didn't know where to start trying to make things right. *How* to start.

He rested his head in his hands. 'Oh, Lucy. I'm so sorry,' he whispered. 'But I don't know if I'm enough for you. I don't know if I can be the man you want me to be, the man you deserve. I just don't know.'

Lucy took one look at the card that came with the bouquet of hand-tied crimson roses and shoved the whole lot straight in the bin. Did Nic really think that sending her flowers was going to make things all right? He'd done a Jack on her, made it ten times worse by virtually suspending her at work, and he thought roses would smooth things over?

Half an hour later, she fished the flowers out again. It wasn't their fault. And fresh flowers would make the cottage look a bit brighter. The roses looked a little sorry for themselves so she cut a couple of centimetres from the bottom of the stems and placed them in a jug of water. 'Here. A bit of TLC's all you need,' she said.

She removed the bruised petals. There were an even number, she noted. 'He loves me—he loves me *not*,' she said.

And then the tears came. Tears that burned like acid in her soul. Tears that she could only hope would burn away the pain for good. Because she could never, never go through something like this again.

The phone rang and rang and rang. Still no answer. Nic knew for certain that Lucy had an answering-machine. Maybe she'd turned it off for some reason.

But she had to be at home. It was half past ten. He knew Lucy wasn't the pubs-and-clubs type. Hadn't she left the hospital charity ball early even? He drummed his fingers on his knee and tried her pager. It was turned off. Of course—he'd put her on leave for a few days. Why should she leave her pager switched on?

Fear prickled down his spine. She wouldn't have done anything stupid—would she? No. Lucy was too sensible, too level-headed. But on the other hand, she'd been hurt. Badly hurt. She'd lost her judgement at work. And what he'd done had only magnified the Jack situation. Had it been enough to tip her over the edge, make her do something completely out of character?

And if she had...it would be all his fault. He'd never be able to live with himself, knowing he'd done that to her. He had to make sure she was all right. He grabbed his car keys, locked up his flat, drove to her cottage and banged on the front door.

No answer. No sign of a light—but her car was there. So she *had* to be in. He banged on the door again. Still no answer. He was about to smash a window and break in to check for himself when a light flashed on and the door opened.

'What the hell do you think you're doing, Nic?' she demanded.

'I came round to see if you were all right.'

'It's a quarter to eleven,' she pointed out. 'Did it not occur to you that I might be asleep?'

'You haven't answered your phone for two days.'

'There's no law against that.'

Cool, crisp and very much in control. The Lucy he knew and had fallen for. Nic was so relieved that she was OK he actually laughed.

'What's so funny?' she demanded.

'Me. Overreacting. I thought you might have…'

At the look of scorn on her face, he had the grace to flush.

'No, Nic, I haven't done anything stupid. You're not worth it.'

'I was worried about you, though.'

'As you can see, I'm perfectly all right. For someone who's been suspended.'

'You haven't been suspended. You're on leave for personal reasons,' he said.

'Which amounts to the same thing. No doubt I'll hear all the different theories via the grapevine when you finally let me come back to work,' she said drily. 'Now, if you'll excuse me, I *was* asleep.'

'Sorry.' And he noticed that she wasn't wearing anything

under the towelling robe she'd clearly pulled on to answer the door.

Just like the time she'd been wearing *his* bathrobe.

When he'd picked her up and carried her to his bed.

She was still the most beautiful woman he'd ever seen. Even though she was looking as if she wanted to stick knives into him, Nic discovered that the so-called space between them wasn't working in the slightest. He wanted her every bit as badly as he had the first time he'd seen her.

'Foot out of the doorway,' she said. 'Now.'

'Lucy…'

She saw where he was looking and pulled the robe tighter. 'No.'

He rubbed a hand over his jaw. 'I wasn't trying to come onto you just then.' He'd stopped himself. Just in time. 'I really did come round just to check that you were all right.'

'Well, now you know. So you can just go away again, can't you?' And she slammed the door in his face.

It served him right, Nic thought ruefully. Not only had he hurt her, he'd been arrogant enough to think she might have done something stupid because of him. 'Niccolo Alberici, you're a first-class jerk and it's time you grew up,' he said. And he promised himself that he'd leave her alone.

Except he couldn't get Lucy out of his head.

CHAPTER ELEVEN

'IF THAT's you, Niccolo Alberici, I'm going to say something *extremely* rude,' Lucy muttered, and picked up the phone. 'Yes?' she barked.

'Lucy—thank God you're in. It's Mal. Look, we've got a bit of a problem on River.'

'Sorry, I can't do anything from here. Bleep Nic.'

'He's not answering his bleeper.'

Lucy heard the note of panic in her SHO's voice. 'What's up?'

'I've got a mum in shock. I'm not sure if it's a retained placenta or something worse.'

'Is she bleeding?'

'Yes.'

'Have you done a check for uterine inversion?'

'I'm not really sure what I'm looking for,' he confessed. 'It doesn't happen very often, does it?'

'No. Cord traction on an atonic uterus can do it, or even if the cord's very short, especially when the placenta's right at the top of the fundus,' Lucy said. If it was an inversion, they needed to correct it fast. She knew she wasn't supposed to be at work—Nic hadn't given her the all-clear to return yet—and she'd probably be up for a disciplinary if she went in and he caught her. On the other hand, this was an emergency, Mal was in trouble and since Nic wasn't available she was the only one who could do something. 'OK. Get some fluids into her, get a line in and give her oxygen to deal with the shock. Bleep an anaesthetist and say we want halothane anaesthesia, and get Theatre on standby in case we need to sort it surgically. I'll be with you in ten minutes.'

'Lucy, you're a saviour!' Mal said in relief.

She put the phone down, drove in to Treverro and was on the ward within ten minutes, ready for action.

'Ah, Lucy, you're here, thank God!' Mal said when he saw her. 'The anaesthetist's ready and waiting.'

'I'm going to need your assistance, Mal, if it's what you think it is, because it's a two-person job.'

'Just tell me what you want me to do.'

'First off, the mum's name?'

'Shauna,' he said. 'Shauna Ogilvy.' He led her to the delivery room where Shauna lay on the bed.

'Hello, Mrs Ogilvy—or may I call you Shauna?' At the woman's tired nod, Lucy continued, 'I'm Lucy Williams, senior registrar. Would you mind if I examined you?'

With the patient's permission, Lucy examined her gently, swiftly but thoroughly. As she'd suspected from Mal's hurried briefing, she couldn't feel the fundus—the top of the uterus—when she palpated Shauna's abdomen. 'It's a partial inversion,' she explained to Mal. 'Second degree—the uterine wall's gone through the cervix but it's still inside the vagina. If it's third degree, it comes out of the vagina and if it's fourth degree, it's complete inversion. This really isn't as bad as it could be. Though we need to act now. A tight ring tends to form at the neck of the inversion—and the longer we take to sort this out, the more firmly the cervix contracts and the harder it is to put the uterus back.'

'So what do we do?' Mal asked.

'STAR management. That stands for Shock—which you're already doing—Treat Aggressively and Repair. I want you to get me some cystoscopy tubing, a silastic ventouse cap and two litres of 0.9 per cent warm saline. Using hydrostatic pressure to put the fundus back is a bit old-fashioned and dates from the 1940s, but I prefer it to manipulation because, in theory, stretching the pelvic viscera again could make the mum go into shock.'

And tonight definitely wasn't the time for risky procedures. She wanted tried-and-tested, conservative management. Something that Nic couldn't fault if he happened to come in and catch her here. She moved to stand beside Shauna and held her hand. 'Shauna, what's happened is that your uterus has turned partly inside out, and I need to put it back. I'm going to try to do it manually so we don't have to give you a general anaesthetic and an operation. We're going to give you some drugs to relax the muscles in your uterus and then I'm going to ease it gently back into place. After that, we'll give you something to make it contract properly.'

'Is it going to hurt?'

'You might be a bit sore tomorrow, so we'll give you pain relief,' Lucy said. 'And we'll be keeping a very close eye on you for the next day or so to make sure it doesn't happen again.'

When Ray Edwards had put the anaesthesia in place and Mal had returned with the equipment she'd asked for, Lucy began the procedure, giving Mal step-by-step instructions.

Gently, Lucy held the cap in place and ran the saline through the tubing. Mal followed her instructions and the hydrostatic pressure of the water gradually pushed the uterus back, allowing Lucy to correct the inversion.

'We're there,' she said with a smile. A few deft stitches and she'd repaired the lacerations to the birth canal. 'Now, we need to make the uterus contract to stop the inversion recurring. That means uterine massage, which I'll do now, and uterotonic drugs. What do you think we should give Shauna, Mal?'

'Ergometrine?' he suggested.

'Absolutely right. And very, very close obs.' She winked at him as she performed the massage. 'We'll make a registrar of you yet.' She removed her gloves and went back to Shauna's side. 'We'll let you have a rest before we check you over again, Shauna—you've earned it. But if anything doesn't feel right or you're worried at all, I want you to use your buzzer to call one of the midwives.'

Shauna nodded wearily. 'I'm just so tired.'

'You've just given birth.' Lucy's eyes flicked to the card. 'A big boy, by the looks of things! Nearly four and a half kilos.' She chatted lightly, reassuring Shauna as the anaesthesia was reversed and Mal administered the ergometrine. 'We'll see you later.'

'Thank you, Doctor.'

'I'd better get going,' she said as she and Mal left the room. 'If Nic catches me in here, he'll have my guts for garters.'

'Too right I will,' a cold voice said behind her. 'What are you doing here, Lucy?'

She turned round to face him. 'Got bored, twiddling my thumbs,' she said lightly. 'So I thought I'd pop in and see how everyone was doing.'

'It's my f—' Mal began.

Lucy placed her hand on his arm and made a warning gesture to keep quiet. 'Time for your break, Mal. Catch you later.'

'Shall we go to my office, Lucy?' Nic said.

Lucy followed him in silence, knowing it was an order, not a question.

He closed the door behind them and waited for her to sit down. 'You're supposed to be off until I think you're ready to come back,' he reminded her.

'And you said I wasn't on official suspension,' she countered. 'Strictly speaking, you didn't ban me from the ward. But it's all right, I've got the message. I'm going now.'

'Why were you here, anyway?'

'I told you. Got bored, twiddling my thumbs.' She shrugged. 'Put it down to my…shall we say, faulty judgement?'

And before he could say another word, she walked out.

An hour later, Nic stood outside Lucy's front door with half a dozen bunches of carnations. They should have been roses, really, but the florist was closed and this was the best the supermarket could come up with at this time of night.

Pathetic.

Maybe he should have bought a white flag instead. She might have seen the funny side. Now, she'd think he was trying to schmooze her.

Well, he *was* trying to schmooze her.

Or at least apologise and persuade her to give him a second chance.

He rapped on the door.

'Come in—it's open,' she called.

Nic walked in and nearly fell over a brown-and-white streak that raced towards him, zoomed round his feet and then bounded back over to Lucy and jumped straight into her lap.

'I didn't know you had a puppy.'

'I don't. I'm dog-sitting for my neighbour while she's at the supermarket so he doesn't turn her dining-room table into a coffee-table—aren't I, Bert? Actually, I thought you were her, come to pick him up.' Lucy rubbed the dog's ears, and the dog leaned back against her, clearly enjoying the attention.

Maybe this was the way to keep her talking to him. Talk about the pup. 'Bert. It's an unusual name for a dog.'

'His kennel name's Treverro Lightning, but Ruth called him Bert. Because of his cheeky little face,' she said, nuzzling the pup, who promptly licked her face.

Nic discovered that it was entirely possible to be jealous of puppies. Especially cute ones like this one.

'I didn't know you were a dog person.'

She shrugged. 'I'd love to have one, but it wouldn't be fair, not with my lifestyle. Changing shifts, never here—the dog'd be on his own too much. Dogs need a family around them. Especially ones like this one.'

'He's a spaniel, isn't he?'

'Yes. One of my stepmothers bred them. I used to...' Her voice trailed off, and he guessed that it was yet another painful memory. One she wasn't going to share with him.

'Why didn't you tell me the full story at work tonight?' Nic asked.

'Nothing to tell.'

'Correcting a uterine inversion isn't "nothing".' His eyes narrowed. 'Mal's told me everything. It seems that Dawn put too much traction on the cord too soon. He knew something was wrong and he needed help. So he called you.'

Lucy shrugged and continued rubbing the pup's ears. 'Don't give him a hard time about it. He was sensible enough to know when he couldn't do it on his own, and you weren't answering your bleeper.'

Nic flushed. 'Flat battery. I didn't realise.' He looked at her. 'I was going to put you on a disciplinary for disobeying my instructions. You knew I'd have to do that if I found out about it, didn't you?'

She nodded.

'But you still came in.'

'The patient has to take priority,' she said simply.

'And you were going to take the flak for it. Even though it wasn't your idea to come in.'

'It *was* my idea, actually. I thought it'd be easier than trying to give Mal instructions over the phone.'

'What am I going to do with you, Lucia *mia*?' he asked.

Lucia *mia*. My Lucy. He'd called her that for a long time, partly teasing. But it was true. He'd thought that it was just for fun, just for now—but it wasn't. It wasn't anything of the sort.

With a shock, Nic realised that Lucy was the woman he'd been looking for all his life. A brave, talented, clever woman who was prepared to put herself on the line for what she believed in. Who put other people first. Who rescued people quietly without making a fuss about it or expecting praise heaped on her. Who'd matched him passion for passion, kiss for kiss, in a way he'd never experienced before.

And he wanted her. He wanted her for always.

But she'd called him 'Mr Dump-them-after-three-dates-if-they-last-that-long'. He'd already let her down. Badly. After she'd been extremely badly burned by her experience with Jack. How was he ever going to persuade her that he was serious about her? That she could trust him?

'I…um…brought you these.' He waved the flowers at her.

'Why?'

She wasn't going to give a millimetre, was she? But he knew he deserved it. 'Sort of another apology. It was the best I could do at this time of night.' He tried for levity. 'Without pinching some from the mums on the ward, that is.'

'No need.'

'Apology accepted?'

She gave him a stony look. 'I didn't say that.'

'Lucy...' Suddenly inspired, he put the flowers on the floor, fished a pen and a white handkerchief out of his pocket and made an impromptu flag. 'Truce?'

He couldn't read the look on her face. He wasn't sure whether she was on the edge of being amused or really, really angry. This wasn't going how he'd planned it—not at all. He shoved the makeshift flag in his pocket and spread his hands. 'I'm sorry, Lucy. I've treated you appallingly. I don't know what to do. I don't know how I can even begin to make it up to you.'

'Forget it.' She made a dismissive gesture. 'We're colleagues. Well, we *were*.'

Nic's heart started to pound. 'What do you mean, were?' Surely she wasn't resigning? Please, no. The idea of her walking out of his life before he'd had a chance to make it up to her, set things right between them...

'I'm off work indefinitely at the moment. A little case of faulty judgement. Being distracted. Putting patients at risk.' She looked up at him. 'Unless, of course, you've changed your mind about that.'

Relief flooded through him. She wasn't resigning. She wanted to come back to work. 'You went for the hydrostatic pressure option. Why?'

'It's easier than lifting the uterus back into the pelvic curve.'

'What if the uterus hadn't gone back?'

'Then I'd have tried manipulation techniques combined with tocolytic drugs, and held the uterus in place until the ligaments had returned to their original state and did the job for me. And if that had failed, I'd have had to go for surgical repair, using the Huntingdon technique. And if *that* had failed, I'd have used the Haultain procedure.' She rubbed the pup's tummy. 'What do you think, Bert? Do you reckon I've passed my viva?'

Nic tried for lightness and gave a soft bark. 'Yes, you have,' he said in a mock-growly voice, as if answering for the pup.

She didn't look the slightest bit amused. His attempt at levity had fallen flatter than a pancake.

'So that's settled. You agree that my judgement's sound. And that I'm not going to put patients at risk.'

'What about Jack?' Nic challenged.

'What about him? I imagine he's back in London by now. Hopefully doing the right thing by Nina. And, before you ask, no, it doesn't bother me. I stopped loving Jack a long time ago. Seeing him again was a shock, I admit. It brought everything back—how bad I felt when he left me. But I'm older and wiser now. I can cope.' She stared at him. 'So can I come back to work?'

Nic nodded.

'Thank you. Have you changed this month's duty roster?'

'No.'

'Then I believe I'm on late tomorrow. I'll see you then.'

She was dismissing him—but he couldn't go yet. Not without asking her... 'Lucy—about us.'

'There is no us.'

'What happened—'

'Was a mistake. A huge mistake,' she cut in. 'You're right. We work together. A relationship between us is completely out of the question. It'd make life far too complicated.' She gave him a tight smile. 'So I'll see you tomorrow. Goodnight, Nic.'

When Nic had closed the door behind him, Lucy stared at the puppy. 'Your eyes are just like his, you know. A mixture of grey and brown. Beautiful eyes. I could fall for you in just the way I fell for him.' Her eyes filled with tears.

'But he let me down, Bert. I thought he cared, *really* cared about me—but I was just another challenge to him. And once he'd conquered me, he lost interest.'

The dog licked her face.

'Three dates and you're out, that's his usual *modus operandi*. I didn't even last one,' she continued. 'And I'm not ever going to let myself get in that sort of situation again. Colleagues, yes; friends, probably not; and lovers, never again.' Her voice broke. 'It'd be so easy to love him, Bert. Look at the way he made that silly flag, just to make me smile. He's like no one else I've ever met. He's got this crazy streak. He makes me laugh. He cooks like an angel. He sings. He…' No. She wasn't going to let herself think about the way he made love. 'But if I let myself get close to him, let myself love him, he's going to break my heart again. And I don't think I'd recover this time.'

She rubbed her face against the pup's soft fur. 'If I give in to the way I feel about him, it'll be wonderful while it lasts—but I know he'll drop me again and he'll hurt me. He won't be able to help himself. He'll always be three-dates-and-you're-out—it's just the way he is. A gorgeous butterfly. So I can't let him get close to me again. I just can't.'

CHAPTER TWELVE

GOING back to work turned out to be easier than Lucy expected. Everyone seemed pleased to see her back but no one said a word about the circumstances leading up to her enforced leave.

Just when she was starting to relax, she hit the first sticky moment.

'Time for a break, Dr Williams.'

She looked up at Nic from her reports and shook her head. 'Sorry. I've got paperwork to double-check.'

'You haven't had a break since you came on duty,' Nic reminded her. 'I need a break, too. Let's go for a coffee at Pat's Place.'

No way. She wasn't going to spend any more time with him than she had to. It was way, way too dangerous. She might start to remember what it had felt like, being in his arms. Touching him. The feel of his mouth against her skin.

No. They were colleagues, nothing more, and she was sticking to that. For ever. 'Thanks for the offer, but I'll pass. I'm cutting my caffeine consumption.'

'Then I'll buy you a mineral water.'

Did he really think they could behave as if the whole mess hadn't happened? As if she hadn't slept with him, as if he hadn't dropped her, as if he didn't know the truth about Jack Hammond and her disastrous attempt at getting married? She lowered her voice. 'Nic—I can't do this. I can't pretend nothing happened and act as if everything's the way it used to be.'

'I'm not asking you to,' he said simply. 'I'm asking my

number two to join me for a quick discussion. Over decent coffee rather than the stewed stuff they drink up here.'

OK, so he wanted to talk about work. But she couldn't handle spending that much time with him. Not on her own. Not yet. Her wall wasn't anywhere near high enough. 'Maybe later.'

He looked at her for a long, long moment. Then finally he nodded. 'As you wish.'

The next week grew even harder, watching Nic chat and flirt with everyone who came onto the ward—everyone from two-year-old toddlers longing to see their new baby brother or sister to great-grandmothers proud to welcome the next generation into the world.

But Lucy noticed that he didn't actually date anyone. Didn't go to lunch with anyone. Didn't go to Pat's Place with anyone.

'The word is, the man's in love,' Mal said.

Lucy flinched inwardly. That was the one thing she couldn't take. The idea of Nic being in love—in love with another woman. Someone who wasn't her.

And had Mal really forgotten her own affair with him that quickly? Given Nic's three-dates-and-you're-out reputation, maybe that wasn't so impossible.

'But apparently she's turned him down.' Mal whistled. 'Can you believe it? I mean, the man makes women swoon from here to John O'Groats and I'd kill to be able to do what he does. But it seems there's one woman in the world who can resist the legendary Alberici charm.'

If only she'd been able to do the same. 'I don't think we should be gossiping about him, Mal,' Lucy said crisply. 'I've got work to do, even if you haven't.'

Nic, in love. Her heart felt as if someone had just asked

it to carry a ten-ton weight. She'd always known she'd have to face the day. She just wished it hadn't come so soon.

Another week passed, this time with Nic switching from the charming flirt to a hard taskmaster who grew more and more short-tempered with his team. Eventually, Rosemary took Lucy to one side. 'Have a word with him, will you?'

'Why me?' Lucy demanded.

'You're his number two. The only one he'll listen to—anyone else, he'll bite our heads off.'

'Come on. This is Nic Alberici we're talking about. The Italian playboy.'

'Who's acting as if someone's just taken all his toys away and he's not a happy bunny. Sort him out, will you?' Rosemary pleaded.

If she protested too hard, people might start to ask why. 'All right. I'll tackle him.' The question was, how to do it without letting him too close to her, without dropping her own barriers.

She waited until the mid-afternoon break, then marched into Nic's office. 'Coffee. Pat's Place. Now.'

'I'm busy. Budgets,' he snapped, not looking at her.

'It wasn't a request.'

That got his attention. His head jerked up. 'What do you mean, it wasn't a request?'

'It means, as your number two, I've drawn the short straw. And I'm definitely not bearding the dinosaur in his den. I want somewhere public where you won't bite my head off—or where someone at least will mop up the blood.'

His eyes narrowed. 'Explain "dinosaur".'

'Tyrannosaurus rex,' she said. 'You know, the stroppy

one who eats people alive for breakfast. Or maybe he just needs a caffeine fix. With one of Pat's muffins.'

Nic stared at her for a long, long moment. She thought that he was going to refuse. And then he sighed and closed his computer file. 'All right.'

'*Very* graciously done, Mr Alberici.'

He gave her a quelling look and they walked in silence to the café. Though this time it wasn't the easy silence they'd always had. This time it was tense to the point where she thought he was going to snap.

'My shout,' she said when they reached the café. Well, the ward's. They'd all given her money and strict instructions to feed him cake. *Lots* of cake. 'Grab a table.'

Nic's eyes widened when he saw the number of muffins she'd bought. 'What's this, one of each?'

'Yep.'

'Lucy, I can't eat all these.'

'There's one from every member of staff.'

'But…' He stared at her, blank incomprehension written over his face.

'You're a pain to work with, Nic. You're grumpy, you don't talk to anyone, you don't smile—the staff are starting to be scared of you, let alone the patients. It's not good for the ward.' She sighed. 'Even cake in industrial quantities clearly isn't going to get you out of this mood. So what's the matter?'

'What's the matter?' He laughed shortly. 'Ah, Lucy. How can you of all people ask me what's the matter?'

'Because I'm not a mind-reader. And neither is anyone else on River.'

'OK. If you must know, I've discovered that a bit of fun, ''right here, right now'', isn't for me any more.'

'You're talking in riddles.'

'Let me tell you a story,' he said. 'Once upon a time,

there was a prince. A spoiled, selfish prince who did nothing but play all day. And then he met someone special. A princess. She lived in the country next door. He wanted her as his playmate—but she was the serious type and he thought everyone would expect him to build an alliance. And he was sure he'd fail. So he got scared. Backed off. And then he discovered she'd already had a broken alliance, and he felt ashamed of himself for causing her even more pain. He wanted to make it up to her, but she didn't want to play with him any more.'

Lucy met his gaze. 'And?'

'And then something happened. Someone was in trouble in his territory and she sneaked in when he wasn't looking and fixed it. And she wasn't even going to take the credit she was due. He realised what he really felt about her. How very, very special she was. And he spent a long time wondering how he could prove to her that if she had an alliance with him, it would never fail. It would be rock-solid until the end of time. He didn't want to play any more. He didn't want "right here, right now". He wanted more. He wanted always. He wanted her to be his princess, his *principessa*.'

His *principessa*. Nic's old pet name for her. Was he telling her…?

No. She wasn't going to buy into it. Not this time.

'So that's what's wrong with me, Lucy. I've met the woman I want to spend the rest of my life with. And I don't know what to say to her.'

Her judgement had definitely gone again, Lucy thought. Nic didn't want *her* as his princess. Mal was right—Nic had fallen in love with someone who'd knocked him back. *Someone else.*

'What do you expect me to say?' she asked, only just managing to keep her voice cool and calm, though she felt as if she were bleeding from every pore.

'I don't know.' He sighed. 'That's one of the problems. We're hardly on speaking terms.'

Lucy stared at her coffee. She was supposed to be doing this for her colleagues' sake. And if he was in love with someone else, it would be better for her anyway. Because it would put him out of her reach and maybe then she'd stop thinking about him, stop wishing for might-have-beens. And, one day, stop loving him.

So why did it still hurt so much?

'Just tell her straight,' she muttered. 'Tell her how you feel.'

'Tell her straight,' Nic mused. 'You think that'd work?'

She didn't meet his gaze. 'It's worth a try.'

'OK.' He paused for long enough to make her look back up at him, and then smiled. 'I love you.'

Lucy's eyes widened. 'You what?'

'I love you, Lucy Williams,' he said simply. Loudly. Loudly enough for every coffee-cup in the café to stop clattering. Loudly enough for everyone to hear him.

The silence was excruciating. Lucy's face flamed. How could he say that? How could he toy with her like this, in front of the whole hospital, after what had already happened between them?

'This isn't the time or the place,' she muttered between clenched teeth.

'Name them and I'll be there.'

'No. No. You're not in love with me, Nic. You're in love with the *idea* of being in love. You were the same at Plymouth.'

'How do you know what I was like in Plymouth?'

'I trained with a doctor on your ward. She was my best friend at med school, actually. And she was always talking about you—how you were a brilliant doctor but the corridors were littered with the broken hearts of the women you'd dated three times and dropped.'

'That's a bit of an exaggeration. I told you before, I'm not a notch-carver. I dated, yes, but everyone knew the rules from the start. It was a bit of fun. And now I'm not in the market for fun any more.'

'That's nothing to do with me.'

'It is. Because you've changed me, Lucy. I love you. No one's even come close to making me feel the way you do. You've eclipsed every memory of every woman I've ever known. And I want you on a forever kind of basis.'

'Maybe I'm not in the market for that.'

'Lucy…I know what happened with Jack devastated you. I know I hurt you, too, and I'm sorry. But it won't happen again.'

'Too right. Because I'm not letting anyone that close to me again,' she said crisply.

'Lucy…you have to take a chance. You'll never find happiness if you refuse to get involved with anyone and cut yourself off from the world.'

'I didn't refuse to get involved with Jack. Or you. And what happened, both times?'

'Don't cut yourself off just because you're scared to try again. If you don't meet happiness halfway, you'll never find it and you'll end up bitter and lonely.'

'There's no guarantee I'll find happiness. And in my experience, looking just leads to heartache.' Lucy pushed her chair back and stood up. 'We're colleagues, Nic. And that's all we're ever going to be. Get used to it. Oh, and don't take it out on the staff any more. Because you'll have found someone else within a week.'

A week in which she avoided him as much as possible. Nic was still mulling over ways to prove himself to her—having rejected skywriting, serenading her or asking her to set him the modern equivalent of the Seven Labours of Hercules— when there was a knock at his office door.

'Nic—have you got a moment?'

Nic looked up from his desk and his heart missed a beat. Had Lucy noticed that her prediction had been wrong and he hadn't even taken a colleague to lunch in the past week, let alone dated or 'found someone else'? Was she about to give him a second chance?

No. Of course not. She'd made it very clear that she'd only talk to him about work. He gave her his best professional smile. 'Sure. What's up?'

'I'm pretty sure I've got a mum-to-be with toxoplasmosis. I wanted to check a couple of things with you.'

'Have you come across a toxoplasmosis case before?' he asked.

'Once, when I was a student. The consultant then said that only about a hundred women a year get tested for it— the rest don't have any symptoms and have no idea there's a problem. It's rare, though probably more common than the official stats show.'

'Yep.' He leaned back in his chair. She was talking to him. About work, yes, but at least she was talking to him. He wasn't going to pass up the chance. 'So what do you know about toxoplasmosis?'

'It's caused by a parasite, *Toxoplasma gondii*—it's usually caught from raw or undercooked meat, unwashed fruit and veg, unpasteurised goat's milk or infected cat faeces. It's easier to prevent it than treat it, which is why we tell expectant mums to wear gloves when gardening or cleaning out litter trays, to cook meat thoroughly and wash fruit and veg,' she recited. 'It's most common in 25- to 30-year-olds and most cases don't show any symptoms. There are around two thousand cases a year in pregnant women in the UK and there's a 45 per cent risk of the baby getting it too. The earlier the mum gets it, the less likely it is to transfer to the foetus but the more severe it can be. It can lead to miscarriage, stillbirth, eye problems or hydrocephalus,' she finished.

'What's the presentation here?'

'She thought she might have glandular fever. She went to her GP with swollen lymph glands in her neck, a headache and general flu-like feelings. He had a hunch it was toxoplasmosis.'

'Could be either—it's not easy to spot.' Nic tapped his fingers on the edge of his desk. 'Did the GP do a blood test?'

Lucy nodded. 'He sent her in with the results. She's got raised IgM antibodies to the parasite—so that means it's a recent infection, not something she caught before pregnancy.'

'OK. First off, we need to find out if the baby's infected. How many weeks gestation is the mum?'

'Thirty.'

'Hmm. It's pretty likely the baby's infected, then—but the good news is that any damage won't be as bad,' he said. 'We'll need to do a scan to see if there's any obvious damage to the foetus. Check with the path lab about the antibodies, because we have to wait four weeks after confirmation of the mum's infection before we can test the foetus. Then we'll need to do a cordocentesis and an amnio, so we can do PCR testing—polymerase chain reaction—on the samples.'

'And in the meantime we give the mum a script for Spiramycine?'

He nodded. 'Four weeks of that, followed by four weeks of sulphadiazine and pyrimethamine—studies show the combination's eight times more effective than the individual drugs on their own, and they also cross the placenta so they'll treat the foetus. Repeat it to the end of the pregnancy. We need to give the mum folinic acid as well, to counteract any reduction in the production of red blood cells. The baby's going to need the same treatment from birth until the end of the first year. We can check his blood for toxoplasmosis from the same sample as the heel-prick test for PKU—' the test for phenylketonuria, a problem with metabolising protein, that was done on all newborns '—and we'll need to keep a check on his eyes for retinochoroiditis.'

'Right. Thanks for your help.'

'You already knew what to do.'

'Just checking. To make sure I'm not being slapdash.'

She left his office before he could respond.

Oh, hell. She was never going to forgive him for that. And it had been partly his fault anyway. He should have seen that she was under too much pressure.

She'd talk to him if she needed him professionally—despite her independent streak, Lucy was sensible enough to know when she needed help—but personally was another matter. He didn't think she'd ever admit it, even to herself.

He'd just have to work harder on melting those barriers around her heart. Find some way of proving to her that she could trust him. That he'd never, ever let her down again. That he loved her more than anything, more than life itself.

Lucy went back to her patient. 'Mrs O'Connor, I'm sorry to have kept you waiting. I just wanted to confirm something with the consultant. Have you heard of toxoplasmosis?'

'It's something you get from cat poo, isn't it?' Danielle O'Connor said.

'Among other things, yes.'

'And that's what I've got?' She frowned. 'But—I don't understand. I haven't got a cat and my husband does the gardening.'

'Have you eaten any meat that's been a little bit pink?'

Danielle shook her head. 'I'm vegetarian.'

'Do you drink goat's milk or eat goat's cheese or yoghurt?'

'Yes. I can't have cow's milk because of my eczema. I get my milk from the farm down the road—but they're ever so good.'

'Unfortunately, it sounds as if that was the most likely source of infection,' Lucy said.

'Is my baby going to be all right?'

'We can do some tests to find out, and there are a lot of things we can do if the baby is affected,' Lucy reassured her. 'I'd like to give you a scan now, if I may. When did you first start feeling ill?'

'Two or three weeks ago.'

'Then it'll be about another week before I can test the baby—we can't do any tests until four weeks after you've been diagnosed. We'll need to take some blood from the baby's cord, and a sample of the fluid from around the baby,' Lucy explained.

She settled Danielle O'Connor back against the couch and performed the ultrasound scan. To her relief, there were no signs of hydrocephalus—water on the brain—or neurological defects on the screen. 'It's looking good from here, but I should warn you now that your baby has a high risk of having an eye problem—though it might not show up until well past his teens. It's called retinochoroiditis. It's when the retina and choroid—that's the light-sensitive surface at the back of the eye—become inflamed and scarred, so there's a slight loss of vision. The good news is that we can give you a course of antibiotics that'll help clear the infection from you—and if the baby doesn't already have it, the drugs will help stop him getting it too.'

'But aren't antibiotics dangerous in pregnancy?' Danielle asked anxiously.

'They can cause problems in early pregnancy, but you don't have to worry as you're thirty weeks,' Lucy said. 'If your baby has it, we'll need to give him the same drugs after the birth until his first birthday, and he'll have very regular check-ups with the eye clinic here. We'll test his blood soon after he's born, but we can use the same sample of blood we use to check newborns for PKU, a condition that affects the way the body uses protein.' She squeezed Danielle's hand. 'We'll do our best by you both, so try not to worry too much. I'll write you a prescription now, so if you don't mind waiting another few minutes we can get the hospital pharmacy to sort out the drugs for you, and I'd like you to come in again in a week's time so we can take the samples from the baby.'

'But I still don't understand how I could have got it. The farm's so *clean*,' Danielle said.

'Goats are more susceptible to the parasite than cows are,' Lucy said. 'And they could have got it anywhere—from their food, or even infected water. It's bad luck, but some people don't even have any symptoms so they don't see us for treatment. At least you've got that on your side.' She squeezed Danielle's hand. 'Start taking your antibiotics this afternoon. If you're worried about anything, give us a ring here, or have a chat with your midwife. And I'll see you next week, OK?'

CHAPTER THIRTEEN

'BLEEP me if you need anything,' Lucy told Rosemary. 'I'm just going to get some fresh air in the park.' To blow the cobwebs away—and hopefully Nic with them. She had to get him out of her head. Somehow.

But before Lucy had even got to the door, there was a blood-curdling scream and a man pushed roughly past her, carrying a wrapped bundle. He ran down the corridor, and as he burst through the doors the alarm went off.

'My baby,' a woman sobbed, staggering through the doorway. 'He's taken my baby!'

'Call Security and look after the mum,' Lucy directed. 'I'll try and catch him up.'

She hurtled through the doors after the man. The display above the lift doors flashed 'G'. It was unlikely that the lift doors had already been open on their floor, and even if they had been, the lift wouldn't have reached the ground floor that quickly. So the man must have taken the stairs. She could hear running feet—had the man headed up or down? She leaned over the stairwell and saw a flash of denim on the stairs above.

Up.

Lucy took the stairs two at a time, using the handrail as a lever to speed her progress, but desperation was clearly driving the man faster. And when he reached the top of the stairs and realised there was nowhere else to go…Lucy swallowed. Please, God, don't let the man do anything stupid. Let him talk to me, give the baby back before someone gets hurt.

But why had he taken the baby in the first place? Who was he? A hundred and one questions flashed through Lucy's mind. And a hundred and one scenarios. If the baby-snatcher went up onto the roof, the baby could suffer from exposure. What about feeding? If the baby was hungry and started wailing for food, would it tip the already unstable baby-snatcher over the edge? Would he jump? Drop the baby?

Be calm. You have to be calm, Lucy told herself. If you confront him and you're panicking, you'll make the whole situation worse. Stay calm, get him talking, and hold his attention until Security or the police can deal with the situation.

Then she heard a door bang and groaned inwardly. It could only mean one thing: the baby-snatcher had gone onto the roof. And it was a bitterly cold November day, the sort with blue skies and bracing winds. Somehow she had to persuade the man to hand the baby back before the infant got too cold. She took a deep breath and climbed the last stairs before the door to the roof.

The man was standing in the furthest corner, close to the edge. Please, no, not a jumper, Lucy prayed.

'Stand back!' he yelled as he saw Lucy.

Lucy lifted both her hands to show she wasn't carrying anything. 'It's OK. I'm not going to hurt you. I just want to talk to you.'

'There's nothing to talk about. Don't you come near me—I've got a knife,' the man warned, 'and I'll use it if I have to.'

Worse and worse. His words sounded slurred. Which meant alcohol, drugs or maybe a medical condition. At this distance, Lucy couldn't tell which. She just had to tread very, very carefully or the baby was going to be in even more danger. And what was the man going to do with the knife? Kill the baby? Himself? Her? 'I promise you, there's no need to use a knife.'

'I don't want you coming near me.'

'I promise I'll stay at a distance. Are you all right?'

'Me?' The man sounded taken aback. 'Why shouldn't I be?'

'Just making conversation,' Lucy said. And if she could keep the man talking long enough, maybe she could persuade him to take the baby back.

'How's the baby?'

'My baby's fine,' the man said, holding the bundle tighter.

'It's cold out here,' Lucy said, 'and newborns lose their body heat very quickly. Can we talk about this inside, where it's warmer—for the baby's sake?'

'Nothing to talk about.' The man half turned away. 'And he's *my* baby.'

'I know. And, sure, you can take your baby for a walk if you want to,' Lucy soothed.

'Don't you talk down to me. You doctors are all the same. If you lot hadn't interfered,' the man burst out, 'she wouldn't have said I couldn't see my baby.'

Lucy thought frantically. Was there a restricted visiting order on any of the patients? She couldn't remember any. 'What's your name?' she asked.

'Why?'

'Just seems funny, talking to someone and not knowing their name, that's all,' she said, hoping that her voice sounded lighter than she felt. 'My name's Lucy. Lucy Williams.'

'Yeah, but you're one of *them*. You won't let me see my baby.'

'There's always a way round a problem,' Lucy said, 'if you talk it through.'

'But *she* won't listen to me. I said I'd change, I said I'd stop drinking, I said I'd go to counselling, do anything she wanted me to. But, no, you lot had been talking to her, you and her parents, brainwashed her into thinking she'd be better off on her own. She said she was getting a new life, one without me, and my baby didn't need me—not now, not ever.'

Lucy waited. Years of training had taught her that if you gave people room to talk, they'd tell you more than if you asked question after question.

'All I wanted was to see my baby. Hold my son.' The man's voice sounded thick with tears. 'She wouldn't even let me see him. I brought her flowers, brought him a teddy, and she threw them back at me. What else could I do?' He cradled his precious bundle against him. 'But now I've got him. She's not going to take him away from me. Not ever.'

'What's going on?' Nic asked Rosemary as he walked back onto the ward and saw several security people. 'What are they doing here?'

'Baby-snatch,' Rosemary said grimly. 'The police are on their way.'

Fear flickered at the base of Nic's spine. 'Where's Lucy?'

'She went after him.'

'Him?' Nic echoed, not understanding.

'The baby-snatcher. Lucy was talking to me at the desk when it happened.'

Nic knew that baby-snatches were very rare, and they were usually done by women. Women who'd maybe just lost their own child and hadn't come to terms with it and were confused enough to think the child they were holding was their own baby. 'So what happened?'

'The baby's father came in and just took him,' Rosemary

said. 'I called Security and Lucy went after him. One of the patients saw them heading upstairs—towards the roof! Even worse, the mum says he's got a knife.'

'A *knife*?' Nic's stomach dived. Lucy was on the roof with a man with a knife?

'She'll be fine. You know Lucy—cool, calm and sensible.'

But what if…? He forced his mind back to concentrate on work. 'How's the mum?'

'Completely distraught. Gemma's with her now, but would you mind looking in on her? Bridget Livesey in room seven.'

'Sure.' Nic didn't dare let himself think of Lucy—or the knife. Was Lucy in danger? Was she a hostage? Was the baby-snatcher threatening to jump? Nic's first instinct was to go up to the roof himself, do whatever he could to save Lucy, but he knew he was needed down here.

Just keep her safe, he prayed. Please, God. Don't let anything happen to her. Don't let anything happen to my Lucy.

In room seven, Bridget was huddled on the bed, rocking to and fro. 'My baby, my baby!' she moaned.

'It's all right, Bridget. We'll get him back for you,' Nic soothed, noting the blue card taped to the baby's empty crib which told him the baby was a boy. 'I don't know if you remember me—I'm Nic Alberici, the consultant. I saw you on my rounds this morning.'

'I don't need you. I just need my baby.'

'I know.' Nic sat down on the bed beside her. 'I'm sorry you're having to go through this right now. But Security are here and they'll get it sorted out.'

'You don't understand,' Bridget sobbed.

'Then tell me,' Nic said gently.

'It's Nigel. I love him, but…oh, I can't live with him.

Not with his drinking. I asked him time and time again to
cut down, but then he'd be out with clients and he said he
had to drink socially, and he'd be home late, stinking of
booze. I told him if he didn't stop, it'd be over between us
and I'd bring the baby up on my own. I even left him—I
thought it'd bring him to his senses, but he just got blind
drunk. He lost his job over it.' Bridget's face twisted in
anguish. 'My parents said I'd be better off without him. So
I wouldn't let him see the baby—and he came staggering
into the ward again today, said he just wanted to give his
son a cuddle. I told him to leave and—and—and—he's got
a knife!' she howled. 'He took my baby, said I'd never see
him again...'

Nic went cold. It was worse than he thought. Not only
did Nigel have a knife, he was unstable and drunk. And
Lucy was trying to talk him into giving the baby back.

Supposing he stabbed Lucy? Supposing Lucy died before
he had the chance to tell her how much he loved her? What
was he going to do without Lucy? How could he bear it if
she died?

'It's OK. He's upset, he's saying things he doesn't
mean,' Nic soothed, trying his best to sound calm even
though he was terrified inside and the back of his neck was
burning with adrenalin and fear for Lucy. 'He'd never hurt
your baby.'

'Not even to get back at me?'

'You said he wanted to see the baby, give his son a
cuddle. That doesn't sound like a man who'd set out to hurt
a child.'

Bridget gulped. 'He brought Harrison a teddy. I...I threw
it back at him, said my baby wasn't having anything from
a drunk. If only I hadn't. If only I'd just let him see
Harrison, hold him...'

'Hey, don't go blaming yourself. It was a tough situation.

You didn't think he'd do anything like that. He's probably scared himself, too. Our registrar's up there, talking to him. Lucy's brilliant. She'll help calm Nigel down.'

'But what if she can't?'

'Trust me. Lucy can do anything,' Nic said, mentally crossing his fingers. He *hoped* Lucy could calm Nigel down. If she couldn't…it didn't bear thinking about. He checked Bridget's pulse. 'Would you like me to give you something to help you relax?' he asked gently. 'I'm not forcing a sedative on you and I'm not saying you're hysterical—just that you're in a situation that would terrify any mother and it's something that might help you while you're waiting.'

Bridget shook her head. 'I just want my baby. Please. I want my baby,' she moaned.

'I know.' Nic squeezed her hand. 'I'll try and find out what's happening for you.' All he knew right now was that Lucy was on the roof, talking to Nigel Livesey and trying to persuade him to give the baby back. Security was probably holding back, waiting for her signal to move. The only way she could find out more about the situation, things that maybe Nigel hadn't told her, would be if Nic went out on the roof himself. But he needed an excuse, something that wouldn't upset Nigel's already fragile grip. 'When did Harrison last have a feed?' he asked.

'Two hours ago.'

'And you're feeding him yourself?'

Bridget shook her head. 'Bottle. I know I shouldn't. I know you're supposed to do it yourself because it's best for the baby, but I couldn't. I just couldn't.'

'Don't beat yourself up about it,' Nic said. 'Yes, breast milk has all the antibodies and a lot of advantages for both mum and baby, but if you don't want to do it you'll only make feeding time really tough for both of you. Do what suits you both, and don't let anyone bully you into feeling bad about it,' he finished. 'How long since it happened?'

'I don't know. Twenty minutes? An hour? I don't know. I don't know anything any more.' A tear trickled down her face. 'I just want my baby.'

'I'll be back with news as soon as I can,' Nic promised. 'I'll take some formula in case Harrison needs a feed. And between us, Lucy and I will persuade Nigel to give him back. I promise.'

'Nic, you can't. You can't go up there,' Rosemary said when Nic returned to the nurses' station and started sorting out supplies. 'Someone, talk some sense into this man!'

'The baby might need feeding,' Nic insisted.

'And the man's got a knife!' Rosemary pointed out.

'Exactly. Rosemary, Lucy's up there and she doesn't know the full story behind the snatch. She needs help—she needs information. I'm not going to stand by and wait.'

'That's exactly what Security will tell you to do. They're handling it.'

'If the man you loved was up there, would you sit back and wait quietly for news?'

'Well—no,' the senior midwife admitted.

'Exactly. And that's why I can't wait and leave Lucy up there on her own.'

'But, Nic, you can't put yourself at risk,' Rosemary said.

'Without Lucy, life isn't going to make any sense. So it really doesn't matter. I'm going up.'

'Nic—'

'We have a day-old baby up there—it's freezing cold, and I don't want him coming back down with hypothermia, frostbite, exposure or dehydration,' Nic said. 'So I'm taking formula, a hat and more blankets. Can someone rustle me up a flask of tea, please?'

'Tea?'

'Tea,' Nic repeated.

Two minutes later, he'd explained his plan to Jeremy, the head of Security, convinced him that he was doing the right thing and was waiting at the door.

'If you're in any trouble, the slightest danger, yell,' Jeremy directed.

Nic pushed through the door.

'Keep back!' Nigel shouted, taking a step backwards, a step nearer the edge.

'What the *hell* are you doing here?' Lucy demanded in an undertone.

'Reinforcements.'

'I don't need reinforcements.'

'Don't argue. You haven't heard the mum's side of things yet,' Nic told her in an equally soft voice. 'Trust me on this.'

Could she trust him?

Professionally, yes. Personally, never in a million years.

And yet this was personal as well as professional. If Nic did the wrong thing now, the consequences could be tragic.

'They need to get together and talk—that's the only way they'll ever be in with a chance of sorting out their problems,' Nic said quietly.

Lucy knew he wasn't just talking about the Liveseys.

'Mr Livesey—can I call you Nigel?' Nic called across to the desperate man in the corner.

Nigel scowled at Nic. 'You've been talking to *her*, haven't you?'

'Your wife told me your name, yes. But I'm not here to judge. My name's Nic Alberici—I'm one of the doctors on the ward.'

'Another busybody,' Nigel sneered.

'Sort of. I've brought something for the baby.'

'What?' He stared at Nic in disbelief.

'The baby. He's hungry,' Nic said. 'Newborns feed little and often. Harrison's last feed was two hours ago. Any second now, he's going to wake up and scream—that's his way of telling you that he wants food. I've brought some milk.' He held up the bottle of formula so Nigel could see it.

'He's *my* baby.'

'I know. So would you like me to show you how to hold him while you feed him?' Nic asked.

'Nic, he's got a *knife*!' Lucy whispered.

'I know that. But he's not going to hurt the baby,' Nic said in an undertone.

'He might hurt *you*.'

'And did you think of that before you came up here?'

'Well—no,' Lucy admitted.

'I came back to the ward and found out that the woman I love was being held at knifepoint! I couldn't just sit back and wait and wring my hands,' Nic whispered back.

'So you just jumped in with both feet?'

'Yes. Just like you did. We're more alike than you think. Just trust me, will you? I'm not going to let anything happen to you. I'm never going to let anything hurt you again.' Nic raised his voice again. 'Nigel—will you let me bring the milk over? And a hat? It's really cold out here, and newborns lose a lot of heat through their head. Harrison really needs a hat so he doesn't get hypothermia.'

'He's *my* baby,' Nigel repeated stubbornly.

'You're his dad. You can give him what he needs,' Nic said. 'Can I bring the stuff over?'

'She can,' Nigel said. 'And any funny business…'

'There won't be any,' Nic promised. 'But I've got a flask of tea for us, too. Can I bring it over?'

'Tea?' Nigel repeated, as if stupefied.

'It's freezing out here. You must be dying for a cup of tea. I was going to bring coffee, but the hospital coffee is so bad you might think I was trying to poison you.' He smiled. 'Sorry, bad joke in the circumstances. I don't mean anything snide by it.'

There was a long, long pause. Then finally Nigel nodded. 'All right.'

'He'll have to put the knife down to feed the baby,' Nic murmured to Lucy. 'When he does, I'll grab it and get rid of it—and then we'll talk him down. Together.'

Once glance at his face showed her that he meant it. He really thought that talking was going to help solve all the problems, smooth things over so Nigel and his wife could make things work.

And he'd come up to the roof, knowing that Nigel had a knife and was unstable—that his own life could be in danger. He'd come here for her sake.

Maybe she'd got him wrong after all. Maybe he wasn't just a gorgeous butterfly. And he certainly wasn't behaving like Jack. In this situation, Jack would have gone straight in the opposite direction, more concerned about saving his own skin. He wouldn't have been worried about her, worried enough to put himself in danger.

'Ready?' Nic asked softly.

'Ready,' she whispered back.

CHAPTER FOURTEEN

TOGETHER, making sure that Nigel could see everything in their hands so he wouldn't panic that they were trying to trick him, Nic and Lucy walked very slowly over towards him.

'Hat first,' Lucy said. 'Are you left-handed or right-handed?'

'Right-handed,' Nigel answered.

'Then you'll need to hold your son with your left arm and support his head on the crook of your elbow, so you can use your right hand,' Lucy directed.

Nigel followed her instructions.

'Now you can put the hat on with your right hand.'

His right hand—the one containing a carving knife—was shaking. 'What about the knife?'

'That's up to you. If you keep hold of it, you might nick the baby's skin while you put the hat on. And scalp wounds bleed very scarily, believe you me. Or you could put the knife down and know your son's perfectly safe in your arms,' Nic said.

Nigel stared at Lucy. She met his gaze without flinching, without moving.

Slowly, he let the knife drop. Lucy smiled and handed him the hat. 'Thanks. Just stretch this over his head.'

As soon as Nigel took the hat, Nic made a lunge, grabbed the knife and flung it over to the ventilation shaft.

'Hey!' Nigel jerked back.

'Nigel, you're going to have to go back downstairs at

some point,' Nic said, 'and it'd be much better for you if the authorities didn't see a knife anywhere on your person.'

'What knife?' Lucy said. 'I didn't see any knife—did you, Nic?'

'No, Lucy, I don't believe I did,' Nic said.

Nigel's eyes narrowed with suspicion. 'Why are you doing this?'

'Because everyone deserves a second chance,' Lucy said. 'I learned that very recently. Sometimes you misjudge people—you think they're going to hurt you when they're really as scared as you are, and the only way things will work out is if you talk things through. If you want to work things out with your wife and your son, you're in a better position to do it if no one can accuse you of holding someone at knifepoint.' She glanced down at the swaddled baby, who was yawning. 'Do you want me to sort out this bottle for you? It looks as if you're going to need it any second now, and it takes a lot of practice to put a teat on a bottle one-handed—Rosemary, our senior midwife, is about the only one I know who can do it.'

'Thanks.' Nigel was still shaking, but both Nic and Lucy knew that the dangerous moment had passed. Nigel was still upset, but no longer close to the edge, close to doing something desperate.

Lucy swiftly took the teat from its sterile wrapping and fixed it onto the bottle of formula. 'It's easier to feed him if you're sitting down. You'd never believe what a weight newborns are,' she said. 'Especially when you're feeding them. Your arm gets really, really tired.'

When Nigel sat down, she handed the bottle of formula to him. 'You just need to keep it tipped up so the teat's always full of milk—that way, you won't get an air bubble,' she said. 'And your son will do the rest of it for you.'

Hesitantly, Nigel put the teat to the baby's mouth. The baby nuzzled, opened his mouth and began to suck.

'This is… It's incredible,' Nigel said, his voice thick with unshed tears. 'My son. My son.'

Nic and Lucy exchanged a glance. 'Shall I be mother?' Nic said, picking up the flask. 'Or shall we all go downstairs and have a cup of tea in the warm, when Harrison's finished?'

'I vote for the warm,' Lucy said. 'How about you, Nigel?'

'I…' He was still gazing in rapture at the baby.

'I reckon that's a second vote for warm,' Lucy decided.

For the first time, Nigel smiled. 'I can't believe you're doing this for me.'

'Like I said, everyone deserves a second chance.' Lucy reached out to touch the baby's cheek. 'Talk it through with Bridget. Maybe you can both compromise, work out what's best for all of you.' She gave Nic a sidelong glance. 'There's a lot to be said for talking.'

'Definitely,' Nic agreed, his eyes warning Lucy that he had a lot to say to her.

The baby finished sucking and fell asleep. 'Do I have to burp him?' Nigel asked.

'Move him so your shoulder's supporting his head, then rub his back,' Lucy said. 'He might bring up a bit of milk—most babies do—so you're better off doing it with a cloth over your shoulder.'

'I didn't think to bring one,' Nic said. 'Shall we go down and get one? All of us?'

The fear was back in Nigel's face. 'What's going to happen to me?'

'I don't know,' Nic said honestly. 'But maybe if you and your wife can talk things through…we'll ask her not to press charges, and you can work something out between you.'

Nigel was shaking. 'I'll never drink again. I swear it. I want to be there for my boy—I don't want to be a weekend dad who hardly ever sees him, never gets to do bathtimes or be there when he's not well.'

'You need to tell your wife that,' Lucy said gently.

'She told me she loves you, Nigel,' Nic added. 'But she's downstairs on her own—she's missing her baby, she's missing you and she needs you both with her. Let's go down and sort it out.'

'All right.' Still holding the baby close, Nigel stood up and the three of them made their way across their roof to the door.

Nic went through the door first. 'Let Nigel carry the baby back to his mum,' he said softly to Jeremy. 'Let them talk. And, please, don't take a statement from either of them until I've had a word with the mum.'

'There are guidelines,' Jeremy reminded him.

'I think this is a situation where we should bend them. We want to keep this family together,' Nic said. 'Give him a chance.'

The silence stretched for what seemed like for ever, and then Jeremy nodded. 'OK. But I'll be keeping a very close eye on them. Are you coming down now?'

'Not yet,' Nic said. 'I have a little unfinished business. Five minutes?'

'Five minutes,' Jeremy confirmed.

Nic ducked back out through the door. 'OK, Nigel. Jeremy—he's our head of Security—is going to go back down to the ward with you. You and Bridget need a couple of minutes together—we'll be with you soon.'

'You're not coming now?'

Nic lowered his voice. 'I need a word with Lucy about

something.' Nic smiled wryly. 'You and I aren't so far apart, you know. And if she's in the mood to offer second chances…'

Nigel nodded. 'I get your drift. Good luck, mate—and thanks for what you did for me. For my boy.'

'Pleasure. See you in a bit.'

'Aren't we going down with him?' Lucy asked.

'Not until I've had a word with you.' Nic's mouth tightened. 'Don't you ever, *ever* scare me like that again—taking risks like that!'

'You took one,' she pointed out.

'Yeah. One rule for me, one for you. You do things the *safe* way from now on, do you hear?'

She glared at him. 'Don't you boss me about.'

'We're fighting again. And we need to talk.' His eyes grew dark, intense. 'I love you, Lucy. And when I realised you were up here with an unstable, frightened man with a knife…I couldn't bear it. I couldn't just sit and wait and hope that everything would be all right. I had to do something.'

'You could have pushed him over the edge,' Lucy pointed out.

'He just needed to know that his wife was going to listen to him. That she'd give him a chance to talk things through, work things out.' He paused. 'And that's what I want. To talk things through. Work things out with you—properly.'

Did he mean it? But if he didn't mean it, why had he taken such a risk? Why had he put his own life in danger?

Almost as if he'd read her thoughts—or maybe they were written all over her face—he asked, 'So will you trust me, Lucia *mia*? I know I let you down before, but I won't let you down again. I swear on my life.'

Could she trust him? Her throat dried. 'I—I don't know, Nic.'

'Lucy, I love you. Truly, sincerely...' His voice deepened. 'Passionately. And I want to share the rest of my life with you. I want everything. Dog, babies—marriage.'

'Marriage?' Slowly, she shook her head. 'No. Not after Jack.'

'I'm not Jack,' he reminded her. 'I know I'm rushing this but...I can't hold back. Not now. Not when I was so near to losing you. I need you to know how much I love you, Lucia *mia*. Now and for the rest of our lives. Will you marry me?'

She pursed her lips. 'Aren't you supposed to ask me that somewhere memorable?'

'I am. We're on the skyline of Treverro.'

'We're on the roof of the hospital, Niccolo Alberici,' she pointed out.

'OK. We'll put this conversation on hold,' he said. 'Until our shifts end. Let's go and sort Nigel and Bridget out. And then...we're going somewhere quiet, to talk it through. Just you and I.'

When they got back to the ward, they ignored all the speculative looks. Lucy guessed that Rosemary had said something to Mal and the rest of the team, because no one asked the obvious questions, even though they were clearly bursting with curiosity.

Nigel and Bridget were both in tears, but Bridget had promised to drop charges and Nigel was going to make an appointment with his GP to ask for help with his drink problem. Harrison was happily cuddled on his mother's lap, his father's finger clutched in his tiny hand. 'I think they're in with a chance,' Nic said softly to Lucy. 'I hope we are, too.'

Then it was time to give statements to the police, after which there was a round to do, notes to write up, anxious mums-to-be to reassure…and finally it was the end of their shift.

'Come with me, Lucia *mia*,' Nic said, taking her hand. 'We need to talk.'

'Where are we going?'

'A little place I know.'

As he drove down the narrow roads to the coast, Lucy realised where they were heading. 'Are we going to Pentremain?'

He nodded. 'I discovered it the day I went doing my tourist bit. The day you refused to come with me.'

'It's my favourite place on earth,' Lucy told him.

'Then I think this was meant to be, Lucia *mia*.'

They walked hand in hand to the cliffs overlooking the small bay. The setting sun was a red ball on the horizon and the sky was flushed rose and gold; a single star glittered above.

Nic's grip on her hand tightened. 'Look, the wishing star's out. Remember the song? Starlight, star bright…' He sang the nursery rhyme, his voice soft and low. 'Are you going to make my wish come true, Lucy?' He dropped down on one knee before her. 'I love you, Lucy. I've never felt like this about anyone before. When I heard you were on the roof this afternoon…I was terrified. You were trying to talk a distraught father into giving back the baby he'd snatched—a man who was unstable, probably drunk and had a knife. I thought you were going to die. And I knew my life wouldn't be worth living without you. That I'd lay down my life for you. Will you do me the honour of marrying me—of being my love for the rest of time?'

Lucy was silent for a long, long time. Marriage. It was a risk. A *huge* risk. Her parents were both divorced—several times. Her half-sisters and -brothers were all divorced. She already knew she had lousy judgement in men. Jack had left her at the altar. Nic had rushed her into his bed and dropped her. Could she really take that risk again? Marry him, only to discover later that he'd fallen for someone else and would leave her, the way Jack had? 'I'm sorry. I don't think I can, Nic.'

'I know you've been badly hurt—by me, as well as by Jack Hammond,' he said. 'I understand that. I'd feel the same in your shoes. But what can I do to prove to you that I'll never hurt you again—that I'll never let *anyone* hurt you?'

'I don't know,' Lucy said honestly. 'I don't know if I can trust again.'

'You already have.'

She frowned. 'How do you mean?'

'This afternoon—you had to trust me then. You had to trust me not to send Nigel Livesey over the edge. To help you talk him down. To grab the knife the second he dropped it.'

'That was professional,' she said. 'Part of our job. Of course I trust you professionally.'

Nic shook his head. 'It wasn't just professional. It was *personal*, Lucy. It was about you and me, not just the Liveseys and their baby. You had to trust me to work with you as a team, make sure we all came back safely. We work as a team in our job and it'll be the same in the rest of our lives. You and me. A partnership.' He continued looking up at her. 'I thought I was going to lose you this afternoon. And that's when I discovered that life without you was meaningless. Completely meaningless.'

'That's how you feel now. But how long's it going to last, Nic? You live for the thrill of the chase. What happens afterwards? Three dates and you're out... That's not what I want, Nic.'

'It's not what I want either. I've learned there's a bigger

thrill than that of the chase. Except it's very, very scary. It means taking a risk. It means trusting your judgement.' When she was silent, he continued, 'Remember I told you, a long time ago, that I was looking for the one I wanted to spend the rest of my life with? I found you, Lucy. Then I panicked that maybe I wasn't the right one for you. That's how I knew you were special, because my judgement went completely haywire around you. It scared me. I don't usually rush into things.'

'No?'

'Only with you. Because…' He raked his free hand through his hair. 'I don't know what to say. I don't know how to prove it to you. But I love you, Lucy. You're the one who makes me feel complete. I used to think they were a bit over the top, those songs that claimed the singer would die for his love…but it's true. It's how I feel about you. That's why I came up to the roof this afternoon. So if Nigel was going to hurt anyone, it'd be me, not you.' He tightened his fingers round her. 'This afternoon, you talked about misjudging people, thinking they're going to hurt you when they're as scared as you are. And I'm scared, Lucy. I'm as scared as you are now. The idea of having to spend the rest of my life without you terrifies me. And that's why I'm asking you to marry me. Be my life partner.'

'But marriage…' She shook her head. 'I can't do it, Nic.' Not after she'd been left standing at the church.

'What if you had absolute proof I was there, waiting for you?' Nic asked carefully. 'Would you risk it then?'

'It's not just the getting married bit.' Though that would be bad enough. 'It's afterwards. How do I know you're not going to fall in love with someone else and leave me?'

'How do I know *you're* not going to fall in love with someone else and leave *me*?' he countered. 'It's a risk,

Lucy. But we take risks every day in our job. We make decisions, judgements that could be fatal if we're wrong.'

'That's different. We've both had years of training, years of experience.'

'And the future is something neither of us can predict. So do you face it on your own, or with someone who'll hold your hand all the way, who'll back your judgement?'

'I don't know, Nic.'

'OK. Let's forget about marriage—for the moment.' He stood up again. 'Do you love me?'

Yes. But dared she say it?

'*Ti amo, Lucia mia.* I love you. Heart and soul. If you walk out of my life now, so be it—but no one will ever take your place. And my world won't be in colour any more. It'll be two-dimensional, black and white, a cardboard shell. Mere existence.' He pointed up at the stars. 'And these—their only saving grace will be that somewhere in the world they'll look down on you as well.' He sighed. 'I love you. But if you don't want me, I have to accept that. And I promise I won't make life difficult for you at work. I'll hand in my resignation tomorrow.'

'You'll resign?'

'Why should you have to leave? I'm the one who's causing the problem, not you. So I'm the one who should go.'

'But you've only just been appointed. It'll be terrible for your career, only lasting a few weeks in your first consultant's post. You won't get another chance like that for years and years.'

He shrugged. 'It's just a job. And it's not important to me any more, Lucy. Not without you.'

He'd really give up his career for her? He loved her that much?

And then she realised. Niccolo Alberici might have a silver tongue, he might be charming and a gorgeous butterfly—but he was also selfless, honourable and a man she could trust. She'd had to trust him this afternoon, and he hadn't let her down.

Lucy swallowed. 'Maybe I need someone to—to hold my hand. Teach me to trust.'

'Someone who'd support you and never let you down,' he said. 'I can do that, Lucy. If you'll let me.' He paused. 'What Jack did to you was unforgivable, but you can learn to take a chance again. Show him you're better than he is—that he hasn't made you into the sort of spineless coward he is.'

'By marrying you.'

He shrugged. 'That's one way. But you've already said no.'

'If—and I mean *if*—we get married, I don't want frills.'

He rubbed his jaw. 'We might have a bit of a problem there.'

'How do you mean?'

'You come from a big family, mine's Italian and very extended—so even if we sneak off and get married at Gretna Green with two witnesses from the street, we'd still have to have some kind of party later to celebrate our wedding or they'd all be hurt.'

He had a point. 'You really want to marry me?'

'Yes.'

'Really, really?' she tested.

'Yes.'

When it had come to the crunch, Nic hadn't let her down. And he wouldn't let her down in marriage, the way Jack had. He wouldn't leave her standing at the altar. 'Dr Lucy Alberici. It has a certain ring to it,' she mused. 'So it's all or nothing, is it?'

'All or nothing,' he confirmed.

It was the biggest risk she'd ever have to take. But she

could see the sincerity in Nic's eyes, despite the darkening night, and she knew that she wouldn't be taking the risk on her own. He was going to be with her, every step of the way.

'Then, yes, Nic, I'll take the risk. I'll marry you,' she said softly.

He pulled her into his arms and kissed her. Thoroughly. When he lifted his head again, they were both shaking. 'This wedding,' he said, 'is going to have to be soon.'

Lucy stroked his face. 'I learned something too today, Nic. *Ti amo*. I love you.'

'*Ti amo, Lucia mia*,' he echoed. '*Sempre*. For ever.'

EPILOGUE

ONE month later...

'I'll get it!' Allie called as the doorbell went.

She returned with a single white rose. 'For you, Lucy,' she said, somewhat unnecessarily, and dropped the flower into her sister's lap.

'Don't bend forward,' Susie said, her fingers curled round a strand of Lucy's hair, 'or it'll hurt!'

Lucy opened the card. Nic's flamboyant handwriting informed her, 'I'll see you in one hour. Don't be late.'

'Hah,' she said with a grin, and let her sister continue pinning her hair up.

Thirty minutes later, when Susie was perfectly satisfied with her sister's hair and make-up, Lucy stepped into her dress. The doorbell rang again.

'I'll get it,' Rach said, and returned with a single pink rose.

'Thirty minutes,' the note said.

'This must be costing him a fortune,' Susie pointed out. 'Roses in December. The week before Christmas, no less. And florists deliver on a guaranteed day, not a guaranteed time!'

'Look what he's getting in exchange,' Allie said. 'He's getting our Lucy. Priceless among women.'

'Oh, shut up,' Lucy said affectionately.

'But look at you. I think I'm going to cry,' Rach said. 'You look fabulous.'

'Because my baby sister is an excellent dress designer,'

183

Lucy said. Rach had designed a simple off-the-shoulder raw silk and ivory velvet dress, with a matching velvet stole studded with tiny seed pearls. 'And my middle sister is a dab hand with a make-up brush. And my bossy kid sister helped Nic and me organise everything in record time.' She hugged the three of them. 'I couldn't have done it without you. Any of you. And you all look fabulous.' Rach had made similar dresses and stoles for all of them in crimson, and a fairy dress for her toddler, Lily, in the same material.

'Organising a wedding is a lot more fun than organising a conference,' Allie said modestly. 'I enjoyed it.'

'And who else would I make dresses for, except the one who used to nurse my dollies better when I was a tot?' asked Rach.

'Only the person who let me practise on her and didn't yell when I turned her hair green by mistake,' said Susie. 'The big sister who's always been there for us. And we're here for you.'

A lump rose in Lucy's throat.

'Don't cry—the mascara's not waterproof!' Susie said in horror.

The four of them exchanged watery smiles.

There was a hesitant rap on the door. 'Can I come in?'

'Yes, Mum—she's finished,' Allie called.

Sheena Roberts came into the room, holding her grand-daughter Lily's chubby hand, and took a shuddering breath. 'You look fabulous,' she said, her voice cracking. 'Oh, Lucy. You're going to knock them all dead.'

'Not literally, I hope,' Allie said, and they all laughed.

'Nic's going to be so proud of you. So am I. And your dad,' Sheena continued.

'And us,' chorused Allie, Susie and Rach.

'Me!' Lily piped up.

'If you lot don't stop it,' Lucy said, 'I really am going to cry.'

'It's your wedding day. The day you'll remember for the rest of your life—and this time for the right reasons,' Sheena said. 'So put Jack Hammond where he belongs.'

'In the dustbin of history,' Allie said firmly.

When the doorbell rang the next time, it was to announce the arrival of the wedding cars.

'Are you OK, Lucy?' Allie asked when Lily, Rach and Susie had gone ahead with Sheena.

'I think so,' Lucy said. Actually, she wasn't. Her stomach was tied in a complicated knot, the back of her neck felt hot—despite the fact that her nape was bare and there was frost on the ground—and she was sure her hands were shaking. The last time she'd done this, she'd got to the church and waited. And waited. And waited. And then finally had had to accept that Jack wasn't turning up.

But Jack hadn't sent her a rose on the morning of their wedding.

Let alone two.

Make that three, she thought as Allie and her father helped her into the car and the driver handed her another rose—this time, a deep crimson one to match the hand-tied sheaf of roses she carried in contrast with her sisters' sheaves of ivory roses and the teddy Lily was carrying. 'Fifteen minutes,' said the note.

As the car set off, a mobile phone shrilled.

'Good. I was expecting this,' Allie said. 'Perfect timing.'

'Allie, you can't *possibly* work in the middle of your sister's wedding!' Lucy's father said sternly.

'Oh, Roger. As if I'd do that,' Allie teased. 'No, this one's for you, Lucy,' she continued, and handed over the mobile phone.

Lucy went cold. No. It wasn't going to happen all over

again, but this time with the groom letting her know just before she walked up the aisle. Please, no.

But Allie wouldn't be smiling if that were the case. Stop panicking, she told herself. Everything's going to be all right.

Even so, her voice came out as a croak. 'Hello?'

'*Mia principessa.* Did you like your flowers?'

'Yes. Thank you.'

'Ten minutes and you'll be here. The organist's playing Bach, especially for you,' Nic said. 'Can you hear it?'

He'd obviously taken the phone away from his ear for a moment; Lucy could hear the faint sounds of an organ. 'OK. I'm still waiting at the church door. Your mum's just arrived—wow, what a hat. You didn't tell me she was wearing a purple velvet hat! And the girls look fabulous.'

Tears pricked Lucy's eyes. Nic had known how terrified she was of getting married—terrified of it all going wrong at the last minute, of him not turning up and leaving her waiting, just as Jack had done. And this was his way of reassuring her that he was there for her, that he'd always be there for her.

'Oh, and Gina and Sofia are planning to chuck birdfood at us.'

'What?' This was getting surreal, Lucy thought.

'Apparently it's bird-friendly confetti. The vicar's happy because his churchyard doesn't get covered in paper, the birds are happy because they get fed and my big sisters are happy because their aim is lethal. Rach, Susie and Lily have just walked up the path. The teddy's got a dirty face because Lily dropped it. Luckily Uncle Nic has a hankie in his pocket. Hang on, Lily wants a word while I sort out Teddy.'

'Pretty Aunty Lucy,' a babyish voice lisped. 'Princess.'

Lucy gripped her father's hand. 'I'm going to cry.'

'No, you're not,' Roger whispered back. 'You're going to be married to the man you love, to the man who loves you.'

'And I can see the bonnet of your car,' Nic said after retrieving the phone from Lily. 'So I'm going in now—because it's unlucky for me to see you before you walk up the aisle. I love you. And I'm waiting for you, *mia principessa*. I'm waiting for you to make me the happiest man in the world.'

Lucy switched off the phone and handed it to her father, who slid it into his suit pocket and pulled her veil down over her face. And as she took her first steps up the crimson-carpeted aisle to the strains of Purcell's 'Trumpet Voluntary', followed by her sisters and her niece, and saw the love in Nic's face when he turned round to watch her walk to join him at the altar, she knew that he meant it. *I'm waiting for you to make me the happiest man in the world.*

'I will,' she whispered, smiling back at him. 'I will.'

MILLS & BOON®
Live the emotion

0207/01b

Modern
romance™

THE SPANIARD'S MARRIAGE DEMAND
by Maggie Cox

Leandro Reyes could have any girl he wanted. Only in the cold light of morning did Isabella realise she was just another notch on his bed-post. But their passion had a consequence Leandro couldn't ignore. His solution: to demand Isabella marry him!

THE PRINCE'S CONVENIENT BRIDE
by Robyn Donald

Prince Marco Considine knows he's met his match when he sees model Jacoba Sinclair. But Jacoba has a secret: she's Illyrian, like Prince Marco, a fact that could endanger her life. Marco seizes the opportunity to protect her…by announcing their engagement!

ONE-NIGHT BABY *by Susan Stephens*

Five years ago, virginal Kate Mulhoon met top Hollywood producer Santino Rossi – but he knew nothing of her innocence, or of the baby they made that one night together… Now Santino is determined to find out what Kate's hiding, and once he does he *will* make her his…

THE RICH MAN'S RELUCTANT MISTRESS
by Margaret Mayo

Interior decorator Lucinda Oliver's latest client is gorgeous playboy Zane Alexander. Lucinda's determined not to be one of his conquests… But when their work takes them to the Caribbean, she's seduced by the exotic surroundings – and Zane's sizzling desire…

On sale 2nd March 2007

Available at WHSmith, Tesco, ASDA, and all good bookshops

www.millsandboon.co.uk

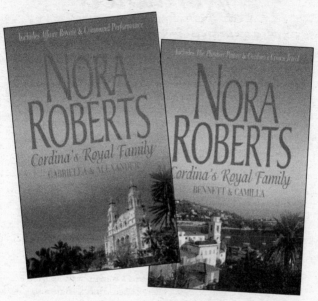